PRAISE FOR

Faker

"A funny, charming, and thoroughly entertaining debut. I couldn't put it down!"   —Samantha Young,
New York Times bestselling author of *Fight or Flight*

"I loved every page of Smith's wonderful debut! The romance was sweet and heartwarming, but it was Smith's ability to write a main character who embraces all of her power that had me cheering throughout this book."   —Alexa Martin, author of *Fumbled*

"Written with insight and humor, Sarah Smith's *Faker* is a charming, feminist, and diverse romance that will have you hooked until the very last page."

—Sonya Lalli, author of *The Matchmaker's List*

Faker

SARAH SMITH

JOVE
New York

A JOVE BOOK
Published by Berkley
An imprint of Penguin Random House LLC
penguinrandomhouse.com

Copyright © 2019 by Sarah Smith

A JOVE BOOK, BERKLEY, and the BERKLEY & B colophon
are registered trademarks of Penguin Random House LLC.

Library of Congress Cataloging-in-Publication Data

Names: Smith, Sarah, 1985– author.
Title: Faker / Sarah Smith.
Description: First edition. | New York, NY: Jove, 2019.
Identifiers: LCCN 2019001219 | ISBN 9781984805423 (paperback) |
ISBN 9781984805430 (ebook)
Subjects: | BISAC: FICTION / Romance / Contemporary. |
GSAFD: Love stories.
Classification: LCC PS3619.M59298 F35 2019 | DDC 813/.6—dc23
LC record available at https://lccn.loc.gov/2019001219

First Edition: October 2019

Printed in the United States of America
1 3 5 7 9 10 8 6 4 2

Cover design and illustration by Vikki Chu
Book design by Alison Cnockaert

For you, Mom.
I love you forever.

one
....

Blinking is underrated. At least I think so. Not only does it keep your eyes from drying out, it serves as a momentary break from unpleasant sights and sensations. Harsh sunlight, a gory scene in a horror movie, a sudden gust of dust-ridden air. Close your eyes, and for a second, you're safe and shielded.

I blink to protect my eyes from the blinding white figure invading my peripheral vision. Behind the black of my lids, I feel relief. As soon as my eyes open again, the nagging brightness is back, whiter than ever.

That whiteness is a pale coworker I don't particularly care for. I pretend like I can't see him. It's no big deal. I fake almost everything else when I'm here.

I have to as a twenty-six-year-old woman working at a power tool distributor called Nuts & Bolts. The company is staffed mostly by middle-aged gruff men who prefer to plaster their cubicle walls with photos of bikini models rather than pictures of their wives or girlfriends. On any given workday, I shift between a limited range of fake emotions: confidence, assertiveness, boldness. I am none of these outside of work. If I were my real self, I'd be roadkill.

When I took this job two years ago, I ingrained fakeness into my work DNA. From 8 a.m. to 5 p.m., Monday through Friday, I force myself to be steely and unflappable. There's no room for softness here. Everything is *literally* nuts and bolts, hard metals, gears, blades. The parking lot is gravel. The halls are covered in a film of dust and dirt.

I have to be hard because working here is no walk in the park. Like when the managers nearing retirement age mansplain information I already know but never do the same to the male employees. Or whenever new hires in the warehouse ask me if I have a boyfriend seconds after they meet me. My pretend toughness—boss-bitch mode, I call it—keeps it mostly at bay. That, along with a strict anti–sexual harassment policy.

Why would I work in such a place? Because things like money, food, and shelter are important to me. Also because a journalism degree only goes so far when you don't actually want to be a journalist.

And to be honest, I like the work. I'm a copywriter who somehow managed to secure my own tiny office in a building full of shared work spaces. I write descriptions about power tools. I manipulate words all day, every day. I make the most industrial, harsh objects sound enticing. I falsify how interesting they are, which is easy for a faker like me.

We all do it. Feigned interest in conversations. Phony hair color. Dishonest proclamations about penis length. Fake orgasms. I'm guilty of that one too.

Fake can be empowering. It's human nature. It's necessary.

And then there's Tate Rasmussen, the pale figure bleeding into my line of sight. The one person at Nuts & Bolts whose presence doesn't require me to pretend. I feel genuine emotions for him, all of which are rooted in frustration, anger, and irritation.

Thankfully, we reside in separate offices. The downside? His office is diagonally across the hall from mine, which means I have an unobscured view of half his face—just as he does of mine—forty hours a week. Only a narrow hallway and two flimsy doors—the equivalent of four paces—separate us.

Shutting the doors would offer more privacy, but neither of our shoebox offices contains vents. Unless we want to roast in the summer or freeze in the winter, we have to keep our doors open.

Tate's in charge of social media for the company. It's an amusing example of irony, as he is one of the most antisocial and eerily quiet people I've ever met. Luckily, we don't interact much. Most of our communication is done via email. Face-to-face words are not often exchanged unless it is to bicker or criticize.

Most days I can ignore him, but this afternoon is proving to be a challenge because I'm enduring Tate's loud pen tapping. When he's not typing or on the phone, it's tap, tap, tap, all day, every day.

"Be quiet, please," I say.

He scribbles something on a sheet of paper before crumpling it and tossing it on my desk, zero trace of emotion on his face. I open it to find a "NO" scrawled in black ink, taunting me. Already I can feel the heat making its way to my face.

That's Tate. Cold, calculating, and hostile. His rude, dismissive behavior is his currency, and I'm the store he chooses to shop at. I'm paid in frowns, grimaces, scowls, and blank stares.

He's never once stepped foot in my office. I'm convinced it's yet another one of his passive-aggressive digs at me, since he waltzes with confidence through every other space in this building. The closest he's ever gotten is hovering around my doorway. I wonder what it would take for him to cross that invisible boundary. Would I need to be choking with bloodshot eyes, begging for him to administer the Heimlich?

I toss the paper into the trash can. It wasn't always this way. Before he started, I was asked by the hiring manager to email him a product catalog so he could familiarize himself with the inventory. His reply was nothing short of impressive.

Emmie,

Thank you for the helpful information. I'm told working quarters will be tight, but I've also heard many wonderful things about you. Looking forward to sharing space with one of Nuts & Bolts' finest.

Sincerely,
Tate Rasmussen

On his first day, I skipped into his office, mesmerized. I couldn't help it. I was a moth drawn in by the glow of his white skin, his curly blond locks, broad shoulders, that sharp jaw. This handsome stranger looked so different from me, with my olive complexion and dark hair.

When I introduced myself, disgust and horror filled his face. Lines jutted into his forehead and his eyebrows pinched together, aging his late-twenties face in an instant. Had we passed each other on the street, he would have shrieked at the sight of me and run the other way.

He weakly shook my hand, then directed his attention back to his paperwork. His instant rebuff hurt, but I chalked it up to first-day-of-work nerves. It wasn't. Every attempt at polite small talk, every invite to lunch was met with rejection.

And then I overheard him on the phone. Through his cracked-open door, I heard, "I don't even know what to say about her. It's only been a week."

I froze. I should have plugged my ears or shoved in my headphones, but I couldn't.

"Just looking at her . . ." Disdain dripped from his voice. "I don't know how long I'll be able to deal."

So that was it. We would never, ever like each other.

I had no idea what I did to turn him sour so quickly. I should have confronted him, but I didn't have the strength. I was humiliated, going out of my way to welcome someone who hated me instantly for some unknown reason. From that afternoon, I quit engaging him unless it was a work-related issue and he was the only one who could help. We fell into a pattern of ignoring and arguing with each other.

I shove away the bitter memory and staple copies of a shopping guide I wrote. A soft squeak distracts me, and I look up to see Tate leaning back against his chair, stretching. His sleeve slides up his arm, and I catch a glimpse of skin. His paleness never ceases to wow me. Living in Nebraska, I was surrounded by countless white children in school, but Tate puts them to shame. His skin practically glows. I want to ask what SPF he uses, how long it takes him to burn when he's outside, but that's small talk, and he refuses to make it with me.

I could say his complexion makes him haggard, but it would be a lie. The lack of color actually suits him. Raphaelian-hued skin, blond hair, eyes so light blue they're almost gray. His photo belongs in a travel brochure for Nordic countries. He's a living, breathing advertisement for that region. It's another reason I can't stand him. A person as unpleasant as Tate shouldn't look that good.

He catches me before I can turn away. Busted.

"Like what you see?"

"Just wondering if you burst into flame the moment you step into sunlight." I can feel myself blushing, but thankfully, my own tan skin conceals it.

His ever-present neutral expression remains. I'd wager his genes have never been infiltrated by a person of color. His ancestors must have been stationed for generations near the Arctic Circle, surrounded by the Baltic and North Seas, no tan people like me allowed entry for generations.

"Not all of us are lucky enough to tan at the drop of a hat like you do, Emmie. What's your secret?"

I ignore his sarcastic question. He's trying to get a rise out of me. I will not give it to him.

This is how most of our interactions go. A mix of snide comments and dismissive quips, with a sprinkle of work-related topics every once in a while. Nothing personal.

Despite this mutual disinterest in each other's lives, I feel like I know him well after eleven months. He reminds me of an android in a sci-fi movie. Cool and polite, but with a machinelike quality. Almost like he's feigning human reactions for courtesy's sake, and you can't tell what's really behind the wall of artificial feelings.

A robot would be a more pleasant coworker.

I once taped a photo of an android on his computer with the words *I'm flattered you work so hard to model your personality after mine* scrawled on the bottom after a particularly infuriating day of snapping at each other. I would have loved to watch him rip it apart in anger, but I was giggling so hard I had to leave the room.

The soft tick of the minute hand on my desk clock pulls me back to the present. Only one more hour until I can go home and shed my work armor. I glance at the lone framed photo on my desk of my younger sister, my mom, and me. Addy is a toddler; I'm just out of kindergarten. We're soaked from running back and forth into the waves at Hapuna Beach in Hawaii. Our mom kneels behind us, hugging us in her arms. All three of us display impossibly wide grins.

My mouth waters for Spam musubi, my favorite childhood snack. I curl my toes inside my sneakers, wishing they were sand. Nostalgia is hitting hard today. I send Mom and Addy quick "I love you" texts, then punch in a reminder on my phone to email Mom this weekend.

Next to the frame is a hollowed-out coconut half, my favorite keepsake from the Big Island that doubles as a quirky paperweight. I run my fingers over the fuzzy fibers on the shell. Inside rests a message scrawled in my mother's trademark cursive handwriting.

For my beautiful anak, *who's as sweet and strong as this coconut.*

My eyes prick, but I blink away the split second of emotion. Remembering how and why she gave this to me will forever leave me choking back tears.

"Missing Hawaii again?" Tate asks.

Curse this heat. I want to shut my door so bad. "You could say that," I concede.

"Wanna talk about it?"

"Nope." I gaze at my computer screen and click indiscriminately on random links.

"Come on. I'm a good listener." He looks at me expectantly, like he thinks I'm actually going to chat with him about my childhood. Fat chance.

"Nope."

The heavy sigh he releases sounds a lot like disappointment, but I have no idea why. Like I'm going to divulge personal details to the guy who spends every workday staring daggers at me in between bicker sessions. He'll just make fun of me. Like how he smirks when I call flip-flops "slippers," or how he frowns when I say "auntie" instead of "aunt."

Five o'clock hits, and Tate's gone before I even log off my computer. I glance at his empty chair, my chest tight with the desire to have a normal work relationship with the coworker sitting closest to me. But I remind myself why it's not possible. He's weirdly hostile, and I'm a big fat phony. As much as I want to be normal with Tate, I don't need it. What I do need is to be hard, focused. Even if I have to fake it.

NO TAPPING TODAY. Instead Tate is loudly guzzling coffee from his thermos. I want to yell after every earsplitting slurp. Every time he brings that silver thermos to his lips, I imagine ripping it out of his grip and chucking it against the wall. But I can't. Because this is a place of business, not a street fight.

Why is he even drinking hot coffee? It's ninety-nine degrees out for the twelfth straight day, one of the hottest Augusts that Omaha has seen on record.

Another slurp. My eyes bulge. There's no way he doesn't know how grating this is. He should think about outsourcing his slurping skills to Guantanamo Bay as a new form of enhanced interrogation. He could get anyone to submit in record time.

Shoving in my earbuds, I crank the volume on the episode of *Eat Bulaga!* I'm streaming, my favorite variety show from the Philippines. The hosts' off-key karaoke rendition of Katy Perry's "Hot N Cold" is soothing compared to Tate's animal noises.

Our boss, Will, glides into my doorway. He occupies a cracker box office on my side of the hallway.

"Emmie! Good morning!" He leans his arm against the doorframe. The weight of his pudgy dad bod pushes the flimsy door back an inch. "I can't seem to find the folder with the photos for that new line of utility knives. I think that software upgrade messed up something on my computer."

I swallow a laugh. Classic Will. He's a bright guy and a great boss who doesn't hover. However, his tendency to lose objects, even digital files, is legendary.

"Can you grab the knives from the warehouse and take some photos of them to go along with the descriptions you wrote?"

The thought of going to the warehouse churns my stomach. "No problem," I say through gritted teeth.

Full disclosure: I'm not some jaw-dropping hottie by any stretch of anyone's imagination. But the fifty-employee workforce here is mostly male with only five female employees. The remaining four are middle aged and married. I'm not ugly and I'm relatively young, so by default I get a fair amount of attention and stares. The warehouse is especially obvious about it.

"Going down to the warehouse?" Tate asks. It's the first time he's spoken to me today.

"Yep."

"How long is that going to take you?"

"Not sure. Why?"

"I have to set up a bunch of promo tweets for those utility knives, and the longer your warehouse fan club keeps you down there, the longer I have to wait for you to add them to the site. I can't tweet the links unless they're on the website, and I have a million other things to do."

I say nothing in response. I loathe how he's trying to make my job about him.

"Do I have to spell it out?" He yanks out his earbuds impatiently and closes his eyes. "I think I should go with you to make sure things get done in a timely manner."

"So this is purely selfish motivation?"

"Precisely."

I cringe. Whenever he speaks to me, he routinely pulls out archaic words only a 1950s rural doctor would use.

"Fine. Let's go."

We trot side by side in silence down the hall to the stairs. Positioned next to each other, our appearances are a stark contrast. My olive skin is ten shades darker than his, thanks to my Filipino mother. My dad is a pale white guy, but the Asian gene is strong. His hazel eyes and light skin did little to dilute such dominant traits. My hair is technically dark brown, but it could pass for black at a distance. My eyes are such a deep shade of brown, I have to endure extra eye drops at the optometrist to fully dilate them.

The only thing not strikingly different between us is our heights. I'm five feet eight inches, which is nothing short of a miracle considering my mom is a tiny five feet one inch. I have my dad's European genetics and his burly six-feet-two-inch frame to thank for that.

I estimate Tate at six feet, maybe six feet one inch if he's standing straight. In the right pair of four-inch heels, I could stand nearly eye to eye with him. However, the fact that our office is casual dress gives me zero reason to wear anything other than sneakers and flats. As often as I fantasize about the opportunity to throw on my favorite killer stilettos and tell him off, it will likely never happen.

Once in the warehouse, I track down the manager, Gus. He's a no-nonsense baby boomer who aspires to run the warehouse with the strictness of a gulag. Raising his fuzzy gray eyebrows is his preferred way to say hello.

Sliding into boss-bitch mode, I do my best Gus impression: I square my shoulders, frown, and keep things short and direct when I talk.

"I need one of your guys to grab these utility knives. Will's orders." I hand him a printed list.

He shoves the paper into the chest of the closest worker and barks directions. The college-aged kid shakes his head in fright before running off. The longer I stand with ramrod straight posture, the more tired I feel. Channeling Gus is exhausting. Shifting my weight between my feet, I almost bump into Tate. He backs up a few inches. It's ridiculous that he felt the need to follow me all the way down here.

"Watch it," he says.

"Then don't stand so close."

He shoots every single warehouse worker around us a menacing glare. Everyone who walks past us leaves a two-foot buffer of space.

"You're a friendly one," I say.

"What are you talking about?"

"Everyone's avoiding us. You look like you'll slit the throat of anyone who comes near. It's quite the vibe."

His raises an eyebrow. So smug. "Who says it's a vibe?" It's like I've complimented him, he seems so pleased with himself.

When he turns away, he fist-bumps Cal, the sixty-something delivery driver, as he walks by. Pleasantries and chuckles are exchanged. I have to blink twice at the scene. Cal is a sweetheart who I count as a friendly work acquaintance, pretty much the opposite of Tate. And I've never seen Tate chitchat with anyone at work. I didn't know they were pals.

A second later Brett from Service and Repairs walks up to us, infiltrating the forbidden force field.

"Fancy seeing you here." He shoots me a sleazy smirk and doesn't even acknowledge Tate.

I know little about Brett other than he's in his late thirties, uses too much gel on his thinning dark hair, and seems to love flirting with any woman in his vicinity. I find him exceptionally slimy. Even though he's never said anything inappropriate to me, I still get an uneasy feeling whenever he's near.

I scowl, recalling the advice I've read in countless blogs and articles on how to be a girl boss when you're working with mostly dudes.

Quickest way to get rid of an unwanted smiler? Scowl. It embarrasses the offender into dropping it.

Brett doesn't seem to know that he should feel embarrassment, because his grin doesn't fade. "Sick of being cooped up upstairs?" He takes a step toward me.

"Nope. Just getting some knives." *Stick to short, terse answers.*

"Knives, huh? Those are pretty dangerous. Don't cut yourself." He winks, but I hold my ground and cross my arms. I may be crawling out of my skin, but I sure as hell won't show it.

"Don't wink at me, Brett. That's creepy." *Call out inappropriate behavior.*

He simply laughs. Nothing short of "fuck off" would make him go away, but I can't do that at work.

"Hey." Tate barks while glowering at him. "Are you done skeeving us out?"

"Huh?" Brett glances at Tate like he's just now noticing him.

"Are you done skeeving us out?" Tate's slow tone implies Brett can't understand basic English.

It seems to throw Brett off kilter. He stumbles back a step. "Jeez, what's your problem?"

Tate hovers over him. "Do you think it's a good use of company time to bother us?"

"Whatever, man. I'll go. Chill out."

I let out a breath, relieved he's gone, but annoyed that Tate felt the need to butt in.

Gus's minion hands me a small box of knives, and we walk back up to the office.

"You're welcome," Tate mumbles as we reach the top of the stairs.

"What is that supposed to mean?"

"Here, let me carry that." He tries to grab the box from me, but I yank it away. We walk down the hall back to our offices.

"I've got it. What are you talking about?"

"I got rid of Brett, didn't I?"

I roll my eyes and march to my office. The slap-rattle sound the knives make when I drop the box on the floor causes me to flinch.

He sits at his desk, shaking his mouse with impatience.

"You think I should thank you for being a jerk to Brett? You're hilarious." I stay standing and turn to face him.

"It seemed like you could use some help getting rid of him."

I squeeze my hands into fists at his patronizing tone, then march to his doorway. "News flash: I don't need your help. I can take care of myself."

"Really? Is that what you were doing down there? Sack up and report Brett to management. He'd get the message real quick then."

"There's more than one way to send a message."

Tate has a point, but how ridiculous would I sound making a complaint about Brett's hard-to-define creepiness? He doesn't say anything that's outright inappropriate and keeps his hands to himself. His off-putting vibe exists in subtleties: standing too close, the way he says certain words. It would be easy for him to say I was taking it the wrong way. Then I would look like the overly sensitive female who can't handle working with men.

"Whatever message you think you're sending? It's failing." Tate frowns at me, and it's pure condescension.

"I'm not a damsel in distress. Back off." I stomp to my desk.

When I glance up, he's staring at me. There are a few seconds where I think he's going to say something, but the hard look in his eyes fades. He turns to his computer instead, the sound of his fingers banging on his keyboard filling the room.

Pulling the camera from my desk drawer, I snap photos while I listen to another episode of *Eat Bulaga!* But even a wasabi-flavored-bun-eating contest set to dance music doesn't ease the frustration coursing through me. I'm strong, I'm capable, and I don't need Tate's help to fend off anyone, not even creepy Brett.

two
·······

The next morning kicks off with a mandatory company meeting. Some surprise announcement. I'm annoyed at first because the last time we had a surprise meeting, it was to scold us about tidying up the break room better. I'm not in the mood for a lecture, but it saves me from listening to Tate physically assault his keyboard for the rest of the morning, so I'm tepidly on board. He beats that thing like it owes him money.

I find a corner seat in the back. The AC kicks on from the ceiling vent above, blowing freezing air directly on me. I glance up and shiver, then slide over to the next chair. There's a soft thud next to me before Tate's blond curls bleed into my peripheral vision. I roll my eyes, but then there's warmth. The fabric of our sleeves barely touches, but I can still feel the heat from his body skimming across my arm. He's like a human radiator. The comfort is so unnerving, I have to lean away.

"Scooting away from me? Are we in preschool?" he says, scribbling on the yellow notepad he always carries. He's a diligent notetaker in every meeting I've ever seen him in.

A faint evergreen scent hits, throwing me further off kilter.

His cologne. My mind flashes to a lush green forest in the Pacific Northwest. The pleasant image it conjures makes me want to smile, but I bite it back. Why must someone so unpleasant smell so delicious?

Refocusing, I side-eye him cattily, zeroing in on his outfit of jeans, gray T-shirt, blue hoodie, and sneakers. "Nice outfit. Are you going for the billionaire douchebag look today?"

Normally, I'm not one to judge when it comes to dress code. My work wardrobe is a special form of armor selected specifically to deter stares in a workplace populated by dudes eager to gawk at anyone appearing remotely female. The jeans, V-neck shirts in muted colors, and assortment of cardigans I rotate every week are as dull as they are predictable. But if Tate's in the mood to start a tiff, I'm willing to bite back.

"I guess it makes sense," I say. "You work in social media."

Several seconds of silence accompanied by a hard scowl prove I've rendered him speechless. I give myself a mental high five and wave at Kelsey from Accounting as she scans the room for a place to sit. It's mostly full at this point, so I scoot over a chair and let her have the seat closest to Tate.

She slides her voluptuous body close to Tate's chair, her head locked to the side as she stares at him. Even though she's mid-forties, she never misses an opportunity to ogle the younger guys at Nuts & Bolts. A gruff sigh leaves Tate's mouth, accompanied by an eye roll. Her shoulder-length sandy blond hair bounces as she slides out of her trance and back to the present. She flashes one more smirk at him, but he's not even paying attention anymore.

Lynn, the Nuts & Bolts special projects manager, stands at the front of the room. "Good morning, everyone!" she says with an impossibly wide smile.

Her cheery and wholesome demeanor is out of place in this

establishment, and that's why I love her. Half of our workforce prefers to keep to themselves while the other half curses loudly with every other word. Lynn is short, adorably curvy with a bob haircut, and always wears dangly earrings. Today they're gold feathers. She possesses a type of fun-mom energy that sets everyone at ease.

"Apologies for the impromptu meeting, but I have a bit of exciting news to share." She clasps her hands in front of her. "Nuts & Bolts has taken on a charity project. We're partnering with the Midwest Family Homes Foundation to build a house for a family in need."

A wide smile splits Lynn's face while she claps excitedly. It takes a few seconds, but the rest of us eventually join in on the applause. I can't help but grin too. This sounds like a worthy cause.

Lynn explains that Nuts & Bolts will be building a single-family detached home at the north end of the city.

"Employees aren't required to participate in this homebuilding project, but we very much hope you'll want to. No outside time will be required for you to take part. Those who choose to volunteer will be doing so Monday through Friday in shifts that fall within the eight-to-five workday. During the homebuilding days, you'll essentially work half a day, then head to the site. Once five o'clock hits, you're free to go home!"

Heads bob up and down across the room. I spot a few "not bad" faces. It seems this hard-to-please bunch is on board with doing a bit of volunteer work to get out of their normal workday duties.

She explains that a small group of employees with construction experience will direct the project while the rest of us will be assigned smaller-scale tasks.

Furious scribbling fills the space to the left of me. Tate's ability

to make noise in a quiet room is surpassed by none at Nuts &
Bolts.

The clipboard Lynn has passed around lands in the hands of
one of the guys from Customer Support. He squints at the sign-up
sheet. "We start building next week? Isn't that when that heat
wave is supposed to hit?"

A sliver of worry flashes in Lynn's eyes. "Unfortunately, yes."

A wave of soft groans echoes through the room. A few people
mutter about crossing their names off the list.

Lynn's formerly cheery face morphs into a frown. "I'd expect
more from a group of professionals."

Awkward silence cuts the room, save for my stifled laugh of
disbelief. I've never seen Lynn turn from joyful to disappointed so
quickly, and it's strangely amusing. I didn't think she had it in her
to be so curt. Both Kelsey and Tate turn to look at me with incredulous expressions. Laughing during awkward moments is a
bad habit that's taken years for me to harness.

Lynn purses her lips. "Everyone in this room possesses skills
that could improve the life of a family in need, and you're worried
about feeling hot for a few hours a day? I'm disappointed in you
folks."

When she tuts, heads droop in shame. A few muttered sorries
follow.

She crosses her arms while scanning the room. Her stance reminds me of a mother scolding her misbehaving teen in an after-
school special.

"I'm certainly not going to force any of you to volunteer, but
let's try to keep in mind that the heat wave will be temporary. I'll
be there sweating it out with all of you every day, and so will the
rest of management. A few days of discomfort will result in a better life for a deserving family." Lynn's arms fall back to her sides.

"Also, food and drink will be provided at the worksite for all volunteers."

Half the room lights up. Nothing like free food to draw people to a noble cause.

Lynn ends the meeting with some words of encouragement. "Be sure to check your email inboxes tomorrow; there's more info on our first day of volunteering to come! And please feel free to come to me with any ideas you folks have. We want to make this project the best it can be!" She points a finger in the air. "Oh, and don't forget, Kelsey is leaving us in a couple of weeks! She's moving to Florida for her husband's new job."

Lynn makes an exaggerated sad face, using her fists to wring fake tears. Kelsey laughs and claps.

"We're having a going-away happy hour for her at Jimi D's next Friday," Lynn says. "Drinks are on Nuts & Bolts till seven. Everyone's invited!"

The room empties, but Tate remains seated. "I have an idea I'd like to run by you, Lynn."

I stand up to leave but halt at the sound of my name.

"It involves Emmie and me, actually."

I peer down at him. "What?"

He gestures to my chair, beckoning me to sit down. Like I'm a toy poodle he's training.

"Oh, how wonderful!" Lynn shuts the door and joins us. I let out a sharp exhale and sit.

Tate clears his throat. "What if Emmie and I spearhead a marketing and social media campaign centered on promoting the charity homebuilding project?"

"Um, what?" I'm unable to hide my shock. Tate wants to work with me on a special project? What in the ever-loving hell?

Lynn claps her hands in merriment before Tate dives into a

laundry list of ideas. There's mention of posting in-progress photos of the house to Nuts & Bolts' social media pages, sending press releases to local media, and a community service hashtag.

"It could take Nuts & Bolts' online presence to the next level while promoting the company within the community. All for a good cause," he says.

He reiterates that he will be in charge of social media, while I will be in charge of writing media releases and pitches. I dry swallow another "um, what?" All that registers in my brain is extra work on top of my day-to-day copywriting duties.

Lynn beams at us, her smile bright enough to power an entire city during a blackout. "Well, I'm certainly impressed at the initiative the two of you are showing. Seeing you come together like this for a good cause is so inspiring. I can't wait to hear what other ideas you'll come up with after you've had time to meet about this project, to really strategize one-on-one."

Lynn continues in full-on excitement mode, suggesting that Tate and I meet weekly and update her periodically to ensure this special project is a success. My throat dries up. Work with Tate one-on-one? Meet with him every week? Hell, no. It's already impossible for us to exist in separate offices across the hall from each other. I have to get out of this.

I whip my head to Tate. "As great as this idea is, I don't know how much I'll be able to contribute. It's your idea, after all, and you just sprung it on me three minutes ago."

Tate frowns.

"Oh, Emmie. Don't sell yourself short!" Lynn says. "Nuts & Bolts' website content has vastly improved over the past couple of years because of you. I know you'll be able to apply those stellar skills to the charity homebuilding project." She gestures to Tate, calling him a social media rock star. He raises an eyebrow when she looks back at me. "This project will be dynamite. I'm sure of it!"

She gazes at us tenderly, beaming with immeasurable hope and excitement. I stutter through a few more "ums," fighting the urge to scream.

After giving us an encouraging squeeze on the shoulders, she claps her hands in delight. "Wonderful! Just wonderful, you two! This idea is so very touching. You know, if you produce some outstanding results with this project, I think I could get you both a week of paid time off each. Maybe even two!"

When I'm back at my office, I plop down in my chair, stunned. I now have to squeeze in bicker sessions with Tate in addition to my regular work during the week. Great.

"That was a weak showing in there."

I stop typing to see Tate hovering at my open doorway. "What?"

"Look, I know you don't want to do this extra project, but it's for a good cause," he says. "Quit whining and suck it up."

I narrow my eyes at him. "Maybe you should have consulted with me before announcing your grand plan to Lynn."

He shakes his head at me. "Like you would have said yes."

My silence is a reluctant agreement. I would have absolutely shot it down.

"How will we even get this project off the ground? We have a hard enough time sitting across the hall from each other."

"Ah yes, here we go with the theatrics. Give it a rest, Emmie."

"Do you know how long it takes to build a house from the ground up? About a year. That means we'll have to work together—one-on-one—for the next twelve months."

He stares at me with a neutral expression, as if he's suddenly forgotten our volatile work history.

"This has disaster written all over it."

"Don't knock it till you try it."

He pushes off my doorframe and runs a hand roughly through his blond waves before looking at me. I glare at him. He glares back. We are beyond ridiculous.

"Fine," I huff. "Let me know how you feel after we've both gone hoarse from yelling at each other."

He rolls his eyes. "Would you prefer if we collaborated over the phone? Or we could do all of our meetings via Gchat, not a single word muttered out loud the whole time. We'd still be four feet from each other, but we wouldn't technically be inhabiting the same space. Would that meet your standards of conduct in the workplace, Ms. Echavarre?"

"Don't even go there. Maybe I wouldn't be so hesitant to work with you if you showcased a smidgen of professionalism, instead of sarcastic comments and snide remarks."

I catch him clenching his jaw before I look away and grab the first object that comes into view. Distracting myself by thumbing through a multi-tool catalog doesn't work. I'm too wound up to come up with anything coherent to write at the moment.

"Quit being so dramatic," he says. "Who knows? You may actually enjoy working with me. Stranger things have happened."

The most obnoxiously smug expression clouds his face. He knows the thought of having to work with him directly is making me crawl out of my skin, and he loves it.

"Fat chance," I say.

"Give it time. I'm quite charming."

"You're not. Believe me. I know charming, and you absolutely are not it."

He raises an eyebrow at me. "Really? And what's charming, Emmie?"

"The exact opposite of you."

He crosses his arms, still facing me. I've still got my nose in the catalog, trying to demonstrate it's more interesting than him.

"Is that so?"

I drop the catalog on my lap, tilting my face up to him. I may be sitting, but we're in a standoff for sure. Our stiff posture and scowls make us look like two cowboys aching to draw our guns and blast each other away.

"It doesn't even matter. When we're together, it's always a complete disaster."

His face drops. I can't put my finger on his expression, but it is no longer smug.

"I see," he says quietly before clearing his throat. Stepping away from my doorway, he walks the few paces to his office.

I flip back around to my computer. We don't say a word to each other the rest of the day. An email pops up on my screen. Tate sent me a meeting request to talk about Nuts & Bolts' charity work promotion project tomorrow afternoon. My first instinct is to decline, but it will just postpone the inevitable. We have to work together whether I like it or not. I reluctantly click "Accept."

three
....

"Photo op?" Tate pins me with an incredulous stare. "You can't be serious."

I bite back the curse I'm aching to let loose and settle deeper into the chair that's shoved in the corner of his office. "What exactly is wrong with that? We take a photo of the family one of the days that they come to see us building the house, then post it on social media. I can include it with the press releases I send to media outlets too."

"It's pretty damn invasive."

I crumple the paper that's covered with my ideas. Twenty minutes into our first official one-on-one meeting for the charity homebuilding project, and I'm already fighting the urge to flip his desk. He's shot down every single one of my suggestions so far. How will we manage these meetings once a week as Lynn requested?

"How would it be invasive? We would ask the family's permission, of course."

I aim for the wastebasket, but the crumpled ball of paper lands a foot away. Tate rolls his eyes, then leans over to throw it in.

"You didn't think this through, did you?"

"How about instead of trashing my ideas, *you* come up with something."

I glance at his yellow notepad, which is covered with red ink. Red is for correcting. What kind of savage writes in red ink?

He drops his pen on his desk. "Did it ever occur to you that this family might be intensely private? Yeah, we can ask to take a photo of them to distribute for media purposes, but they might feel like they can't say no. We're the ones building their house, after all. Maybe they don't want their faces plastered all over Twitter and Facebook."

I frown, but inside I'm thinking that's actually a good point. He didn't have to be so cruel in his delivery, though.

He tilts his head to the side. "This family has little kids. School-aged kids. What if their classmates see them on social media, and they make fun of them for being poor?"

I shake my head. Given how I grew up, I should have thought of this.

"Fine. No photo of the family. But I think posting photos of Nuts & Bolts employees working on the site would be good press."

"If you insist." His hardened face accompanies the uncaring shrug he gives me. "I'm of the opinion that it would be better to convince the Nuts & Bolts owners to make a donation for the kids' college fund after the home is built. We post about that on Twitter and Facebook, it's an instant hit."

I frown at my notepad. "Doubtful." It comes off more like a scoff than the mutter I intended.

"Oh, that's a helpful reaction." His face turns red. "Any other brilliant ideas?"

"Nope. I'm done." I bolt up from the chair and dart back to my office.

I hit the space bar on my keyboard until my screen springs to life. Out of the corner of my eye, I see Tate standing in my doorway, facing me.

"What's the problem?"

"It's pointless to meet with you if all you're going to do is criticize my ideas. Don't bother setting up another meeting until you're ready to get something done."

When I focus back on my computer, Tate is still standing. There's a soft huff of breath, then the rasp of his voice. "Noted."

He walks back to his desk while I deep breathe my way through the frustration. A minute later, Perry from the Purchasing department walks into my office. He doesn't even bother to knock.

"Miss Emmie, a word if you will."

Perry's politeness is an act. Once a month, he drops by someone's desk to correct a supposed mistake, no matter how insignificant, and launches into a condescending explanation. August is my month, apparently.

"I see you posted on the website that we've got a dozen of those new hammer drills in stock. You know, those green ones."

Perry says "green" like I don't know the brand name. It triggers my boss-bitch mode.

"They're called *Hitachi*, Perry." My back is ramrod straight and I stare at him without blinking.

He rolls his eyes. "Unfortunately, we have *zero* in stock. I don't know why you would even put them online. Remember that email I sent you?" He lifts a smug brow at me. "I guess I get it. You're new after all."

I'd laugh if I weren't so pissed. I've worked here for two years. "New" is code for female, and he's used it on me before.

I employ techniques from every article I've ever read about how to be bulletproof when working in a male-dominated environment. My steady eye contact, my posture, my firm tone. It all works together to assert, to say, *I know my shit, Perry, and I don't have time for yours.*

"First of all, Perry, lose the eye-rolling. It's unprofessional, and I won't stand for it. Second, no, I don't remember that email because you haven't emailed me in months."

The words flow out in a hard rhythm that's so unlike how I normally speak.

I pull up a message from three months ago and turn my screen to him. "As for those *Hitachi* hammer drills"—I emphasize the brand name once more before pulling up the inventory software and pointing to the screen—"you most definitely ordered them because those are your initials, PP, right next to the inventory info."

PP. As in Piss Poor. Perpetual Pesterer. Perry the Plague.

His chapped lips purse before he exhales, clearly annoyed. Good. I want to frustrate him; I want to showcase his mistake; and I want him to think twice before confronting me with his mansplaining incompetence again.

"I don't remember entering it in the inventory system," he mutters.

"Don't remember?" Tate chimes in.

Perry and I both twist around to look at Tate. He tosses Perry a death glare from behind his desk. Tate is the only person in the company who Perry hasn't tried to confront. From the corner of my eye, I could swear Perry flinches.

"I don't believe I was speaking to you, Tate." There's a barely detectable tremor in his voice.

Tate's frown is like a bullet to the face. I have to look away, it's so uncomfortable.

"That's irrelevant." Tate's low grown booms. "If you haven't noticed, Emmie's office is just a few feet from mine. You're practically in my office."

Perry opens his mouth but seems to lose his nerve after waiting a second too long.

"When you come here to speak to her about nonexistent mistakes, I have to deal with your voice. Your volume. Your presence. It's all unnecessary."

Perry shuffles out of my office, head hanging low.

A ping of longing hits my chest. It's times like this that catch me off guard, when we unwittingly work together to show up the company know-it-all. It makes me wish that despite our history, we could get along.

Writing boring descriptions about drill bits for the next hour is the only way I can distract myself from that hopeful feeling. It's pathetic to want to be liked by someone who has made it clear they don't like you. Forty-five minutes later, Tate crowds my doorway once more.

"Hey." His jaw clenches, but his eyes are soft. "Try again? We need to get this done at some point. May as well be now."

The urge to scoff is strong, but I shove it aside. He's right.

"Okay," I mutter and follow him to his office.

I notice he's moved the second chair from the corner to in front of his desk. It's a tight squeeze in this microscopic space, but I manage. When I stare at him, I refuse to blink. The way we sit across from each other—our backs straight, our eye contact unbroken—it's more like we're in the middle of an intense salary negotiation rather than a brainstorming session.

"What ideas do you have?" I employ my most polite, even voice. Maybe feigned professionalism will work this time.

His eyebrows lift in what I assume is surprise, but before I can decide for sure, he narrows them back to his standard frown. He consults his notes.

"I came up with hashtags for all the social media posts regarding the charity homebuilding project." He slides the paper so I can see the list he's compiled. "That way our message is consistent and clear at all times."

"I like it," I force myself to say.

The look on his face is one of slight shock, but again, it disappears before I can be sure.

He stares at me blankly. "Your turn."

"We take photos of how the house is coming along a couple times a week and post to social media. We'll attach the hashtags you came up with to stay on message. People pay more attention when they can visualize progress, even if it's little by little."

He nods. "Okay, then." That's as close to a "good job" as I've ever gotten out of him. I feel myself start to smile, but I pull my lips back into a straight line.

"I also thought we could partner with the local food bank and do a food drive at the worksite. I already emailed one of the coordinators there." I slide a printout of the email across the table to him, like a lawyer handing over a crucial document to opposing counsel. "Nuts & Bolts folks can bring nonperishable food items to the site. We'll promo it hard on social media for anyone else in the area who wants to donate. We'll get some excellent cross promotion with the food bank by doing that, in addition to helping a good cause. I'll write up a press release about it and send it to local media for more exposure."

Tate nods. "This could work," he mutters as he scans the paper.

This is a strange dance we're attempting and a far cry from our earlier shit-fit. We're both able to remain even, unemotional, and succinct in our exchange. We've never done that before, and I want to see how long we can maintain this pseudo-professionalism. It happens so infrequently.

"What other ideas do you have?" I say, keeping eye contact with him.

"Random act of kindness day. We'll make it a hashtag to encourage Nuts & Bolts' social media followers to do something nice for someone on a specific day of the week. We'll tell them to tag themselves in a selfie and post it online. Hopefully, it'll be a weekly thing followers will look forward to, which will help promote Nuts & Bolts and the homebuilding project."

I raise my eyebrows. That's actually a great idea. "That could work," I say, borrowing his words.

Tate scribbles something on his pad. I jot down notes on mine. We look up at the same moment and say nothing. This must be some kind of record. Fifteen minutes into a meeting and we haven't lashed out at each other. We'd better quit while we're ahead.

"If you don't have anything else, I can head back to my desk," I say.

"That's all I've got." When I stand up, I spot a speck of notebook paper hanging from his curls, just above his forehead. "You have something in your hair."

I stretch my hand out to his face to point it out, but he jerks away.

"I've got it." His lightning-fast movement away from me is a punch to the gut. I know we're not on good terms, but I was just trying to be decent.

"I wasn't going to do anything. I was just—"

"I said I've got it," he snaps.

My face heats on the walk back to the desk. Even the most pleasant meeting we've ever had still results in hurt feelings on my

FAKER 31

end. I rub my temples with my fingers, failing to massage away the tension. Faking my way through more weekly meetings with Tate will be a whole new challenge.

FOUR MILES INTO my evening jog and I still can't shake my frustration. I can endure almost anything, even a run in ninety-degree heat and ninety percent humidity—but one-on-one meetings with a temperamental Tate for the foreseeable future? Not a chance.

I give up and head back home to my duplex. I'm stripping off my soaking wet clothes in my bathroom when my best friend Kaitlin rings me.

"Emmie! What are you up to?" Her singsong greeting chirps against my ear. No matter how annoyed or angry I am, the sound of her voice always perks me up.

"Just trying to give myself heatstroke by going for a run. How about you?"

"Show-off. Libby's teething, which means she's a howling, restless mess. I'm taking her to the indoor playground at the mall to hopefully help her burn off some energy. Wanna come? I need to be around an adult for a while."

Spending time with Kaitlin and her baby daughter is my favorite pick-me-up. "Let me get cleaned up. Meet you there in a half hour."

When I arrive, I spot Kaitlin sitting on a bench near the main play area. Baby Libby bounces happily on her lap. I bend down to hug Kaitlin and then scoop up Libby. She squeals with delight.

"I swear, you are the only person she will let grab her out of her mama's arms," Kaitlin says.

I scoot next to Kaitlin on the bench while Libby balances her impossibly tiny feet on the tops of my legs.

"I consider that to be the highest compliment a person could ever receive." I kiss Libby's chubby cheeks, and she giggles. "You love your auntie Emmie, don't you?"

From my purse, I fish out a small container of ice cubes and hold one up to Libby's mouth.

Kaitlin squeezes me in a one-armed side hug. "You're amazing. I completely forgot to bring the bag of ice cubes I set aside in the freezer."

"You're busy remembering a million things every day. I can manage a single cup of ice cubes."

Kaitlin hands me a box of my favorite chocolate truffles. "For babysitting last weekend. You're an angel. Ethan and I needed that date night like you wouldn't believe."

I toss the gold box in my purse. "Of course. I'm always on call as a babysitter for you guys."

"I mean it. You're more of an aunt to her than my own sister is. That blanket and plushie you bought her are her absolute favorites. And the baby shower you threw." She shakes her head, a wistful smile on her face. "Everyone still raves about it, and it's been over a year. No one's ever done something so thoughtful and sweet for me in my life."

She gives my leg a soft squeeze, and I can't help but grin. Kaitlin's shower was a blast. Pink streamers and balloons everywhere, and a multitiered cake from her favorite local bakery. I stayed up until two a.m. the night before baking macarons for the gift bags. It was exhausting but worth it. Anything for my amazing best friend and her perfect baby.

"You're wonderful for spending your free time with this little one." Kaitlin tickles Libby's socked foot.

Spending time with baby Libby is a joy, and I'm more than happy to be her go-to babysitter. Besides, it's not like my Saturday nights are all that busy since I'm a single woman with zero dating prospects.

"I can't believe she's almost a year old already," I say. "She's going to be walking soon, you know."

Kaitlin groans. "I know, oh God. Then she'll be running around, crashing into things. She's growing so fast."

"She looks exactly like you."

When Libby finishes her ice cube, she's all smiles. I turn her around on my lap so she faces the playground area. Both Libby and Kaitlin have honey blond hair, green eyes, and angelic rosebud mouths.

"Is Ethan annoyed his baby looks nothing like him?"

Kaitlin laughs and shakes her head. "Not at all. He says he's happy to have a beautiful baby girl who looks just like her mom."

I laugh through a bittersweet tinge. It's an odd feeling being the last single one in my circle of close friends. Whenever they talk about their lives or I spend time with their families, it's a gentle reminder of how far behind I am in the relationship department. Nearly a yearlong dry spell and counting.

I blow a raspberry on Libby's back and she giggles. "The sound of a baby's laughter is exactly what I need to hear after the day I've had," I say.

"What happened?"

"Just annoying work stuff. I have to do a project with that jerkoff coworker I told you about. We had a planning session today, and he was a total prick. Shoot, sorry." I shouldn't use such salty language in front of Libby and the surrounding little ones.

"Don't worry about it," Kaitlin says with a wink. "You should hear the words I use when I'm on two hours of sleep and this little diva is screeching like a beast."

"Like, the project was his idea in the first place. Why did he even suggest working with me if all he's going to do is insult my ideas and make cutting remarks? How we'll get through this without losing it on each other, I have no idea." I press a kiss to the back of Libby's head.

"Do you think you should report him to management for how he's acting?"

"There's an idea." Reporting Tate seems like such a tattletale thing to do. Kaitlin is right, though. I have every right to stand up for myself if he crosses a line.

"Is work going well otherwise?"

"Still surviving as the steely ice queen."

She nudges me lightly with her elbow. "Ice queen? No way. You're a girl boss who works hard, kicks butt, and lets no crap slide. I admire you so much."

I purse my lips. It's sweet of Kaitlin to rave about me, but part of me wonders if it's a little sad that this trait she respects about me is actually something that I have to fake. I shove the thought aside.

"How's Addy doing?" Kaitlin asks.

"Fantastic. She's a month into her yearlong backpacking trek with Ryan. I'm having a hard time concealing my jealousy."

"Where are they now?"

"Costa Rica. I'm supposed to Skype with her in a few days to catch up."

"To be twenty-four and traveling Central and South America with your boyfriend." Kaitlin smooths her hand over Libby's hair.

"Tell me about it." I bounce Libby gently on my lap. "Though they're going the affordable, minimalist route, staying in hostels. No resorts or hotels on their itinerary. Not sure if you'd be into that."

Kaitlin gives me a playful nudge.

"But I'm happy my little sister was able to find a guy as crunchy granola as her," I say.

Addy and I are typical close sisters with vastly different personalities. I'm reserved and quiet while she's bold and outgoing. She lives for off-the-grid adventures, while I'd rather laze around on a beach. She saves money to take a year off work and travel abroad with her boyfriend. I can't imagine being away on vacation for more than two weeks. I live for the comforts of home.

Kaitlin rubs my shoulder. "Are you doing okay? I know it was hard when she moved in with Ryan."

"I miss living with my baby sister of course, but Ryan is a great guy, and I couldn't be happier for her."

Despite my humdrum tone, it's all true. Ryan is a catch and is one of the sweetest guys I know, but I'd be lying if I didn't admit to feeling lonely in my two-bedroom duplex without Addy. I've tried my best to keep it to myself, though. Addy doesn't need to worry about her antisocial big sister missing her too much.

Kaitlin's phone rings, and I play with Libby on the playground while she chats. Crawling on the floor with a one-year-old is surprisingly therapeutic. Once she's off the phone, we head to the food court. Watching Libby destroy a plate of chicken nuggets in her high chair is exactly what I need to get me out of my frustrated funk. I drive home feeling more centered and calm. I'm myself again.

four
....

Tate's banged-up face greets me from across the hall the follow-
ing morning. My jaw drops the moment I fall into my chair.
His left eye is swollen, and his cheekbone is scraped to hell. Shades
of green, purple, and red speckle his ivory skin. I try to remain
discreet in my gawking, but he catches me before I can look away.

He gazes back at me, unblinking. Classic irritated stare.
"What?"

I turn to my computer and log on, wondering if I should ignore
him. I can't. I'm too curious.

"What happened to your face?"

"I mouthed off to the missus."

"Ha ha. You're not even married."

"Brilliant deduction, Emmie." He shakes his head. I wonder if
he's hungover too. He looks like it. "Rugby. Had a match last
night."

"How very un-American," I say, raising an eyebrow. He glances
up at me, a hint of amusement on his face. I wonder how close I
am to making him laugh.

A second passes and the amusement is gone. He's serious

again. "During one of the scrums, a guy in the pack got especially jerky with his elbows, and I caught one to the face."

"Maybe you should be more mindful of where you position your face." I shrug at him.

"Jesus, Emmie." The scowl he shoots me could melt rust from metal.

"It was just a joke," I mutter. And with that, he's back to full-on irritation.

Will struts out of his office to Tate's door. "Hey, did that tweet you sent about the circular saw sale— What in God's name happened to your face?" He jolts back, bumping into the wall. I stifle a laugh.

"Rugby," Tate says with a huff. "Got a little rough last night."

Will whistles through his front teeth. "Yikes, my man. You okay?"

"I'm fine."

He shakes his head while shutting his eyes. "You sure? You want some ice? A Band-Aid?"

"I said I'm fine," Tate growls through what I assume are gritted teeth. I don't see why he has to snap at Will when he's just trying to be nice.

"If you say so."

A soft buzz echoes through the tiny space. Will looks down at his cell. "Ah crap. Hey, would you . . ."

Will clams up when he notices Tate pick up his office phone. He walks the four steps to my office, his face in a worried frown.

I've got a mountain of product descriptions and press releases to write for the charity homebuilding project this morning, but I can't help but take pity. "Need some help, Will?"

"Yeah. Sawyer Custom Contracting is donating some building supplies to us for the homebuilding project. I promised Lynn I would meet their rep downstairs and thank them for the donation, but I forgot I've got a conference call. Can you maybe run down there and shake hands with the guy and tell him thanks for me?"

Oh, Will and his forgetfulness.

"No problem."

Heavy footsteps follow me when I walk down the hall. I twist around and see Tate shuffling to catch up.

"I thought you were on the phone?"

He shrugs, darting to walk ahead of me. I lengthen my stride to keep up.

"Will said the guy would be dropping off supplies. You probably don't want to haul all that by yourself, right?"

When we reach the loading bay downstairs, I zero in on a guy sporting a maroon T-shirt with "Sawyer Custom Contracting" printed in white on the back. He turns around, and I get a proper close-up. Light brown hair with sparkling caramel eyes. He's an inch or two shorter than Tate and built like a concrete wall. Muscles bulge from everywhere. Chest, thighs, calves, arms, shoulders, back. The short-sleeve shirt he's wearing is doing an excellent job of showing off all the long hours he must put in at the gym. I catch myself smiling at him. He grins back through a well-groomed beard. I've never been so happy for Will to double-book himself.

He extends his hand to shake, and I accept. Rough, calloused skin glides against mine. I swoon internally.

"I'm guessing you're not Will," he says with a half smile.

I shake my head, swallowing back a laugh. "You'd be correct. I'm Emmie. I work in Will's department. He's in a meeting, so he sent me instead."

"I'm so glad." His half smile turns whole. "Jamie. Pleasure to meet you. You have a beautiful name, by the way."

"Oh gosh, thanks." I gaze into his perfectly straight white

teeth, which glow against his healthy tan. Trying to keep my grin from growing too comically big is a struggle. "Will wanted me to say thank you for donating the supplies and hauling them all the way over here."

"No problem at all. I just—"

Tate's throat-clear interrupts us. Jamie's gaze moves to my left, recognition hitting his eyes. "Whoa, hey, Tate. How's it going? I didn't know you worked here."

"You never asked," he says in his trademark no-nonsense tone. Why does he always have to be so curt?

I glare at him for a second, then blink it away. Jamie rubs the back of his neck, clearly jolted by his response.

"You two know each other?" My eyes bounce between them.

"We go to the same rock climbing gym," Jamie says.

That would explain Jamie's killer physique.

"No way," I mutter. They both offer silent nods.

Jamie hooks his thumb toward the pile of supplies lying nearby. "I took the liberty of unloading them so you wouldn't have to."

"How sweet." I employ a smidgen of fake work confidence and hold his gaze. My intensity is a bit lower than the boss-bitch toughness I save for difficult coworkers, but the same boldness is there.

"Don't get too excited," Tate mutters. "We still have to haul it to the warehouse."

Jamie points to a nearby dolly. "I'd be happy to help you do that, man."

"Nah. I've got it." Tate's stern response is practically a bark. He stomps to the warehouse, leaving Jamie and me alone.

"Pretty cool that your company is building a house with Midwest Family Homes. My company is too. I'm one of the lead contractors on the project."

"Really?" My stomach jumps at the thought that I might see handsome Jamie again, hammering away at the worksite, hopefully sweaty and sans a shirt.

"If our worksites are anywhere close to each other, you'll have to stop by and say hello."

"Definitely."

We keep eye contact a beat longer than you normally would with someone you've just met. I give myself a mental fist bump for the fun result this bout of faking it brings me.

The squeak of metal wheels dragging against the floor yanks us away from our flirty banter. Tate pushes a massive platform truck in our direction.

"We ready to haul this stuff?" Tate parks it so close to Jamie that he has to take a step back.

Jamie frowns at him. "I thought you said you didn't need any help."

Tate chucks box after box of supplies onto the flatbed. "I changed my mind."

Together the three of us load it up and deliver the supplies to the warehouse to be unloaded. We follow Jamie back to his truck.

"All that rock climbing must have paid off. You two made light work of that."

Tate scowls while Jamie graces me with a half smile. I blush.

He pulls a pen and paper from his back jeans pocket. "Can I get your signature on this form? Just so I can prove to my boss I dropped the supplies off at the right place."

I sign it.

Tate takes a drink from the nearby water fountain before doubling back. "We done here, then?" He crosses his arms while scowling at Jamie and me. "We've got plenty of work to do today.

No sense wasting time standing around and staring at one another."

Instead of rolling my eyes like I want to, I blink. My normal daily to-do list at work has grown. In addition to those press releases, I have a marketing plan to flesh out for the charity home-building project, thanks to Tate.

I lift my hand in a small wave to Jamie. "It was nice to meet you." I start to walk away behind Tate, then flip back around. "Your pen. Sorry."

Jamie takes the pen, brushing my fingers for a long second. I feel my cheeks heat, then he hands it back to me. "Nah. You hang on to it."

"Why?" I giggle like a giddy schoolgirl who's been noticed by the hot guy in class. What a dork I am.

"Because it'll give you an excuse to find me at the worksite." The slick way he raises his eyebrow, it's like he's smirking without moving his mouth.

"Can't wait."

I tuck my hair behind my ears, fumbling with Jamie's pen in my free hand. My response makes me sound weirdly gung ho. I manage to keep a polite smile on my face while I cringe on the inside. My God, am I out of practice at this flirting thing. For a moment I try to think of something witty and cute to say to recover, but instead I let the pause rest between us. What would a confident, unflappable woman do? Let him think of something to say.

He lets out a soft laugh. "I can't wait either." I swear there's a cheeky gleam in his eye before he waves good-bye and climbs back into his truck.

By the time I'm upstairs, I'm officially on cloud nine. It's silly how a minor exchange with a handsome stranger has my insides all mushed up, but I'm currently in the middle of an eleven-month dry spell. I may be jumping the gun a bit, but I'm sick of waiting around.

"You're flirting with contractors now?" Tate says the moment I pass his open door.

When I look up at him sitting behind his desk, he's flipping through his notepad, not even looking at me.

The smile drops from my face. "Excuse me?"

"I overheard the meathead chatting you up around the corner."

"Wow. Eavesdrop much?" He is the king of rude today.

"I have to say, I never thought of you as someone who goes gaga over office supplies."

"What is that supposed to mean?"

"He gives you a *special* pen and you're all smiles. It's a bit much is all I'm saying." His fingers make air quotes when he says "special." Sarcasm drips from his voice with a biting undercurrent of contempt.

My sudden happiness is smashed. "No one forced you to listen."

"It was hard to ignore. His voice carries."

"Whatever. You were so rude to him."

A hot flash hits my skin when I sit at my chair. I peer over my computer monitor at him. Tate finally pays me eye contact.

"He's not as dreamy as you seem to think."

His words sting, and the eye roll he directs at me only deepens the burn.

"Oh, come on. It was so obvious how giddy you were. You think you're the only woman who's ever captured his attention? You should see how women throw themselves at him at the gym."

His words punch me in the gut. I have one happy moment in front of him, and all he can think to do is tear it apart. I shake my head, annoyed that yet again I'm allowing him to infuriate me. I wonder what shade of red my face is right now.

"Of course you would say that," I say after a hard swallow. "You're so pissy and hostile, you wouldn't know how to handle a normal, pleasant interaction if it fell in your lap." It's not until I'm done speaking that I realize how bitter I sound.

"All I'm saying is, up your standards a bit. Find something else in life to bring you joy other than a muscly guy with a pen."

Maybe he's right. Maybe I'm just another cute thing for Jamie to flirt with, and I'm so out of practice that I didn't even realize it.

I shake my head to halt the negative thoughts. No. It was a short, fun, flirty exchange, and I enjoyed it. Nothing more, nothing less. Tate has no right to ruin it.

"I was just being nice. And he was just being nice, which is more than I can say for you."

When he rolls his blue-gray eyes at me once more, my hands ball into fists. He tilts his head to the side, like I'm a child and he's an adult teaching me a valuable lesson.

"Is that all it takes?" He grabs a pen off his desk and stretches his arm out, offering it to me. "Here's a pen, Emmie. Will you be nice to me now?"

"Not in a million years. I'd have to like you first."

"Oh, Jamie likes you all right," he spits out before tossing the pen back on his desk. He sets a pile of product catalogs on his lap and shifts his focus from me to them. "He likes you enough to give you his pen, flirt with you on a loading bay, and then promise to flirt with you at a construction site later. Lucky girl."

"Of course you would say that. You don't like me, so you dismiss anyone who does. Makes total sense."

"You're so full of shit," he mutters while thumbing through a stack of catalogs.

My jaw drops. He's insulted my integrity and sworn at me. I won't stand for it. "What did you say?"

"I said, you're full of it." One by one, he drops the catalogs onto the floor next to his feet. From this angle, I can see the mound of paper piled high underneath the open space of his desk. His gaze is still glued on the stack, like he couldn't possibly waste precious eye contact on me.

"Watch the way you speak to me."

He's silent now, still surveying the catalogs on his lap, still refusing me his eyes.

A second later, I bolt out of my seat and dart to his office. Rounding the corner of his desk, I yank the catalog out of his hand. He gazes up at me in shock as I stand inches from him.

"Don't speak to me like that. Ever." I'm fuming.

"What do you think you're doing?"

"If you think you can swear at me like that, insult me, you are dead wrong." I emphasize "dead wrong." If he suddenly lost his hearing, he would still know exactly what I said, I speak it that slowly.

He raises his eyebrows at me in an expression that indicates both surprise and fear. He probably didn't think I'd accost him. To be fair, I didn't think I would, either, until moments ago.

I'm leaning over him now, taking stock of his features up close. I don't think we've ever been this close to each other before. His forehead showcases a smattering of soft wrinkles, likely earned after spending a year frowning at me. Now that I'm inches away from his face, I notice how pink his lips are.

Then the intoxicating evergreen cologne he wears hits me. This close to him, it smells spicier. One deep inhale almost throws me off. Damn the power of scent.

"Calm down." He says it softly, like he's soothing an angry dog.

And just like that, I shift back to angry and annoyed that he chooses to use that tone.

"No, you . . ." I struggle to finish my sentence. The ache to scream a long list of obscenities at him is strong, but that won't fly. Not after scolding him about swearing. I scrape the innards of my brain for the right non–curse words to spew, but I can't find any. His face reddens and his chest stills. He must be holding in his breath. I take a step back and drop the catalog at his feet. Finally, he exhales.

I dart down the hall to the single-occupancy women's bathroom. Locking the door, I steady myself against the sink. I was seconds away from either lashing out at Tate or slapping him in the face with a tool catalog. A few deep breaths and a splash of water to the cheeks later, and I'm almost back to my steely self.

I don't have to stand for this. I have every right to report him to Will. He's our supervisor after all, and a boss needs to know when one of his employees is out of line. But when I make it to Will's office, his door is still shut. Low murmurs echo from behind it, indicating he's probably still on his conference call. I can't wait, though. From the corner of my eye, I spot a flash of white blond at the far end of the hallway.

The urge to confront Tate takes hold before I can think to do anything else. I don't need Will to do my bidding. I'll confront Tate myself. My rage from minutes ago has cooled to simmering, a promising sign. I'll be able to face him sternly yet professionally.

The heavy metal door to the staircase swings shut, and I have to scurry to keep up. I'm probably thirty seconds behind him. Hustling down the stairwell, I dart through the door to the warehouse. In the distance amidst the endless towering carousels loaded with inventory, I spot Tate's unmistakable blond curls.

He turns the corner, and I nearly lose sight of him. I open

my mouth to call after him while rounding the last carousel, but my breath catches at the sight in front of me.

In the darkened corner of the warehouse is Cal, the delivery driver. He rests on a stool, a wide smile filling his face. Tate is crouched down next to him, paper lunch bag in hand. He hands it to Cal before patting him on the back. Cal gives a nod, then digs into the bag. He fishes out a giant plastic container filled with some sort of casserole, a bag of chips, some fruit, and a packet of cookies.

I'm impressed. That's a far cry from the megahealthy lunch I see Tate eat every single day: an organic turkey sandwich with lettuce, tomato, and mustard on multigrain Ezekiel bread. Always with carrot sticks, an apple, and a giant bottle of water. He's a glutton for monotony. If I ate the same sandwich every day, I'd raze cities. And I know it's organic because when I offered him part of my ham sandwich his first week of work, he inquired if it was organic. There was definite nose crinkling when I said no, and then he muttered something about the harmful effect of nitrates.

Cal must be his one exception.

I stumble back behind the carousel so they can't see me. In the distance, the beeping of a forklift chimes through the warehouse. I squint for a better look while the two chat in hushed tones. I can't hear much until the beeping stops.

"I appreciate it. More than you'll ever know," Cal says in a gruff voice.

"I'm happy to. And here." Tate pulls some bills from his pocket.

Cal frowns before waving a hand at him. "No way. That's too much."

"You fixed my taillight. It's what I owe you."

"That's triple what I charge."

I didn't know Cal did auto repair on the side.

"This is what I want to pay." Tate's cash-filled hand stills. I have a feeling he's going to win this standoff.

A shy smile spreads across Cal's face. "What am I supposed to tell Miriam when I come home with a wad of twenties?"

In the dim light, Tate's mouth lifts into a smile. I nearly choke. I didn't know his face could look so gentle, so soft. "Tell her you won a radio contest."

I have to bite my lip to stifle a chuckle. I don't do a great job keeping quiet, though, because they both twist their heads to look around. Quietly, I suck in a breath and hold it. They turn back to each other.

Tate backs away from Cal. "I'm breaking out the slow cooker tonight, so be ready for pot roast the rest of the week."

With a nod, Cal waves good-bye to Tate. He exits the side door on the opposite end of the warehouse. Leaning my back against the carousel, I huff out a breath. When I straighten up to walk back upstairs, I trip on a rogue electric cord and fall into the carousel in front of me. A box of hammers spills from the bottom shelf, causing an epic crash and echo that I'm sure half of the warehouse hears.

I scramble to pick up the hammers and shove the box back on the shelf when a set of leathery hands comes into view. When I look up, Cal is crouched down to help clean my mess.

"You all right?" Together we slide the box back on the shelf.

I nod. "Sorry, I didn't meant to interrupt your lunch—I mean, I didn't see you eating . . ."

It's official. I'm the world's worst sleuth. Cal waves a hand at me, and a flush of pink flashes across his wrinkled cheeks. There's no use in me stammering through another lie. He knows I saw

Tate bring him lunch and give him money. And there's probably a reason why he's choosing to eat lunch in a darkened corner of the warehouse instead of the break room.

He takes a step back, his eyes falling to the stained concrete below. "Things have been tight for the wife and me lately. She's had some health problems, and there's not a lot of money for much else other than doctors, bills, and rent."

In my head, the blocks fall into place. That explains why Cal, who is pushing seventy, is still working instead of retired like most people his age. It explains why he apparently does auto repairs in addition to his full-time job.

"I'm so sorry."

When he looks up, he's smiling. "Don't be. That Tate fellow is something else. Kept asking me why I never took a lunch break. He saw past all my excuses. Then one day, months ago, he started dropping off bagged lunches for me. I didn't say a word. He just knew." A wistful look passes across his face. I pat his arm. "Son of a gun even tries to give me cash sometimes. I used to refuse it, but he started hiding it in the lunches he brings me."

Warmth courses through me. "Don't be afraid to ask for help, Cal. We're here for you."

His eyes widen for a second, but then he nods. He's probably surprised at my offer, seeing as we haven't spoken more than polite pleasantries to each other since I've worked at Nuts & Bolts. But Cal is someone who's always been kind and respectful to me at work, and I want him to feel comfortable approaching me if he needs help.

"Appreciate it." He walks back to his lunch.

When I make it back to my desk, I see that Tate's office is still empty. He must be out on an errand or an appointment or something. It's just as well. I don't know if I could even muster the courage to look at him right now. Much of the fire and fury inside of me from our argument has melted away, leaving something unfamiliar behind.

I ball both fists in my hair, unsure of what to do or how to feel.

five

·······

"So wait, Tate's been delivering lunch to your elderly coworker? And giving him money?" My little sister, Addy, stares at me through my laptop screen. Her chocolate brown eyes are as big as saucers as I fill her in over Skype about my fight with Tate and creeping on his random act of kindness.

"Yeah. For the past few months now, apparently."

"Huh." A confused frown crowds her face. Anything other than a beaming smile appears unnatural on her. She is one of those people whose resting neutral face radiates warmth and friendliness, unlike me. My resting bitch face suffers no fools.

"I feel kind of bad about freaking out on him now."

I down the last of the green smoothie I made in preparation for this evening's Skype session with Addy, hoping it would reset my cloudy head. It doesn't. Excluding his first week of work at Nuts & Bolts, I've never felt anything other than negative emotions for Tate. But after seeing him act so kindly to Cal, I'm at a loss. The past few days have been quieter than usual because I don't know what to say or how to look at him. We got through our latest one-on-one meeting for the charity homebuilding project with quick answers, minimal questions, and short bouts of eye contact. After ten minutes, it was back to ignoring each other.

"Don't you dare feel bad," Addy scolds.

"Maybe my empathy is seriously lacking," I say, ignoring her comment. "Maybe I've been so blinded with rage and irritation that I missed out on little kind things he's done these past eleven months."

Addy pins me with a frown. "Your empathy is perfectly intact. Can you honestly think of one instance where he showed kindness to you?"

I open and close my mouth a half dozen times, yet nothing comes.

The empty glass makes a loud clink when I set it on the table. Addy wags her finger at me. "Just because he was kind to someone else doesn't take away the fact that he was an utter douche nozzle to you. Do you honestly think that he'll suddenly be nice to you too?"

It actually speaks volumes that he went out of his way to be nice to Cal but can't seem to show me the slightest bit of courtesy in our everyday interactions. Yes, we've maintained a courteous silence lately, but we're bound to bicker about something soon. We always do. And it's only a matter of time before he says just the right cutting words to me, leaving me frustrated and hurt.

That knot of annoyance seeps back into the pit of my stomach. "You're right."

"He'd better be more professional at least, especially if you have to meet with him every single freaking week for that project."

"I wouldn't count on it." I shake my head, hoping it clears away all remaining thoughts of Tate. "Enough about work. Tell me about Costa Rica."

"It's absolutely incredible here. Like, otherworldly." Addy gestures wildly. "Lush green everywhere, crystal blue ocean. I wish you could be here to see it."

Her olive skin is even tanner than before. That combined with her dark hair makes her pop against the beige and yellow background of the room she's in.

"Your gifts are being put to good use too!"

She holds up the pink visor I gave her. "Thanks to this, my face stays covered, which means no blemishes or sun spots. Yay for staving off future wrinkles!"

I flash her a thumbs-up. "How are your feet holding up?"

"Amazing! Those gel inserts you gave us make all the difference when we're walking for hours and hours. You're seriously the best."

She mentions how much she loves the translation app I bought for the one phone she and Ryan are sharing during their trip.

"When you get the chance, check your PayPal account," I say. "I left you a little something."

Addy's jaw drops. "Emmie! Come on, you've already done enough."

"I know you saved money for this trip, but you're still my little sister. It's my job to look after you. You don't even have to use it if you don't want to. Save it for an emergency, just for your peace of mind."

She crosses her arms, but her beaming smile gives away her delight. Seeing her expressive face and wide smile is a delightful comfort. We haven't talked since she left for her trip last month, and I've been dying to catch up with her.

"I swear, you're more like a mom than my big sister. We owe you. Seriously."

"The only thing you owe me are regular Skype sessions while you're away," I say. "Internet access permitting, of course. Speak-

ing of Mom, I emailed her and let her know that I'd be Skyping
you today, so be prepared for an onslaught of questions from her
delivered through me for our next Skype session."

"You're an angel for how you accommodate her when she travels overseas." Addy crinkles her nose in mock frustration. "Way to
make me look bad, by the way. Even when she's out of the country
and you can't do your weekly phone call with her, you email her
regularly instead."

"You're traveling. She understands you're not available. And
every time I offer to pay for international coverage on her phone
when she visits Auntie Marla in the Philippines, she rebuffs me.
Says it's not worth the money and that emailing is better anyway
since we don't have to pay extra for it."

She chuckles. "I wish you were here."

My throat squeezes with how much I miss her.

"We'd have a blast together and you'd be thousands of miles
away from that jerkoff at work."

I let out a heavy sigh. "It's fine. I'll survive. If you could send
some good thoughts my way, though, I'd appreciate it. It's our
first day volunteering at the jobsite tomorrow. I have zero construction experience and will probably embarrass myself in front
of everyone."

"I'll wish for a million construction hotties to magically show
up and offer to help you." She waves her hands in the air, like she's
casting a spell.

Her joking words make me think of Jamie.

"Oh, that face! Tell me!"

I curse the wide grin I let slip. "It's nothing, but you know that
hot guy I mentioned who dropped off the supplies? His company
will be volunteering at the worksite too."

Addy claps her hands. "Perfect opportunity to flirt some more, maybe even ask him out."

Heat hits my cheeks. "We've only met once. I'm probably reading too much into it."

"Come on, think positive! You're a pretty girl. Give him a show while you hammer away in front of him tomorrow." She winks, and I burst into a laugh.

"Enough about that. Enjoy the beach. Get a tan for me. And eat all the yummy tropical fruit you can find."

She peers down at her watch. "Shoot, I'm supposed to meet Ryan at the market. I'd better get going. Miss you! Skype again in a few weeks, okay?" She waves at the screen and I wave back.

"Absolutely. Be safe. Love you!"

I shut my computer. Chatting with Addy was just what I needed to regain perspective. Tate isn't some faultless saint. Yes, it's wonderful that he's helping Cal, but it doesn't erase his treatment of me. Tomorrow I will be a beacon of professionalism, but I will take no crap from him if he tries to pull anything.

NUTS & BOLTS employees scatter around the worksite, eager to get started. Despite the nearly triple-digit temperature, everyone is in surprisingly good spirits.

A foundation for the house has already been laid by Midwest Family Homes. According to the emails Lynn sent out, we're building a four-bedroom home with a basement. The entire block this house is located on boasts a half dozen homes in various states of progress. Volunteers from other companies and organizations hammer away around us.

Lynn finds an empty bucket to stand on and hollers for everyone's attention.

"Everyone, thank you so much for volunteering your time to help with this worthy cause."

Soft clapping follows, as well as more of Lynn's encouraging words. I'm half listening, gazing at the neighboring worksites, wondering if the universe will smile upon me and bless me with a visit from Jamie. I even tucked his pen in the outer thigh pocket of my yoga pants. In my head, I play out our run-in. I retrieve the pen from my pocket while Jamie indulges in a full-body scan. I'm wearing an oversize T-shirt, but I've tied it into a side knot. Hopefully, that will make him think—

"You ready to work?"

The sound of Tate's voice yanks me out of my midday fantasy. I twist around and am greeted with him scowling in ripped jeans and a loose-fitting gray T-shirt. He grips a drill.

"What?"

Lynn jumps off her bucket and the crowd disperses. She waves while darting past us, her thick bangs peeking from under a yellow hard hat.

Tate lets out a slow exhale. "Weren't you listening? We're working on the frame, and those of us with construction experience are supposed to buddy up with the clueless—I mean, inexperienced volunteers."

Now it's my turn to scowl. I don't have it in me to work with Tate on the construction site in addition to our marketing project *and* still share office space.

"Just because I haven't built a house before doesn't mean I'm clueless."

He shakes his head before turning to walk away. I lengthen my stride to keep up.

Sweat beads across every inch of my skin as I sort through the lumber. I can't believe he's taking a potshot at me when we've barely broken ground on today's work. I wipe my face with my forearm, wondering how on earth I'll survive working this close to Tate.

I gaze around the worksite. The Nuts & Bolts crew seem to have fallen into volunteer mode quickly. Most of the workers are huddled by the foundation, working on the frame. A handful of people examine blueprints on the hood of someone's truck parked nearby. Another pickup pulls up to the site loaded with more two-by-fours. Two guys I recognize from the warehouse jump out of the truck and unload the lumber.

Tate joins the nearest group of people sorting through two-by-fours. To avoid looking like the inept volunteer that I most certainly am, I copy the people near me and help line up the rows. Tate works like a machine, drilling together the segments in no time.

"So you're a secret homebuilding expert in your free time?" I ask.

He pauses, leaning up to wipe the sweat from his forehead. "I'm hardly an expert. But I did spend my summers in high school and college working for a homebuilder."

When he reaches up to stretch, I peek at him. His forearms glisten in the unrelenting sun. I've mentioned before that he's a nonugly entity. However, now that I see him in work clothes, there's no avoiding the fact that he's undeniably in shape and attractive. Life is so very unfair.

I move to line up another row of lumber, and he follows. I twist around to reach a faraway two-by-four and catch Tate midgawk. He was staring at the slim peek of my midriff with a half-open mouth. A second later, he clamps it shut. His eyes fall away, but not before I catch a cloudy look I don't recognize. He tries to appear busy messing with the drill bit despite his chest rising and falling rapidly.

This is an amusing change of pace. Showing a bit of skin works a lot better at throwing him off than being combative. I step toward him until the tip of my tennis shoe touches the tip of his work boot.

He lets out a garbled grunt, and the faintest pink color creeps up his cheeks.

"So unprofessional. Keep your eyes to yourself, will you?"

He backs up before almost tripping on an uneven dip in the ground, his face tomato red. I can't help but smirk to myself at how thoroughly I rattled him.

"Hey, you." Jamie's voice sends happy goose bumps across my sweat-soaked arms.

Behind the dark lenses of my sunglasses, I take stock of him. The tattered white shirt he's donned displays his muscular arms nicely. Ripped jeans hug his legs, while a well-worn tool belt hangs off what I can only assume is a killer set of obliques. He looks like a sexy contractor straight out of a romance novel.

"Hey," is all I can say. I can't think of any other words to speak, I'm so flustered.

Kelsey halts midstep on her way to the water cooler to gawk.

"Come to mama," she mutters from behind me. She elbows my arm, and I bite my lip to keep from grinning too wide.

Jamie must have heard, because he lets a soft chuckle slip.

"You weren't trying to get away without saying hi, were you?" He gives me the same killer smile he did last week, and he's maintaining the same eye contact. Definite flirting tells.

"Wouldn't dream of it. I have a pen to return after all." I pat the side pocket of my yoga pants. He takes a glance at my legs, just like I hoped he would.

When he finally meets my eyes, he's grinning even wider. "Happy to see that. But I'd be even happier if I could see you outside of here. Maybe someplace cooler?"

"Oh. That sounds—"

The grind of a circular saw drowns out my voice. Jamie and I twist around to see Tate slicing segments of lumber just feet away. I glare at him and point to the stack of unused two-by-fours, wondering why on earth he thinks we need more.

"Do you have to do that right now?" I try to yell over the scream of the metal blade slicing through wood. Tate squints up at me, mock confusion on his face. He points a work-gloved hand to his ear and shakes his head, indicating that he can't hear.

I hold up a finger to Jamie, then dart around to the extension cord trailing from the portable generator. I yank it from the outlet before narrowing my eyes at Tate. His jaw muscles bulge when he bites down, probably out of frustration.

I step back up to Jamie. "I was saying, that sounds great. What did you have in mind?"

"If you're free tonight, I'm going to hit up the rock climbing gym. Stellar air-conditioning even on the hottest days. Makes you feel like you're scaling the Rockies in the fall. Care to join?"

My giddiness has morphed into full-fledged joy. Jamie the hunky contractor just asked me out. Score.

"I'd love to."

Just a few feet away, Tate has given up on slicing lumber and instead is chugging from his gigantic water bottle. He stares at Jamie and me with repulsion. I wonder what his problem is now.

"I was hoping you'd say that. Here, let's exchange numbers, and I'll text you later with the details."

I nearly melt at the way he tilts his head to the side. I manage a nod. After we return our phones to each other, he flashes me another heart-melting smile. The scrape of plastic on concrete jerks my attention away. Tate's hard hat tumbles to the concrete base of the foundation while he stomps off. One of the warehouse workers picks it up before hollering at Tate, "What gives?" But Tate doesn't even acknowledge him while walking away. He's probably angry Jamie and I interrupted his sawing session with our grotesque unprofessional flirting.

Jamie waves good-bye to me as he jogs back to his company's worksite nearby while I jump back in with the others.

THE EXCITEMENT OF my rock climbing date propels me through the rest of the afternoon, but the moment I arrive at the gym, I'm petrified. It finally registers that I'll have to scale some pretty serious heights on this date with Jamie. One problem: I have a numbing fear of heights.

Jamie greets me at the entrance. I try to zero in on his perfectly straight teeth to distract myself, but even that won't do.

When I step inside, I immediately feel inadequate. Every single person sports a lean, muscular frame and impressive upper body. Climbers hang ten feet from the ground by their fingers, bent at the knuckles. I can't even do a chin-up. I'm screwed. Thank God the floor is covered in inches-thick rubber mats. I'll be cozying up to those face-first real soon.

When I stare up at the climbing walls, my stomach churns. Each one is dotted with multicolored knobs, denoting the various difficulty levels. The walls look like they have Muppet measles. My throat tightens until it's sore.

"It's something, isn't it?" Jamie nudges me. I'm too terrified to speak. "Want to head up first? I'll spot you."

"Uh, no."

"I know the climbing walls look intimidating, but I actually think it's easier to get your feet wet doing this first. Then we can try out bouldering."

"Okay," I mumble. I look down at my hands. They're trembling. I cross my arms to hide it.

"Here. I'll go first and show you."

I watch Jamie as he explains how to put on the harness and strap on the safety cord. His mouth moves, but I register no words. A faint ringing noise is all I hear while nerves crackle under my skin. He claps some chalk onto his hands and scales to the top in record time. He must be part mountain goat. An easy grin crosses his face when he gazes down at me, looking like he just graced the cover of *Outside* magazine.

Sweat pools under my arms, in my palms, on the inside of my elbows. I have a sinking feeling that I will die if I try to climb this wall. It's a completely irrational thought, but I can't help it. Heights bring out worst-case-scenario me.

Jamie is rappelling back down when I hear a familiar voice.

"You okay?" I turn to my left and see Tate.

"What are you doing here?" My fear is now tainted with annoyance. He is the last person I need to see.

"Working out. I'm here most Mondays, Wednesdays, and Fridays."

"Oh." Just speaking that single word leaves me out of breath. My nerves are officially shot.

"Hey, are you all right?" he asks.

I shake my head. "I don't do heights."

"Then why are you here?"

The urge to rebuff him overtakes my fear. Of course I would run into Tate at the rock climbing gym when I'm on the verge of having a panic attack, and of course he would be here to witness it.

"Jamie invited me," I say defensively.

"If you don't feel comfortable doing this, you shouldn't." I notice he's wearing a gray tank top dotted with his sweat. His arms are encased in sculpted muscle and thick veins. I had no idea under all those hoodies he had the pipes of a Greek god.

I blink and shake my head. "I'm fine. I'll be fine."

Jamie drops to the ground. "Oh, hey, Tate. What's up?" How he can be so cheery after scaling a forty-foot wall, I'll never know.

"I'm trying to talk her out of climbing the wall." Tate brushes his hands on his shorts, leaving chalk residue on the navy blue jersey fabric.

"That's silly. Why?"

"Because she's clearly freaked out. Look at her."

I try to smile, but it comes off like I'm being forced to grin at gunpoint.

"No way. She'll be fine. It's easy," Jamie says as he straps me into the harness.

"Emmie, you don't have to do this." Tate's voice is soft. It's strange. It's the opposite of the irritated tone he employs during work hours.

"No. I want to," I say. I'm such a liar, but I can't let him see me fail. I want to impress Jamie, too, but the urge to prove Tate wrong outweighs even that. I will fake bravery, and I will climb this terrifying wall.

From the corner of my eye, I catch him shaking his head when he steps away. I follow Jamie's instructions and push myself up the wall with my legs. As I climb, he shouts out directions.

"Grab the yellow knob on your right," he says. I obey with trembling arms and legs. "Green one on the left. Okay now, push yourself up a bit with your legs. Nice!"

I don't know if my pulse has ever soared so rapidly. Even when I do sprinting drills, my heartbeat is nowhere near this frantic.

"Don't look down. Don't look down," I chant quietly to myself as I hug the wall.

"You're doing great!" Jamie yells from below. He sounds far away. Curiosity gets the best of me, and like a blockhead, I peek down. I'm well over halfway up the wall. Fucking hell, this is high. My arms begin to violently tremble.

"Now go for the blue on your left," Jamie directs.

My vision blurs, my mouth hangs open, and I'm huffing like I'm having a panic attack.

"No!" I yell.

Jamie's laugh echoes. "It's okay, you've got this!"

"No! I can't!" My panicked, deafening tone ricochets off the wall.

Every single person in this gym must have heard me. I don't care. I'm paralyzed with fear. There's no way in hell I'm moving an inch higher on this wall. I want to go back down to the floor, but I can't move. I can't even will myself to lift one finger from either knob in each hand.

"Emmie. Take a breath," Tate shouts from below. "I'll lead you down. Just listen and follow my directions, okay?"

I nod, knowing that if I try to speak I'll burst into tears.

"Look to your left. See that orange knob? Put your left foot on it."

I do it.

"Good. Now lower your left hand to that gray knob below. Yes. Nice job."

The next few minutes Tate directs me back to the floor. I've never been so happy to hear his voice. The moment my feet touch the ground, my heartbeat slows. It's still fast, but I can discern that there are individual beats taking place. It's an improvement from the single thrust of adrenaline against my rib cage while I was glued to the wall.

Yanking off the harness and cord is impossible with shaky hands. "Get me out of this. Now."

"Okay. It's okay. Easy." Jamie is wide eyed at my frantic showing. If my meltdown halfway up the wall didn't turn him off, the freaked-out way I'm kicking off the climbing gear certainly will.

"Hey, it's fine. You did great." Jamie pulls the harness off of me.

"I need a minute." I jog to the front door, suddenly aware of all the strangers staring at me.

I'm pacing back and forth in tears across the parking lot when Tate approaches me.

"What a loser, huh?" I say in a raspy whisper.

"You're not." His tone is strangely kind. I don't think I've ever heard his voice this soft or seen his eyes this concerned. He seems genuinely worried for me.

I let out a half-cry, half-laugh sound. "I had a panic attack on the rock climbing wall in front of everyone. My freak-out will be posted on YouTube in no time, I'm sure."

"Don't say that."

I shake my head. "I honestly thought I could do it." I rub my arms. They're covered in goose bumps even though it's eighty-eight degrees outside and insufferably humid.

"You tried something you were scared of. That's commendable." He moves his arm like he's going to pat my shoulder, but it lands on his hip.

"And I promptly had a meltdown. It was pathetic. I am pathetic." My voice shakes.

"You are not pathetic, Emmie." The way the words fall out of his mouth sounds like he's reading from a heartfelt greeting card. Those are the kindest words he's spoken to me.

I glance at him. He glows under the parking lot lights. "Thanks for helping me get down," I say. "Sorry, I should have said that sooner."

He nods, his mouth curving into a not-quite-smile. "You're welcome."

The yellowy light reveals a smudge of chalk on his forehead. Slowly, I reach my fingers to him. He doesn't jerk away like I think he will. In fact, he doesn't move at all, not even when my thumb glides against his hot, wet skin. He simply stands, still as a tree, his eyes on me the entire time. A wave of comfort washes over me. Touching him feels like the most natural thing in the world right now.

"Chalk on your face." I wipe my hand on my thigh.

"Thanks." That not-quite-smile remains. He turns away and walks back inside.

My hand falls on my chest, and I gasp for air. Tate Rasmussen saved me tonight. Color me surprised.

six

·······

I guzzle a Cherry Coke and rum while listening to Kelsey chatter on during her going-away happy hour at Jimi D's Bar and Grill. Lucky lady is moving to Florida for her husband's new job. After sipping, I sigh. I'm going to miss her high-pitched giggles and the fun-loving personality she brings to Nuts & Bolts.

"Don't get me wrong. I love it here. This is the heartland after all." She clutches my arm like she's worried I'll take offense.

I wince. The multiple rings she's wearing dig into my flesh. I shake my head, pulling my arm away as I laugh along. My phone dings. Jamie texts that he's running late but will be here once he's done with work. Luckily, my recent rock wall freak-out didn't cost me the flirty edge in our text conversations. After Tate disappeared inside, Jamie came out to check on me. I explained how heights weren't my cup of tea, and he said he appreciated how I gave climbing a shot. He still seems into me, and I'm definitely still into him.

The Nuts & Bolts crew has taken over half of the bar. Almost everyone from work is here, even antisocial Gus, because no reasonable person would decline free alcohol paid for by their employer. Surprisingly, I don't see creepy Brett. I would have thought he'd be first in line at the bar, but I'm delighted to not have to deal with him.

"But the beach!" Kelsey's pitch reaches glass-shattering levels. "I've been dreaming about this for years. Sticking my feet in the sand, closing my eyes, and just forgetting about it all."

Her hair spray–stiff curls bounce when she throws her head back. I nod absentmindedly, wishing I could teleport to Hapuna Beach right about now. I'd give anything to dive under those crystal-blue waves.

Kelsey turns to the group next to her, regaling them with a tale about Florida beach hotties.

"Joke's on her. Pensacola is a shithole." I flip around to see Tate on the stool next to me.

Other than our weekly meeting, this is the most he's spoken to me since the rock climbing gym. His momentary sweetness was a blip, evidently.

"She's moving to Panama City." I frown at him.

"That's even worse." He grips a small glass of clear liquid and ice.

"Water?"

"Vodka."

"Wow. You drink like a Russian mobster."

"And you drink like a sorority girl who's scared of hard liquor." He gestures to my half-empty glass with a cherry floating in it. Yup, he has definitely forgotten any temporary kindness toward me.

I stand up and move next to Will. The rest of the evening carries on in loud conversations about sports, work woes, and whispered gossip. The Nuts & Bolts crew slowly trickles out of the bar a few at a time. The company agreed to pay for drinks until seven, and I assume most will leave then. I check my phone periodically for a text or call from Jamie, but nothing so far.

"You didn't let me finish," Tate says. I glance up from my phone and notice he's planted himself next to me again.

"Can't you take a hint? I don't want to sit next to you," I groan like a petulant child.

"Too bad. This was the only free seat left."

I scan the room and see two empty seats on the other side of the bar. "There's an empty seat over there." I point. "And there."

"I meant it as a joke."

I drain the last of my second Cherry Coke and rum. "What are you talking about?"

"I was joking when I called your drink a sorority-girl drink. You left before I could say it." His tone reminds me of how he spoke to me after rock climbing. "I actually really like Cherry Coke and rum."

"Good for you." I refocus on my phone. I'm not in the mood to play games.

"You seem distracted."

I ignore him, but then he pushes another Cherry Coke and rum in front of me. "Thanks." I take a long sip, finally considering him. I'm not above accepting a free drink. "Jamie's supposed to meet me here tonight."

The edge of his jaw tenses. He must be biting down. "You two hit it off."

"We did." If I remain short in my replies, maybe he'll get the hint and leave.

My phone hits seven o'clock, and I look up. Almost all of Nuts & Bolts is gone, like I predicted. Lynn and Kelsey are the only ones left beside Tate and myself. I give Kelsey a hug good-bye before she walks out with Lynn, then resume the staring contest with my phone.

"He's late, huh?" Tate says. What a nosy parker.

"It's fine. I told him I'd wait and have a drink with him." My foot shakes against the metal footrest on the stool. I wish he would leave so I could have a moment to myself before Jamie comes. That way I could finish my drink in peace and then run to the restroom to freshen up my makeup.

"Good thing I'm here to keep you company."

I frown at his smug face. "I don't need you to do that."

He has the gall to look hurt. I can't tell if it's fake or real. Before I can decide for sure, the bartender blows a whistle. We both cover our ears and glower at him. He dons a bright red shirt with a pink heart on it, whistle dangling around his neck. I can't remember what he was wearing when I got here, but it sure as hell wasn't that.

"Folks! It's August and you know what that means! It's our Halfway to Valentine's Day contest! If you want to play, please sit at the bar. This is a couples contest, so only couples at the bar."

I guess the rabidly enthusiastic bartender is supposed to be Cupid? I roll my eyes, but I'm also relieved. This crazy contest is my ticket away from Tate. We can leave the bar, he can go home, and I can wait for Jamie. I try to stand up, but Tate's hand on my arm keeps me in place. A light bulb seems to go off in his head the moment I look over to him. There's a knowing expression behind his eyes. It's the look of a mischievous child who just caught his sibling in a tattletale-worthy act. I bet that's exactly the kind of kid Tate was.

"Let's play, shall we?" he says.

"What? No."

I try to maneuver myself away, but his arm wraps around me, pulling me closer to him. The heat from his body disarms me, just like during the company meeting. It's been so long since anyone's held me like this. Even in the shock of this moment, I could be tempted to stay under his arm, content and warm.

He hollers to the bartender to sign us up. "Come on. It'll be fun. The prize is a hundred-dollar gift card. We can pretend to like each other for a hundred bucks, right?"

A text from Jamie lights up my phone, and I pull away. Jamie says he'll be here in a half hour. I scan the bar to see if there are free single seats anywhere, but now everything is taken. I sigh. If I walk away from this ludicrous game like I want to, there will be nowhere else for me to sit. I could wait outside, but this August heat wave is unrelenting. I don't want to greet Jamie all sweat soaked and smelly. Sitting in my car with the AC cranked seems like a hassle. I guess I'm stuck here.

"Fine." I scowl at Tate, silently cursing his existence, but he's staring ahead and doesn't seem to notice.

The bartender hands us a dry-erase board and a marker, and just like that, we're a fake couple.

"Okay, people, here are the rules," the bartender bellows. "I'll ask a series of questions relating to either the holiday Valentine's Day or the word 'Valentine.' The couple with the most correct answers wins the gift card. Understand? And no using your cell phones. Keep them on the bar top facedown so I can see them and make sure you're not cheating."

Everyone obeys, placing their phones out in full view.

"Okay, first question: The small town of Valentine with a population of approximately twenty-eight hundred people is located in which state?" the bartender bellows.

Participants scribble answers on their white boards. Tate gives me an unsure look.

"Seriously? Come on." I snatch the marker from him.

I write *Nebraska* on our whiteboard. When we hold it up, we're one of the few who correctly guessed it.

"Nice work," Tate says.

Bartender Cupid continues. "Next question: What country is home to the Valentine Falls waterfall in Kosciuszko National Park?"

I shrug, taking another gulp of my drink. "No idea."

Tate scribbles *Australia*. Point for us. "I guess when we put our heads together, we're halfway decent at geography," he whispers to me. I can't help but chuckle.

"You guys are killing it!" bartender Cupid shouts at us. "In what city did the infamous Valentine's Day Massacre happen?"

"New York?" Tate mouths to me. My eyes fix on his lips. Are they always this pink and plump? I shake my head and write *Chicago*.

"That one was easy," I say, looking around the room. "Almost everyone got it right."

"According to a recent survey, what is the most popular gift given to women on Valentine's Day?"

I whisper, "Jewelry," at the same moment Tate whispers, "Flowers." I stifle back a laugh. This is more fun than I thought it would be. We agree to toss out both our guesses and write down "chocolate" instead.

"Oh, come on, you guys were doing so well!" Bartender Cupid frowns at us. "It's jewelry."

I elbow Tate. His flesh is hard, solid. I swallow. "Told you. Get it together." It comes off more playful than I intended.

He raises an eyebrow at me, and it sends a foreign tingle through my stomach.

"Admit it. You're having a good time," he says.

I don't answer. Instead I take a sip and silently admit to myself that he's right.

His phone dings with a text message, and he leans over to check it, dropping the eraser on the floor. I bend down to pick it up and notice my name in the message above what he's typing. My eyes wander, skimming the text. I freeze as the words register in my brain.

I can't handle this. It's worse than I thought. She is . . . fucking hell, I don't even know.

Heat rises to my face. I can't decide if I'm more angry or humiliated. Serves me right. The moment I go against my better judgment and let my guard down around Tate, he reminds me exactly why I shouldn't.

His negative feelings toward me are no surprise. What I don't understand is why he forced me to stay for this pointless game if he planned to make fun of me behind my back. I bite the inside of my cheek to keep from shouting at him. Or maybe I'm on the verge of tears. I'm too caught off guard to know for sure which way I'll fall.

I slam the marker on top of the board and glower at him. "Screw you. I'm done."

"What?" he says. I've never seen a more convincing look of feigned confusion in my life.

Jumping off the stool, I weave through the maze of sweaty bodies crowding the bar. I register Tate's voice calling after me, then I hear the bartender.

"Hey, wait! I was only kidding! You two can still make a comeback!" bartender Cupid shouts. The last of his words are swallowed into the background noise of the bar as the door closes behind me.

Before I can stomp to my car, a hand grips my arm. I shove it away.

Tate holds his hands up in front of him. "Hey. Stop. Why did you leave?"

"You're a dick, you know that?" The words come out in a controlled hiss.

His brow furrows, the lines in his forehead deeper than I've ever seen. "What are you talking about?"

"I saw your text. I saw what you wrote about me. 'I can't handle this'? 'It's worse than I thought'? 'She is . . . fucking hell, I don't even know'? What the hell is your problem?" I'm able to keep a reasonable volume, but my voice shakes with fury. Any moment it could switch to tears.

What little color his face retains drains completely. His eyes widen, then drop to the ground. He's the definition of utterly dejected. I've never seen him react this way.

"You saw that?"

I nod slowly.

"You weren't supposed to."

"Of course not. Shit-talking normally occurs behind someone's back. That's what you were doing, right?"

"Listen. It's not what you think." He holds both of his palms up at me, as if he's talking down an out-of-control mental patient.

"Oh really?" I slip up and the words come out in a shout. I pull myself back to a normal volume. "I saw my name right above that text. I know you were talking about me. Don't you dare lie."

On the outside I manage to maintain my composure, but on the inside I'm rabid and foaming at the mouth. I should be muzzled. It occurs to me there are people outside the bar smoking and watching us. Maybe I'm not as composed as I think I am. When I swallow, I feel how sore the base of my throat is from straining to keep my voice at a non-yell. The blip of shouting seconds ago must have caught everyone's attention, though. That and our obviously hostile body language. I'm gesturing like a crazed palm reader; he's got his hands up in a futile attempt to calm me. We are quite the Friday-night shitshow.

I continue my tirade. "You forced me to play that game just to screw with me behind my back."

"Okay, just . . . just let me explain." His face warps in agony. "Here, let's sit in my car. I can explain it in there, okay?"

"No way I'm going anywhere with you."

"We won't go anywhere. We'll just sit down for a minute. We can't talk out here. People are staring."

I'm too afraid to do a full-on head turn to see our audience, so I rely on my peripheral vision. He's right. Everyone is watching. Embarrassment finally catches up to me. I should book the *Maury* show next week. I'm displaying daytime–talk show–worthy behavior.

I huff a sigh. "You have two minutes."

seven

....

Tate gestures for me to follow him to his car.

"Jeez, man, let her cool off first," a male voice calls after us. Cackling follows. We are the laughingstock of the parking lot.

I climb in the passenger seat of his nondescript gray car. It's such a contrast to him. He's a striking, tall, broad man. The four-door sedan he drives is a car that fugitives would kill to have as a getaway car. Unnoticeable and unremarkable in every way.

He starts the car, and I shoot him what I can only imagine is a look of sheer terror. "I'm not driving anywhere. I'm just turning on the AC."

I place my phone on the dashboard and set the timer. "Two minutes. Talk."

He's gritting his teeth so hard, the muscles in his jaw pulse. "I admit, I was talking about you in that text. But it wasn't anything bad, I swear. I can't tell you the full story, but nothing bad was said about you."

I almost laugh, but I'm furious so it turns into a snort. "You think I should just take you at your word? After tonight? After all

the crap we put each other through every day at work? You're
something else."

The death grip he has on his steering wheel is turning his
knuckles an even starker shade of white. "I can't go into detail, but
what I told you is the truth."

The irritation in his tone makes me want to scream. I can't take
it anymore. I try deep breaths, then swallow. I blink again and
again. Nothing works.

"I want to flip out right now." I speak to the dashboard through
gritted teeth.

Slowly, he turns to me. "I want to kiss you right now."

"What?" I jerk to face him.

If his intention was to throw me off, it worked. I'm not sophis-
ticated enough to harbor two intense emotions at once. The anger
is replaced by confusion. He must be joking.

"I'm not kidding," he says softly, like he can read my mind.

The gaze he gives me is game changing. I've never, ever seen
him display such tenderness, not even when he consoled me at the
rock climbing gym. Right now, in the darkness of his car, he is
illuminated only by the residual light from a nearby streetlamp.
It's perfect though. His face has gone soft. All the skin and muscles are relaxed. Not a trace of tension, anger, or frustration can be
detected anywhere. Something else is there. Something foreign.
Something beyond kindness. The longer I let my eyes linger, the
clearer it becomes. I think it's affection.

When he reaches a hand to my face, I am perfectly still. When
he pulls his mouth closer to mine, I don't flinch. When he presses
our lips together, I let him. He kisses me, and it's the lightest,
softest, most gentle kiss in the world.

He leaves his mouth on mine for several seconds, but I can't be totally sure how long. I'm completely out of sorts and lose all sense of time. The unexpected feel of his mouth has short-circuited my brain. A warm tingle spreads from my lips to the rest of my face.

When I feel his tongue run lightly against my bottom lip, my body tenses and my brain finally catches up. Holy hell, Tate is kissing me. An alarm bell is going off in my head, alerting me to the lunacy of this moment. I immediately smash it. Yes, it's crazy, but I can't deny how divine it feels. I want this. I need this. Screw anyone—even me—who says otherwise.

When he jerks away, I'm left hovering over the center console, my mouth half-open and my eyes still closed. I fall back into my seat, letting the cool air wash over me.

"I'm sorry," he mumbles. Jerky movements take over his body. He's rubbing his eyes, yanking at his hair, shaking his head back and forth. "I don't know what . . . I don't know why I did that." He buries his face in his hands, then sits back up and turns to me.

His expression is his trademark neutral once more. I'd be impressed at his ability to slide so seamlessly from embarrassed to cool if I weren't so aggravated. He springs a kiss on me, then pulls away just as I was getting into it? No. Hell, no. This kind of behavior is not allowed in this parallel universe we're currently residents of, this strange world where Tate is a dynamite kisser and has the sudden nerve to make a move.

In this new world, I turn bold. With my fist on his collar, I yank his face back to mine. I can tell by the shy way he keeps his tongue in his mouth that he's not sure about it. I slide my tongue through his pressed lips. *Too bad for you, Tate. You started this. You will damn well finish it.*

This time, I relax. I enjoy it. The sensation of the tip of his soft tongue teasing mine, the smoothness of his mouth. He tastes like nothing. There's the faintest hint of vodka, but after a few seconds it disappears. Just wetness and flesh and the blank flavor of saliva. It's strange, but I love it. Every guy I've kissed has a particular tang to his mouth. Tobacco, coffee, mint. It must be all the water he guzzles nonstop. Gallons of water washing away any semblance of flavor, leaving the unmistakable taste of Tate behind. I'm in awe of how much I love it, this clean kiss.

His teeth clink against mine, and my eyes jolt open. His do too. The sudden eye contact throws me off.

Just breathe, I think. A slow hiss of air escapes my lips.

"Mmm, oh, mmm." It comes out as a soft, breathy huff. I'm in the middle of a surprise hot kiss with Tate Rasmussen, and that's the sound my brain delivers to my mouth?

My eyes fall down in shame. I remain in place, my face still touching his. What an unbelievable dork I am. I bite my bottom lip. It's a reflex when I'm embarrassed.

He says nothing. His eyes showcase the same cloudiness I remember from our first day on the worksite when my shirt slid up in front of him. I bet I know exactly what he was thinking in that moment, because I'm thinking it now too.

Our faces stay still, our lips barely touching. His tongue finds my bottom lip again, and a switch flips. Our mouths collide once more. This time it's sloppier, more desperate. We're downright hungry for each other. The last time I had a man's lips on mine was almost a year ago. It's obvious how much I've missed it. The way Tate kisses me, I wonder if it's been a while for him too. What a way to end a drought.

When we breathe, our exhales crash. The wetness of his breath is like water. I could drink it forever.

I slide my hand through his curls. His hair is thicker than I thought it would be. I moan in delighted surprise. These white-blond ringlets are the perfect spot for my fingers. Better than gloves, better than the steering wheel of my car, better than the warm manicure bath at my favorite nail salon. I curl them against his scalp and pull. The groan he lets out is like crack to my eager ears. I let go, then pull once more. Again he groans. My eyes are rolling back behind my eyelids. If from this moment on, my life consisted of nothing but kissing Tate and touching his curls, I would be satisfied.

His hands cup my face in such a surprisingly affectionate way that I whimper. He makes an "mmm" sound, and the vibrations of his lips pulse through mine. I could pass out from shock. I had no idea Tate could be so passionate, so gentle in his kiss. I was dead wrong. An android he is not.

There's an ache between my legs, and I nearly yelp. Shit. That's never happened to me during a first kiss before. It rarely happens even when I'm in more advanced stages of fooling around. I wonder if I'd have to fake it with him, like I've had to with other men I've been with. The heat of this kiss and the excitement it brings make me think that maybe, just maybe, I wouldn't have to.

I turn my head to whip my hair out of my eyes and lose a moment of contact. His hands clamp me to his face. His body makes a convincing argument. Don't move away, not even for a second, it says. Stay right here, keep kissing, and enjoy the delicious twinge in your lady parts. You earned this.

The ache settles into a warm tingle and floats through my body.

The melodic ring of my phone interrupts our car interlude. We release each other at the same time. We both seem to understand, even in the heat of arousal, the importance of promptly answering a phone call.

Jamie's name flashes across the screen. For a moment, I wonder why he's calling me, then I remember I invited him to meet me for a drink. Funny how a single tantalizing kiss can destroy the brain cells responsible for my short-term memory.

I answer, out of breath. I register Tate's panting as well.

"Hey! I'm finally here," Jamie says cheerily. "Are you somewhere in the back? I don't see you."

"No, I um . . . I stepped outside for a sec. Hang on, I'm about to walk back inside now." I reach for the handle, but Tate pulls me away from the door.

"I can just go outside—"

"No!" I nearly shout, freezing in Tate's grip. "Stay inside. I'll be there in just one minute, okay?"

I hang up, then yank away from him. "I have to go," I say without looking at him. I'm afraid if we make eye contact, I'll end up lunging at him mouth-first again.

"Wait." He sounds desperate.

"Jamie's here. I have to."

"You can't go. Not yet." His hands rest in fists on top of his legs. He seems to be putting considerable effort into not grabbing me right now. I can't decide if that's good or bad.

This kiss. This crazy kiss, as incredible as it was, has killed my capacity to think clearly. All I know is that I need to get out of his car *now*.

He shakes his head. "Just please listen to me."

He wraps his hand around my arm, but it's not a firm hold. Just pure softness. I stare, mesmerized by the way his creamy arm overlaps my tan skin.

"No," is all I can manage to say.

"Please." His eyes beg me to reconsider, but I can't. I have to get out of this car, I have to meet Jamie, and I have to screw my head back on straight to make sense of what the hell just happened.

"I can't."

Sad eyes are all he gives me. His hand falls away, then I'm gone.

I walk back to Jimi D's, catching a glimpse of myself in one of the glass windows. Matted hair, swollen lips, flushed cheeks, smeared eyeliner. The top of each hot-pink cup of my bra peeks up from the black scoop-neck top I'm wearing. I look like I just auditioned for a porno.

Using the window as a makeshift mirror, I try to quickly salvage my appearance. Luckily, there's a giant shade pulled over the wall on the inside so none of the patrons can see me. Not that they would notice if they could see anyway. Judging by the booming music, cheering, and laughter, it seems like everyone is having a jolly good time. Everyone except me. And Tate, too, probably.

I smooth my hair with the minibrush I keep in my purse. It's tangled to hell, but I manage. I wet a tissue and wipe clean the black smudges under my eyes, then adjust my shirt to a more respectable position. My lips and cheeks will have to calm down by themselves.

When I reach for the door, Jamie pops out, almost running into me.

"There you are," he says. "I know you said to wait in there, but it was getting a bit loud and crazy. Can you believe they're doing a Valentine's Day contest? It's August."

I attempt a chuckle in return, but it sounds like I'm being strangled. I clear my throat. "Sorry for making you wait. I was just getting some air."

I grip my purse in one hand, then the other. Then I jerk the strap all the way up my arm. This is some suspicious fidgeting I'm showcasing. I try to focus on Jamie's face. His kind caramel eyes are an anchor for my wayward emotions. They center me for a half second.

"No worries at all. Feel like going somewhere quieter? Maybe the tavern across the street so we don't have to drive?"

I nod and scurry across the parking lot to the sidewalk, half listening as he chatters about the importance of walking ten thousand steps a day.

"You okay? You look a little flushed."

"No. Yeah. Yeah, no, I mean, I'm fine. Just hot is all." I shake my head, hoping I can disorient myself into forgetting the impossible kiss in Tate's car just minutes ago.

"You look beautiful, by the way."

My mouth freezes in an "O" shape while I breathe. "Oh. Thanks." If only he knew what a tangled mess I am inside.

He raises an eyebrow. "Sounds like you could use some convincing."

"I'm sweating like a pig. I don't feel very beautiful right now." I wonder if Tate thinks I'm beautiful. Is that why he kissed me? I bite the inside of my cheek. Don't think about him. Focus on Jamie.

He tucks a chunk of my hair behind my ear. "Stop. You're beautiful."

He takes my hand and leads me to the crosswalk. A car idles next to us while we wait for the light to change. It's dark gray, four doors, with a dent in the hood. I let go of Jamie's hand when I spot the reflection of Tate's eyes in the rearview mirror. Two full seconds of blue-gray sky until he blinks, then speeds away.

eight

·······

Monday morning arrives after an entire weekend spent replaying the kiss with Tate. I couldn't focus at the tavern when Jamie chatted about his upcoming camping trip. Something about hiking in the Rockies or the Andes. Even drinking a Scotch and water couldn't settle me. After slurping it down, I bade him farewell with a hug and chaste kiss on the cheek. If only he knew where my lips had been.

Staring at my computer screen, I run my tongue along my bottom lip. I swear I taste Tate's clean flavor. All weekend I was a ball of stress thinking about him, our kiss, and what the hell I'm going to do about it all. How embarrassing that a single make-out session has derailed me so thoroughly. I blame the best kiss I've ever had, and the ache it caused between my legs. The sensations linger over me like fog.

Footsteps echoing through the hallway snap me out of my haze. Tate settles in his office, logs on to his computer, and stares ahead. A full minute passes. With each second that ticks by, my shoulder muscles tense. My fingers are useless. I can't type my name, let alone full sentences in this awkward loaded silence.

I guess it's up to me to break it. I walk to his desk. "Hey," I finally say.

"Hey, yourself," he answers in an identical tone.

After plopping in the corner chair, I gaze over at him and nearly gasp. His expression is completely tender. Not a smidge of anger or irritation can be detected anywhere. I don't think I've ever seen him sport such a nonthreatening expression at work. Small bags sit under his eyes. I wonder if he had trouble sleeping this weekend like I did.

"About Friday night," we both say at the same time. I smile; he purses his lips. Typical.

I clear my throat. He rests his palms on the tops of his thighs. I make a mental note of how much more handsome he is when he's not actively scowling. The gentle shading of silvery-blond stubble along his jawline does me in.

"So . . . we kissed," I stammer.

"We did indeed." His tone is one of casual observation. He looks away and slowly licks his lips, like he's lost in thought. The sight of his pink tongue emerging from his mouth is a shot of adrenaline to my heart.

For a second, I let myself remember how solid he felt under my hands. I recall his taste, his lips, the feel of his hair. God, his hair. It's a tousled mess today, and it's hypnotizing. The way the curls fall seems more reckless. It takes every ounce of self-control to keep myself in this chair. My hands would rather take a touch-tour of his hair and body.

I silence my dirty mind. "What should we do about it?"

"What do you mean?" He sounds surprised.

His gaze shifts from my face to the bottom of my neck, then to my chest. It lingers there briefly, then he looks away.

I open my mouth and for a moment I feel bold. I itch to tell him that the clean taste of his mouth is all I've been thinking about, that he's the only guy to ever make me ache between the legs during a first kiss. I'm dying to climb on his lap, wrap my arms around his neck, press my forehead against his, and sink into his eyes until I pass out.

But when I fixate on his gaze, I lose my nerve. There's an intensity behind the gray-blue that I've never seen before. Clarity hits for the first time in three days. It wasn't him who initiated this conversation. I did. I walked to his office. He didn't dare set foot in mine. If he felt any inkling of what I feel for him, he would have brought it up. He would have come to me. Instead, he walked to his desk without so much as a glance in my direction, like he does every morning. Today is just another day for him. It's like Friday night never happened. If that's not indifference to our kiss—to me—I don't know what is.

If his actions just now weren't evidence enough, his stare is. Wariness has replaced cool. Whatever affection I witnessed from him earlier is gone. I understand him now. He wants to ignore what happened between us and move on.

"It was a mistake, right?" I let out a quiet, defeated breath.

He looks at the floor and nods. "Yeah." There's an edge to his voice that wasn't there before. I tuck it away in the back of my mind along with the fleeting boldness I felt.

I take the hint and start to walk back to my office.

"Good weekend for you, then?" he asks while facing his computer.

I pause at the doorway. "It was fine. How about you?"

This is one of the first normal exchanges we've had, and it feels phony. Maybe the two of us are incapable of anything but bickering and smart-ass comments.

"My weekend was okay." He assaults his keyboard with re-newed intensity. "You and Jamie have a good time on Friday night?"

I cringe, remembering that he saw us holding hands at the crosswalk while driving away. When I peer over, I can see the muscles of his jaw push against his skin. The way his mouth clenches indicates that this is probably the last time he will ever make small talk with me.

"It was okay. I mean, good." Apparently "okay" is the word of the day. "We're terrible at small talk, aren't we?" I try to make it sound like a joke, but it comes off more like a sad observation.

A full five seconds pass before he answers me. "Obviously, it's quite the ordeal for us to converse casually. Why don't we go back to normal? Silence unless we need to talk about work." The stony expression I'm used to seeing on his face is gone, replaced by one I can't recognize.

Even though he's right, I can't help but feel hurt.

"Sounds perfect," I say flatly, hoping it hides the despair in my voice. He can probably still hear it, though. I walk back to my of-fice, an invisible cloud of rejection hanging over me. No matter how hard I try, I can't seem to fake anything with him.

IT'S WEEK TWO of building the house, and the heat wave hasn't loosened its grip in the slightest. Even at nine a.m. it's scorching hot, but I welcome it. Avoiding heatstroke is a necessary distrac-tion after four days of tense silence with Tate. We've missed this week's meeting for our social media and marketing project be-cause he never bothered to schedule one. I suppose I could have done it, but I can't bear to look at him, let alone meet him face-to-face. Ever since our kiss postmortem, there's been an unspoken tension that coats the air between us like smoke. The less we interact, the better.

Even sitting across the hall from him, listening to his deafening keyboard punches and tapping is too much. At least out here, physical space separates us.

Unexpected moments of eye contact are the worst, though. Even during our daily volunteer shifts at the worksite, we still manage to accidentally catch sight of each other, then awkwardly look away. Jamie would be a fun diversion, but he left for his hiking trip the morning after we met up for a drink and won't be back until tomorrow. We're due for a proper date that doesn't involve rock climbing or a predate kiss from Tate.

To stay busy, I'm taking progress photos of the worksite. Hopefully, sending them with the pitches I've written to local media outlets will drum up community interest in the charity homebuilding project.

I take a panorama shot, shrugging through the dull ache in my side that's been plaguing me since yesterday. I blame the heat wave, which seems to be cooking me from the inside out. Or maybe it's stress induced from the silent standoff between Tate and me. A weekend of resting is the cure, I suspect. I just have to stay preoccupied for the rest of day, avoid Tate, and I'm golden.

"Can you believe how the frame is coming along?" Lynn claps her hands in delight. She's exchanged her trademark costume jewelry for jersey walking shorts and a pink hard hat. She looks downright adorable, like a mom in a Hallmark movie helping with a home renovation.

I gaze around, my professional mask in place. "It's definitely something."

In a few weeks, the family we're building the house for is

scheduled to stop by and view the worksite. Lynn mentions plans for a swing set in the backyard for the kids. What a thoughtful surprise that will be. I hope the family loves everything we put together for them.

"It was Tate's idea," Lynn says, waving at someone behind me.

When I turn around, I'm rewarded with the sight of Tate. Beautiful, exquisite, toned Tate. I try not to stare, but I fail miserably. He's wearing this long-sleeve, skintight silver workout shirt that clings for dear life to his muscled arms and torso. I can't say I blame the shirt. I'd cling to that body too.

If only the designer of this shirt could see Tate wearing it, doing it incredible justice. The way his torso cuts through the fabric is how that shirt is supposed to look on a body. He sets the hammer clutched in his fist on a nearby sawhorse. The visual reminds me of Thor decked out in all his superhero costume glory: hard, chiseled mass bulging through every inch of fabric. The shiny gray color is the perfect counter to his glowing white skin. He is the god of thunder dipped in a milk bath.

I'm not the only one who notices. No fewer than a dozen women and a couple guys at the surrounding worksites whip their heads around to gawk at him as he walks up to me.

Lynn is called away to answer a question, leaving us alone.

"What?"

Crap. I'm staring, and it's obvious.

"Long sleeves," I say quickly, shaking my head. I focus on the grass. "Interesting choice. A little warm for that, don't you think?" I manage to sound seminormal after four days of not speaking to him.

"It's moisture-wicking fabric. I'll be fine. Besides, I need the sun protection."

My memory bank pulls up an image from the beach next to

the neighborhood I grew up in, of tourists encasing their children in sunscreen and thin long-sleeve T-shirts. Tate would fit right in.

He squints at me, and for a moment, I wonder if he can tell just how much I'm drooling over him. "Any reason why you're standing around taking photos instead of helping with the frame?"

I roll my eyes before directing my gaze back down to my phone. "I'm taking progress photos of the worksite for our special project." I swipe through the pictures I've already taken.

When I rub my forehead, my fingers pull away coated in sweat. Damn, this heat. Already I'm drenched, and I've only been here an hour. I can't wait for the roof to go up so we'll have a reprieve from the unrelenting sunshine.

Tate crosses his arms, his brutal stare still aimed at me. "Get any good shots, Annie Leibovitz?" And there's the winning sarcasm I know so well.

Mimicking his stance, I lean closer to him. "This extra project was your idea, but you seem to have lost all interest. Someone has to stay on top of it. I guess it falls on me."

Brushing past him, I make my way across the wide space to the area that will eventually be the kitchen and dining room. I drag a nearby ladder outside so I can get some exterior photos and hopefully a cool aerial shot.

Tate grabs the other end of the ladder, despite me trying to tug it away from him. It's no use. The ladder is too heavy, and Tate is too strong for me to do anything other than drop my end at a random spot. I set it up at the back corner of the house and walk around. Tate looms like an overprotective bodyguard. I climb up the ladder for the aerial shot, ignoring the ache in my side. All this physical labor from the last few days is leaving me with soreness in muscles I didn't even know I had.

"Jesus, Emmie." Tate curses from several feet below. "Don't lean over like that."

When I glance down, he's gripping the ladder to steady it. "You can let go. I know what I'm doing."

He remains planted below me. "Oh really? You're afraid of heights. Don't be so careless."

A tiny punch lands in the middle of my chest. He's right. I have no idea what I'm doing, but it still hurts to be scolded by the jerk I spent an entire postkiss weekend fawning over. A very handsome jerk who looks like a calendar model in his work clothes, while I look like a frazzled mess in yoga pants and the only clean tank top I could find in my laundry pile. Invisible steam pumps out of my ears.

"No worries, man. I've got it." My jaw drops when I look down and see Jamie standing below. Tate's left arm remains on a middle rung, but he pulls away when I make my way down.

The moment my feet touch the ground, Jamie pulls me into a hug. I grip onto his massive arms, which are nicely on display in a sleeveless shirt. A glowy tan covers his skin. He must have gotten a ton of sun on his trip.

"What are you doing here?" I can't help the cheesy grin on my face.

"A storm was moving into the Rockies, so we left a day early. Thought I'd come over and say hi."

"What a great surprise."

He removes his hard hat, placing it on my head. "To satisfy the safety police over there."

Tate stares daggers at the two of us while leaning on the ladder.

Jamie beams at me. "I'm sorry I didn't call or text while I was gone. Doing a week of off-the-grid camping and hiking in the Rockies was a blast, but there was no cell service."

"No worries at all. You're here now."

Jamie brushes my ponytail over my shoulder, and I let out a soft chuckle. Weirdly, Tate hasn't moved since Jamie arrived. It occurs to me I'm flanked on either side by two very handsome, very strapping men. For a fleeting moment, I can't remember which one I like more. There's something hypnotic about Tate's milky glow, how it highlights his cut musculature. I can't seem to shake it. Then Jamie smiles at me, and heat creeps up my face. Oh, that's right. I like him too.

"You look lovely, by the way." Jamie takes a step closer.

I'm blushing hard core now. Jamie's killer charm has me feeling fab.

Tate scoffs loud enough to scare a nearby bird into flying away, then walks off. Jamie frowns, tipping his head in Tate's direction, then shrugs at me.

"I have no idea what his problem is," I whisper.

From the nearby worksite, a low voice hollers for Jamie.

"I should say hi to the guys, but you up for lunch later?"

My insides mush together. "Absolutely."

I try for a sweet smile. He returns a sly one before jogging away.

Scooting the ladder over, I climb back up to take a few more aerial photos, but the sun glare makes it tough to get a clear shot. Even though I'm only about ten feet from the ground, my hands start to shake. No more height-related activities after today. I step down and hear a softly muttered curse float up from below.

Tate scowls up at me. "You really need to be more careful. There's gravel all over the concrete around here. The ladder isn't steady."

Faint concern rings at the end of his words, almost like he cares. It softens my resolve, but just barely.

Stomping down the ladder, I yank it out of his grip and drag it to the other end of the house. The harsh sound garners confused stares from surrounding volunteers, but I don't care. If the only time Tate cares to talk to me is to lecture me about what a construction noob I am, I don't want to speak to him at all.

"I'm just trying to look out for you, okay?" he calls after me.

I roll my eyes in an attempt to mask my embarrassment.

At this opposite corner of the home's exterior, the sun is behind me, meaning I can get a much clearer photo. I set up the ladder and make the wobbly climb once more, nerves shooting through my stomach. I should have made sure the ladder was on sturdy ground before I scaled it. I can't ask Tate to run over and hold it steady, not after rejecting his help. I'd look like a fool.

With shaky hands, I adjust my hard hat, take a bunch of quick photos, then scale back down.

"Emmie, wait! It's not steady—"

The whine of metal scraping against concrete shrieks against my ear. Then I hit the ground.

nine
....

When I open my eyes, I'm lying facedown on the concrete. Slowly, I lift my hand up and touch my cheek. Bits of gravel dot the side of my face. My limbs are numb, but then the fiery burn sets in and radiates through my body. It's not just my right side anymore; I'm aching everywhere now.

I try to push myself up, but I don't get more than an inch off the ground before I fall back down. My head is spinning, and white dots cloud my vision. A meek, pitiful yelp leaves my mouth. Firm hands on my back and shoulder gently haul me up to stand.

"Are you all right?" Tate asks.

I try to push him away, but he holds me tightly. I give up and lean into him. My head is as unsteady as a spinning top toy.

"Hey, answer me." His voice is urgent, but not unkind.

"Obviously not. I just ate concrete."

"I can see that."

The sunshine is blinding, and when I squint up at him, I can barely make out his face. He seems to notice and moves, blocking the glare with the back of his head. I get a better look at him and am surprised at the deep crease of concern in his forehead.

He brushes the gravel off my face. "Your hard hat slipped partway off when you fell, and you hit your head." Worry fills his eyes. It's the strangest sensation knowing that it's meant for me.

I wiggle out of his grip for a moment, wobbling on my own. "Um, I . . ."

"Here. Sit down."

He lowers me down to the ground, leaning my back against the wood beams of the house. I search my brain for words to speak, but I can't seem to find any. It's like an invisible blanket has covered all the words I want to use.

Blinking over and over is my only clarity. Then I notice that the entire Nuts & Bolts homebuilding crew has stopped working to stand around me. Seconds later, my ears register an angry tone. Tate's angry tone.

"So no one thought it would be wise to make sure the worksite was cleared of debris?"

Slowly, I spin my head to look at everyone. They all have frightened, wide-eyed stares. I don't fault them. Hostile Tate is scary.

Tate crouches down to me. When he speaks, his tone is now soft, an impressive flip from the anger he displayed just seconds ago. "You look like you have a concussion. You need to go to the hospital."

I rub the left side of my head, which I now realize is faintly sore. "What are you, a doctor?"

"No, but I'm taking you to see one right now."

"I can go on my own."

"Like hell you can. I'll take you."

"Crap, Emmie, are you okay?" Jamie appears out of thin air on my right side.

I open my mouth to speak, but Tate beats me to it. "She fell off a ladder and hit her head. She's clearly not okay."

Lynn scurries over, and the three of them stand above me, converging in urgent tones. I try to focus so I can properly eavesdrop, but my head is a cloud. Nothing seems to make sense. I pull my phone from my outer thigh pocket and scroll through my texts. I can't make sense of any of it. Slowly, panic sets in. Why can't I read the words on my phone? Why can't I process what everyone is saying around me?

I elbow Tate's leg and hold my phone up at him. "I can't read what this says."

The horror in those three pairs of eyes is too much to take. Tears burn at my waterlines as I shed every bit of my professional facade. I don't understand why or how, but I'm in a dire state, and I don't care who sees me falling apart right now.

Not even a second later, I'm hauled up by Tate's hands. Calloused, firm, warm hands. Hands I want to hold me forever. When I take a breath, the spice of his cologne mixed with the musk of his sweat fills my lungs. In all the chaos of this moment, it's strangely soothing.

Jamie reaches for me, but Tate turns me away from him. "It's fine. I've got her." The tone he uses makes it sound like a warning. Jamie steps away, crossing his arms against his chest.

"I'll call an ambulance," Lynn says.

"No way." I may be out of it, but I know that if I step foot inside an ambulance, I'll fully lose it. The fluorescent lights, being strapped to a gurney, paramedics poking and prodding at me.

"It's fine. Your insurance will cover it," Jamie says.

"No, just . . . no. No ambulance. I mean it." The pain hardens my voice into a strange mix of terrified and no-nonsense.

"I'll drive her to the hospital," Tate says. "It'll be faster than waiting for an ambulance anyway."

I nod my head in agreement. A car ride with Tate sounds infinitely better.

Lynn puts her phone back. "Let me grab her purse, and I'll help you walk her to your car."

Lynn is barely five feet two inches, and I don't want to crush her as I wobble, so I lean most of my weight on Tate. Jamie offers to help along the way, but Tate snaps a refusal. The steady way Tate walks, he seems to support me with ease. The urge to retch hits, and I let out a single dry heave. Lynn asks if I need to stop, but I shake my head.

"This is definitely a concussion. She needs to see a doctor now." Tate's blunt words register just as his car comes into view. More bickering follows.

"This isn't a two-person job. I said I've got it," Tate barks as he lowers me into the front passenger seat.

"Look, I'm just trying to help. Dial back the intensity, will you?" Jamie's impatience sounds on the cusp of anger. I try to speak, but instead I heave a wad of spit onto the concrete below. I shut my eyes.

"I don't have time to argue with you," Tate says. "I need to get her to the hospital." When he touches my cheek, I open my eyes. He's crouched down, staring at me. His entire milky forehead fills with a half dozen concerned creases. "She's completely out of it. She needs to be at the ER now."

Jamie says something about calling me, but Tate shuts the door and I can't make out the rest. Tate speeds out of the parking lot. I bounce between the door and my seat with each urgent turn and press of the gas pedal. If social media doesn't work out, he'd make one hell of a getaway driver. We're paused at a stoplight when he seems to remember that I'm unbuckled. He straps me in with my seat belt.

"It'll be okay," he says calmly. "We're almost there."

The panic filling me is in direct opposition to the slow-motion gears crowding my head. "Do you promise?" I peek up at him from under a mess of sweaty hair.

"Promise." He holds my gaze for a long second. "Don't fall asleep though, okay?"

After pulling into the parking lot, he leads me to the ER with easy strength yet again. I'm clutching at him like an injured lemur, but judging by the firm way he grips my body, he doesn't seem to mind. In the waiting room, he takes the chair next to me and fills out my paperwork, consulting my ID and insurance card when needed. I try to say thank you, but a lump lodges in my throat.

"Here. Come here." He slinks his arm around me, and my face falls into the space between his shoulder and chest. How he could sense the silent panic within me, I don't know. I'm grateful he could though, because being cuddled into him is pure divinity. I could nuzzle forever in this perfect crook.

My eyes fly open when I remember that he said not to fall asleep. Instead, I huff a deep breath. The spicy forest aroma of his deodorant is a needed distraction. I'll have to ask him later what brand it is. I inhale deeply, keeping my eyes shut. Not a hint of sweat in his scent. Even in the heat and humidity of this morning, he managed to stay BO-free. He is a machine.

When I glance at the form, I notice he wrote the wrong date. I point to it. "No. That was yesterday's date."

Pure relief washes over his face when he gazes at me. "You can read this?"

I nod, then smile when I realize what a good sign that is. My gaze floats to an elderly woman across from us, smiling kindly. We must look adorable huddled together.

Soon a nurse fetches me. Tate props me up once again, and we follow her through glass doors to an empty exam room. As I'm settled into the bed, Tate stands in the corner, staring at me in silence. The creases in his forehead remain. I want to tell him to stop frowning because it will cause premature wrinkles, but I don't have the energy.

The nurse takes my vitals, gives me a gown to change into, sticks an IV into me, then tells me I have to give a urine sample before the doctor can see me.

"I don't know if I can even pee," I mumble. I couldn't stomach anything other than a glass of water this morning, the pain in my side was so bad, and I sweat it all out during the first five minutes on the worksite.

"Well, you have to try. If you can't pee, I'll have to take it from you with a catheter, and trust me, you don't want that," she says flippantly while gazing at her watch and checking the pulse in my wrist.

She hands me a plastic cup and walks out of the room. Tate glowers at her; I assume because of her impersonal bedside manner. I lean up from the bed.

"Don't stand up by yourself." He rushes over and slides my legs over the edge. "Do you need help?"

With what little strength I have, I roll my eyes. "No way in hell you're helping me pee. Or change."

He sighs and leads me to the toilet despite my false claims that I can walk on my own. I take a moment to steady myself against the closed door. After undressing, I toss the flimsy gown on and tie it in the back. A measly amount of dark yellow urine is all I'm able to squeeze into the cup, which I leave on the ledge of the sink before washing up. Tate practically carries me back to the bed.

The nurse returns, this time with a forty-something man wearing a white coat and stethoscope around his neck. The doctor, I assume. He introduces himself before asking what happened, and I explain my fall. He inquires about any pain or injuries. I mention the allover soreness and the ache in my right side.

The doctor presses and prods me, asking me to move various limbs and describe the pain.

"Nothing seems broken, which is good. There'll be bruises and scrapes, but the soreness will fade after a few days. Can you tell me what your name is?"

"Emmaline Echavarre. I go by Emmie, though."

"Good. Emmie, can you tell me what day it is?"

"Friday."

"Very good. And where are you right now?"

"The hospital emergency room."

From the corner, Tate huffs a sigh. He seems relieved.

The doctor flashes a penlight in my eyes, then presses around the injured side of my head. "I don't see any bruising on your head, which is good. Did you throw up?"

"I dry heaved once and spit saliva, but I didn't throw up. I haven't eaten anything today, though."

Tate explains how I was able to read the registration form in the waiting room. The doctor nods and scribbles some notes in his clipboard. "It sounds like you've had a minor concussion. It's an excellent sign that you seemed to have regained cognitive ability after about fifteen minutes of feeling out of sorts. I think you'll be just fine, but we'd like to keep you overnight at the hospital for observation, just to be extra sure. That sound okay?"

I nod and close my eyes. Then I remember the warning about sleeping and peel them open.

By the way he chuckles, the doctor seems to read the thought tumbling through my mind. "Tired?"

"A little."

He squints at the clipboard. "It's okay to sleep if you feel tired, actually. The nurses will check up on you periodically once we admit you to a room upstairs. We'll wake you up every couple hours to make sure you're doing okay. If your boyfriend can stay with you and keep you company, too, that's even better."

"Oh no, he's . . ."

The gentle frown crowding Tate's face halts me. The doctor and the nurse probably don't care that he's not my boyfriend, just a coworker who I shared a hot car make-out with.

When the doctor leaves, the nurse says someone will be in soon to fetch me and take me to a room upstairs. She walks out the door, leaving Tate and me alone once more.

"I wasn't trying to make it seem like you and I—I mean, I didn't want to get into . . ."

He holds up a hand, then a half smile crawls across his face. "Don't even worry about it."

"You can leave. I'll be fine here alone."

His smile drops.

"I'm sorry. I didn't mean it like that. I just, I assumed you'd be tired from all you did today. And that you'd be sick of me."

"I'm not," he says quietly.

There's eagerness behind his eyes, and I realize he truly wants to stay with me. My stomach flips with excitement and relief. And then it hits me: I want Tate here with me, too, no one else.

"Then stay here with me. If you want."

With his calming blue-gray eyes, he holds my gaze. They're the perfect hue to warm up this sterile white room.

"I'd love to," he says.

ten

....

One hour later, I'm in a private room on the fourth floor. Tate walks to the window, whipping open the curtains before walking back to my bedside.

"What time is it?"

He checks the clock on the wall. "Almost six."

I mouth, "Wow," silently to myself. I should have known from the dark orange sunlight shining behind the concrete tower crowding my window view. Tate has taken care of me and been by my side for the past few hours. He's watched me fall, smoothed my hair back, consoled me, held me, propped me up when I couldn't walk. Now he gets to watch me struggle to relax while I recover from a concussion.

"And I called Lynn to update her on everything. She says everyone is relieved you're okay. They all say hi. Wanna try to take a nap?"

Hearing the word "nap" is like the opposite of a trigger. My body unclenches, and fatigue rushes through me like air. "What will you do?" I say through a yawn.

"Hang out right here." He pulls a chair up to the side of the hospital bed. When he sits down, he's facing me, his knees inches away. If he reached his arm out, he could touch my face. "Don't worry about me."

His fingers brush the top of my hands for two seconds before he returns his hand to the top of his leg. I close my eyes.

SHORT NAPS ARE all I manage until the sky outside my window turns indigo, indicating the dead of evening. Tate still sits by my bedside, like a patient guardian. He alternates between reading something on his phone and skimming through a stack of magazines he found near the nurses' station.

Through a handful of blinks, I study him. His eyes are heavy with fatigue. Then they cut to me.

"No reading over my shoulder. You're not supposed to tax your brain. Rest like a good patient, okay?" A yawn follows his gentle warning.

"You're tired."

"A little, but I'll be fine. I've slept in worse places before, believe it or not."

When I open my mouth, I expect to hear myself ask what places are less comfortable than a shoddy plastic chair, but then I hear myself say, "That chair is no good to spend the night in. Stay up here with me."

Dread fills me when I realize how desperate I sound, but it quickly dissipates. His eyes don't widen in surprise like I thought they would. Instead, a relieved smile appears. "Okay."

It brings warmth to my chest, setting me at ease. It's a welcome counter to the soreness lingering in my body. I slide to one edge of the hospital bed and shift to my side. He says nothing while kicking off his shoes and climbing next to me. With his back flat over the covers, I cuddle into the crook of his shoulder and chest. It's the same cozy position we practiced in the ER waiting room, only better because now we're lying down. For a moment, I wonder what plans he had for today and if he had to cancel anything to look after me.

"Don't worry. I won't try anything," he teases in a whisper.

"Even if you did, it wouldn't make a difference." I yawn. This hospital bed must have been made for a giant, because even though it's a tight fit, it's not uncomfortable. In fact, I feel a million times more comfortable snuggled next to him than I did while lying in it alone.

"Why do you say that?"

"I'm difficult to excite in that way."

"You mean . . ." He drifts off.

"I'll give you a hint: I'm not often able to reach the top of the mountain." I yawn again. "We'll see how long it takes you to figure it out."

A minute passes. "Does it start with an 'O'?" he asks.

I nod.

"Sorry to hear that."

"It's fine."

"So you've never had an orgasm?" he says after several seconds of silence.

"No, I have. Just not with most people I've been with. I fake them usually. I can give myself one just fine."

He nuzzles the top of my head and takes a long whiff of my hair. The knotted muscles in my shoulders relax. I can't remember the last time I was this comfortable, this content against a male body.

"You are a fascinating being, Emmie."

I let out a tired moan. With each blink, my eyelids stay closed longer and longer. Feeling Tate's solid body against mine is an instant relaxer. I'm not far from sleep. "Thank you for taking care of me today. You didn't have to."

"I wanted to. Thank you for letting me."

My ear presses against the side of his chest, the slow rhythm of his heartbeat lulling me to sleep.

THERE'S ONLY PITCH black when I open my eyes. It's a handful of moments before my vision adjusts and I spot the crack of yellow light between the door and the wall. The nurse must have shut it while we slept. She also must not have minded the way we disregarded the visiting hour policy, because Tate is still cuddled up next to me. I zero in on his faint wheeze above my head. I tilt up for a look. When I move my shoulder slightly, he stirs. His eyes open, and even in the darkness, their soothing color is visible.

"Hey there," he whispers in a raspy voice. My ears tingle, giddy at the sound. I wonder if this is what he sounds like first thing in the morning.

"Hi," I whisper back. "Are you comfortable? Do you need me to move?"

He closes his eyes again and gives me a sleepy smile. He shakes his head. "Nope. This is perfect."

A tiny spot in the center of my chest bursts. I've never seen a grin that was as adorable as it was sexy. I try to scoot closer to the railing to give him more space, but his arm keeps me firmly against him.

"Cognitive wellness check," he whispers. "Tell me your name, the day, and where you're at."

A sleepy chuckle falls from me before I answer the questions perfectly, just I like I did when the nurse checked on me.

His massive hand gives my upper arm a single soft squeeze, then his thumb rubs up and down my skin. He doesn't want to let me go.

"You passed with flying colors."

Goose bumps spring up all over my body. It occurs to me I've never, ever felt this comfortable and safeguarded with any man I've been with. No boyfriend has ever cuddled me the way he does. Whenever a guy has tried to spoon me in bed, I pull away. I feel smothered and contorted, and I can't escape their grip fast enough. But one night in this bed with Tate is changing me. I think I'm a born-again cuddler.

With my body sunken into his, I burrow my nose in his chest. "You sure you're comfortable?" I peek up from under my eyelids to steal another glance.

Even though his face shows all signs of being in a restful sleep, he answers. "Very."

The dull pain in my right side sharpens. I've been curled in the fetal position too long, and my sore body's not happy about it. I shuffle around so my back is cradled by his front, and in an instant, I'm asleep once more.

When I wake in the morning, I'm still wrapped in Tate's left arm, but the minor ache in my side has morphed into something worse, like I'm being stabbed with a dull butter knife. I touch my forehead, and my fingers come away covered in cold sweat. Why the hell am I burning up? Momentary shivers cause my teeth to chatter. I try to straighten my legs against the bed, but the cramping worsens. I have to take several deep breaths. Did my concussion cause this?

Tate's peaceful snoozing tickles my ears, the only source of comfort I can latch onto right now.

"Tate," I whine.

There's a soft grunt. "What is it? Are you okay?"

I shake my head. Seconds pass. The more awake I feel, the worse it gets. There's an invisible vise twisting the side of my stomach, eviscerating my insides.

I feel his warm, firm body peel away from me. The bed rattles, and there's a thud. Tate jumping out of bed and falling to the floor, I assume. He rounds the foot of the bed and crouches down so he's eye level with me.

"God, you look pale."

"That's rich, coming from you."

He frowns. "Don't joke. I'm serious. Hang tight, I'll be back with one of the nurses."

Deep breaths help, but only marginally. The ache from the fall, the sore spot on the side of my head, is nothing compared to the invisible machete in my right side.

Soon Tate returns with a nurse I don't recognize and a dark-haired woman in a crisp white lab coat. The doctor on call, I think.

She leans down over me, then gently presses me flat on the bed. "Emmie, I'm Dr. Tran. Can you tell me about the pain you're experiencing?" Her deep brown eyes study me.

I explain how it feels like psychotic-level PMS cramps and how it started as a dull ache in my right side a couple days ago. Dr. Tran presses her gloved hands all over the side of my lower abdomen while I bite back squeals of pain. I rack my brain to try and remember if I landed on something when I fell that could have caused an internal injury.

Behind the cloud of pain that consumes me, I hear Tate ask if my fall could have anything do with this. It's a trickle of comfort in my physical agony that he's somehow so in tune with me.

The doctor says something about not ruling anything out be-fore turning back to me. "I'm going to order a CT scan to get a better look at what's going on in there."

I nod and close my eyes.

"I know you're in intense pain right now, so we're going to give you some morphine. It'll take a few minutes to kick in, but once it does, you'll feel a lot better."

The promise of no more mind-blowing pain is the best thing she could have told me. I'm approaching kid-on-Christmas-morning levels of happiness. The nurse administers the morphine and leaves with Dr. Tran.

Tate walks to my side. "You'll feel better in a few minutes. Just breathe with me until the morphine kicks in, okay?"

"Okay. Thank you," I say softly. The sharp stab gradually fades back into an ache.

"That's it. Just keep breathing. Slowly. In and out." He must notice that I'm death-gripping the edge of the bed, because he places his hand over mine. Instantly, my fingers loosen.

I follow his instructions. The intensity of the ache decreases as the seconds tick by. When it reaches a dull soreness, I almost smile.

"Wow," I say in a drawn-out whisper.

His eyes widen. "What?"

"I feel better already."

This time when I close my eyes, I fall asleep. I wake up to the jolt of my bed wheeling down a hallway. A large tan man pushes me into a darkened room filled with expensive-looking medical machinery. A tiny blond woman with a cheery smile and her hair in a bun greets me before saying something about hauling me onto the bed of the CT scan. With the morphine coursing through me, I tell her I feel strong enough to climb up by myself. She nods for

the man to stand next to me just in case I fall, but I make it un-
assisted.

Slowly, my body is slid into the darkened tunnel. It stops so just
my head and upper chest jut out from the opening. For five minutes I lie there, staying as still as possible. Slow, deep breaths tide
me over until I slide out and climb back into the hospital bed. I'm
wheeled back to my room.

"How was it?" Tate asks, seated in the chair at my side.

"Glorious." I run my palms lightly over my stomach.

"I wonder what weird things they found in my stomach." The
morphine leaves me floating in a cloudy haze. "Maybe a pack of
tiny elves is hunkered down in my gut, stabbing me with samurai
swords. That's what it feels like."

He chuckles. "Those ninja elves need to come up with better
things to do with their time than bother you. Like fighting crime."

"Or making cookies in a tree."

"Or repairing shoes."

I laugh, then I narrow my eyes at him. He stares back, studying my face as hard as I'm studying his.

"You're impressively pale," I say.

"So I've heard."

"I love it."

"You do?" His cheeks turn a gentle shade of pink. He sounds
genuinely surprised.

"You remind me of the Scandinavians who travel to the Big
Island for the Ironman race. When I was a kid, I'd see them jogging and swimming all over the island to practice for it. They were
milky white and ripped to hell, just like you."

The truth-serum effect of painkillers is impressive. I'm telling
him things I would normally never dream of saying out loud.

He lets out a half chuckle. "How do you know I'm ripped to hell?" His elbow rests on his knee, his chin propped on his fist.

"You wore a tank top when I saw you at the rock climbing gym. Your arms are . . . delightful." I catch him with an amused smile. It's heaven knowing I caused it. "And the shirt you're wearing now leaves little to the imagination."

Now that he's hunched over a bit, he's within touching distance. I reach over and grab his biceps in my hand. Even under fabric, it's hard as steel. The firmness makes my insides ache in a good way. Normally, I would never be so bold as to feel up a man's arm. I blame the morphine.

"This spandex or Lycra or whatever it is, the way it hugs your body, I can see all the muscles."

He shifts in his chair. His cheeks are full-on red now. I think I'm overdoing it in the compliments department, but I can't help it. The painkillers are holding the filter between my brain and my mouth hostage. I am no longer myself. I am Morphine Emmie who is making my coworker feel self-conscious by showering him with compliments about his body.

"The other day at the worksite, you lifted your shirt up a couple times to wipe your face. I got an excellent view of your stomach. Very muscly. Muah." I kiss my fingertips like I'm complementing a delicious Italian meal.

"Jesus Christ." He laughs. "That's enough out of you." The chuckling fades, but his smile remains. "You should sleep now."

"Aren't you going to ask me what my name is?" I'm in a cloudy haze, but it's different from the confusion I felt during my concussion. It's a light, airy feeling that reminds me of laughing gas at the dentist.

He shakes his head. "I overhead Dr. Tran telling the nurse

FAKER   109

she's pretty positive you're fully recovered from your minor concussion."

His words are the green light my body seems to need to fully relax. At least my first health crisis resolved itself before the next one arrived. Soon that cloudy haze turns into half sleep. I don't know how long I'm out, but when I open my eyes, self-awareness makes an appearance. My face heats when I remember how I grabbed Tate's arm. Whatever momentary gall it was that came over me then has gone into hiding now.

I don't know why I feel so self-conscious all of a sudden. We shared a bed last night and this morning after all. But that was tender and sweet. My drugged-up comments to him were downright outrageous.

Dr. Tran glides back into my room. "I just wanted to pop in and let you know that we believe you're suffering from appendicitis."

My mouth falls open so fast, my jaw pops. That's a hell of a way to announce a serious medical issue. Straight to the point, not even a hello to soften the blow.

She seems to sense the fear coursing through me and quickly explains in laymen's terms the results of my CT scan, specifically how my appendix is inflamed. A simple surgery scheduled for this afternoon is the chosen course of action.

Appendicitis. Inflamed. Surgery. Her words incite a slow-motion freak-out inside of me. All I can do is ball my clammy hands into fists and remind myself to breathe. When I ease into an inhale, I realize I've been holding my breath the entire time she's been speaking.

"Surgery?" is the only thing I can say.

Dr. Tran's kind brown eyes focus on me when she finally picks up on my fright. "It's a routine procedure, and I'll be performing it. You have no reason to worry."

"Sorry, I'm just a little scared. I've never been cut open in my life. Ever." My meek voice is a dead giveaway for how terrified I am. Tate grabs my hand, interlacing his fingers with mine. The warmth of his skin is the most soothing thing in the world.

"I understand." When she nods, her shoulder-length black bob moves in a single perfect swish. "But you're young and you're healthy. I have every reason to believe you'll recovery quickly from this."

"I don't understand . . . How did my concussion cause this?"

"I can assure you, it didn't. From what you described, the symptoms started before your fall. The shock of the concussion seemed to cloud things for a bit. In all likelihood, you mistook the appendicitis pain as soreness from your fall." She taps my blanket-covered leg with her hand. "I know it's a lot to process, but you'll be fine."

She tells me the aides will fetch me around one thirty to bring me down to the surgery ward. When she leaves, ringing fills my ears. I stare at the clock. Exactly one hour until I'm wheeled to the OR.

"Emmie."

I finally register Tate's voice.

"You have nothing to worry about," he says in a calming tone. "I'll be right here with you the entire time." He traces the top of my knuckles with his free hand.

At work, I find his unrelenting gaze unnerving. Right now, it's pure comfort. There's an invisible, unbreakable line between my eyes and his. The longer I look at him, the surer I feel. The more I trust him. The comfort deepens, seeps into my chest, then spreads to everywhere else in my body.

"Do you want me to call your family and tell them you're here?" I shake my head. "I don't want to worry them."

He raises an eyebrow at me.

"My mom is in the Philippines for the next month visiting my aunt, my dad is on the road for work, and my sister is jungle hopping in Costa Rica. It's hardly worth the trouble."

I silently thank the heavens that my mom is out of the country. If she were home, she'd drive like a bat out of hell to my hospital bed from the nearby suburb where she lives. Then she'd camp out at my bedside babying me, just like she did when I would fall sick as a kid. It would be sweet for sure, but too much.

"Someone needs to know where you are," Tate says.

"Why? If things are routine like you say they are, I don't need to worry anyone by calling them and telling them I'm in the hospital."

"Don't be ridiculous. Your family and friends would want to know what you're going through."

"I'm exhausted. I'm on painkillers. I don't feel like chatting or texting."

"I'll do all that. You rest. Just tell me who to contact."

I let out a frustrated sigh. His persistence is legendary. I both hate and admire it. "Fine. I have my email up on my phone. My sister's name is Addy; she should be one of the first names in my inbox. When you mention me being in the hospital, please make it clear that I'm okay."

His fetches my phone from my purse. His fingers move across the screen at lightning speed. "Email has been sent to Addy. Who's next?"

"No one. She's it."

The way he throws his hand on his hip, his jaw tense, illustrates what a frustrating and uncooperative patient I am.

"Give me the name of a friend to call or I'll call the first name I come across in your contacts list."

The muscles in my neck and shoulders tense. I grip the railing again but let go as soon as his eyes dart to my hand. "Do it. I don't care." I fail in my attempt to sound tough.

"You're a terrible liar, you know that?" He glides his thumb across the screen.

"Fine," I groan. "You can call my friend Kaitlin, but she's a new mom and busy as hell. I shouldn't bother her."

"I'm sure she'd want to know how you're doing."

I shake my head. "She's listed in my contacts as 'My Best Mate Kait (lin).'"

"Cute."

I hear Tate leaving what sounds like a voice mail message before I slip into a light sleep.

eleven

·······

A shrieking gasp jolts me awake. I squint my eyes open and see Kaitlin standing over me. Her mouth hangs wide and her eyebrows are pinched together. I know that expression well. It's her signature horrified look.

"Oh my God." She covers her mouth with her hand and grips the bed railing with the other. "I rushed here as soon as your co-worker called me."

"Um, why?" I look around for Tate, but he's nowhere to be found.

She shoots me an annoyed, dumbfounded look. "Because you're in the hospital."

"Didn't he tell you that I'm fine?" I'm half speaking, half moaning.

"Emmie, get real. You are not fine. You're in the hospital, for crying out loud."

I hold up the morphine drip button. "I have pain meds. I'm set."

She rolls her eyes and crosses her arms. She's wearing a pink hoodie zipped over gray yoga pants and flip-flops. Guilt hits. She must have dropped everything and rushed to see me the moment Tate called her. I feel bad for being the cause of her worry.

"I'm sorry."

"For what?" Her frown is one of utter confusion.

"For making you worry. You didn't need to drop everything to come here. I know you're busy with Libby—"

She cups her hand over my mouth. I smack it away.

"Stop. You're my best friend and you're sick. Of course I'm going to drop everything to check on you."

"What about Libby, though?"

"She's with Ethan's mom." She pulls a chair to the bed and sits, then sniffles.

"Cold?"

She shrugs. "Libby caught a cough and runny nose from day care. And, of course, that means I get it too." She pulls a tissue from her pocket and wipes her nose. "I feel terrible you're going through this alone. You should have called me when you first got to the hospital yesterday. I would have driven like a bat out of hell to be with you."

"I wasn't alone. Tate drove me here and checked me into the ER. He waited with me the whole day while they examined me and admitted me, and when the doctor talked to me."

She flashes a relieved smile. "I'm glad." A moment later her lips purse. "Wait, you said Tate helped you? *Tate* is the guy who called me?"

I nod.

"I thought you didn't like him? I thought you said he was insufferable?"

I shift, pushing the covers off my chest. "Yes to both of those statements."

"Did something happen to change things between you two?"

I contemplate telling her about the kiss in his car, but I don't want to get into it here.

"He's just trying to be nice."

"I wonder what brought on the sudden kindness."

I'm wondering the same thing. "Where did he go?"

"There was no one else in the room when I walked in."

"Maybe he went home." An unexpected ping of disappointment hits. I have no right to feel this way. He's done more than enough for me and deserves to enjoy what little is left of the weekend.

Kaitlin starts to ask another question, but Tate walks back in, cup of coffee in hand. "Oh. Sorry."

"Don't apologize!" Kaitlin pulls him into a hug. He's wide-eyed as his arms hover over her back, barely touching her. I chuckle at how his large, muscled frame swallows her petite body.

"This is Kaitlin," I say.

She returns to my side. "Thank you for taking care of Emmie."

"Of course. Here, I'll step outside and give you two some privacy."

Tate walks out of the room. When Kaitlin turns to face me, her jaw is wide open. "Holy hell," she says in a loud whisper.

"What?"

"He is gorgeous. Why have you never mentioned how good looking he is before?" She steals another glance at the doorway.

I roll my eyes. "I never really thought about it. I was too busy being annoyed at him to notice."

She plops on the foot of the bed and raises an eyebrow at me. "I'd bet good money he likes you."

"Don't be ridiculous."

She counters with a knowing smirk. "A man would never spend an entire Saturday taking care of a woman he can't stand."

I shake my head, but inside I wonder if what she says is true. She pats my leg and checks her phone.

"Thank you for coming to check on me, but you should go pick up Libby."

"I told you. I can stay."

"It's fine. I'm fine."

"You sound like a broken record."

I clutch her hand. "Kaitlin, don't push yourself. You're sick. You should be home resting. You don't want to end up in the room next to me, do you?" I wink, and she lets out an exasperated sigh. "As soon as I get out of surgery, Tate will text or call you."

"You are too stubborn, you know that? You're lucky I love you."

"And I love you. Thanks for checking on me."

She leans down to give me a kiss on the cheek. She waves bye and stops at the door, smiling at an unseen person before walking out. Tate walks in the moment she's gone.

"She's nice," he says before sipping his coffee.

"She is. She's the best."

He scoots his chair closer to the bed.

"Why did you make her leave?"

"I didn't need her to stay. It's not necessary." I close my eyes. "Also, thanks for eavesdropping, by the way. Good call hanging right by the open door like that."

"I wasn't eavesdropping."

"You're quite good at it during work hours. Why not do it at the hospital too?" I keep my eyes shut, thinking back to when Tate overheard me flirting with Jamie.

"I guess I deserved that." He sighs heavily, then gulps. "I gotta know, why do you do that?"

"Do what?"

"Pretend like you're fine when you're not? Like you don't need anyone's help even though you do? Like you're some tough-as-nails warrior who is above other people helping you? You do it at work. You did it at the worksite. You did it with Kaitlin just now." He's not accusatory. He sounds more curious than anything.

I open my eyes. The dull ache creeps back to my side. I press the morphine button before it has a chance to grow into full-fledged pain.

"Because I'm full of shit."

"No, you're not."

I shrug.

"Then explain why. I don't get it at all."

This gentle back-and-forth is new. We're not arguing. Things aren't tense between us. We're simply having a casual conversation about the root cause of my behavior. I don't know how much longer I'll last, though. I'm dead tired and aching. I'm sliding back and forth between normal reality and the slow-motion one that takes over whenever another dose of morphine glides through my veins.

"Of course it would be nice if Kaitlin stayed longer, but she's not feeling well and her baby's sick. What kind of a jerk best friend would I be if I made her stay with me when she's dealing with all that?"

I let my eyes wander over him. His head is drooped slightly, and he's staring at the coffee cup in his hand.

"And as far as work goes, come on. You couldn't fathom why I would try to be tough and unfeeling in a workplace staffed by mostly gruff men? I have to be that way. If I were myself, I wouldn't survive."

"No 'try.' You *are* strong and tough. Give yourself some credit."

I think he's trying to coax personal information out of me by being nice. It's working.

"It's pretty damn cute, though. Your face, the way you reset it before you respond to people sometimes. Like your natural expression happens first, then you have to remind yourself to act hard." He follows with the hint of a smile. It's gone after a second.

I have to look away, I'm so flustered. I had no idea that he even noticed. I wonder when he picked up on it. And I wonder if other people notice too.

"It must be exhausting, doing that all the time."

I sigh but say nothing. It used to be. I used to have to jog after work or chat with Addy or Kaitlin to crawl back to my real self. Now, it's like slipping into a second skin.

"You have me figured out. Congrats." I attempt to sound bored, like I couldn't care less that he's noticed this telling habit of mine, but I'd bet anything he can decipher my real tone.

I try to scoot out of bed, but Tate leads me gently back against the pillows. "What are you doing?"

"I have to pee."

He squints at me.

"I do."

He helps me out of bed and to the bathroom. Behind the door, I breathe deeply to steady myself. It's my go-to boss-bitch exercise, but I need it to work now. I can't afford to freak out. I need to keep my heartbeat and breathing under control. Going into surgery with an off-the-charts heart rate while hyperventilating can't be good. When I crawl back into bed, I press the button to my morphine drip for the millionth time.

"You're doing it again," Tate says.

"Doing what?"

"Breathing slowly, resetting, trying to mask your natural reactions."

"Thanks for the play-by-play." I turn away, hoping he can't see my face.

With gentle fingertips, he turns my face to his. I crumble at his touch.

"I'm scared," I whisper. A lump hits the back of my throat.

"It's okay. I'm here."

I scoot closer and press my cheek against his palm. I zero in on the thickness of his skin, and how it soothes me.

Soon I'm wheeled out of the room to the elevator. By the time I make it to pre-op, Tate is there waiting for me. He sits in the only chair in the space, and just like he did in my hospital room, he scoots it as close as he can to the bed to be near me.

A clown car of medical staff filters into my room to check my vitals and explain the procedure. Then a late-twenties man with short dark hair steps in.

He smiles politely and gives me a quick wave. "Hi, Emmie. I'm Brendan, the resident who will be operating on you with Dr. Tran."

At first I think it's strange that he doesn't call himself doctor, but then Tate stands up to shake his hand.

"We're old friends," Tate says, patting him on the back.

"Oh." The seconds-long way I respond makes me sound like I'm living in slow motion. Pain meds have quite the relaxing effect on my vocal cords.

Brendan chuckles. "I'm sorry you're not feeling well, but we'll fix you right up."

He stands in place for a moment without saying anything. He raises an eyebrow at Tate, then smiles. Tate shakes his head as Brendan leaves the room. I wonder what that silent exchange was about.

"Do you know *everyone*?"

He sits back down, grinning wide. There's a burst of joy in my chest at getting him to smile so big.

"Very funny. We go way back."

"That knowing look between the two of you just now. Don't think I didn't notice it."

His feet shuffle between the chair legs. "I texted him yesterday to let him know that I was at his hospital with you. He tried calling me during his break last night, but I didn't answer. I think he was amused to see I was still here."

"You mean you don't spend all your free nights at the hospital cuddling with random women?"

"You're hardly random." He gazes up at me, exhaustion detectable in every feature of his face. Even when they're fatigued, his eyes are powerful enough to floor me. If I look too long, I start to feel stripped down.

I divert my gaze to the morphine button.

"Careful with that," he says. "No overdosing on my watch."

"I couldn't even if I wanted to. There's a limit programmed into it. It locks up after that."

I contemplate pressing it again but hold off. Noises from behind the closed curtain fill our silence. There's a faint beeping from an unknown medical machine as well as a steady stream of squeaky footsteps. I count the loud ticks from the clock on the wall. Only minutes until I'm sliced and diced.

"Tell me about Hawaii." His soft voice interrupts the background noise.

"Why?" I'm surprised at his odd request.

"You seem like you could use a distraction."

The cynic inside of me is uncertain. He's asked me about Hawaii before, but always in a way I didn't fully trust. I don't want to indulge him if his plan is to just make fun of me.

"Or maybe you just want more things to tease me about."

He shakes his head, clearly annoyed. "No, of course not. I want to know." He closes his eyes for a moment. When he opens them, he seems sincere. "I swear I won't. I honestly want to hear about your life there."

I swallow, the inside of my mouth grainy with dryness.

"Please?" His eyes sparkle with anticipation. The genuine kindness in his voice melts me.

"Fine." I try to sound unfazed. "I grew up on the Big Island."

"Where exactly?"

"Kona side. Kailua, specifically."

"Did you go to the beach every day?"

"That's the first question everyone asks me. Not every day. Probably every other day."

"Sounds amazing."

"It was. Sunny almost every single day. A few rainy days here and there. Sometimes we'd have an off year where winter was rainy, but it never lasted longer than a week or so." I mark "winter" with air quotes since there is no such thing as winter in Hawaii, only more rain.

"What are the beaches like?" He scoots his chair closer to the bed until his knees touch the edge.

"Beautiful, but rockier than you'd think. Especially on the Hilo side."

"That's the eastern part of the island?"

I nod and glance up at him. He's staring at me intently, like I'm telling a suspenseful campfire story.

"Magic Sands and Hapuna are my favorite. They're on the west side."

"What else?"

"The waves of the water are crystal blue. There are sea turtles everywhere, on almost every beach. The farmers markets are the greatest. You can get so much fresh tropical fruit for cheap." My mouth waters at the thought of strawberry papayas and ice cream bananas. This is the first time I've felt hungry in days.

"What's your favorite fruit?"

"Papayas. Actually, mangoes. Mangoes from the Big Island are the best. You'll fall on the floor crying after one bite."

"Did you ever see a lava flow?"

"No. We went to Volcanoes National Park once. I was maybe seven, and we only stayed for a few hours. The most we ever saw was steam coming out of the lava fields."

"Still pretty cool though," he says.

"Standing near them felt like being in a steam shower. My sister and I shredded our flip-flops walking all over the lava rock. They were ruined. Our mom was pissed."

He lets out a quiet chuckle, and I try to memorize the joyful shape his face takes.

"Did your family have a house near the beach?"

"Nope. Too expensive. My dad never had a steady job, so we basically shuffled from crappy apartment to crappy apartment, miles away from any beach. Sometimes we couldn't even finish out a lease because my parents wouldn't have enough money for the rent, and we'd get evicted."

My chest squeezes at the memory.

"I'm sorry," Tate says.

"It's fine. First-world problem."

"It's not. That's a terrible thing to have to go through as a little kid."

"I survived."

"Just like you are surviving now." He reaches for me, his hand landing on my arm. With his index finger, he rubs the underside of my wrist. My eyes focus on the tiny patch of skin-to-skin contact.

"We'll see if I make it out of surgery," I say, closing my eyes.

"Don't say that. It's a simple operation. You heard what Dr. Tran said." His finger glides all the way down to my fingertips. He touches them one by one, and I nearly stop breathing. It's weirdly intimate telling him about my childhood while he touches me.

"You'll survive." He gifts me a half smile. "And when you come out of surgery, maybe I'll tell you a bit about my life here in the Great Plains, pretty much the opposite of the beach." His eyes fall to his shoes. "As a kid you must have hated it at first, leaving a tropical paradise for boring flatlands."

"I did hate it, but not because of the scenery. When we moved, I was in junior high and had to transfer schools in the middle of the school year. Kids were mean. I was one of a handful of minority students in the entire school. In the entire town, actually. They called me names."

"What kind of names? Like racial slurs?" He sounds concerned. It's sweet.

"No, not that. Things like Pocahontas because some kids thought I looked Native American. Then when they realized I was from Hawaii, they called me Lilo, like from *Lilo and Stitch*."

"Fucking jerkoffs." He pushes a chunk of hair away from my face, tucking it behind my ear.

"I know. Not even the right race." I twist my fist into the bedsheet as more memories surface.

Once I can trust my voice to sound normal, I speak. "You'd burn the second you step off the plane if you ever go to Hawaii."

He makes an amused scoffing noise. "You're probably right. I'm a haole after all. It sounds incredible, though. I'd like to go some day."

"You know the word 'haole'? I'm impressed." I let myself laugh.

"One of my college roommates was Hawaiian. It was his favorite nickname for me when he spotted me doing 'white boy things,' as he put it."

"What are 'white boy things'?"

"Watching or playing lacrosse. Eating Jell-O. Drinking Red Bull and vodka. Driving an Acura."

He chuckles, and I laugh even harder.

My eyes settle back on him. "You are very fair, though. If you ever go, shellac yourself in sunscreen, put on a hat and sunglasses, and you'll be fine."

"You sound like my sister. Sunscreen is serious business for her, and she never lets me hear the end of it when I forget to put it on."

"Smart woman. Protecting fair skin from the sun is no joke."

That tidbit of personal info is like catnip. I want to hear more from him, to learn as much as I can.

He speaks before I can even open my mouth. "What brought you all the way here? I've always wondered."

I shake my head. "No. More about you first."

He gives me a handful of blinks before his face splits into a smile. "Why?"

"Because I'm giving you a hell of a look into my life right now. Sick in the hospital, dispensing personal info like candy. I've got nothing from you, other than you have a sister and you used to live with a guy from Hawaii."

When he pauses, he takes the time to purse his lips. Then there's a soft smile. "Ask me anything."

"Do you have any other siblings?"

He shakes his head. "Just me and my twin sister."

I nearly choke. "You're a twin?"

"Is that a problem?"

"No. Just processing the fact that you're almost a clone. Christ, you're a steel trap for information. What's she like?"

"Sweet. Kind. Outgoing. Easy to get along with. Pretty much the exact opposite of me."

"That's not true. You can be sweet and kind, but only when someone is deathly ill and on their way to the hospital."

He grins, then purses his lips once more.

"Tell me more about her," I say.

"Her name's Natalie. She's fiercely loyal and protective of me."

His face perks up slightly at the mention of her. I picture a lively, curly-haired blond little girl refusing to leave the side of kid Tate.

"Then she would hate me for all the crap I give you at work," I say.

"She'd like you a lot. I have no doubt." He shuffles his feet. "What else do you want to know?"

"Relationship status?" I can't help my curiosity. It's something I've wondered the entire time I've known him, but I've never felt comfortable enough to ask.

"Single."

"Interesting."

"Is it?" He squints at me.

"A bit. You're so damn handsome. I would think women flock to you like flies to honey." Normally, I'd be too embarrassed to say such a thing, but my morphine courage helps.

Pink creeps up his neck and his cheeks just as his mouth quirks into a smile. "I think the pain meds are messing with your head."

"Way to dodge the subject."

He shakes his head and runs a hand over his face. His lips resume their straight line the moment his hand falls to his lap.

"I think you know why I'm unattached." His eyes bore into mine.

I shrug. "You're too broody, too intense. Ladies dig it to a point, but I'd bet anything you intimidate them with your constant scowling and staring and jaw clenching. Remember before I fell off the ladder, when you walked up to me?"

He nods.

"Every single woman in our vicinity was gawking at you like you were something to eat. A couple guys, too, actually. You didn't notice. Too busy death staring at me. If you just eased up on the steely facade, they would approach you."

I expect him to chuckle, to roll his eyes at my assessment. I think it's pretty accurate, but I'd love to hear the real reason a hottie like Tate doesn't seem to be interested in any woman around him. Yet he doesn't speak, not right away. All he does is swallow and stare.

"Maybe I don't want them to," he says.

There's a flutter in my stomach. It surges up my chest and to my throat, making it impossible to talk. He sets his hand over mine and gives it a soft squeeze.

Just then a nurse pops in to up my morphine dose before wheeling me to the operating room. With each blink, I grow more and more groggy. The feel of Tate's hand on mine is the last thing I remember before slipping into the darkness.

twelve

....

A woman dressed in scrubs with a cap over her hair is shoving thick socks onto my feet when I wake. I'm guessing she's a nurse. She's speaking, but I can't make out what she's saying. It's hard with a cloudy head and ringing ears. After a minute, I finally understand a handful of the words she speaks. *Laparoscopic. Post-op. Successful. You did great.*

Ten seconds after that, I begin to process full sentences.

"You had a hot appendix, honey. It probably would have burst had you waited any longer to come to the hospital," she says.

Coming out of general anesthesia is surprisingly exhausting. I try to say "okay," but I can't open my mouth. I can barely tilt my head. I feel like I've been shaken awake from a coma. Every blink is a battle. I just want to wake the hell up and go home.

I'm wheeled back to my hospital room. When I turn my head and see no one is there waiting, I stare at the ceiling and space out, on the verge of unconsciousness. Soft patting against the bed wakes me. It's Dr. Tran. She explains that surgery went well and that since I'm recovering so well, I can go home tomorrow morning.

I try to sit up, but sharp pain shoots through my right side. I fall back down to the bed.

"Try not to strain your abdomen," she says. "You need to heal."

"Okay." I sound like a sleepy toddler.

Alone in the room, I wonder where Tate is. I crawl back in my memory, going over the conversation we had before I was wheeled into surgery. I try to recall all the things we said to each other this morning and yesterday. I remember telling him about growing up in Hawaii and about being bullied in school. I remember Kaitlin marching in, brimming with worry. I remember gushing about how handsome he is. And then I remember telling him about my big "O" problem.

Fuck. I press my eyelids shut, grimacing at the memory. I can barely recall it. But he can. I bet he remembers it perfectly. Oh dear God.

Every other candid admission I made to him over the past day and a half floods over me. He opened up, too, but nowhere near the scale that I did. Fiery warmth consumes me, even under these paper-thin bedsheets. Before today, I didn't know my entire body could blush with humiliation.

When he walks into my hospital room, I tense. A gentle smile spreads across his face. He's done so many thoughtful things for me the past day and a half. The urge to thank him over and over hits, but I stop myself. I would just sound weirdly grateful, which would add to my growing list of pathetic qualities he's now aware of.

"You're back," he says, slightly out of breath.

"Where have you been?"

"With a friend. We just got back from moving your car to your place."

"Oh." What an incredibly nice thing for him to do. "Wait,

how did you know where to take my car? You don't know where I live."

He plops on the chair. "Your driver's license. Your address is printed on it."

"Right. Thank you for thinking to do that."

"No problem at all." He heaves a breath. Bluish bags rest under his eyes. He hasn't changed since he brought me to the hospital yesterday. I wonder if he's eaten.

"I, uh . . . I survived. Surgery, I mean," I stammer. I'm so thrown off, I can't think of anything else to say.

"I guess I owe you some chitchat about me," he says.

Part of me wants him gone, so I can be alone to fight through the worst of this embarrassment. But the other part of me burns with curiosity. His comments about ignoring the interest of other women were the last words I heard before I went under anesthesia. I wonder what that means in relation to me.

"Chat away," I say, trying my best to keep my cool.

He swallows, and his face turns serious. "Sitting next to you has been what gets me through every single workday. I'd rather have a bad day at work with you in the office across from me than a good day without you."

His words hit my ears like a banging cymbal. That same surge of hope I felt when we saw each other at work after our kiss surges through me. That same dread follows. For the past thirty-six hours, Tate has been unexpectedly caring and attentive. Now I realize why this new side of him is as unsettling as it is wonderful. It's completely unlike him, and I hate not knowing how long it will last. He will eventually switch back to his abrasive self, just like he's done every other time he has showed me any kindness. All of this will just be a blip of sweetness on his radar of hostility.

"You could have fooled me," I say.

"I know I've been an asshole to you. I just . . . It's hard to explain."

I shake my head. "I'm used to it. Middle school prepared me well."

Slowly, he stands up, walks to my side, and grabs my hand again, this time in a grip so tight I couldn't let go if I wanted to. It still tingles. "Please don't say that."

"It's who you are, Tate. You made it clear to me on your first day of work that you don't like me."

"But you don't—"

"It's true, and you know it. I fake like it doesn't hurt my feelings when it does. I pretend like I don't want to be your best work buddy, but I do."

It's cathartic to finally admit this to him. I wait for him to let go of my hand, but he holds on.

"It's all fine. I can pretend like I don't care." When I admit it out loud, I want to cry. But I can't. Not here in front of him, not now when I'm desperately grasping for my bearings in this post-surgery haze.

His fingers trace my cheek. My pain isn't physical anymore. I need something more powerful than painkillers to ease it.

He takes my hand in both of his. My eyes are slits at this point, but I catch a glimpse of his head lowering down to the bed. His velvety lips press against the back of my hand, giving me the softest, most gentle kiss in the world. Instantly, I melt.

"Things could be different if we start being ourselves." His gaze turns tender. He kisses my hand again.

I shake my head. "Maybe, but too much has happened. We've been jerks to each other for too long."

"It doesn't have to stay that way," he says.

"We don't know how to be anything else to each other."

"That's not true. Right here, right now, we're not at all like we are at work. We've been so much better."

He's right. In this hospital, we've been so good to each other. But in a few hours it will end, and all I'll have is a morphine-induced memory of him touching my hair, holding my hand, kissing my cheek, cuddling me to sleep. I should be thankful I've gotten this much.

I pinpoint him with drowsy eyes. "We're in a vacuum. We can say and do whatever we want here in this hospital, but it's not reality. How could we make this work in our normal lives?"

When he doesn't say anything, I know I'm right. Even though I ache for him to tell me that I'm wrong, that he can be this kind person forever no matter where we are, it's not possible. He can't be something he's not.

I close my eyes and let the silence bury me.

Tate's husky voice cuts through to me. "Let's stay here, then."

"Ha." I moan. "Impossible. My insurance won't cover it."

"Then let's go away and start over. Fix ourselves, make things right, and then come back. We can be just like this, how we are now. How does that sound?"

I gaze up at him. I want it more than he knows. If we could figure out a way to be our kind selves in front of each other always, I would say yes in a heartbeat.

Tears brim behind my eyelids. I keep them closed until I know they won't fall.

"More drugs, please," I say.

"I'm serious." His tone is impatient.

"I'm serious too." My eyes are barely open.

His sigh is heavy, but still he holds my hand. Somehow no tears fall. I inhale with relief.

A getaway, a do-over with Tate so we can be friends or maybe even something more. If only it were that easy.

Closing my eyes, I turn my face to him and manage a whisper. "I'm in. Let's do it."

Tense silence fills the space between us. Despite my words, the anxiety bubble in my chest is about to burst. I can't bear to sit in the same room with him anymore, staring at him until I'm discharged. I've said too much, he knows all my dirt, and I am officially exposed.

I clear my throat. "You don't have to stay here. I'm not getting discharged until tomorrow morning anyway."

He lets go of my hand and skims the railing. "It's fine. I want to."

"I can call Kaitlin or someone else to take me home."

"That's not necessary. I brought you here. I'll drive you home." He sounds surprised that I would suggest such an idea.

"Don't you want to go home and rest? Aren't you hungry? I haven't seen you eat since you've been at the hospital."

"I'm okay." He shrugs. When he leans back against the wall, he lets out a tired sigh. Even in the trenches of exhaustion, he's exquisitely handsome.

"Go get something to eat. Please." I try for a gentle tone. "And after that, feel free to go home and shower or whatever."

His face falls. "Okay, then." He walks out of the room.

I let out a breath, thankful to be alone again, but I'm itching to get the hell out of here. I need to be home, someplace familiar so I can sort myself out and feel like me again.

I can't do anything about that until tomorrow morning though. All I can do now is sleep.

When I wake, it's dark. A few hours of rest leaves me feeling slightly more refreshed. I prop myself on my elbows to stretch out, but the killer soreness in my lower torso reminds me I have to be careful with every single move I make. I wince, inhaling through my teeth when my ears home in on a soft wheezing to my left.

Through the darkness, I see Tate hunched on his side while propped in the chair next to me, sound asleep. He came back to be with me, even though I told him not to.

Somehow, I don't panic. Probably because deep down, I'm grateful. As mortified as I am that Tate now has such an intimate knowledge of all my insecurities, my lizard brain feels flattered. He cares enough to watch over me after all this. His sleeping body won't pity or judge me, or turn into a jerk when I least expect it. That silent presence is exactly the comfort I need. I wish I could have it all the time. After tomorrow though, it will disappear.

I sink back into my covers and drift to sleep.

THE NURSE COMES into my room for my midmorning check. I reiterate how stellar I feel and how I'm ready to go home. After an hour of waiting and consulting with Dr. Tran, it's decided I can leave.

She fetches my discharge papers and an info packet on how to take proper care of myself postsurgery. I text Tate, who's been camped out in the cafeteria ever since he woke up, that I'm ready to go. It's a relief that I didn't have to ask him for time to myself when he woke up, that he just knew to give me space on his own.

He replies in seconds:

I'll be up in a sec.

I can't take more coddling. Right away I reply:

Not necessary. Just meet me out in front with the car, please.

I change back into my sweaty worksite clothes, grimacing every time I have to lean or bend to contort myself into my clothing. I never knew just how much I used my torso for mundane movements.

When I open the door, I jump at the sight of Tate. He's re-gained a bit of the pinkish hue in his skin, probably due to eating something. In front of him is a wheelchair.

"I said I could do this on my own." There's a strain in my voice I didn't intend.

He flinches. A pinch of guilt hits me.

"You need help whether you admit it or not," he says.

He wheels me to the elevator, then to the entrance, where I wait while he fetches his car. He tries to take my folder of papers and purse from me, but I clutch them to my chest.

"I've got it."

The drive to my duplex is mostly silent. He peppers me with questions about the temperature of the car and if I want the win-dows down. When he parks in my driveway, I try to wave him off, but he insists on helping me out and seeing me inside. His kind-ness is so damn sweet, but all I want is to be alone in my groggy, sore state.

"I don't want you to fall or trip," he says as I unlock the front door. He follows me in before I can shut it.

"I'm fine. Really. I just need to get cleaned up, and then I'll go to sleep," I say.

Stuffy hot air hits me in the face. I switch on the AC.

"You like it warm, then?" Tate trails behind me.

"We never had AC in Hawaii. When we moved to the main-land, my parents always turned it off when we weren't home to save money. Old habits die hard."

He nods before peering around. If I weren't mortified by my super-personal confessions to him over the past couple days, I'd have the decency to feel ashamed of the state of my home. The decor of my duplex is college-grad minimalist. Hand-me-downs make up the bulk of my furniture. Tea mugs and books are strewn everywhere. My laundry basket sits in the middle of my living room, overflowing with clean clothes I neglected to fold days ago.

"Nice place," he says.

"Thanks." I drop my purse and papers on the couch. "The thrift-store coffee table and bookshelf really tie the room together."

He chuckles. I turn around and see his face just as it transitions back to blank.

"Well, thanks again. For everything," I say impatiently. A film of dried sweat pulls on my skin when I move. I ache to scrub it away under a stream of scalding hot water.

He doesn't budge. "You sure you don't need anything else?"

"Nope. I've got it from here." I can't remember ever having such a difficult time getting someone to leave my place.

I step around him to the front door and open it. He turns around to face me and shuffles. I notice he does the same thing with his feet when he's sitting.

"You're absolutely sure? I can stay and help out. It's no problem."

"Do you honestly think I need you to help me take a shower?"

He shakes his head, flustered. "No, no, that's not what I meant. I didn't know you were going to take a shower."

"What do you think 'clean up' means?" I rub my forehead, sounding more curt than I mean to.

He sticks a hand in his hair, pulls hard, then yanks it out. "Right, yeah, sorry."

"It's fine. I'm just crazy sore and tired. Thank you for your help these past few days, but I'll be okay on my own. I just need to rest." I cross my arms, then uncross them, then cross them again.

"I get it. I'll take off." He exhales and walks quickly out the door. I lock it before he even makes it off my porch.

A wave of exhaustion hits, as do the words printed on the info packet. No showering allowed for forty-eight hours. I stumble to the bathroom and give my body a half-hearted wipe down with a wet hand towel, then collapse on my couch.

I think about how Tate left, embarrassed and very clearly wanting to stay longer. I grimace at how short I was with him, how I practically pushed him out my front door. I should have been nicer. What would have happened if I had shoved aside my embarrassment and insecurity, and let him stay? It's my last thought before I drift off.

Sleep is delirious and deep. A faint thud jerks me into a confused and groggy stupor, but I can't be bothered to open my eyes. Probably the mailman dropping off a package. When I finally wake, it's early evening, meaning I slept for a few hours.

Gripping the coffee table to pull myself up, I yelp in pain. Surgery has rendered my core ineffective. Evidently, my torso is made of Jell-O and Silly Putty. When I'm finally standing, I walk to the kitchen for a glass of water. I trot back into the living room, but then I remember the mail. I open the front door and see a small crate of mangoes sitting on the porch. Holy shit.

There's a note card on top of the dozen or so greenish-orange fruits. There's no name signed on it, but I know they're from Tate. It's his distinct all-caps handwriting. I crouch down slowly to pick it up:

These aren't from the Big Island, but they'll have to do.

I'm not risking destroying my abdomen muscles to pick up the crate, so I cradle a few in my arms and bring them to the kitchen. It takes three trips, but I manage. By the time I'm finished, mangoes litter the counter. I stare at them in disbelief, then arrange them into a "T" shape. It seems appropriate given who they're from.

Pressing each with my fingertips, I find the ripest one. I peel and slice it, then devour the sweet, juicy chunks. I'm wide eyed, dumbfounded, and ravenous. I'm chomping on the final piece when I realize I'm smiling.

The next morning, I'm buzzing with a fructose high. The gift of mangoes was a shock. Maybe Tate's kindness wasn't short lived. Maybe this is a turning point. Maybe the care and attentiveness he showed me when I was sick is who he truly is. Or maybe the mangoes were a final thoughtful gesture before returning back to our status quo of arguments and loaded silence.

I spend the better part of the day wondering about it. Nothing I do eases my anxiety. I lie on the couch, YouTube my favorite *Eat Bulaga!* episodes, browse Etsy for antique jewelry I can't afford, then take a slow walk around the neighborhood for a couple of blocks. Tate hovers at the back of my mind the entire time.

By the time evening rolls around, I'm lying on the couch again. The recovery packet says to rest and ease back into walking long distances. I'm a terrible patient. Luckily, today is Labor Day and our workplace is closed, but I need more time to recover. I call both Will's and Lynn's office extensions to leave messages about my unexpected surgery and how I'll need the rest of the week off and part of next week to recover. And to think more about Tate.

I'm still at a loss as to what to do, torn between apologizing profusely and thanking him, or ignoring him and going back to normal. I'd also like to hug him. Maybe share a mango with him. I'm clearly on the brink of insanity.

I'm making my way through the mangoes like a starving monkey. Six are left, and the stem of the "T" is gone. They're all I've been eating. Every time I eat one, I think of Tate. With each peel, slice, and bite, my brain floods with memories of his gentle, caring demeanor. How he cradled my body when we fell asleep together, the way he stayed by my side even when I told him to leave. The sense of comfort I felt around him that I've never felt with any guy before. All of it leaves me breathless and wanting. Every time I think of his lips against my skin, there's a tremor inside me.

I'm washing my hands of mango juice when I realize I can no longer deny it: I have feelings for Tate.

The realization tumbles around my head, giving way to other blush-inducing thoughts. I'd trade all the mangoes in the world to crawl under bedsheets with him again, this time sans clothing. I think I've felt this way since the moment I left his car the night we first kissed. I was just too stubborn and flustered to admit it.

Once my hands are dry, I grab my phone to text him. I start, stop, erase, and edit a half dozen messages. They're all wordy variations of "I'm sorry" and "thank you." I suppose I could have just written that, but it sounds robotic. Even if this weekend was a one-off in his behavior, I want to be sincere in my gratitude. I finally settle on:

Hey. Sorry it took me so long to get in touch with you . . . it's been a rough couple days . . . thank you for the mangoes. And thank you for taking care of me.

Not terrible, but not great. I'm brushing my teeth when my phone buzzes with a response from him:

You're welcome. I hope you feel better.

Relief hits me, followed by disappointment. It's an appropriate reply. Something's missing, though. I can't tell if it's because we're communicating via text and the nuance of emotion is impossible to convey, or if it's because he's back to his rigid, stern self. It's hard enough admitting this in the privacy of my mind, but I wanted a more personal response from him. I wanted him to say what a pleasure it was to hold my body, how honored he was to play nurse to me for the weekend, that he was sleepless until he heard from me.

I rinse and spit in the sink, annoyed with my irrational desire.

I thanked him, and he acknowledged me. I lay in bed tossing and turning, confused as to why I expected anything more.

The glow of my phone screen cuts through the darkness of my bedroom, interrupting my thoughts. I turned it to silent but forgot to set it facedown on my nightstand like I normally do. When I check it, I have to bite my lip to keep from splitting my face in half with a grin. At 11:47 p.m., Tate's text to me has sent all my doubts flying out the window.

Tate: No reply? Aww, Emmie. I was hoping I'd get a smiley face, or a "good night." You're killing me :P

God in heaven, that colon with a "P" is my new favorite emoji.

Me: Sorry. Recovery and all that has my brain in an odd mode.

Me: :D:D:D

Me: Is that any better?

Tate: It will suffice. I can rest easy knowing you have the energy to be a smart-ass to me via text ;)

Holy shit, a winking face. My heart thunders through my chest. Before I can reply with another silly emoji, he replies.

Tate: Is it okay if I check on you every day? I know you don't want to be smothered, but I'd like to be there for you. If you want me. I've been thinking about you.

Tate: Maybe I can come over too?

My heart has ceased thundering. Currently, it's at the base of my throat along with my stomach, my lungs, my liver, and probably both of my kidneys. My entire body is in a giant knot at his sweetness on full, unquestionable display. I worried for nothing. He cares. I've been on his mind, and he wants to be close to me, just like I want to be close to him.

Yes, please.

thirteen

·······

"You sure you're okay?"

It's the millionth time Kaitlin has asked me that in this ten-minute phone call. No matter how many times I say it, she doesn't believe me.

"Because I can dart over there no problem. Ethan is home from work. I could stay with you tonight and fetch things for you, make sure you don't fall."

I lean on the kitchen counter, checking the clock on the wall. I need to get off the phone ASAP. "I'm fine. It's been three days since the surgery, and I've somehow survived. You've done enough. I have a full refrigerator thanks to your grocery run this morning."

"Do you need help in the bath?"

I swallow back a laugh. "I should be able to bathe myself at this point. Thank you, though. Why don't you spend the rest of the night relaxing with Ethan and Libby? I'll text you if I need anything else."

I thank her once more, and we hang up. Three days post-surgery, I'm still sore, but improving. I can stand, sit, and lie down without groaning in pain. I can chuckle during *Eat Bulaga!* without my stomach hurting too much, and I can walk for a half hour around the neighborhood before getting tired. The only thing left on my list is to shower. Finally. And it's for the best possible reason: Tate is coming over soon to check on me.

I'd like to be fresh and clean for his arrival. Our late-night text session led to an all-day exchange today while he was at work. And it wasn't just checking-in texts asking how I felt, but full-on conversations complete with jokes, emojis, and one video of a bunny and kitten falling asleep together in an Easter basket. I squealed out loud when he sent me that one.

I make my way to the shower, letting the wonderful weirdness of the past few days wash over me. My once work enemy is the guy causing all these butterflies in my stomach. And I want these butterflies swarming through me every single day.

Steam from the hot water transforms my tiny bathroom into a sauna. As soothing as the wet, warm air feels, a flash of panic hits. The bottom of my white porcelain tub glistens like it's iced over. Kaitlin was right. What if I slip and fall?

A knock at the front door saves me from finding out. Carefully, I pull my tank top and shorts back on before opening the door to greet Tate.

"Hey." He shoves his hands in the pockets of his jeans.

Butterflies and warmth hit me square in the gut at the sight of him. "Thanks for coming over." I take a step back, hoping he can't smell my stench.

"Is there water running?" His eyes dart over my shoulder.

"I was about to take a shower."

He frowns. "You sure that's a good idea?"

I cross my arms. "The pamphlet the nurse gave me advises to wait two days after surgery before bathing, so I'm in the clear. Hang on."

I leave him standing in the doorway and go to turn off the tub faucet. The water level is halfway up the tub, perfect for a shallow bath. When I return to the living room, Tate hovers by the couch, frown still on full display.

"You could slip. And what about your stitches? Getting hot water all over them can't be good."

I yank up my tank top and point to my lower abdomen. "I had a laparoscopic procedure. There are three tiny incisions. One in my belly button, one near my right hip, and one . . ." I trail off before I can reveal the location of my third incision, which is right above my pubic bone.

Tate's cheeks take on a crimson hue. By the way he clears his throat, I think he has a good idea where that third incision is.

I straighten my shirt to its rightful place. "Besides, Dr. Tran used tissue adhesive to seal me up. It's like clear, super strong glue that protects my incisions. It's perfectly safe to bathe at this point, as long as I don't directly scrub at the incisions."

Tate's eyes fall to my midsection. "Oh."

This is new. We're bickering, but not because we're mad or frustrated with each other. Because Tate cares about me. Emotion hits the center of my chest. He's living out the text he sent last night, the one I read over and over until I fell asleep, phone in hand.

"Do you want to help me?" I ask, my voice soft.

He nods, then stops himself. "I won't try anything, if that's what you're worried about."

I don't doubt his words or the tender expression on his face, the way his eyes plead when they look at me.

"You said that when we slept in the hospital bed too." His gentle tone conveys the same care and sweetness from that day. It makes me wish I were one hundred percent recovered so I could jump him.

"Whatever you need to make this more comfortable, tell me. I just want you safe."

Safe. Never before has that word make me tingle.

As much as I want him here with me, I don't want him to see me in my birthday suit. "You can't see me naked."

"Of course not. That's not why I— I wasn't even thinking . . ." His red face pulls into a grimace, something in the realm of shocked and nervous.

I wink at him. "Here." I hand him the hot-pink sleeping mask I've been wearing while napping on the couch. "Wear this. Sit on the toilet lid. I'm going to pull the shower curtain so it closes off the back half of the tub, so you can't see anything. If you hear me scream, cry, or shout for help, take off the mask and help me. Otherwise, if all you hear are normal splashing noises, just sit there until I say I'm done. Sound good?"

His toned chest heaves with a single breath. And then there's a small smile. "Got it."

He waits in the living room while I undress in the bathroom, only a rickety wooden door separating us. The hot water laps at my lower half when I settle in. I moan. It's heaven on my roughed-up body. The water level barely hits my hips, which is perfect because according to the pamphlet I'm not supposed to let the incisions sit in stagnant water for long periods of time. After another few seconds, I pull the shower curtain forward until it covers half the tub and prop up on my knees. Using my hands as cups, I splash the water across my stomach.

"You can come in now."

The bathroom door squeaks open. Tate's soft footsteps make

my heart pound. There's a loud thud, then an "oof" sound from Tate.

I stick my head around the curtain. He stumbles backward from the sink, rendered blind by my hot-pink eye mask.

"What are you doing?"

He bumps ass-first into the towel rack and groans. "Crap."

I swallow back a laugh. "I meant for you to put it on after you came in."

He faces me. "Oh. I guess that makes more sense."

"Here, just take the mask off and sit down. I'm already in the back of the tub behind the curtain. You can't see me anyway."

Through the white of the curtain, I observe his shadowy silhouette sit down.

"Mask is on," he says.

We're maybe four inches apart, sitting side by side, only an opaque sheet of plastic separating my naked body from Tate's clothed one. A deep breath centers me, and I let out a soft moan. Tate clears his throat.

I splash some more until my entire body is soaked, then lather soap into my hands. Soon I'm covered in pineapple-scented body wash. I breathe in, eyes closed, and for a minute I'm back on the beach. My wet skin pebbles, and I open my eyes. No. This is even better. I'm bathing next to my coworker. My coworker who I used to loathe. My coworker who I most definitely don't loathe anymore. Nerves are certainly present, but so is anticipation and joy. A strange, yet wonderful cocktail of emotions.

"Doing okay?" he says.

"Yep." I slide back on my bottom and lie down in the tub so I can wet my hair. Slowly, I prop myself back up into a kneeling position and lather shampoo through it. "I feel so naughty."

The second the last words leave my lips, I bury my face in my hands and groan.

Tate's soft chuckle floats past the curtain. "How so?"

"Sorry, I mean that it feels naughty to take a bath. They're pretty indulgent, using all this water for one person. Growing up on an island, showers were the rule. My mom would get pissed if she caught my sister or me taking a bath. Said they wasted so much fresh water, and we needed to be less wasteful."

"I see."

The world's most awkward laugh falls from my lips. "This is weird."

"Kind of, yeah."

"A good weird, though. Don't you think?" I bite my lip. Thank goodness for the security this shower-curtain barrier gives me.

"'Good weird' is the perfect way to describe it." It sounds like he's smiling.

"Tell me something about yourself," I blurt out.

"What do you mean?"

"Something that shows me you're vulnerable too." It's an odd request, but I want it. I *need* it. "I'm sitting next to you, naked. I'd say that's a pretty vulnerable position. Tit for tat, right?"

My face burns at my phrasing. *Tit.* Excellent word choice.

"Okay," he says. "I'm deathly afraid of spiders. Whenever I see one, I freeze."

I smile. "I would have never pegged you for an arachnophobe."

"It's not a phobia," he says sternly. "I just don't like them."

"I get it. I'm the same way with snakes. Though I'd say that's a definite phobia for me." Lying back in the water, I run my fingers through my hair to rinse out the shampoo. The scent of fruit hangs in the humid air. "What else?"

There's the soft tapping of his sneaker against the tile. "When I was eight, my parents planned a birthday party for me and invited all my classmates. My birthday is February twenty-fourth. There was a blizzard and none of the kids could come because the roads were iced over and there were accidents all over the city. So I spent my birthday alone."

"What about your sister?"

"She wanted to see *Disney Princesses On Ice* in Kansas City that weekend, so our grandma took her."

Pain hits my chest. I lean up and turn to my right to face him. Even though we can't see each other, the movement makes me feel closer to him. "That's awful. I'm sorry."

He lets out a soft chuckle. A handful of silent seconds follow before he speaks. "It ended up being perfect. I didn't want to have a birthday party in the first place, but my parents made me invite all those kids because they didn't want me to celebrate alone without Natalie. But honestly? I just wanted to have the day to myself. They thought it was weird. I remember when my mom told me none of the kids could come, I burst into this huge smile and ran to my bedroom. I built a blanket fort and stacked my favorite comic books inside it. My parents felt so bad at the party fail that they let me eat as many slices of cake as I wanted. So I ate, like, an entire Funfetti cake in my blanket fort while reading comic books all day."

When he finishes telling the story, I'm grinning. "That's hilarious. And wonderful."

Through the shower curtain, I see the silhouette of his arms run along the tops of his thighs. The soft sound of fabric rubbing fills the bathroom.

"It always cracks me up to remember that day," he says.

All those times I've seen Tate eat lunch by himself in his office spring to mind. He doesn't approach anyone at work unless he has to for a work-related reason, and he always sits by himself at meetings. It makes sense now. He's a lifelong loner.

"I guess I should cancel the surprise party I have planned for your next birthday," I say.

Another chuckle. I wish I weren't stuck behind the shower curtain so I could witness his expression and the way his body moves when he laughs.

The mood in my sauna bathroom is light, easy. This closeness is new, but when we chat, we're like old chums sharing stories.

After I finish scrubbing and rinsing, I stand. The sloshing noise of the bathwater streaming off my body causes Tate to sit up.

"Mask is still on, right?"

"Of course."

I step out of the tub and onto the bath mat, carefully toweling off. When I look down, I see my shin is inches from his knee. With the soft cotton wrapped around me, I stand and stare. He sits perfectly still, hands on the tops of his thighs, his back straight as an arrow. For a moment, I wonder what he would do if I sat on his lap, if I leaned into his ear and whispered, "Thank you." Would he run his hands over my cold, wet skin? Or better, his mouth?

My foot slides toward him, but I stop when my toes are less than an inch from his shoe.

"Everything good?" he asks.

In an instant, my back finds the wall. "Yep."

When I open the door, steam flows into the living room. I slip on a loose-fitting tank dress from the laundry basket still in my living room.

"Decent," I call out to him.

"Cool. Give me a sec."

I collapse onto the couch. It's a minute before he steps out of the bathroom. He walks to the end of the sofa, his face red.

"You okay?" I ask.

He nods, sporting a flustered expression. His chest heaves, and he coughs a few times, his watchful gaze on me. It makes me feel as naked as I was in the bathtub minutes ago.

"Feel better?" he asks.

"Much."

He hands me my sleeping mask. "Would it be okay if I came over again tomorrow?"

"I'd like that."

Leaning over me, he plants a kiss on my forehead. His hand grazes my cheek. "Best if we keep things PG, don't you think? For the sake of your recovery."

I nod, despite my hope for something mouth to mouth. He's right though. If our first kiss was any indication, our mouths are dangerous weapons when left unchecked.

I nod.

"Get some rest, okay?"

Quiet footsteps lead him back out the front door. When the door shuts behind him, I sink into the couch. The throb between my legs is back with a vengeance. This feeling is more than arousal, though. It's a spark, a connection, the beginning of something new.

fourteen

·······

Every single day since our bathtub session last week, Tate and I have connected. Days are spent texting each other sweet comments, jokes, or silly videos. Most evenings we cuddle on my couch. He always leaves me with a forehead kiss and a caress on the cheek, just like that first day he visited me. We both remark, usually with huffy breaths, that we prefer kissing with tongue, but I've got a body to heal.

The one time he couldn't make it, he texted to let me know, then I received a grocery store delivery of pineapple and young coconut. I didn't even have to hack away at the impossibly hard coconut shell. It was peeled and sliced, ready for me to chow down.

Seeing this whole new side of him is the reason for the ever-present swarm of butterflies in my stomach and why I wake up with a smile on my face each morning. Who knew Tate Rasmussen, the no-nonsense hard-ass, could be devastatingly sweet?

This morning is sweeter though. My first day back at work. Ten days postsurgery and I'm aching to return, not because I miss Nuts & Bolts, but because I'm itching to see Tate at work. We can finally spend all our working hours in this new bliss bubble we've created.

Through nerves and residual soreness, it's a wobbly walk to my office. I scale the stairs fine, but the moment I turn the corner, my knees forget they're supposed to bend. Forcing myself forward, I make my way to my office and sit at my desk. When I look to Tate's open door, he's turned away, his broad back and curly hair in full view. A tickle-kick hits my gut. The last time I laid eyes on him in this building, tension, frustration, and a bevy of other negative emotions pulsed through me. Everything about this day—the section of building we share, how we look at each other, the way we talk—will be different after our time together.

He stands up and disappears, but a split second later, he's back in my line of view, exiting his office. Then it happens. He takes his first ever step into my space. I look down at his sneakered feet, which stand a full foot inside my doorway, four inches from the edge of my desk. Let the record show Tate Rasmussen entered my office for the first time this second Tuesday of September. Snowflakes are forming in hell. Winged pigs are soaring above. I never thought I'd see the day.

"Welcome back," he says softly.

"Thanks. Hi."

"Hi. How are you feeling?" It's the same question he's asked me every time he's visited, but it still gives me shivers. His smoke-hued eyes pull a full-body once-over on me. Every day he's seen me, he's done that, and every day it's given me goose bumps. Tingling, thrilling, delicious goose bumps. He's examining me, in a caring, watchful way, like he's making certain I'm okay.

"Fine. I mean, good. I feel good overall."

"I'm glad." His smile goes from toothy to lips only. Even after seeing him beam every day this past week and a half, I still can't decide which one I adore more. Both slay me. Even more so now that he's doing it in my office.

"Thank you. For everything." I remember I haven't thanked him in person for the mango delivery. I've seen him almost every day since, yet not a word. What horrible manners I have. "Especially the mangoes. And the pineapple and coconut. That was . . . I don't even . . ."

For someone whose profession is to formulate words forty hours a week, I'm doing a dismal job of articulating myself. Flustered, I rub the back of my neck.

"They're all I've been eating. Sorry, I forgot to say that on the days you came over."

He breaks eye contact with me to stare at the floor. He shuffles his feet and meets my eyes once again before lowering himself to the chair in the corner. "I hoped you'd like them."

We stare at each other in silence for the next few seconds. This is the first time we've spoken under this roof with zero animosity tumbling between us. Before we can say anything else, there's a muffled thud from inside Will's office. Our heads twist in his direction.

"Ow, ow, goddamn it!" Will shouts.

We burst out in laughter at the exact same moment. I clutch my abdomen, whispering, "Ouch!" between breaths. Cackling this hard kills, but it's worth it. I'm finally laughing at work with Tate. He's looking at me with affection in his eyes. There's a soft burst in my chest. It's my own affection for him.

He catches his breath. "Are you okay?"

"Yeah. Just very sore still." I wince. "Laughing is surprisingly painful when you've had surgery on your lower abdomen."

"I'm supposed to forward you an email about a new line of chain saws, but maybe I shouldn't. The cutting, the sharpness. That could bring on some terrible flashbacks for you."

The fake worry on his face sends me into a fit of painful giggles.

"Shit, sorry," he says a moment before Will bursts out of his office.

"Oh, Emmie! How are you? We were worried about you." Will wrings his right hand as he walks toward me.

"I'm fine, thanks. Are you okay?"

"Yeah. I was trying to take some photos of those *Star Wars* figures I've been meaning to sell online for ages, and I accidentally dropped a box of them on my hand."

I bite the inside of my cheek. I don't think my stomach can handle another cackle.

Tate sits silently while Will asks me questions about my hospital stay, then I ask him about his toy sale on eBay.

"It could be great side money for me," Will says. "Loads of people love *Star Wars*. Who knows how much they'll pay for vintage toys."

I chuckle along with Will. After a week and a half away, I've missed his antics. I nod while listening to Will and peek at Tate pursing his lips, failing miserably to keep the wide grin off his face. There's nothing overly funny in this moment. Will is just being Will, but there's something lighthearted, something giddy in the air. It's clearly having an effect on the two of us.

"My cousin made a killing selling one of his. What was it? Not Chewbacca . . ." Will says, gazing at the ceiling deep in thought.

I shoot a playful helpless stare at Tate. I need him to keep a straight face if I have any hope of doing the same. Otherwise, I'm going to bust an incision. I point at my stomach and make a sad face. He takes a breath. In no time his neutral face is back. He winks at me before turning his focus to Will. A breath catches in my throat; my heart pauses before resuming its regular beat. I had no idea Tate could be this playful at work. I can barely take how much I adore it.

Will's phone rings, and he darts to his office to answer it.

"Your trying-not-to-laugh face is incredible. I thought I was going to rupture one of my incisions." I shoot him the first non-serious glare I've ever given him.

"I guess I'll have to practice that one more. Excuse me for a sec."

His hoodie-clad shoulders take up a good chunk of the open doorframe as he walks out of my office and in the direction of the men's bathroom.

A minute later, a teddy bear the size of a toddler fills my doorway. Lynn's head pops from behind the fuzzy brown mass.

"A little get-well present!" she announces excitedly.

I let out an embarrassed laugh. "Wow, Lynn. You shouldn't have." The teddy bear is almost half her size. It must have cost a pretty penny. She's a sweetheart, but this gesture is above and beyond.

"It's not from me. It's from Jamie from Sawyer Custom Contracting." She winks before setting the stuffed bear at my desk. "I ran into the delivery guy downstairs and offered to pass it along to you."

My jaw drops. Jamie. The sexy contractor I've been flirting with. I haven't thought of him in days.

There's a white card stuck to its paw with a short message: *Thinking of you. Get well soon! Jamie*

"What a sweet young man to send such a thoughtful gift. I didn't know you two were an item." She lingers in my office, like a mom coaxing information from her child about their significant other.

"Whoa," Tate says before settling behind his desk.

"Isn't it something?" Lynn claps her hands before twisting around to address Tate. "It's not often we see such a romantic gesture around here."

"Romantic gesture?" Tate blinks away the warmth on his face. Needlelike goose bumps hit the back of my neck.

Lynn turns back to me. "That Jamie fellow must be smitten."

I need to say something, anything, to make Tate understand this teddy bear business is one big misunderstanding, but I'm too flustered to formulate the proper words.

"We're not an item," I bark. Judging by the scowl on his face, I'm about a minute too late with that crucial piece of information.

Lynn's sweet high-pitched giggle claws at my ears. "Well, he must think so by the looks of it." She nods her head toward the gift.

A frustrated breath booms from my chest. I look past her to focus on Tate. He's giving the bear his best death stare. I'm surprised it doesn't crumble into itself.

"Tell Jamie nice job." His voice is hard again. My heart sinks.

"They're not . . . It's not . . . I don't know why he sent me this." My tongue feels too big for my mouth. Why can't I translate the dread I feel into the proper words?

The longer I stare at Tate, the harder he clenches his jaw. He turns away to his computer before I can say another useless word.

"We are not involved, I promise." My volume is a beat under a shout. Lynn jumps slightly at the tone, while Tate remains perfectly motionless in the space behind her shoulder, still staring at his computer screen.

"Oh. Okay, then." Lynn's wide-eyed stare indicates my sharp

tone is totally work inappropriate. "Actually, would you mind popping into Will's office for a sec?"

I follow her inside and shut the door. Will's eyes go wide at the sight of Lynn, who gives him a disapproving glance. He nods and kicks a box of action figures under his desk, like a little kid who's been told to put his toys away. I'd laugh if I weren't about to get reamed by two managers for raising my voice in the workplace. Fantastic.

I take one of the chairs across from Will's desk, while Lynn takes the other. I'm in full-on work mode. It's a struggle to contain my panic about what Tate saw and heard, but first I need to throw on my professional mask and get through this meeting.

"How are you feeling?" Lynn asks with concern.

"Fine. Still a little sore, but I'm doing well otherwise. Sorry about how I sounded earlier. I just—the gift was a surprise, that's all."

"No, I understand," she says. All prior giddiness has left her. "If Jamie's actions make you feel uncomfortable, you should tell someone."

I shake my head. I just want to move past this teddy bear debacle and get out of here. "It's not that at all. Jamie and I have become friends since meeting on the worksite. The gift was a friendly gesture. I'm sure of it."

That's a blatant lie. I'm positive Jamie sent it with romantic intentions, but I don't want to get into that mess. Downplay and move on is the only way I can think to move Lynn off this topic.

"I see." She looks relieved. "It was partially my fault for getting so excited about it. Like I said, you don't see too many big romantic moments around here. In my day, a gift like that equaled romance. I've got a lot to catch up on it seems."

I dig my claws into the arms of the chair. I need to get out of here and rush back to Tate so I can explain how that stuffed bear means nothing.

"Also, Will and I want talk to you about a different matter. I meant to meet with your first thing this morning, but the gift delivery distracted me."

She pulls her glasses off and inhales, like she's about to break bad news. I cease breathing.

"Brett from Service and Repairs has been fired. Now, we wouldn't normally divulge information about a firing to another employee, but this concerns you."

Lynn looks to Will, who clears his throat.

"Tate brought to the managers' attention a couple weeks ago that Brett was speaking about you inappropriately. He overheard him in the break room and reported it to me and Brett's boss. The language used was lewd and unacceptable. Tate demanded that Brett be fired, but we had to investigate first," Will says.

Lynn nods along. "We discovered this wasn't an isolated incident. Apparently, Brett made inappropriate comments to a couple of other female employees."

"Wait, what?" I'm light headed. This is information overload.

"I know this is difficult to hear. You're a young lady working at a mostly male company." Lynn sighs. "Tate was on our case the entire time we investigated. It was a bit much at times how often he would check up on it, but I can certainly understand where he was coming from."

My head is spinning. Tate demanded that Brett be fired for me? I shake my head, hoping it somehow centers me and I can come up with a well-worded reply. It doesn't.

"That's a shocker," I say.

Lynn folds her hands on her lap. "I suppose it is. However, given how he took care of you when you fell on the worksite, I don't think it's a shock at all." She gives what I think is a knowing look, but it disappears before I can be sure.

This impromptu meeting has me feeling like I'm riding a roller coaster with no safety bar. I look to both Will and Lynn. "I appreciate you telling me."

I shoot up from the chair, shut the door to Will's office behind me, and leap to Tate's doorway. He's glowering at a photo of a chain saw on his computer screen.

"We need to talk."

"I'll forward you the chain saw info in a minute." He keeps his eyes on the computer. His harshness is back.

"No, not that. I need to talk to you right now." The words punch out of my mouth in a harsh whisper. I glance behind to Will's office door. "Not here. Come on."

I speed walk down the hall to the stairwell door. I open it and point for him to step in. The metal door clanks shut, and we're left standing at the landing at the top of the stairs, silently staring at each other.

"That gift, it's not what you think." The waterlines of my eyes burn. I can't cry. Not here, not now.

His arms rest at his sides, each fist clenched. His face is a sheet of white steel. "I don't think anything."

"Yes, you do. That's why you're upset."

"I'm not upset." His strained tone gives away his lie.

"Stop it. I'm going to call Jamie later and clear things up. I'm not interested in him in that way."

"Based on that adorable stuffed bear, he may need some serious convincing." His bitter tone makes my throat squeeze.

I grab his arm and pull him away from the door, hoping the

few extra inches will serve as effective insulation, because I don't want anyone overhearing us. We're so close that if I move my arm in front of my body, I'd graze his.

"Tate, you stayed with me at the hospital. I bathed next to you. I spent almost every day with you this past week and a half. We've been texting every single day. I thought it was clear just how much I like you."

He crosses his arms, the defensiveness melting from his face.

"Look, I'm not sorry for chatting with Jamie or getting to know him or having a drink with him. That happened before this stuff with us."

He starts to shake his head, but I stop him.

"You're mad about all that. Or jealous. Don't try to deny it."

His jaw clenches, and I can count every muscle pressing against his skin. He's frustrated. So am I. But all I want to do is take his face in my hands, touch his jaw muscles one by one, and kiss him. What a mix of emotions he brings out in me.

"Fine. You're right. I just . . ." He trails off before huffing out a tense breath. "Look, I know I have no right to be jealous or upset. But after all that's happened with us, the thought of you and him . . ."

He shakes his head and looks away.

"I know."

"I'm sorry for how I reacted."

I sigh and smile. Crisis averted after one ill-timed teddy bear delivery.

"I had no idea about Brett."

His eyes widen. "Management told you?" he asks, his tone softer.

I nod. "You did that for me?" It comes out more like a question than a statement like I intended.

He shrugs. "I don't want to work in a place where an employee thinks he can speak about his coworkers like that."

I ease to a whisper. "It means so much, what you did."

I place the palm of my hand against his chest and take another step toward him. I've been aching to touch him all morning. Feeling how hard his body is when I'm not delirious with pain has been the highlight of my evenings lately. In my alert state, I relish this flesh. His heart beats swiftly against my hand. I wonder if it's my touch that causes it. I hope so.

"Working here, around all these guys, I have a shield up every day. Knowing you were looking out for me means everything." My voice is a soft rasp.

Gently, he grabs my hand and pulls it off his chest. My stomach twists, but then he laces his fingers with mine and pulls me closer, pressing my torso against his.

"I fucking hated that guy," he says in a low whisper. A slight smile catches the edge of his lips.

"Me too." I grin wide.

"Every time he looked at you, I wanted to smash his head into the side of a table, the floor, the wall."

"I kind of wish you had."

His smile grows. "If I had done that, then I'd be in jail, and we couldn't have this awkward moment in the stairwell."

"I don't think it's awkward." I tilt up my head. My lips inch closer to his.

Our stairwell interlude almost feels like progress. We've shared truths and worked out a misunderstanding, and now we're better. Closer.

The sound of the metal door slamming open at the bottom of the stairs below us jerks us apart. We're pressed against opposite walls now, arms crossed over our chests. Heavy footsteps thud up the staircase. Gus darts between us to walk through the door. I wonder if he even saw us. He sure didn't act like it. We glance at each other and laugh at the same moment.

A hint of worry creeps into my brain. "Do you think he noticed anything?"

"Nah. It's Gus. He doesn't pay attention to anything outside of the warehouse."

I step back into his reach, and he gently wraps his arm around me. I touch my lips against his. He pecks me but stops before we can properly kiss. I pull back, disappointed.

"Believe me, I want to. I'd press you up against the wall right here, right now, but we can't get caught. Not like this," he says. The hard swallow in his throat lets me know he's telling the truth.

"You're right." I'm embarrassed for letting my hormones dictate my behavior in this stairwell. "Come out to lunch with me, then. We can find a spot someplace away from here where you can press me against a wall." I trace my fingers across his chest, hoping to convince him.

He leans his head back and groans. "I wish I could, but I have a dentist appointment over my lunch hour."

Backing away again, I shoot him a pouty face. He pulls me to him, leans down to nibble my bottom lip, then licks it lightly with the tip of his tongue. My knees buckle.

"What about after lunch?" I'm shameless in my desperation.

"I should have told you: I have to go to a social media seminar this afternoon at the DoubleTree. Today's a half day for me."

I groan and pound lightly on his chest. "You're killing me."

He grabs both of my arms and pins them behind my back. Something hard and blunt pokes me from the front of his pants. "I'll make it up to you. Promise."

He releases me, then folds his hands in front of him to conceal his pants tent. "Okay. Back to work for us. You go first."

I walk back to my office, a giddy skip in my step. Five minutes later, he returns to his. I can't help but feel flattered at the thought that it took him five minutes to collect himself after pressing against my body. Leaning around my computer, I steal a quick glance. He's smiling to himself. When he catches me peeking, he rewards me with a wink. My mind races with all the ways he will make it up to me.

fifteen

....

By two o'clock I'm deathly bored and turned on. My cell phone rings, and I jump to answer it, hoping it's Tate. When I look at the screen, I freeze. It's Jamie. Crap.

"Emmie! How are you? Are you okay?" He sounds concerned.

"Hi, yeah, I'm good. Thanks."

"I was so worried when I didn't hear from you after you went to the hospital."

"Well, I'm fine now." It's like I'm reading from a cue card. I wonder if he can pick up on the disinterest in my voice. I register the plush bear propped against the chair in the corner of my office. "And thank you so much for the gift."

"I thought you'd like it." I can tell he's smiling. "How'd your surgery go? Are you recovering okay?"

"It all went well. I'm crazy sore, but I'll live. Wait, how did you know I had surgery?"

"Tate answered your phone one of the times I called to check on you."

"Oh."

"Yeah, he was a little short with me. I offered to come see you, but he wouldn't tell me what hospital you were at. He said he had everything under control and didn't need my help. And he told me to leave you alone during your recovery, so you could rest. Can you believe that? He's got that stone-wall jerk personality down."

I feel a pull of defensiveness for Tate but push it aside.

"Can I see you? It's been a while, and I'd like to see your pretty face."

His attempt at a sweet comment makes me cringe. "I don't know if that's a good idea. Look, I appreciate the gift, but I don't think I'm interested in—"

He chuckles. "Oh no, I don't mean that. I was hoping to give you some pointers for when you're able to go back to the worksite. I was chatting with Lynn the other day, and she mentioned the social media project you and Tate are in charge of. She was worried it would fall by the wayside with you being out the past week and a half. I told her I could talk to you and help. I do marketing and promo work in my job too."

"Oh, that. Sure."

"Great! How about we chat about it tonight over ice cream? You know what they say. Ice cream after surgery is a must."

I frown at my lap. I've never heard anyone say that. "I, uh—"

"Please? Don't make me beg." The whiny, drawn-out way he says "please" is like nails on a chalkboard.

"Shouldn't Tate be part of this meeting?"

"Sure, if he's free."

I glance at the clock. He'll be at the seminar the rest of the day, maybe the evening. I have no idea; he didn't give me a time frame.

"Actually, I think he's busy," I say.

"That's okay. You can fill him in on what we discussed."

"Fine," I finally concede. "I can meet you at that ice cream shop in Dundee after work."

"I'll pick you up. You shouldn't have to drive after what you've been through."

I'm too exhausted to fight him, so I agree and give him my address. We hang up, my head spinning.

"ARE YOU OKAY?" Jamie asks while seated next to me on a bench outside of the eCreamery Ice Cream. I assume my phony smile is not convincing.

"I'm fine. Like I said on the phone, still very sore."

I finish the last of my vegan chocolate ice cream and toss the container in a nearby trash can. This past half hour with Jamie has been an awkward mess. Awkward side hug when he picked me up, awkward small talk in the car, sitting in awkward silence while eating our ice cream. I check my phone. Still no message from Tate. I text him that I'm meeting with Jamie for the charity home-building project, but that I'll be free afterward if he's up for another cuddle session at my place. I want him to know he's on my mind. I wonder if I'm on his.

"What ideas did you have?" I ask.

The half smile Jamie shoots me has lost its intriguing luster. The guy who set my pulse on fire when we first met doesn't even register on my internal Richter scale. Whatever chemistry we had has fizzled.

He takes a bite of his raspberry sorbet. "What's the deal with Tate?" he asks, ignoring my question.

"What do you mean?"

"Is he into you or something?"

"I thought you wanted to discuss promoting our homebuilding project."

"I'm having a hard time getting a read on him."

Now I'm annoyed. That's twice he's ignored my questions.

I pin him with what I hope is a stern stare. "Look, I appreciate the teddy bear and ice cream, but I thought we were meeting to talk about work, not Tate."

He frowns. "I didn't mean to offend you. I just wanted to know what I was up against."

"Up against?"

With a flick of his wrist, his empty ice cream container lands in the nearby trash can. "Well, yeah. I thought that we . . . that you and I were—"

"Friends," I finish for him. "I'm sorry if you thought it was more, but honestly, all I want right now is a friend."

The letdown is hardly kind, but I'm not interested in kind. Jamie dragged me out here under the guise of work talk when all he really wanted to do was eliminate Tate as dating competition.

"A friend," he repeats with a raised brow. He scoffs, then smiles. It doesn't look happy though, more like regretful. "Well, then. Let me take you back home, friend."

When we return to my place, I start to let myself out of the car, but he insists on opening it for me. He gestures to the porch, but I stop at the giant birch tree in the front yard. He stands on the pavement below me.

"Thank you again for the ice cream and the stuffed bear." I cross my arms. "We'll have to figure out another time that Tate, me, and you can chat."

He sighs. "Sure. Have a good night." He leans in to kiss my cheek, but I jerk my head to the side and end up bumping my head into a low-hanging tree branch. His wet lips land on my ear. He backs away into the street, a disoriented look on his face. The whole scene is a mess and a half.

"Sorry, I— Friends can kiss on the cheek, right?" he stutters.

I wipe my hand along the side of my face. "I don't."

"Uh, good night, then." He gives me a limp wave before climbing into his car and driving off.

When I look up, the streetlight at the corner of my block catches my eye, but not because of the glow it casts on the darkened street. Because it perfectly highlights Tate's silhouette as he walks over to me.

My breath comes out in a rough blow. Now we're both standing on my lawn in the dark.

"I got your text." His tone is nonchalant, casual, and every bit a surprise.

"Your timing couldn't be more perfect. Or awful, depending on how you look at it."

He shrugs. "I take it the meeting with Jamie didn't go well?"

"You caught the tail end of it, didn't you?"

He nods.

"'Didn't go well' is putting it nicely. I'm pissed. We didn't talk about work at all. He wanted to talk about you and me. And then me and him."

He clenches his jaw, which shifts his expression into hard territory. When I cradle his face in my hand, he immediately softens. There's a gentle moan.

"I told him I wasn't interested in him other than as a friend."

"A friend?" He lifts an eyebrow. "Friend" is the buzzword of the day.

"We have to work next to him for several months. You have to see him at the rock climbing gym. It's best if we stay on friendly terms. You understand, right?"

"Not my favorite thing in the world to see him try to kiss you, though." There's an edge to his voice, but he seems to understand.

I can tell by the softness in his eyes and how his hand squeezes my hip.

"I didn't like it either."

"Maybe you'll like this."

He places a giant orange and green papaya into my hands. My jaw drops at the sight of my second favorite fruit. I didn't even notice he was holding anything. This is what he meant earlier in the stairwell when he said he would make it up to me.

"Can I ask you a question?" he asks.

"Of course."

He takes my hand and leads me to sit down on the curb with him. "Why did your family move all the way out here?"

The randomness of his question nearly makes me laugh, but then I remember that he asked me this in the hospital. I never answered him, bombarding him instead with personal questions of my own.

"You don't give up, do you?"

He nuzzles my neck, wetting my skin with his breath. "Not when it comes to you."

I swoon from the inside out. "Money. My parents couldn't afford to live in Hawaii anymore. My dad has family in the Midwest, and he and my mom decided it would be better to live here since it's cheaper. And my dad's family offered to watch my sister and me so my parents could save money on babysitters. So we moved, but it didn't help things all that much. My dad still could never hold a job for long."

"Why?"

"He has a difficult personality. Very stubborn. He got into arguments all the time with his bosses and coworkers. He'd get fired or quit. It drove my mom nuts. She eventually got sick of it and divorced him. My little sister and I lived with her from then on and saw him every other weekend."

He stares at me with tenderness and sympathy. I realize now he's been looking at me with those emotions in his face ever since I fell at the worksite. It makes something in my chest flutter.

"That must have been hard," he says.

"It was for the best. They're better apart."

"You're so strictly business. About everything. I like that about you."

My cheeks flush at his compliment. "It killed my mom to leave Hawaii. She loved it there." My chest aches thinking back on how sad she was when we first moved.

"Do you think she regrets moving?"

"I think so. She would never admit it, though. She cried most nights our first few months living here. She waited until she thought my sister and I were asleep, but I could hear her sometimes."

"How awful."

"If she didn't have kids to support, she would still be living there probably."

"You don't know that."

"It's true. She always worked, always had a job. Supporting herself was never a problem. Maybe if my dad had been a harder worker like her, or more ambitious, we could have stayed. She would have been happier."

"Your mom loves you and your sister. Part of being a parent means making sacrifices for your kids. She may have been sad at first, but I bet having two wonderful daughters means more than living in Hawaii."

"You sound like a therapist." I rest my head on his shoulder. When his arms slips around me, I moan. I've never felt this comfortable talking about these tough moments of my childhood with anyone before. "You know that coconut shell I keep on my desk?"

I feel him nod against the top of my head.

"She gave it to me when we moved from Hawaii. She knew I would take the move pretty hard, so she wrote a note on the inside for me to look at whenever I felt sad."

"What does it say?"

"'For my beautiful *anak*, who's as sweet and strong as this coconut.'"

"That's perfect."

I can hear the smile in his voice. It sends goose bumps across my skin.

"She has the other half. She said she held on to it her first few months of living in the Midwest, to remind her to be strong for me and my sister. It's like my security blanket, reminding me to be strong like my mom whenever I feel weak."

"You're never weak, Emmie."

"So wrong. You have no idea."

"Can I ask you something else?" A deep sigh follows his frown when I nod. "How long until your classmates finally called you by your real name?"

"Most never did." I wince at the memory of kids calling me Pocahontas and Lilo in class and in the halls of my middle school, my face blank as I tried to ignore it. But another part of me feels joy. Tate remembers me telling him this at the hospital, and it stuck in his mind. *I* stuck in his mind. I'm important to him.

"Seriously?"

"Yeah. All through middle school. High school was better. I made friends with people who were nice enough to call me Emmie."

"Jesus. Little fucking assholes."

"It was a learning experience. I ignored them. Or pretended I couldn't hear them." I clear my throat. It was years ago, but every time I think about middle school, the feelings of embarrassment and hurt crash over me in waves.

"It still bothered you though, didn't it?" he says softly.

"It hurt to know they wanted to be mean to me, make me feel like an outsider, just because I looked different. I was this dark Lilo-girl from a place they only knew about from a Disney movie." I bite my lip. "I cried about it sometimes, but never in front of them. Always hidden away in the auditorium or the girls' bathroom. I never wanted to give them the satisfaction."

I've never told anyone how I used to cry alone in middle school. Tate is the first and only to know.

He grabs my hand, and I swear I feel tingling where our skin touches. "Forget them. They didn't know you. They didn't deserve to know you. They were probably jealous of you."

I scoff. "You don't have to butter me up."

He cuts me off. "I'm not. I swear I'm not."

I roll my head on his shoulder. With his fingertips against my cheek, he pulls me closer. His gaze is gray and intense.

"I know for a fact they were jealous. They saw you, this beautiful girl from Hawaii who looked different from them, and they didn't know how to handle it. So they acted like jackasses."

There's an achy pulse in my chest at the kindness of his words. Again, he frowns. Again, it sends my heartbeat into a tizzy.

"And for the record, I think it's sweet your mom gave you that coconut, but you're strong on your own."

My breath catches. As close as our bodies are, I feel closer to him emotionally after this intimate exchange. He cares about me and wants to know so much about me. It's not just that I'm attracted to him; it's that right here, right now, I'm the happiest I've been in a long while. No worldly destination compares to sitting on this curb with Tate, except maybe my bedroom.

"Want to come inside?" I grin up at him. My hand is already digging in my purse for my keys. He stands, then helps me to my feet.

A hint of a smile is dancing at his lips, and I feel like I've won the lottery. He rubs the back of his neck. "Maybe we should wait."

Disappointment hits. "Why?"

"You're still recovering from surgery. And a concussion."

"It's been almost two weeks," I say. I'm shameless in my need to be with him.

He runs a hand through my hair. "Believe me, I want to." He turns to glance at my front door. "But I have a feeling the moment we walk through that door, we won't be able to control ourselves."

"That's not true." He frowns at my lie, but I press on. "We spent almost every night together while I was out from work, and we managed just fine."

"True, but every day you feel better and stronger, you'll be tempted to test the waters. So will I."

I let out a pouty scoff.

"Emmie, I want you. There's no question about that. You have to rest, though."

I tug at his hand. "Wait, is this because you saw Jamie and me just now? I thought we cleared that up."

Tate shakes his head before raking my hair from my face. "No, of course not. Look, I know I came off like a jealous jackass this morning, but you explained everything. I realize I was wrong to feel that way. What happened just now didn't bother me."

I raise an eyebrow at him. His jaw clenches.

"I get it. There's nothing between you two. I'm just . . . I take time to process things, longer than most people."

"You're introspective," I say. "I respect that."

His lips press against my forehead. My eyelids fall closed. I can't do anything other than hum.

"Let's take our time, okay? You need it, and I need it."

When he pulls me in for a hug, I press an openmouthed kiss against his chest.

"Emmie," he chuckles. "Please. Don't."

My teeth graze his shoulder in a soft scrape.

"Fuck," he groans. "If there's anything harder than walking away from you, I don't want to know what it is."

I eye the crotch of his jeans. "Speaking of hard."

He ruffles his hair with his hand. "And that's my cue to leave."

Watching Tate walk away is an exercise in patience that I don't possess. So instead, I lunge forward and grab his hand. I let myself press into him and breathe in deep. That spicy, woodsy scent that seems to follow him everywhere will be the death of me.

"Have dinner with me tomorrow night."

Surprise laces his smile. "Dinner?"

I nod. "Maybe we can't do the physical stuff yet, but we can eat together, can't we?"

Even in the darkness, there's a spark in his eye, like he can't believe it either. Weeks ago it was a struggle just to be in the presence of each other. Now we have to walk away to keep from tearing each other's clothes off.

Under the faint gleam of a half moon, he smiles. It's brighter than all the stars in the sky.

"Sounds perfect."

sixteen

·······

When I walk into Three Happiness Express, I spot Tate at
a small table for two in the back. This local dive is apparently his favorite place for Chinese food. I wind through the haphazard configuration of tables and chairs, and take the seat across
from him.

"You made it." He points to my left hand. "Snack time?"

Heat climbs up my face when I hand the loaf of Ezekiel bread
to him.

"You've given me so much fruit, and I love it. I wanted to give
you something too." I recall how quickly I devoured the perfectly
ripe papaya after I raced home from work to clean up for dinner.

But now before him with a loaf of bread, my nerves are shot.
"Bread as a gift. What the hell was I thinking?"

His mouth scrunches between a purse and a smile. "Stop. I like
it. Thank you." He handles it with care, like it's made of glass.
"How did you know this is my favorite bread?"

"You eat the same turkey sandwich every single day. It was easy
to figure out."

His half smile reads amused. "What else have you figured out?"

"I have a sneaking suspicion that you rarely drink anything other than water. It's all I ever see you guzzle. You're the only person that Perry doesn't dare confront. Must be nice, by the way. And you're a loner to the core. Striking up casual conversations is a no-go. You only talk to people when they ask you questions or you need clarification. You grind your teeth when you're annoyed or angry."

Wrinkles crease his forehead when his brow lifts. "How do you know that?"

"Your jaw bulges every single time."

"Anything else?"

"Deep down, under that bulletproof facade, you care. It's why you got Brett fired, why you helped me at the rock climbing gym, and why you took care of me at the hospital."

"Damn." Blushing, he runs a hand through his curls. They're perfectly tousled when he lets go.

And there it is once more. A crack through his hard exterior. More proof that the guy who pretends to be an industrial-strength jerk on the surface is actually a sweet and endearing mush on the inside.

"I didn't mean to freak you out. I swear, I haven't been stalking you."

"It's okay." His face resumes the confident, knowing expression I've seen so many times. "I've noticed a few things about you too."

I recall how he shared his observations about me in the hospital. Before I can comment, a baby-faced server delivers two glasses of water to our table along with menus. I thank him, then fixate on the specials. I gaze around the restaurant. It's bustling for a weeknight with loads of other diners. People dart in and out to pick up to-go orders. The local news channel blares from the TV mounted in the corner. The decor is tacky as all get-out with laminate tabletops that haven't been replaced since the early '80s and red-and-white-tile walls reminiscent of a public restroom.

"I really know how to woo a lady, don't I? Look at this place." He focuses back on his menu.

"You've already done some excellent wooing with those evening cuddles and surprise fruit deliveries." He looks away before smiling, and my heart slides back to my chest. "I love it. This place reminds me of all the dive Chinese food restaurants my mom used to take my sister and me to on the Big Island. No frills, but food so good you don't care."

"Really?"

I nod. "Instant nostalgia the moment I walked in."

"The food here is the best."

"I'm getting peanut butter chicken. What about you?"

"Either Szechuan tofu or sesame beef." He closes the menu and rests his chin on his palm.

"Wow. That's pretty unhealthy for someone who eats the same organic turkey sandwich every day for lunch." I raise an eyebrow at him.

"Now that I have a huge loaf of Ezekiel bread, I can make all the organic sandwiches I want, which should offset this meal."

The server returns, and we order. Tate surprises me by requesting both the tofu and sesame beef.

"You are quite the glutton," I remark before sipping my water.

"Leftovers from here are the best. You can take mine home."

"Did I say glutton? I meant to say generous fellow." His mouth curves into a full smile. A burst of pride hits me for getting him to break for the millionth time.

I let my eyes wander from my glass to his side of the table. He's sitting board-straight against his chair, and he's wearing the same outfit of dark jeans and a gray T-shirt that he wore to work today.

I feel a tad silly for changing before meeting him. Denim shorts and a black tank top aren't exactly dressy, but I don't want to come off like I'm trying too hard.

"You look handsome."

He blinks, then squints, giving off the impression he's confused.

"I think you're handsome," I repeat.

"Oh. Thanks." He tucks a loose curl behind his ear and cranes his neck to the side. He's flustered and it's adorable. "You're very pretty."

I roll my eyes. "You don't have to pay me a compliment just because I gave you one."

He frowns. "That's not it at all. I've always thought you were pretty. It's just not professional to tell your coworker that during office hours."

"Um, thank you," I stammer. "But if that's true, why were you so hostile to me for so long?" And there's the million-dollar question.

"I'm an asshole." He says it dismissively, like it's a no-brainer.

I reach across the table and set my hand on top of his. "Don't deflect. Talk to me."

His chest rises and falls with a single slow breath. "Nicer folks would probably call me an intense introvert."

"I kind of noticed that."

"You remember how I said my sister Natalie and I are total opposites? That's putting it lightly. She's Miss Congeniality. The most welcoming, friendly person you'll ever meet. Everyone loves her. She's been like that our entire lives. I don't hold a candle to her." He swallows hard, and I'm hypnotized by the way his throat moves. It makes me ache.

"It's okay if you're not like your sister. You're two different people. No one expects you to be exactly the same just because you're twins."

"Tell that to my parents. And the rest of my family. And most people who know us." He rubs the side of his face. "I have a few people I'm close to. My sister; Brendan, the doctor from the hospital; a couple of other people. That's it. Going out, meeting new people, it's exhausting. I'd rather get a prostate exam. During parent-teacher meetings in school, my teachers consistently complained to my parents that I never participated in class discussions. I had a hard time making friends. I still do."

I'm overcome with the urge to console him, to tell him he is wonderful just the way he is, but I stay silent. He's opening up to me, and I don't want to interrupt. Instead, I keep hold of his hand.

"My whole life everyone—mutual friends, teachers, coaches, relatives—everyone made it a point to remark to me how different I was from my sister. They'd always have this bewildered look on their face, like they couldn't believe we were siblings, let alone twins. It made me think there was something wrong with me."

There's no anger or bitterness in his voice when he explains. Only the slightest bit of embarrassment coating his words.

"There's absolutely nothing wrong with you." I squeeze his hand, hoping I'm giving him some comfort.

"I know that now. I didn't as a kid, though. It's tough when you're little and almost everyone you meet raves about your much more pleasant sibling, then makes a comment about how you're the polar opposite."

Letting go of his hand, I caress his perfectly stubbled cheek. He turns his head to kiss my palm.

"I'm so sorry."

"Don't be." When he smiles, I want to take a photo and keep it forever. Such a far cry from the way he used to look at me.

When I close my eyes, I can recall perfectly the harsh expression on his face the day we met. It could blast nails from concrete. It's nothing like the way he looks at me now.

"Honestly, I could have handled all that fine if my parents weren't part of it. Over and over my whole life they always said, 'Why can't you be more like your sister?' That sort of malarkey. They didn't understand me or my personality. They still don't. We argued a lot. They thought it was simple to go out and make friends or be friendly and talkative like Natalie, but it's a huge obstacle for me. It's like they took my introversion as an insult to them. I was never as fun loving or affectionate toward them as my sister was, but believe me when I say no one is."

"I believe you," I say.

"Logically, I know they didn't mean to hurt me. It just stings. They wish I could be more like Natalie. I can't say I blame them. She's the absolute best."

"So are you." I reach over and stroke his curls. He moans softly. "You're amazing. Getting to your amazingness just takes a bit longer. You make people earn it. They have to dig a little, but it's there."

I ache with the hope that my words quell his self-doubt.

"What does your sister think about all this?"

I'm a nosy jerk to keep asking all these questions, but I can't help it. Each nugget of info I get from him feels like a gift. Every time Tate opens up to me, it's akin to earning a gold star. We're growing closer by the second, and it's the most enthralling feeling in the world.

"That's the kicker. She always sticks up for me. Whenever someone would try to compare the two of us or make me feel bad for being closed off, she always shut them down. Even our parents. She tells them over and over to quit comparing us. It's yet another reason why she's the greatest. She has a giant heart and she goes out of her way to protect her grumpy, unlikable twin brother, who doesn't deserve her support."

"Stop. You deserve it. It's proof you're an incredible person that your sister would defend you so adamantly, especially to your parents."

"It's why I got into social media, actually." He lets out an amused laugh, then stops to stare at the open kitchen behind the front counter. One of the cooks is flipping sesame chicken over and over in a massive wok. The aroma of sesame oil and peppers wafts over to us. We both watch for a long moment, hypnotized.

He pivots his focus back to me. "I wanted to prove to everyone who ever thought of me as a standoffish prick that I could be social. In my own way, of course. As it turns out, you don't actually have to be all that social to work in social media. You just have to be good at Twitter, Facebook, and Google Analytics."

"What a devious rebel you are."

"It's a huge yet acceptable middle finger to them all," he says. "The irony of my profession is not lost on me, believe me."

He runs his fingers up and down my arm.

"This explains so much. Thank you for telling me. I know it wasn't easy."

Our food arrives, and we chow down. I'm savoring every bite, but it's not just because the meal is delicious. This conversation, this dinner, it's a level of comfort I'm not used to on dates. Even our awkward moments I adore. It's only our first meal together, but I already know I want to do it again.

Staring at his plate, Tate spears a chunk of fried tofu. "Thanks for listening."

"It's my pleasure."

He chews, swallows, then offers a lips-only smile. "It's easy telling you difficult things. I feel so comfortable around you. Like I can be myself."

I beam at him, then at my half-eaten plate. All the gold stars in the world can't compete with the bliss his words give me. This new comfort floating between us gives me the confidence to ask him about another difficult thing, to see if we can cross over from comfort to intimacy.

"If I ask you something, will you promise to answer honestly?"

He levels me with a you-should-know-better frown. "Okay."

"Why didn't you tell me Jamie called when I was in the hospital?"

seventeen
. . . .

He opens his mouth but is drowned out when a gaggle of little kids dressed in T-ball uniforms enters the restaurant. All we hear are giggles, endless babbling, and high-pitched shrieks.

"What?" I shout.

"I said—"

A half dozen screaming five-year-olds push together the three tables next to us. Four of them immediately haul themselves onto chairs and begin jumping up and down. Two crawl under the tables and start smacking each other.

"Fucking hell," Tate mutters under his breath.

"Hey. Language," I scold.

"Like they can hear me."

He stabs his fork into a strip of beef, then levels the lone adult in charge of this mini motley crew with a death glare. The man flinches when he makes eye contact with Tate, and I feel a pang of pity for him. Dining out with six rambunctious five-year-olds is a punishment I wouldn't wish on my worst enemy.

He attempts to reason with the kids in a hushed, unsure voice. "Guys. Hey, guys. That's enough. Sit down. I said sit. Come on now." The kids continue to yell while treating the tables and chairs like a jungle gym.

"We should just leave," I say.

"And go where?"

An earsplitting scream invades my eardrums. Two kids are warring over the same chair.

"To the Dumpster, into a sewer, I don't care. Anywhere but here."

He packs up our leftovers, we leave cash on the table, and we bolt out the door.

"Dear God," I say while rubbing my ears. "The best birth control you could ever ask for is in that restaurant."

Tate lets out a proper belly laugh. My heart stops for a split second. I could listen to him laugh forever.

"Wow. And you had the nerve to lecture me in there?"

"I didn't drop the f-word in front of a bunch of kindergarteners. I get points for that."

"So what now?" he says after chuckling.

I think about repeating my question about Jamie's call, but I lose my nerve. He's opened up plenty to me this dinner. I feel good about where we are in this moment.

I gaze across the parking lot to the street. "It's dark. I should probably head home. I've got a bit of a walk." The moment I say it, I realize that I don't yet want to leave him. I don't know how to say it and not sound like a desperate weirdo, though.

"Let me drive you." Tate points to his car.

"Remember the first time we were in your car?" I let out an exasperated laugh. "I'm supposed to be resting and recovering, right?"

We let the intensity of our first kiss in his car shuffle in the air between us. The instant I mention it, I'm reminded of his soft tongue and lips, the way he moaned against my mouth.

Even in the darkness, I can see the faintest hue of pink on his cheeks. "I promise to keep myself under control if you do."

I slide in the passenger seat. He starts the car and blasts the AC. When I buckle my seat belt, I wait for him to pull out of the parking lot, but he doesn't move.

"Do you honestly want to know why I didn't tell you about Jamie's call?" His eyes fix ahead.

I nod.

He shoves both hands in his hair, pulls, then lets go. "I was afraid that if I told you he called, you would ask him to come take care of you and tell me to leave. I wanted to be the one there with you."

He doesn't look at me when he speaks. His admission sends a wave of all-consuming warmth through my body. The intimacy I was so curious about is right there in this admission. He trusts me enough to open up about a vulnerable moment. I grab his hand, hoping my touch reassures him.

"Tate, no. I'm grateful you were the one with me. You shouldn't have been afraid to tell me he called. It wouldn't have changed anything."

"You can honestly say that?" His eyes bore into me. "You can say in that moment, without question, you wouldn't have wanted Jamie there instead?"

"I wanted you there and you only. No one else." I squeeze his hand, hoping he believes me.

With a nod, his gaze falls to his lap. I wonder what he'll say next, what he'll do. Seconds pass and he doesn't budge. The air in the car grows frosty. I rub the goose bumps on my arms.

"Sorry. I always crank the air. Bad habit." He turns off his car and cracks the windows open, then refocuses on me.

It's another long, aching second before he leans to me. Softly, he presses his mouth to mine, then pulls back. It's only our third lip-to-lip kiss, and I immediately regret holding off for so long. One touch of his lips is the first hit of a mystery drug. All I want is more of him on me.

I laugh softly to myself. "Such a tease."

"Excuse me?" he scoffs through a smile.

"You're not leaving me with that sorry excuse for a kiss, are you?"

He grabs me by the chin, leading me in a full-blown, tongue-heavy kiss. A proper kiss. It's our first kiss at Jimi D's cranked up to eleven.

Twelve seconds in and the world around me is forgotten. The wetness of his mouth, the firmness of his tongue, the way he seals his lips against mine makes me forget everything that isn't this kiss. It's hungry, electrifying, soul shaking, and can convert even the most stubborn bodies, mine included.

His hands don't let me off the hook either. One is thrust into my hair, fisted against my scalp. The other is loosely gripped on my shoulder, daring me to pull away. Joke's on him though. A raging bull couldn't pull me from his mouth and this kiss.

I balance myself with one arm on the center console. My other one pulls at his hair. We're at it like starving creatures whose mouths are food. I was wrong. This is not a proper kiss. It's a fucking dynamite, earth-shattering kiss.

He jerks back. "Are you in pain?" He sounds completely robbed of breath.

"No," I blurt, then pull him back to my mouth. He continues

the desperate rhythm for what feels like minutes, then pushes me away.

"Good. Because I need you on my lap. Now." He reaches under his seat and slides it back all the way.

"Fine," I snap, as if he just inconvenienced me with a request to take out the trash. It's an understandable request, and now that I think about it, I would most definitely love to plant myself on top of his thighs. But that means fewer seconds to kiss, and I can't say I support that.

Nevertheless, I maneuver myself awkwardly on top of him. I'm all elbows and knees for several seconds until I'm straddling him. He chuckles at what I imagine is an amusing scene.

"Quiet," I scold, but smile at him immediately after. It's a cramped fit, but it'll have to do.

He guides me back to his mouth with a hand at the back of my neck. The tip of his tongue teases the tip of mine. This time it's slower, deeper, more controlled. He's showing me what he likes, what rhythm he wants me to mimic. I'm more than happy to follow his lead.

Now that I'm firmly on top of him, he lets his hands wander. First my neck, then my shoulders. He fingers both straps of my bra for a beat, then slides his thumbs under each one. I open my eyes to peek at him. His eyes are covered in a hypnotic film. I reckon he's equal parts aroused, fascinated, and comatose.

One of my legs starts to fall asleep, and I shift in his lap slightly. I feel an unmistakable hardness underneath me and smile against his mouth.

"Enjoying yourself, then?" I ask. His hands wander up and down my back.

He laughs in the middle of our kiss. "Hell, yes."

I nibble at his bottom lip, and he groans. One more nibble, and he groans again, this time louder. The guttural sounds coming from his throat are like catnip, and I'm the greedy feline who can't get enough.

Soon I feel his grip on my ass. It's a long, gratuitous squeeze with both hands. He throws his head back, bumping his headrest. He gazes at me with cloudy eyes.

"Your little shorts. Your tank top. Fucking hell, Emmie," he says between desperate breaths.

"You like my outfit?" I trace my fingers down his throat while he's leaned back, then bite lightly at his neck. A sound somewhere between a deep yelp and the word "fuck" slips out of his mouth. I bite again, this time harder.

He growls, leans up, then smiles. "Fuck, I love it when you're rough."

"Seriously?"

"Fuck, yes. I go crazy for you when you're hard with me, when you're a boss at work, laying down the law."

I press a light kiss to his lips.

"I like your soft side too," he rasps. "Every bit of you. I can't get enough."

His words would be an epiphany if I weren't so turned on. My boss persona may be more a part of me than I thought, and in this moment, with Tate writhing under me, the thought drives me wild.

I continue my kissing trail to his collarbone. My finger hooks over the neck of his shirt and I gently pull, exposing more of his stunning skin. A small tuft of curly white-blond hair peeks out. I nuzzle it with my nose.

Finally, I get to enjoy all the parts of him I missed during our first kiss. There was no time for any horsing around that night. It was rushed and desperate and shocking. Tonight is different. We exist in this car and can do whatever we want. In this car, there are no rules, no time limits, no etiquette to abide by. Only whatever our mouths and hands feel like doing. And right now, I feel like digging my fingers into the meaty muscle of what I assume are his impressive pectorals. At least, they feel quite impressive under the thin cotton shirt he's wearing.

His body flexes under me, pushing my fingers back. I quiver at how solid he feels. His eyes drop from my face to my chest to my legs.

"Look at you. Fuck. The moment you walked into the restaurant, I wanted to do so much—"

My tongue meets the base of his neck, and his voice drops. I give him another soft nip and he lets out a deep, hot breath.

"You need to wear this every day. Every single goddamn day."

I giggle and look up at him. His eyes remain clouded over, signaling he's in a pleasure-filled state and it's all my doing. What a strangely empowering feeling. This tough, imposing man has been rendered helpless by little ol' me. With his size and strength, he could normally push me up or hold me down with ease, but not now. Not in this hot and blissful moment. If I could bottle this smug, satisfying rush inside of me, I could sell it in department stores. I'd call it Domination and charge fifty dollars a bottle. People would kill to feel this desired and in control. I'd make out like a bandit.

Burying my face in his chest, I take in the musky, spicy scent of his skin. I'm gently biting him over his clothes when he leans up and pushes me against the steering wheel. He locks eyes with me and smirks. The rush it gives me makes my legs buckle. I yelp. Good thing I'm already sitting. My back is arched at an unnatural angle, but it somehow makes this moment hotter. He's got me by the waist; I've got him by the shoulders.

He doesn't blink once while he presses his forehead against mine. "Emmie," he says, like he's just now remembering my name.

He kisses me before I can say anything in response. It's seconds before he lets me up for air.

"Yeah?" I finally gasp.

His head dips down to my neck, and I'm shaking as he licks and nibbles. He stays on the left side of my neck at first, then lightly blows on my clavicle before starting at the bottom of my right side. The licking and nibbling commence. I'm moaning and squealing like a wounded animal. I can barely handle this. He laughs against my neck. The vibrations reverberate throughout my chest and head, intensifying the pleasure.

"Tate, please," I whisper. I open my eyes for a moment and my vision is blurry. I don't know how much more I can take.

Instead of easing up, he dips his head lower. He softly bites my left breast outside of my shirt.

"Fuck," I cry. That bite is the single hottest thing that's ever happened to this part of my body. What inventive use of his mouth. Clever boy.

With slow-moving yet sure fingers, he pulls down the front of my tank top. Both cups of my black bra spill over, and his index finger traces the top of my breasts in a steady, deliberate line. Goose bumps rise up on every inch of my exposed skin, even in the heat of this stuffy car.

"What are you . . ."

My breathy, incomplete question is answered with his tongue on my nipple. By the way I nearly choke on my breath, I'm clearly shocked. Tate Rasmussen is a freaking master with his tongue. Slow, wet, warm circles soon turn into rapid, desperate ones. Then he dials back the speed and slides to the other one. Again I nearly choke on air. My eyes cross every time I try to focus my vision on the mass of snowy waves planted right in front of my face, so instead I shut them.

A warm ache spreads from my abdomen up my chest, to my legs, my arms, my fingertips. I'm writhing, whimpering. I say his name over and over. Not once does he stop. How Tate can deliver this much pleasure to my body with just his tongue on my breasts is a mystery. It makes me ache for more. A shiver pulses through me, ending at my lower abdomen. The ache intensifies, and suddenly, I want his tongue anywhere he wishes to put it.

"Yes," I moan. "More."

I take it back. *This* is the single hottest thing that's ever happened to this part of my body.

My head hangs over the top of the steering wheel, my pulse hammering at the bottom of my throat. When I open my eyes again, I notice there's condensation coating the windows. I wonder if anyone can hear us with the windows cracked. A sweaty film covers my skin. I lean up, my face brushing against Tate's glorious curls. He raises his head and our gazes meet once more. I could do this forever. I'm sweaty, cramped, bent out of shape, and painfully turned on. This could last for days, weeks, months, and never go any further and I would be eternally happy.

The sharp beep of my phone interrupts our wholly inappropriate parking lot interlude. We pull apart instantly, and I nearly laugh. It's impressive how quickly we stop ourselves at the sound of a phone.

I fish it out of my purse and see an email alert.

"Everything okay?" Tate asks.

"Yeah. It's just an email from my mom asking if I remember what her Facebook password is."

Pearls of sweat dot his chuckling face. As muggy as it is outside, it's worse in the car. Any residual cool air from when he blasted the AC has now disappeared.

"Sorry. We normally talk once a week when she's home, but when she's out of the country visiting her relatives, it's messages like this almost every day."

He laughs harder. I chuckle, then wince. The position I'm in must be aggravating my incisions.

I push off Tate and move back to the passenger seat. He braces me with his arms, making sure I don't fall. When I'm back to sitting, I notice how the sweat highlights his physique. His arms are a perfect blend of thick muscle, veins, and golden hair.

"Still pretty sore?" he asks hesitantly, short of breath.

"Just a little." I rub the side of my stomach. "It's getting better. I just probably shouldn't be in a position like that for long."

Side by side, in separate seats, we steady our breathing. Tate turns on the car and cranks the AC once again. My scalp is soaking wet, as is the back of my neck. I gaze up at him, curious as to what the next step is for us.

He speaks before I do, and I'm relieved. "As much as I want to continue this, you need to rest."

I'm crestfallen. Even so, I nod at him. Doctor's orders are to refrain from any intense physical activity for four weeks after surgery, sex included. Even though my lower half is on fire and the only way to extinguish it is to engage in a bevy of lewd acts with Tate, it's not possible right now.

I look down at my lap, trying to hide my disappointment. "I wish it weren't the case, but you are correct."

"I'll take you home, then." The dissatisfaction on his face does not match the politeness of his words. I'm grateful to see his expression though, because it means we're both equally disappointed.

He drives the short distance to my place. When he parks in the driveway, he reaches for the bag of food. He insists I take all the leftovers, but I convince him to accept a container.

I dawdle a bit before opening the door. "So. Thanks." I have no words in my head, and the ones spilling from my mouth manage to sound woefully inadequate compared to how I feel.

"That was fun." He rubs the back of his neck.

"Pretty epic first dinner."

He joins me in a laugh. We gaze at each other again, affection in our stares.

I reach for the door handle. "Good night."

I expect to hear him say it back, to say, "Bye" or "See you in the morning." What I don't expect is for him to grab me by the wrist and say, "Wait."

eighteen

·······

s everything okay?"

He gazes at me with wide eyes, his stare emboldened. "Was this a date?"

"Honestly? I have no idea. Do you think it was?"

He swallows, and I watch the muscles in his neck flex. "I kind of hoped it would be."

"I hoped so too." My feelings for Tate rush through my body, settling in my chest.

"What I said last night, about wanting to take things slowly, is it too difficult for you?" When he speaks he looks pained, like he's worried to hear my answer.

"It's definitely not easy, but it's the right thing to do. I'm still pretty sore."

He shakes his head. "No, I mean, what I said last night about needing to take my time with this, with us. Does it bother you?"

"Honestly?" I clear my throat. "It wouldn't bother me if I knew why."

He ruffles his hair. "I've always been a slow mover. I take my time; I don't rush; and I only do things I want to do. I've been this way ever since I was a kid. I hate it when people try to pull me out of my comfort zone. I'd rather quietly work things out on my own."

"I can respect that. There's something more though. I can feel it."

He sighs. "It's made dating and relationships difficult. I'm not an easy guy to be with. It took me a while to figure out why."

"My money's on your introvert personality."

His half smile reappears. "Bingo. The women I've dated hate that I don't open up about everything right away, that I'm so reserved. I've tried forcing myself to be open, but it's always ended in disaster. It always felt so rushed, unnatural. It led to arguments, resentment, strain. Eventually, we'd break up because they couldn't handle my personality long term."

He reaches for my hand and laces his fingers with mine.

"With you it's different. Comfortable. You set me at ease." He points between us, then pauses to swallow. "I don't want to mess up by jumping into things too fast. I've made that mistake too many times before. I don't want to lose you too."

There's a tiny fireworks show happening in the middle of my chest, like a rainbow with every color in the world surging through my body. Tate is the champion of making me feel things I've never felt before.

"What if I said that tonight was a date?"

I bite back a smile. "Then I would say it too."

"And what if I said I wanted to date you, but still take things slow? Would you be up for that?"

I've done the normal jumping-in-too-fast routine with exes, and it's always failed. This time with Tate, I want to do things differently.

"I can do slow," I say.

Relief seems to be the undercurrent of the lips-only smile he flashes me.

A single doubt lingers in my head. "The stakes are pretty high though, don't you think? Even if we're careful and do everything perfectly, there's still a chance it won't work out. If that happens, we'll have to work together in the aftermath. Hurt feelings, failed expectations. It won't be pretty. It might even be worse than it was before. Doesn't that worry you?"

No frown or grimace like I expect. Instead, he flashes the easiest, most relaxed smile. "You're worth the risk."

With my eyes still on him, I feel for the door handle. I need to steady myself after praise of that caliber. He grabs me for one more kiss. It mimics the filthy kisses we shared in this car just minutes ago, but this time it's slower, charged with more emotion.

"I don't plan on failing," he says through a grunt. "Do you?"

I run my hand against his stubbly cheek. "No way."

I step out of his car on wobbly legs. He waits until I'm inside before he pulls out of the driveway. Sleep will be impossible tonight, but it doesn't matter. What matters is that Tate Rasmussen and I are dating. I couldn't be happier.

RAINBOW SPRINKLES ARE the only thing I see. They dot my kitchen counter, the bowl of cream cheese frosting, the floor. Bits are even nestled in my hair. Tonight I'm baking Funfetti cupcakes to surprise Tate after his Wednesday evening rock climbing session. A dating-appropriate activity, if I've ever known one.

It's been a handful of days since our first date. Almost three weeks since our very first kiss. A few flirty words, cheesy grins, and prolonged stares are exchanged at work, but that's it. I'm still recovering from surgery and the car contortion session, and we shouldn't tempt ourselves. Sugar temptation, though? Totally acceptable if, due to health reasons, you're trying to avoid sex with your broody coworker-turned-dating-interest.

While I frost the last cupcake, I wonder how Tate's cake looked on the day of his favorite birthday, and if these cupcakes are anywhere close to satisfactory. Would this beautiful, health-conscious man even allow himself the indulgence?

With my index finger, I swipe a lump of the frosting from the bowl. Under the sunlight filtering through the nearby window, it glistens. Just like Tate. I pop it in my mouth, taking my time licking it off. My cheeks heat. It's perverse what I'm doing, allowing his childhood memory to fuel this naughty moment.

I load them into a plastic container, zip to my car, and drive to the rock climbing gym. When I spot his trademark gray sedan, I park a few spots away, walk over, and try the doors. They're all locked. I sigh. Of course. I set the container on the roof of his car and turn back to mine. Pulling out my phone, I type out a text to him:

Left a surprise for you on top of your car. Happy climbing!

After returning home, I clean up the mess on the kitchen counter and fold the basket of laundry I've been putting off for a week. I am contemplating a hot soak in the tub when there's a knock at my door. When I open it, Tate's focused face greets me, along with a bottle of wine in his hand. The plastic container of cupcakes rests in his other. Three cupcakes are already gone.

"Up for turning your surprise into date number two?"

I've never seen his face this bright before. His eyes sparkle, his cheeks flush, and it is divine.

"Yes, please."

He follows me to the kitchen, gushing about the cupcakes. "They're my favorite. Best surprise ever."

I pour us glasses of water and fetch two wineglasses. "It's just a box recipe." I blush. My eyes fall to my glass. "I'm awful at making anything from scratch. You should have seen the macarons I made for Kaitlin's baby shower."

He's standing on the other side of the counter, which is the perfect distance for him to stretch out his arm and rest his hand under my chin. He tilts my head up.

"None of that disparaging talk. They're delicious."

When he licks his lips, I shiver. "A little more than two weeks," I mumble.

I don't have to explain what I mean. He understands that I'm counting down the number of weeks I have to wait until I can engage in certain physical activities.

His fingers glide down the side of my neck. A soft moan is the least obnoxious noise I can manage.

"I should probably stay on this side of the counter." He demolishes half of a cupcake in one bite.

I watch him chew and swallow. "Good idea." For a few seconds, my eyes scan his sculpted upper body, which is displayed nicely in a sleeveless workout shirt.

He pours both of us wine, then clinks his glass to mine. "So what's your typical second-date activity?"

"Usually dinner. First date I do drinks or coffee. That way we don't have to spend an agonizing meal together if we don't hit it off. You?"

"I take her to the rock climbing gym to see if she can hang."

I bite into a cupcake. Tate's eyebrow raises and his hand twitches in my direction, but then he rests it on the counter.

"Frosting. On your lip."

With the back of my hand, I wipe it away. I bet if my body weren't in such cock-blocking condition, he would have taken care of the frosting with his mouth, which could have led to a rather sexy make-out.

I stare at the hemline of my cotton tank dress. "You're hard core, putting dates through physical labor."

"If rock climbing goes well, third date is Chinese food."

I pause midchew. Lucky me got to experience third-date Tate on our first.

"What else do you want to know?"

"Anything and everything."

He doesn't answer right away.

"I broke my wrist playing soccer when I was in third grade," he finally says. "I studied abroad in England when I was in college. I wasn't used to driving stick then, and I crashed into a round-about."

My jaw falls. "Seriously?"

"Dead serious. My parents were livid. Their car insurance went through the roof because of me."

"What other un-fun stuff don't I know about you?"

He nods without breaking eye contact. The intensity is as unnerving as it is mesmerizing.

"You mean like, relationships, exes?"

"You already know about my un-fun stuff." I think back to how I admitted my "O" problem to him and resist the urge to shrink into myself.

"Fair enough." Silence fills the air between us. It's loaded on his end, and I think I know why.

"Someone broke your trust, didn't they?" I ask.

He nods. "I've had a few serious relationships in my life. The longest one, we dated senior year of high school into senior year of college."

"Wow, four years? That's a long time when you're that young."

"It was. We went to different colleges, so we were long distance, too, which was awful. The whole thing was a terrible mistake looking back on it now. We moved pretty quickly into committing to each other. We argued all the time. We'd break up, get back together, over and over. She liked going out with big groups. I preferred one-on-one dates. We'd get jealous of each other. She hated any female friends of mine. I hated most of her guy friends. It was pathetic." He lets out an amused scoff.

He opens his mouth as if to continue, but there are no more words. Just a tired chuckle. I want to prod, to ask for more detail, but I don't want to push him. It's a monumental step for him to reveal this much to me, when he's so hell-bent on taking it slow.

"I was an imbecile," he says. "We both were."

I can't ever remember hearing a person in our age group use such an old-timey word. It makes me smile, despite the serious topic.

Tate glances up at me. "People in their late teens and early twenties are clueless when it comes to relationships. Don't hold it against me."

His hand rests flat on the top of the counter. I move my hand over his and he sighs. It sounds like satisfaction. Every time I've rested my hand on his whenever he goes deep into a conversation, he seems to loosen, to relax. Such a tiny gesture, but it feels enormously intimate.

"Why'd you stay together so long, then?"

"She was my first love, my first long-term relationship. There were lingering feelings on both sides, and we were too young to know how to handle them properly. I didn't know when to call it quits. Neither did she."

"How did it end?"

"She lined up another guy to date, then broke up with me. One of her guy friends. I never liked him. There was definitely some overlap from me to him. That sucked."

"I'm so sorry." I squeeze his hand softly.

"It's fine. I'm over it now." He rubs my fingers with his thumb before taking a long swig from his water bottle. "It sort of stunted me, though. I guess I've been conditioned to expect the worst after that mess."

"Not all women are the same," I say. "You're a smart guy. You should know that."

"Logically, I do, but old habits die hard. It's hard to explain. Almost like a reflex."

"I get it."

He reaches for my hand. "I like you. I like this."

The shaky breath I let out nearly blows my napkin off the counter. His stormy blue-gray stare has me by the throat.

Hearing Tate say he likes me is a formality at this point. I've known it for a while, but it doesn't make the admission any less special. His words are a song I want to listen to over and over.

"I like you too." I bite my lip to keep my gigantic grin at bay. I hope hearing me say it, too, makes him feel just as giddy.

We indulge in one last cupcake together. He offers me the first bite, then he takes one, then I go again. We're doing our best *Lady and the Tramp* impression sans the spaghetti nose-bump.

He insists I have the last bite. I suck a dollop of frosting from my thumb when I finish. "I knew it. You're all talk. You're a sweet guy to the core."

He laughs, then coughs. "Can I ask you something?"

"You just did."

"Smart-ass." He tops off both of our wineglasses, and I take a long swig.

"How is your last name Echavarre? That's not your dad's last name, is it?"

"It's not, but how do you know that? I'm pretty sure I never told you." I wonder for a moment if maybe it slipped out when I was drowsy on painkillers in the hospital.

"You didn't. I overheard you mention a while ago how your dad is so pale he fries almost every time he's out in the sun, but Echavarre doesn't sound like the name of a pale white guy who sunburns easily."

"It's my mom's maiden name. It's Filipino-Spanish. When I was in college, I got this idea in my head that since she raised my sister and me, we should change our last names to hers. My mom was always the one to take care of us. It felt like she got shafted in a way. She gave birth to two daughters, raised us, and we ended up with our dad's last name. It didn't seem fair."

"Excellent point." He tips his glass to me. "What's your dad's last name?"

"Walden." I gulp the rest of my glass. "We're on good terms, but we're not close. Not like my mom and I are. He lives five hours away, but my mom is just a twenty-minute drive from me. You get the idea."

He nods.

"She had been wanting to go back to her maiden name ever since she and my dad got divorced, but never got around to it. I convinced her to do it with me. After I graduated college, we went through the entire name-changing process together, filled out all the paperwork."

"I bet that meant a lot to her."

"It did. She cried when I showed her all my new legal documents with Emmaline Echavarre printed on them."

"You win daughter of the century for that. What about your sister?"

"My mom didn't want her to change her name as a minor. She wanted Addy to make her own decision about it when she was old enough."

"Did she?"

"Yeah. As soon as she graduated college, she changed her name. She's Addison Echavarre now."

"My God, you and your sister have epic names."

"Thanks, I guess?"

He wags an eyebrow at me. "I like your name. I always have. And I admire your conviction. A lot of people wouldn't legally change their names, not even for their mom. It shows what integrity you have."

I beam from the inside out. It's divine, winning the admiration of someone who is historically impossible to please.

"I was very into sticking to my guns and living out my convictions at that age."

"Are you different now?"

"Yes. Not everything needs to be a powerful statement about character or society or whatever. Sometimes, things are the way they are and nothing more."

My words are strangely relevant in this moment. We have a hell of a hostile past, but right now, we're content. Just two people on a date, enjoying the company of each other in the presence of wine and cupcakes.

"Echavarre is much better. Emmaline Walden sounds like the name of a little girl who attends boarding school in Wales."

"I look the exact opposite of a Welsh school girl."

He gives me a side glance that radiates warmth. "I love the way you look, especially in that dress."

His empty glass clinks against the counter when he sets it down, probably because his gaze is fixed on me. "Come here."

"I thought you said to stay on opposite sides."

"Just for a sec. Promise I'll behave."

I wish upon all the stars in every galaxy that he's lying. I round the counter. In a hot second, his hands are on my waist, I'm pressed up against him, and I've forgotten how to inhale.

"Breathe," he whispers, his breath moistening my mouth. My tongue runs along my bottom lip, and I take in the sticky air around us.

Eyes open, he presses his lips against mine. Their velvet feel delivers a lightning bolt to my heart. Before we can get our tongues involved, he pulls away.

"That's all I can do. It's all we *should* do," he huffs.

I nod. Heat simmers between us, but our brains know better. He lets me go and takes a step back. With the cupcakes tucked under his arm, he walks to my front door.

I should see him out, but instead I stay put and open my mouth.

"How about you stay the night?" I've never gone this deep on a second date before, but this is unlike any second date I've ever had.

He turns to me with his brow lifted.

"A reward for how good we've been. We've behaved ourselves pretty well so far, don't you think? We can sleep in my bed and cuddle, just like we did on the couch those nights you came to check on me after my surgery. We won't take it further than that, of course. It's just, I—I know we're only at our second date, but it feels like so much more, don't you think? Probably because of our history." The hurried way I babble gives away my nerves. I swallow to steady myself. "I'll be good if you're good."

His stare gives nothing away. First there's a frown, then a sigh, then dropped eye contact to the floor. I brace myself for the excuse, for the letdown, for the embarrassment I'll nurse with the leftover wine sitting on my counter after his rejection. But then he looks up, a grin on his lips and something extra in his eyes.

"Let me shower first. Then we can head to bed."

nineteen

·······

t's a darn shame." Perry's nasally voice cuts through the song playing in my earbuds. "You'd think Tate would know how to schedule tweets properly."

The noise drifts from Will's office. I yank out my earbuds so I can eavesdrop. It's not often that I hear Perry trash-talk Tate. He wouldn't dare do such a thing to his face, but Tate's running late this morning, because after spending last night kissing, cuddling, and dozing in my bed, he had to drive back to his place to get ready for work.

Rules were set to preserve my recovery. We had to stay fully clothed and couldn't go further than making out. Despite the no-fooling-around policy, I've never had a more satisfying night.

I smile to myself, remembering the way his body was the perfect big spoon to my little spoon, how his sleepy grin and his perfectly tousled bed hair greeted me when my alarm went off. I could get used to that endearing sight every morning.

Will's voice pulls me back to the present. "The storage product promo shouldn't have started until next week. He knows that. I told him." There's the sound of papers shuffling.

"Well, Will, you can only do your best. You've always maintained excellent communication between your department and us folks in Purchasing, but that guy seems to have a mind of his own. Never really works well with others. I'm wondering if he needs a talking-to."

My blood simmers. Perry speaks as though he has authority over the Purchasing department. He doesn't. He's the same level as Tate and me. Lorenzo is head of Purchasing, but he's gone today, which explains Perry's sudden appearance in our section of the building.

He sputters more nonsense about Tate's supposed shortcomings. The urge to defend the man I'm dating is strong. This exact same defensiveness has hit me before when protecting my little sister from a bully or my best friend from criticism. It signals a turning point. Tate is now part of my tribe, and no one messes with my people.

I scroll through my emails. I remember Tate messaging me about those toolboxes a few weeks ago when I wrote descriptions for them.

Perry's nasally vocal assault continues. "Now we have a slew of customers pissed that they won't be getting the discount that was promised. The manufacturers only gave us permission for discounts on those specific dates, and the call center's having to deal with their complaints. We'll probably have to honor the sale by eating the cost ourselves. The manufacturers sure as heck won't pay the difference between the sale price and the actual cost."

The email I'm looking for pops up. Right there in bold, the incorrect date is listed, which means that Perry sent Tate the wrong information.

I print off the sheet, highlight the date, and dart to Will's office.

Perry drones on. "I think that Tate should be the one to take the customer complaint calls. Don't you—"

"Really?" I interrupt, standing in Will's doorway. Perry frowns at me while Will looks up from behind a pile of scattered papers.

"You think Tate should apologize for your mistake? You're completely in the wrong on this one, Perry. As usual." I scowl at him before handing the paper to Will. "The only reason Tate set up the promo tweets for this week is because Perry told him to."

"Let me see that," Perry mutters. Will hands him the paper.

An expression between indignant and embarrassed clouds Perry's face. "I don't see why you needed to involve yourself in this discussion, Emmie."

Classic Patronizing Perry. He's used this tactic before when I've tried to correct him in the past. Always trying to make me feel like an outsider. He wouldn't dream of taking that tone with Tate.

"I do." I cross my arms, stand tall, and square my shoulders. I don't even have to remind myself to slide into boss-bitch mode. I'm already there. "You're only mad because I called you out on your latest blunder. Stop coming into our office and trying to get other people in trouble for your mistakes. We all have better things to do."

Perry the Plague, meet next-level Boss-Bitch Emmie.

Will straightens in his seat before raising his brow at him. "She's right, Perry."

"Be more careful next time. We're all a little tired of your un-professional antics." It's my best professional screw-you tone. Clear and deliberate, almost slow in delivery, yet strong and hard in volume. It says don't mess with me ever again unless you're pre-pared to die on this hill.

Perry's face reddens. He has no words, and it's delightful. The few seconds of tense silence in Will's office feel like a triumph.

"Ridiculous," he mutters.

I slide to the side to let him exit the office first. He walks out the door, then freezes.

With wide eyes, Perry stammers at an unseen person around the corner. "I was just . . . You know, it's a funny story—"

"Is it?" Tate's hard tone hits my ears. He must have heard everything.

"I wasn't trying to—"

"Weren't you?" Tate is calm and steely in his no-nonsense tone. I know he's standing up straight, arms at his side, giving Perry a stare-down that will haunt his nightmares.

"There's not much to add. Emmie said what needed to be said, and I heard it all."

I crane my neck to peek out the door. Perry's back blocks my view of Tate, except for the top of his face and the right side of his body.

"I think we're done here, Perry." Not even a blink mars Tate's stony face. He extends his arm to Perry, and I look down. He's holding the container of Funfetti goodness. "Cupcake?"

Perry shakes his head and scampers out of our office and down the hall.

"Did someone say cupcakes?" Will says.

Tate walks the few steps to Will's office and hands him one.

"Thanks, man! This is one for the record books. I don't know if I've ever seen you eat sweets in the office."

The corner of Tate's mouth quirks up. "Thought I'd add some sweetness to my life. Best decision I ever made."

I have to clear my throat to disguise the gasp I let loose.

Will peels away the cupcake wrapper, seemingly oblivious. "Just don't overdo it. Too many sweets is bad for you."

Tate's knowing stare finds me. "No such thing as too many when it's the right kind of sweet."

In a single bite, half of Will's cupcake is gone. Unlike me, he remains unaware of the subtext of Tate's comments.

"And don't worry, I'll send an email to Perry's boss to warn him about pulling that sort of crap again. His errors aren't our problem," Will says through a mouthful.

I hand him a second cupcake. "Thanks, Will. Seriously."

Will may be forgetful and silly from time to time, but he always has our backs. For that I'm thankful.

He pops a thumbs-up. Tate follows me to my office. I'm all smiles. Tate is too.

"You were pretty impressive back there," he says, leaning against the doorway.

"I've had it with Perry's quest to make everyone look bad, even though he's the one who is famously incompetent."

Warmth softens the angles of his face. "You defended me."

"Of course. I wasn't going to let him trash you."

"Thank you," he says in that low tone I go crazy for. His intensity is back, but only in his eyes this time.

He's bare in his gratitude, utterly stripped down in this moment, and it's my doing.

"I can't believe you were going to give Perry one of your cupcakes," I say once I refocus.

"Not to eat. If he had said yes, I was going to smash it in his face."

I cover my mouth to keep from laughing, but then his face shifts to serious. "We've got our meeting for the Midwest Family Homes Foundation in ten. You ready?"

"Yup," I say.

I grab my notebook with the ideas I jotted down the other day. But then he lowers his head and along with it his tone. "Seriously, Emmie. Thank you."

Tenderness accompanies his soft expression. I grow so weak in the knees, I have to sit down in my office chair.

All I can do is whisper, "Sure thing," turn to my computer, and watch him walk back to his office. We can't kiss; we can't hug; we can't rip each other's clothes off. But we can share this new silence, heat and triumph tumbling between us, and enjoy our latest moment of intimacy.

NINA SIMONE'S GRAVELLY voice is the soundtrack to my soak in the tub this evening. Anything to take the edge off the fire engulfing my insides. It's been burning full blast ever since I defended Tate at work last week. We're two dates, one sleepover, and a million kisses in, and I'm properly smitten.

The tiny incisions glisten in the water, the glue from the tissue adhesive shining bright. From my phone, the melodic sound of "Feeling Good" bounces between the walls. Too bad my body isn't keeping pace with our speed. I'd be ready to throw down right now, but postsurgery recovery and all.

I dry my hand off on the bath mat and grab my phone from the lid of the toilet. I contemplate texting Tate to ask what he's up to, but instead I snap a photo of my freshly shaved legs dangling over the side of the tub. My thumb hovers over the screen, ready to text him the photo in hopes of piquing his interest. Sexy texts are what couples do during the honeymoon stage. *Couple.* We're only two weeks into officially dating and haven't had the label discussion yet. It's been a month since our first kiss, though. We're acting like a couple, but is it jumping the gun a bit to send a seminude pic before the boyfriend-girlfriend discussion? Possibly.

I stretch my arm to set my phone back on the toilet lid, but I slip on the slick edge of the tub. My thumb hits the button, and the photo sends, just as it drops out of my hand and onto the floor.

"Shit," I jolt up, my abdomen throbbing in pain. "Ow, shit."

A slow hiss of breath eases me through the soreness. It's gone in seconds, but the realization of what I've done lingers. Two breaths later, my phone rings. Tate's name flashes across the screen. I'm tempted to ignore it, but that will just make for an awkward workday tomorrow. May as well get the humiliation over with now.

"Yeah? I mean, hello?" I pound a fist to my head, my eyes pressed shut.

"You're in the bathtub." There's a low growl when he speaks. A smidgen of my humiliation disappears. I guess he liked what he saw.

"I am." I try for a nonchalant tone.

"You're taunting me."

"Am not." My nonchalance is now a breathy huff that mirrors his rasp.

"Liar. What are you trying to do to me, Emmie?" There's a frustrated chuckle at the end.

"Nothing. I'm innocent. Just simply bathing by myself."

"By yourself? That should be a crime."

I let out a breath. "I have to say I'm relieved."

"What do you mean?"

I press my eyes shut, even though he can't see me. "I thought it would seem desperate, maybe jumping the gun a bit, sending you a photo of my half-naked body."

He huffs a breath. I think he's smiling. "Come on. We're going on dates; we're spending the night together; we're getting physical to the point of having to set rules so we don't injure ourselves. Desperate isn't even on the radar for us."

Us. The way he says it sounds official. "Us," I repeat.

"Us. As in you and me."

"*Two* of us."

He chuckles. "We're a couple, Emmie. Is that what you want me to say?"

A giggle hits the base of my throat. I have to lean back to laugh properly. "You said it, not me."

"Come on. Tell me you haven't been thinking the exact same thought. I sure as hell have."

"I have," I groan. My hand slips from my stomach to between my legs. "We should celebrate." A moan escapes. Even though I'm talking to him on the phone, the pulse between my legs is back. Just the sound of his voice, that perfect low growl, gets me going.

"How?"

"Just listen."

The pressure of my hand leads to a single quiet moan. I swirl my fingers round and round. The clench in my abdomen doesn't aggravate my soreness like I thought it would. I'm relieved because I don't think I could stop, even if I had to.

I put the phone on speaker and place it on the edge of the tub. Eyes closed, I let my hand work in slow circles. Quick, even circles. Every muscle in my body shakes. A minute passes, then another. The heat and pressure always build quickly when it's just me, but with Tate on the other line, the sound of his heavy breath echoing against the walls, my pleasure comes lightning fast. A long, pitchy, breathy moan pulls from the bottom of my throat and out of my mouth. Panting, I clutch the side of the tub and bring the phone back to my ear.

"How was that?" I say, still short of breath.

He lets out a groan. "Fucking hell, Emmie. The way you breathe, the way you moan . . ."

I can picture his face perfectly. Shy, dilated eyes, half smile, face an undiscovered shade of red. I wonder if he got a bit handsy with himself too. A soft chuckle falls from me. I'm the one doing all of this to him, and it is a whole new realm of satisfying.

"Can we call that date three?"

"We can call it whatever you want. Thanks for letting me listen."

"It sounded like you did a bit more than listen."

A pause follows. "Can you blame me? You drive me wild, Emmie."

We share a chuckle, then say good night. I lie back and submerge myself under the water, still on fire. It's official. We're a couple. Tate Rasmussen is my boyfriend.

I WALK INTO Lynn's empty office, mimicking the slow, quiet movements of a cat burglar. The word "couple" bounces through my head. It's the reason why I'm creeping in an office that isn't mine.

Luckily, what I'm looking for rests in a neat stack on top of her desk: the Nuts & Bolts relationship disclosure forms. Just the sight of the bold black text makes me grin. I won't ask Tate about it, not today at least. But as of last night's bathtub session, we're officially a couple. The conversation about making us "work official" is sure to come up soon. I may as well be prepared.

Soft, swishy footsteps echo down the hall. With shaky hands, I swipe a form, fold it in a hurry, and shove it in the outer thigh pocket of my yoga pants.

I spin around to the open door just as Lynn spots me.

"Oh, hey, Emmie." Her wide smile is devoid of any suspicion. God bless Lynn and her wholesome nature. "Were you looking for me?"

I nod frantically. "Uh, yep. Today's the day the family is visiting the worksite, right? I was just wondering if you needed help with that."

I blink like I'm sending Morse code. I hope she believes my lie.

"Oh, how sweet of you to ask! I do actually." Lynn's grin grows even wider.

She asks me to hand out goodie bags to the kids once they tour the home. "I've been so impressed with what you two have managed so far on this social media and marketing project. Have you seen how well Nuts & Bolts is trending on Twitter and Instagram?"

When I tell her I've scored a feature in a local industrial magazine for Nuts & Bolts, she high-fives me.

"You, Tate, Will, and I should meet next week to talk more about the amazing progress of this project. How's next Monday morning sound?"

I nod yes before heading to the worksite. Since I'm not allowed to do any physical labor yet as part of my surgery recovery, I've been throwing myself full force into media promotion. All those press releases and pitches I sent out have paid off, with local news stations and the newspaper wanting to cover Nuts & Bolts' home-building project.

From the side of the unfinished house walks Tate. The slow burn inside me slides into full-blown fire. He's wearing a tattered gray shirt, worn jeans, and a tool belt. I take in the sculpted glory of his upper body with hungry eyes. Holes dot his T-shirt, giving me delicious glimpses of the perfect flesh underneath. I lick my lips.

He saunters up to me. "Looking at me like I'm a piece of meat? How very unprofessional, Ms. Echavarre." His smirk leaves my face on fire.

Behind him trail a trio of dark-haired elementary school–aged children. Their mom, a petite woman with a kind face, follows. He introduces me to the family who we're building the house for. The kids flash shy smiles while the mom pulls me into a hug, then sways gently back and forth. Emotion hits, and I have to swallow back a lump in my throat. She hugs a lot like my mom. When I pick my mom up from the airport in a couple of months, it'll be nonstop bear hugs for sure.

Tate grins down at the kids. "You guys wanna see where we're going to put up your swing set?"

His cheery tone and exaggerated smile have me swooning hard core on the inside. All those times I listened to Kaitlin and Addy raving about how attractive it is to see a man with kids, I would roll my eyes and shrug. Never understood the appeal. I do now, though.

It's an endearing balance to his hard exterior, a peek into his ever-growing soft side—a side I didn't think existed for the year that I've known him. There's so much goodness within him that I didn't even realize. It makes me want him more than ever.

I offer their mom the goodie bags. She thanks me, then beams at the sight of Tate pointing out the empty swath of dirt that will eventually be planted with grass. Each of the kiddos stares up at him with wide eyes. He says something we can't hear, but it causes a raucous round of giggles among the kids. Flicking off his hard hat, he hands it to the oldest one, who tries it on before letting his younger sisters wear it. Tate high-fives them before darting to his car. He returns with a rugby ball and tosses it to the kids. They play a rousing game of catch with loads of laughter.

"What a sweet young man he is. My kids were asking him all sorts of questions about the house and the yard. He was so patient with them."

I smile to myself. "He is something else entirely."

I introduce her to Lynn when she walks over to us. The kids scurry over to us, excited to dig in to the bags. Lynn takes the family to say hello to the other volunteers. Tate wanders over to me, one hand on his hip, the other gripping the ball.

"Man, kids have a lot of energy," he wheezes.

"You seemed to keep up with them just fine." Sweat glistens over his arms. I have to bite my tongue to keep from licking him.

"Last night left me feeling pretty damn energized."

He pins me with a stare that's knowing and sneaky. Behind his cool facade, he's thinking of our naughty phone antics from last night, and it has me in a tizzy.

"I've got to get back to work. But no work for you. You, Ms. Echavarre, will be heading back to the office. Your recovery comes first."

"I think I'd rather stay and watch you." My knees wobble when I say it.

He winks at me. "Last night you were all about listening. Today you want to watch. We're developing quite a kink early on."

"Call it date number four if that makes you feel better." I keep my voice low enough so no one else can hear.

His face twists. "It might have to be. I've got plans tonight. I really want to see you, but maybe tomorrow?"

Disappointment hits, but I say it's fine.

"Trust me, I'd rather spend time with you. I just can't get out of it."

Lynn returns with the family, who tell us thank you once more. Each of the kids dons the tiny hard hat included in their gift bags.

We wave good-bye to them as Kip from Purchasing walks up to Tate. "You're a champion, man. Tiring out three kiddos is impressive. I should have you over to entertain my crew. What's your secret?"

Tate mumbles something about weekly rugby matches at Memorial Park, rock climbing, and weight lifting. Kip's impressed whistle follows.

Lynn jogs up to me. "I think that went wonderfully, don't you? The family is so excited about their home. And Tate! Who knew he's so good with kids?"

I sneak another glance at him. I have to plant my feet on the ground to keep from lunging over and licking him.

"He's been in a great mood lately, don't you think?" Lynn says. "Such a positive influence on this project."

She steps away before asking the volunteers to gather around for a progress update. As she runs down the worksite to-do list, I'm left alone to bask in my bliss bubble. Tate is happy, and it shows. And I'm the reason.

He trots up to me. "Did you get any photos from the far end of the worksite?"

I shake my head.

"Come on."

He leads me to the back of the unfinished house, behind a pile of lumber. Someone's truck is parked right next to it. It and the pile of wood create a tiny secluded spot in the middle of a bustling worksite. With everyone else gathered at the front of the house, all we hear are soft muffled voices. If I close my eyes, the hollow sound reminds me of the lava tubes I explored as a kid on the Big Island.

Tate turns me so my back is to the wall. He grips my waist; I press my hands against his shoulders.

"I needed a moment in private. With my girlfriend." His lips shift into a half smile. "Hope you don't mind."

A rush of warmth floods my cheeks, and he inches closer to my face. When his lips hit mine, it's an electric shock. His mouth parts, opening my lips, his tongue slides in, and I can't breathe. His trademark clean taste fills my mouth, and I moan. I try to keep up with his heavy and urgent rhythm, but I can't. His hands are a soft clamp over mine, pulling my body against his. Thankfully, no one can see us, because this kiss is pure pornographic lust.

He pulls away after what feels like a solid minute, though I can't be sure. I'm so dizzy after that soul-shaking kiss that I sway a bit. He steadies me with his hands, which are now circling my rib cage.

"I thought about you all last night," he whispers. "In the bathtub, wet, naked."

The low hum radiating from the base of his throat makes me grin like the Cheshire cat. I nibble his bottom lip. "You should have come over. It would have been a nice surprise."

"I am not a smart man."

Again he captures me in a kiss that leaves me breathless. When I come up for air, he's gasping as well.

"Did you make yourself come again after we hung up?"

I shake my head, too dizzy to speak.

"Why not?" He studies me with pleasure-drunk eyes, his lids halfway closed.

I lean into the hard bulge at the front of his pants. With my hand over his chest, I steady myself. If I weren't holding on to him, I'd be a puddle on the ground. The truth dances on the tip of my tongue, waiting for me to be brave enough to say it.

"I wanted you instead."

One of his hands stays at my waist; the other glides up my arm and stops on my face. His forehead falls against mine. Our stares lock. In an instant, my throat dries up.

"I'd love to make you come, Emmie."

He presses his lips to mine but leaves out his tongue. I miss the soft, clean wetness already. Even without the kiss, I'm rendered weak. How he manages to constantly floor me with sexy comments, I'll never know.

"You only want me for my body? How shallow."

His hands tighten around my waist. It almost feels like he's holding me steady just so he can hypnotize me with the storm brewing in his stare. There's no way I'll ever tire of looking into those eyes.

"Hardly. I want you for so many other reasons. Your smile, your laugh, your thoughtfulness. Your strength and sweetness. The way you make me feel at ease every single time I'm around you. You tick all my boxes. There's no one in the world like you, Emmie."

I breathe, but it doesn't feel like any oxygen is making it inside my body. I'm floored once more, but this time it's the obvious affection in his face, the way it laces all the words he speaks.

"We'd better head back," he says.

We join the rest of the Nuts & Bolts crew. Lynn lends a few final remarks, and the crowd disperses. I mill around the house snapping progress photos for another press package I'm working on. When I near the far edge, I hear Kip's laughter echoing around the corner.

"I hear ya, Tate. Good luck at the rugby game tonight."

With Kip's perfectly timed words, the most brilliant idea pops into my head.

twenty

·······

Images of Tate from earlier today bounce around my head while I walk along my evening jogging route. The way he played and joked with those kids all the while decked out in sexy contractor cosplay gave me a whole new fantasy to obsess over.

But it's his words doing me in. Maybe he missed a chance to surprise me last night, but I'm not missing my chance to surprise him. Six words loop inside my head, making it impossible to focus on anything else.

I'd love to make you come.

It's so Neanderthal of me, but I can't help it. Tate brings out both the sentimental part of me and the cavewoman part that wants to be taken against a wall. Every time his low, velvety voice repeats those words in the privacy of my mind, there's a starburst at the bottom of my gut. Fire engulfs my cheeks.

Every minute spent with Tate makes me want a hundred more. Every time he says something sweet, I want to hear it over and over. I've never been this level of smitten in any prior relationship.

Each footstep is a struggle to stay on course. I want to sprint instead, but I manage to keep walking until I reach the end of the street. My brain orders me to keep a slow pace, but my legs tell it to go to hell. I blame restless leg syndrome. I blame the boredom brought on by doctor's orders to take it easy. I blame Tate's pillowy lips that must be laced with crack.

I continue speed walking, take a hard left, and pick up the pace. The end of my route is only a mile from where his game is. I'll surprise him with a hello, a hug, maybe a kiss, and then be on my way.

In exactly fourteen minutes and forty-seven seconds, I reach Memorial Park and spot a group of men milling around a huge field. I discreetly mosey around the edge of what I assume is the perimeter of their game. There are no markings, just plain grass. When I'm about twenty feet away, I stop and watch.

Even in the chaotic crowd of rugby players, it's easy to spot Tate. The white-blond curls peeking out of his scrum cap give him away. Currently, his arms are interlocked with a dark-haired guy who's shorter and stockier than he is. After a bit of violent tussling, Tate shoves him away using his shoulder. He takes off in a full sprint, tackling the guy with the ball. The spot between my legs aches as I observe my boyfriend. He's sweat drenched, grass stained, and fueled by testosterone. Everything about the way he moves is carnal and masculine. It is divine to watch.

The game ends, and he chats with his doctor friend, Brendan, who assisted during my surgery. They high-five a few teammates. The longer I stand on my own, the sillier I feel. This is clearly male bonding time, and I'd be intruding, even if it were to just say hello.

Twisting my head, I scan the park in search of a discreet path to walk away. I spot Tate chugging water before toweling off, then he begins to walk in my direction. I dart the opposite way, pausing behind a tree, hoping he can't see me. The sun is setting soon, meaning it will be dark before I make it back to my place. I cross a nearby field, but then I hear Tate call my name. And I thought I was so slick.

"Emmie, I know that's you," he hollers.

I spin around, wondering if my face is as beet red as it feels.

"Oh, hi," I say, as if I'm shocked to see him.

"What are you doing here?" The sweat on his body shines bright, making him appear like a chiseled Roman statue.

"I was out for a power walk and happened to pass by. Thought I'd say hello," I say quickly.

"Power walk, eh? So that's why you're so red." His breath steadies.

That's right, Tate. I'm red because I was walking in the late summer heat. It's not because I'm ogling your sculpted physique, which is showcased exquisitely in a sweat-soaked white T-shirt.

"I lied. I wanted to surprise you."

Tate gives my body a visual once-over. I feel on display, but in the best possible way.

"Damn, do I love surprises from my girlfriend."

Giddiness pools at the bottom of my throat. I have the sudden urge to giggle like a schoolgirl. Instead, I beam at him.

He wipes the sweat off his face with his upper arm, careful to avoid a small cut on his brow. "I like your outfit."

I'm wearing the rattiest tank top I own over a highlighter-yellow sports bra and the same yoga pants I wore at the worksite today. Based on the whistles and car honks I received during my stroll this evening, I look positively indecent.

Brendan waves and walks up to us. "Hey. Emmie, right?" he says with a smile. "Look at you out and about. You're looking great. How do you feel?"

"Tons better. Thanks again for all you did when I was in the hospital."

He nods. "Glad you're recovering well. Did you catch any of our game?"

"The last bit, yeah. How'd you guys do? Sorry, I'm a rugby noob and I had no idea what I was watching."

The two of them laugh. "We won thanks to Tate." Brendan gestures at him with his thumb just as Tate looks away at the other side of the field. "He stopped the other team from scoring at the end with a killer tackle."

"Way to go," I say. Tate smirks at the ground.

"Well, I'll leave you two, then." Brendan grabs his car keys out of his pocket and walks past me. "Do me a favor, Emmie, will you? Tell Tate to reconsider about this weekend. And don't take no for an answer."

Tate's face slips into twisted frustration.

"I'll do my best."

Brendan pats me on the back and walks off. We're left standing across from each other again.

"What's this weekend?"

He crosses his arms and purses his lips like he's eaten something sour. "I'll tell you once we get to my place."

He wraps an arm around my waist and walks. His body is still hot from all that glorious physical exertion minutes ago. I bite back a cheesy grin and relax into his hold. The sour scent of sweat laces his usual evergreen spice. I breathe deeply, giving his chest a quick nuzzle. This surprise walk to his place is way, way better than my surprise.

"You smell so damn good. Like a man's man. Rugged and sweaty."

He lets out a low laugh. Two blocks later, he leads me to a brick duplex and lets go of me to unlock the door. The places on my waist where he touched me tingle.

It's a decidedly bachelor dwelling. In the living room is a faux-leather sectional and a massive flat-screen. There's a beat-up wooden coffee table in the middle. No dining table, just a couple of wooden stools sitting by a counter that juts out from the open wall, which divides the living room from the kitchen.

"Nice place," I say, walking around the living room.

"Have a seat." He gestures to the couch and walks to the kitchen sink. "Water?"

"Yes, please." I hover over his sectional, not wanting to press my sweaty self on it. Instead of sitting, I walk to the kitchen. "How long have you lived here?"

"A couple years."

"Really? It doesn't look like it. There's not much to it." Rock climbing shoes, a harness, and a bag of chalk litter the floor of what I assume is the dining room.

He hands me a glass of water, and I chug half of it. "What a rude thing to say." He winks, then raises an eyebrow. The throbbing between my legs commences.

"I didn't know you lived in a duplex too. Yours is nicer than mine, though. More modern. Mine looks like a tiny red barn from the outside."

He drains his glass of water in two quick swallows and turns around to refill it. The back muscles poking through his wet shirt are a tractor beam for my eyes. It is physically impossible to look away. Instead I force myself to finish my water.

"I lived here with Natalie until she moved out about a year ago."

"Did she take all of the furniture with her when she left?" I gesture to the sparsely furnished space.

"Precisely why it looks like this." He waves his hand around the room. "She started dating the guy who owns this building. They hit it off, it got serious, and he asked her to move in with him."

I'm floored by how many random things we have in common. We both have sisters who lived with us. We both live in duplexes. We're both terrible decorators.

He leans against the counter and gazes at me. I try to brush away a chunk of sweaty hair that's fallen over my forehead, but he stretches out his arm to take care of it for me. He sweeps his hand down my cheek and holds my chin with his thumb.

"What's going on this weekend?" I ask.

"Nothing major."

I trace my finger along the tight muscles of his jawline. "This tells me different." I lightly press the skin around the fresh cut on his forehead. "Let me clean this for you."

He directs me to a nearby drawer, and I grab peroxide and Band-Aids. I dab a soaked paper towel against the cut, taking care to blow on it to ease the burn. To my surprise, he smiles when I secure a Band-Aid over the cut.

"You didn't jerk away this time." I remind him of how he recoiled when I pointed out that speck of paper in his hair all those weeks ago.

"I'm much happier, more relaxed these days. Thanks to you." A kiss on my cheek seals his compliment.

I inquire again about this weekend.

He sighs. "It's our high school reunion. Brendan, my sister, and a few other people have been hounding me to go, to catch up with old friends, but I'm not into it."

"You're not into spending time with your friends?"

"I spend enough time with my friends. I just don't want to spend a Saturday evening at my old high school surrounded by people I couldn't stand ten years ago."

"Well, it obviously means a lot to your sister and Brendan."

He leans down, rubbing his face in his hands, then stares ahead. "I wasn't the most popular person in high school. I was moody and quiet and pissy."

"You're moody and quiet and pissy now. What's the difference?"

"Most everyone hated me. Except for a handful of friends and my sister."

"So just go and hang out with your sister and Brendan. It's a few hours of your life. Then leave."

He leans his head against the cabinet behind him. "They'll spend the entire reunion catching up with old friends about the good old days while I'll be the quiet weirdo in the corner."

His chest heaves when he inhales. I resist the urge to lick his stomach.

"At least you'll be a hot quiet weirdo in the corner."

He chuckles and skims his thumb along my arm. "That's the first time anyone's called me that. 'Hot,' I mean."

I rest a hand on his shoulder. Never in a million years would I have pegged Tate as the type of person who's too insecure to go to a high school reunion. He seems ruthlessly confident. I assumed being nervous was beneath him.

"What if I go with you?"

He squints at me. "You'd do that for me?"

I run my fingers through his soft curls. He closes his eyes and moans.

"Absolutely. That way you won't be alone, and you'll be doing something nice for your sister and Brendan. Think of it as a date, if it makes things more enticing." With both hands on my waist, he pulls me against him. "We're a couple now. We should be there to support each other."

He pecks me on the lips, then leans back to gaze at me. His mouth is a flawless line of pink. "No one's ever gone out of their way for me like this."

He gives me a proper kiss this time. Pulling away, he types a text on his phone.

"Don't make plans for Saturday evening because you'll be my date to the reunion."

His hand falls to my waist, and he runs his thumb along my stomach. It causes the most divine shiver. He pulls me closer.

"Watching you play a full game of rugby would have been a fun date."

He swallows, his Adam's apple moving slowly along his neck, daring me to lick it.

"I'm covered in sweat and dirt, crashing into a bunch of dudes. We're all grunting and shouting. Sometimes we fight. That would be the worst date ever."

"You are sorely mistaken about what I like to do on dates."

Now his gaze holds me hostage. The fronts of our bodies are still pressed together, but I want to press something else. I nibble his bottom lip, and it's like a match falling in gasoline.

He grabs me by the sides of my face and pulls me in for a deeper kiss. Instantly, we sink into each other. My arms are wrapped around his neck. His hands wander all over my body. First my waist, then my hips, then my ass, then up my back. My fingers are tangled in his curls by the time he reaches my breasts. When his mouth reaches mine, I bite his lip playfully and he backs off, leaving his hands to set up camp at my waist. I want to give him all the hard and soft stuff that he wants.

Minutes pass as we kiss. I bite again, he nips me back. I slurp, he sucks. Every morsel of contact I have with Tate's lips and tongue is heaven. His mouth is the best taste I've ever known, and

I can never get enough. I want more, as much as he's willing to give me.

When his hand wanders to my right lower abdomen, there's a squeeze. I squeal at the sharp pain.

"Shit, sorry!" he cries out.

"It's fine." My pained tone is not convincing. I'm leaning over, holding the side of my stomach. "It's still a little tender. Hard pressure aggravates it."

He kneels down and looks at my stomach. He's eye level with my navel, pulling up my tank top to examine me. My breath catches. This is an interesting position. The flesh between my thighs aches again when his exhale bounces off my stomach.

He presses a featherlight kiss against the tiny incision before standing back up to face me. I almost choke.

"I guess I got a little carried away." He blushes, and it's adorable.

I clear my throat. "I like how carried away you get around me."

"Can I make it up to you?"

"How would do you that?"

He leads me by the hand to his sectional, and I take a seat. When he kneels on the floor in front of me, my breath catches.

"I know you've still got a couple days left until you hit four weeks, but you feel good, right? As long as there's no hard pressure on your abdomen, you're okay?"

"That's exactly right," I answer too quickly with a smile that's probably too wide for my face.

"I'd like to make good on my comment from earlier today."

Goose bumps flash across my skin. I hope that he's talking about those six words that propelled me to sneak to his rugby game this evening.

He asks if I'm okay lying down on the couch. Instead of answering, I fall flat on my back. Slowly, his hand glides up my thigh to the hem of my leggings, then the waistband.

"Okay if these come off?"

I moan an "mmmhmm."

Lycra fabric soon pools at my ankles, and the hot moisture of his breath is all I feel on my thighs. I lean my head up to gaze at Tate. Cloudy eyes and kiss-swollen lips greet me. Then he scoots closer between my legs, his face at my thighs.

"Let's see how I compare to your hand."

twenty-one

....

H e raises an eyebrow, smug confidence seeping into his expression. "If anything hurts or feels uncomfortable, just say so, and I'll stop."

Christ almighty, I've been aching for this. Another "mmm-hmm" is the only sound I can make when my heart is beating this fast. Tate is about to explore a part of me that hasn't been touched by another person in nearly a year. My mind goes straight back to our car make-out after our Chinese food date, to the moment his tongue slid over my breasts. A shiver pulses through me.

"I haven't even touched you yet," he says.

"Nerves and all that," I babble. "I was thinking of us in your car, when you pulled down my shirt and bra and—"

He reaches up and puts a hand over my mouth, pushing me back down flat. The ache between my legs spreads. I moan, then chuckle against his palm.

"Get out of your head. Let me in for a bit."

This tiny show of dominance drives me wild. His stubbled cheeks slide against my inner thighs, and a satisfied sigh pushes my mouth open. Pleasure and anticipation pulse through me.

Then he mumbles something I can't hear. For a moment, I wonder if I should ask him to repeat himself, but then I feel his finger hook over my panties, pulling them to the side, and I forget how to use my words.

An instant later there's contact, followed by softness, wetness, circular motion. Delicious, divine circular motion. It starts slow in a teasing, clockwise manner. I try to count the seconds, but I forget what number comes after six. All I can focus on is the wet slide of his tongue. Then he has the audacity to change to counter-clockwise movement and speed up.

My head falls back, my mouth falls open, and I make a noise. It doesn't sound human, but it is human since it's coming from me and I'm a human being.

Time passes. I'm not sure how long because my brain is trapped in a pleasure fog. When I finally muster enough strength to speak, I sound desperate.

"How . . ." I gasp. I press my eyes shut, hoping it helps me concentrate on speaking. "How are you . . ."

A little further, but still a challenge. I can either speak or moan. My brain won't let me do both.

I inhale. "How are you so good at this?"

He stops and lifts his head. I tilt up, and our eyes meet.

He shoots me a heart-melting smirk. "Practice."

"Fucking hell." It's all I can say without losing it.

Without another word, he lowers himself back down. He's a man of few words when it counts, and I like it. I like it even more when I feel his teeth gently bite the inside of my thigh. When he resumes, I'm a yelping, writhing mess.

It doesn't take long before I'm screaming and shaking, a convulsing heap on top of his couch. One of my hands grips the back of his head. The other wrenches the cushion above me. I start to speak, but the sounds I make are muddled and incoherent. I stare at the ceiling, my vision blurry and my ears ringing. Spots of black and white speckle my field of vision. I've never orgasmed that hard, that quickly with anyone before.

It's a minute before I can see clearly.

"Are you okay?" Tate's head pops up from under my thigh. His lips glisten in the dim light his living room lamp casts. He swipes the back of his hand over his mouth, his brow crinkled in concern.

"Holy shit," I finally say. My hands are useless flesh gloves compared to the pleasure Tate just delivered to my body.

"Emmie." The soft palm of his hand finds my knee. He props me into a sitting position, but I'm so dizzy, I nearly topple over. "Easy," he coaxes.

"Water," I rasp.

He darts up to the kitchen and fills a glass. I follow him on wobbly legs. When he spins around to find me standing behind him, his worried frown turns into a frustrated one. He touches my forearm. "What are you doing up?"

I grip the counter to steady myself, glass of water in one hand. It's drained in seconds. Leaning my butt against the edge, I break out into a string of pitchy giggles.

He pulls me into a hug. "You're okay, then?"

The water seems to have restored a bit of the strength that Tate pulled from me just minutes ago, because I have the energy to push him back while still laughing.

"Of course I'm okay. I'm freaking fantastic. Tate Rasmussen, that's one hell of a mouth you have on you."

Gripping his chin with my hand, I pull his face to mine. Our foreheads touch, and he finally lets a smile break free.

"You had me worried for a sec."

"The only thing you should be worried about is how I'm going to get you back for that."

My free hand falls to the waistband of his gym shorts, which are highlighting his rather impressive hard-on. I begin to tug his shorts down, but Tate stops me with a soft hand on my wrist.

"Not tonight."

"Why not?" I whine.

"This was enough for one evening. You should rest."

"But what about you?" I point my eyes back down to his bur-geoning erection. Even in the passing seconds, it loses zero steam.

"I'll be fine." Pink cheeks flank his flustered smile.

"I want to, though."

"I do too. But tonight I wanted to just focus on you."

I bite back my grin, but my face still heats. He is too good to be true. Again my gaze falls to his nether regions.

"Your concern is sweet, but I'm a dude. I've been waiting out boners since I was eleven."

My head falls back in a laugh. In this moment, it's like we're horny high schoolers aching to round the bases.

When I turn my head, I catch a glimpse of a paper taped to one of his cupboards. A list of Ilocano words are printed on it, along with their English definitions. *Manang (older female sibling or cousin). Ading (younger sibling or cousin). Wen (yes). Escuela (school). Ubbing (child).*

I step away from him to get a better look. There's a faint image in the background of the paper. As I move closer I realize it's the backside of the android picture I pasted on his computer screen all those months ago.

"Why do you have this?" I point at it, stunned.

He swallows hard. "I thought it was funny, so I saved it."

I lift an eyebrow at him. "So you could write Filipino words on it?"

"I've always wanted to learn," he stammers.

I walk up to the dark cherry cabinet and touch the paper. "You could have fooled me. You looked pissed that day. I assumed you tore up the picture and threw it away."

I turn my gaze back to him. He's sporting that adorably flustered look again, only this time with crossed arms. I can't believe he kept that android picture. And I can't believe he's teaching himself Ilocano.

"I'll explain in the car. I should drive you home anyway."

He grabs his keys from the kitchen counter and heads for the door. As much as I want to demand he carry me up to his bedroom this instant so we can finish what he started on the couch, he's right. All of my limbs tingle, and I feel the faintest tinge of soreness at the lower part of my torso. My body has enjoyed enough thrashing pleasure for one evening, it seems.

Comfortable silence accompanies our drive back to my place. It's the perfect time to bask in my afterglow.

"Teaching myself a different language is on my bucket list," he says, parking behind my car in the driveway.

"Ilocano is an interesting choice. I would have assumed you'd choose Tagalog. It's more widely spoken."

"I can't lie; you were my inspiration. I remember you saying to Will around the time I started at Nuts & Bolts that your family spoke Ilocano, not Tagalog."

I can't believe he remembered.

He turns off his car. With our heads leaning against the headrests, we turn to each other. The green and yellow glow of the dashboard lights bounces off his skin. He looks like a beautiful alien.

"You could have asked me, you know. I'd be happy to help you learn some phrases and vocab."

"I was too nervous to ask when I started learning months ago. Introvert problems. Like you said before, I'm a loner to a fault."

"I never said it was a fault."

The dashboard lights have faded, and now it's the gleam of a nearby streetlamp hitting us. The silver-blond hair on his arms makes him shine like a diamond.

"You sure you're okay with it?" he asks.

I frown at him. "I don't know if you've noticed, but I'm not the most outgoing person either. Introverts unite."

Worry clouds his face. "I just don't want you to be disappointed when you meet everyone at the reunion."

"Why would I be? Brendan is great, and your sister sounds lovely."

"No, I mean, disappointed in me."

I hold his hand in both of mine. "I could never be disappointed in you."

He finds my gaze. Again my touch seems to unlock something inside of him. "I'm nervous that you'll see how great my sister is, and then realize how awkward I am. I'm scared you'll be turned off. I like you so much, Emmie. I don't want to drive you away."

I lean forward, my lips falling against his in a soft, chaste kiss. Such a far cry from the filthy kiss he gave me on the couch.

"Never in a million years would I think that about my boyfriend."

I plop onto his lap. It's the same straddling position I assumed when we fooled around in the Three Happiness Express parking lot.

He pats the sides of my calves. "Nice try. We're done for the night. Rest and recover, remember?"

I shoot him my best pouty smile when I plop back into my seat. He grins, then his gaze narrows at his lap.

"What's this?"

I squint to see black text on crumpled white paper. When he unfolds it and the bold letters come into focus, my stomach falls to my feet. It's the relationship disclosure form I tucked into my pocket earlier today. It must have fallen out when I straddled him.

My brain sends a million panicked messages to my hands to seize the paper from his hands before he can read it, but I'm frozen in shock. It's too late anyway. He grips it in both hands, gazing at it with a frown of concentration. What is he thinking? Probably that his new girlfriend is commitment obsessed and wants to take things to the next level way the hell too soon.

When my hands finally get the message, I snatch the paper from him and shove it back in my pocket.

"Well, have a good night then . . ." I stutter, tumbling out of the car.

He does the gentlemanly thing and waits until I'm inside before he drives away. I stumble into my bathroom and splash cold water on my face, wondering if I've ruined everything.

twenty-two
·······

Lying on my couch, I'm still a bundle of nerves from last night's slip-up. I wanted to talk to Tate about it at work today and apologize for jumping the gun, but he was stuck in meetings with Will and Lynn, then took off for the worksite.

I tangle both hands through my hair. Last night could have ended on such a high note. It had the makings of an epic night, what with a mind-blowing oral session on his couch and plans to meet his sister and friends at his high school reunion. And there I go, ruining the mood of it all because I got carried away thinking about the future.

The truth is, I'd love to make things official at work. I'd love more dates, more fooling around, but I can't do any of that if I've scared him away.

I silently curse myself for the millionth time for shoving such a bulky piece of paper into my yoga pants pocket. Those types of pockets are designed to hold a phone or a key, not folded-up papers. I make a fist in my hair and groan.

I stare at my phone, aching to text Tate a million versions of

I'm sorry for jumping the gun! I'm TOTALLY not planning our future like a commitment-obsessed psycho LOL! We're still cool, right??? I have a feeling this is not an issue to be resolved via text, though.

I glance up at the mountain of *pansit* still sitting in the giant wok on my stove. A sorry attempt to take my mind off the likely mess I've made. I'll probably eat one plate of that, then put the rest in the freezer, where it will sit along with the two dozen *lumpia* I rolled the moment I arrived home from work. My mom would be so annoyed. The only time I cook her recipes is when I'm trying to distract myself from self-inflicted humiliation.

Jolting up from the couch, I throw on my sneakers. Walking off this restlessness is the only way I can think to deal.

When I open my front door, I get another jolt. Tate is halfway up my driveway.

His face blank, he holds three yellow, lemon-sized fruits. "*Lilikoi* delivery."

"Yay." I smile, swallowing back all the nerves wreaking havoc on my system.

He follows me to the kitchen and sets the fruit on the counter. Normally, I'd squeal at the sight of my favorite brooding pale hunk delivering more delicious tropical fruit, but all I can do is stand across from him and bite my tongue to keep from babbling like a nervous nitwit.

He peers at the *pansit.* "Yum."

"Are you hungry?" When he shakes his head no, I grab a handful of plastic containers and pack up the mound of fried noodles with pork and veggies.

"I already ate dinner, though I'm regretting it now. *Pansit* is my favorite."

"You'll be taking most of that home with you."

He pumps a fist in the air. "My college roommate would always get on my case about how I would eat half of the *pansit* his mom cooked whenever she visited."

"My sister and I used to have *pansit*-eating contests when we were little."

His mouth quirks up. "Really? Who won?"

"It was about fifty-fifty." The casual chitchat eases me slightly. I wonder if suggesting a *pansit*-eating contest right now would help him forget my faux pas from last night.

"We should chat, don't you think?"

His words send me into a low-key tizzy. I guess not. Here it comes. The talk I've been dreading.

I turn back to him. Keeping my breathing even seems to help. The hay bale of nerves simmering in my gut is now fist sized. "About last night, I didn't mean to—"

Before I can finish, he closes the gap between us in a single wide step. With both hands around my waist, he hauls me up onto the counter. Our faces are barely an inch apart. I can taste the heat of his breath, and I could swear I hear his heart beating. Or maybe that pounding in my ears is the sound of my own heart. When his lips crash against mine, it's heated, wet, desperate, and everything good.

He leans away, then pulls a folded-up piece of paper from his pocket. "I was afraid you threw your copy away yesterday, so I got another one today. We can fill it out together." The smile he flashes me is practically a smirk. "But first I want to take my girlfriend upstairs to her bedroom, if she's up for it."

The wide grin that splits my face is equal parts ecstatic and relieved. Tate Rasmussen is a commitment-obsessed freak, too, and I couldn't be happier.

"So no more taking it slow, then?" I tease.

"I'm done with taking it slow." He skims his palm over my stomach so that he's barely touching the fabric of my top. "If you feel up for it. I know tomorrow is technically the day that marks four weeks since your surgery. If you want to wait, just to be sure, I completely understand . . ."

Nearly four weeks since surgery. Five weeks since our first kiss in his car. A month and a half since we started working one-on-one. It's all more than enough time.

I cup my hand over his. "I don't want to wait. I feel perfect. And I want you right now."

I hop off the counter and lead him by the arm up the stairs to my bedroom. My fingers dig into dense flesh. It's like his cotton T-shirt isn't even there. When I spin around after closing the door, he's sitting at the foot of my bed. He scoots up and nods his head for me to follow his lead before lying down. I do the same. With his head propped up on his right hand, he gazes down at me.

He places his hand gently on my stomach. Like a Pavlovian dog, my body is at his beck and call. I'm back to swallowing desperate pants, doing my damnedest to stabilize my ragged breathing. I've reached the point where a simple touch from him leaves me hot and aching.

His face is stern with a hint of aroused urgency. A flush fills his cheeks, and his eyes are hazy. I recognize that look. Every man I've ever been with has attempted that take-control attitude, but none has done it while looking as delicious as Tate.

Off his T-shirt goes, falling to the floor. I'm sure I have the cheesiest grin on my face, but I can't help it. He's cut like a brick wall. Hard, bulging muscle peeks through milky skin. There are lines everywhere. I want to bite, suck, and lick everything. My hands drag across his flawless torso; I can't help but inhale sharply.

"Holy hell. Look at you," I whisper in undisguised awe. Tufts of blond hair cover the center of his chest, then curve into a line that trails underneath his pants.

"I'd rather look at you."

The process of him peeling my clothes off is an arduous one. He starts with my tattered tank top. I lean up, and he slips it gently over my head. I do my best not to tremble, but I can't help it. It seems every time Tate makes contact with my body, there are fireworks, no matter how insignificant the touch. I'm still in awe that he is the one to make me feel this way. Everything about this moment is surreal.

"I feel silly," I say.

"Why?" He presses his lips to my stomach. I let out a high-pitched moan. It's nowhere near as dramatic as the noises I made last night on his couch, but it still echoes against the walls.

"I was so worried that you'd freak out when you saw I had that form, but you were fine with it."

"More than fine." He's talking to my stomach now. His lips refuse to leave my midsection, and I couldn't be more ecstatic. I hope they make their way to where they left off last night.

His head pops up. "Dating you has been a dream. I've been wanting to make us work official for a while. I didn't want to rush it though because I thought you wouldn't be into it."

"Seriously?"

"Seriously," he says in a slow hiss.

"Oh, go on." My attempt to sound in control of my speech fails because I'm all hot sighs and moans. I'm also shameless. I want to hear more.

"The chemistry between us has been off the charts. All those months of bickering has led to some pretty hot times so far, don't you think?" He begins a trail of kisses from my clavicle to my belly button, then slides a hand across my stomach.

"Yes. I want more though," I whimper. I'm practically salivating.

He scoots his face to my right hip bone.

One deep breath later and I sound halfway normal again. "So what's it like being in a work-official relationship with Tate Rasmussen?"

"Lots of foreplay, for starters."

I blink, and my mind flashes back to a visual of last night, his mess of blond curls peeking from between my legs. I run my hands through the soft ringlets. "I can live with that."

"Dates at the rock climbing gym."

I slap his arm playfully. "No chance."

"Damn. Tough crowd."

His face is mere inches from the achy epicenter of my body. I wonder if he can hear it throbbing. I can.

"What else?"

"Late nights spent mostly in bed. Sleeping in the mornings after. More fooling around on my couch. Shower shenanigans. Making out in the stairwell at work. Flower deliveries on birthdays and anniversaries. Naked Skype sessions when one of us is out of town. Romantic weekend surprises."

"Holy hell."

I run my finger lightly along his sculpted jawline, buzzing at the thought of doing every single one of those with Tate. A shudder runs through him. This is all a preview of what's to come for sure, but already I feel like I know. We're weeks into being together, but it's the happiest, the most content I've ever felt with anyone.

"Where do I sign?"

"Here," he says.

He switches course and covers my mouth with his. For an untold number of minutes, his hands roam wild as he kisses me. He alternates between squeezing my breasts, tracing my nipples through my sports bra, and lightly skimming my stomach. He takes extra care not to touch the lower part of my torso, just like last night. I smile against his lips, impressed at his mindful technique.

He pulls away for a moment. "Nothing hurts, does it?"

"Nope." Not even soreness registers. Arousal is a powerful drug.

He licks his lips, then thumbs my bottom lip when I smile at him. His right hand is tangled between my hair and my scalp. He scrunches it into a fist, and I moan. I tug at the waistband of his gym shorts, desperate for what's underneath. The shrill ring of his phone in his pocket interrupts our flow.

"Ignore it," I say midkiss. He nods.

The beeping and vibrating continues.

"Hang on." He pulls out his phone, resting his head against the headboard while he glances down at it. He shuts his eyes, his chest puffing up and down. "Crap, it's my sister. She never calls me this late. I have to take this."

I stand up to leave the room so he can talk in private, but he gestures me back. I sit down on the bed. We're an awkward sight for sure. He's perched at the head; I'm at the foot. My hair is a tousled mess, and I'm down to my sports bra and shorts. He's still shirtless.

"Eli's still out of town? No, it's fine. I'll be there. Give me fifteen minutes, okay? Hang tight."

He hangs up, and I force a smile. I'd rather cry in frustration at how our night is ending, but I want to maintain some degree of civility.

"My sister is stuck on the freeway with a flat tire and needs me to help her put on the spare. I guess her boyfriend's work trip ran long; otherwise, she'd be calling him."

Now I feel like a baby for being upset. "Do you need me to help? I can add it to the list of girlfriend duties."

He shakes his head and laughs. "It's okay. It's dark now, so it wouldn't be safe to have a bunch of people standing at the side of the freeway."

I pull down the strap of my sports bra, giving him a view of more flesh. "You sure I can't convince you to stay for a bit longer?"

He surveys my body with hungry eyes, then ends with a pained smile, like he's seriously reconsidering.

"I'm joking. You will not leave your sister stranded on the side of the freeway for sex. That's unforgivable."

"I can always beg for forgiveness."

I throw my head back in amused exasperation. "No way in hell. Go help your sister."

He throws on his shirt, I throw on mine, and we hustle downstairs. "You have no idea how sorry I am to have to leave like this. Believe me, I don't want to," he says.

"Oh, I know. The front of your pants is proof of that."

He glances down and blushes, then adjusts his shorts. I press up against him, pushing a kiss to his lips.

"Starting tomorrow, we'll have all the time in the world," I say. "I can wait one more night."

He pulls on his sneakers with a grin that makes me suddenly question if I have the willpower to wait.

"I'll make it up to you," he says. "We'll spend a couple hours at the reunion, then we'll leave and pick up where we left off."

Just when I think he's headed for the door, he lunges back and pulls me to his mouth. We're a tangle of tongues, saliva, and growls.

"We'll fill out that form too. We can hand it in on Monday."

"I love it when you talk dirty," I say against his lips. "Go."

I finally pull him off my mouth by his hair. It's a battle against every natural urge to drag him back to my couch and finish what we started. His hands are glued to my hips, his fingers digging into the soft flesh. He finally releases me.

I fetch him two giant containers of *pansit*. "Give one to Cal when you see him on Monday."

He frowns. "How did you know?"

"I saw you bring him lunch a while back. And then Cal spotted me and told me everything. That's sweet of you, Tate."

His eyes fall to the ground, and he shrugs. "Just trying to be decent."

"You're more than decent. You're amazing."

His smile is all I see before he heads out the door. I make my way back to the kitchen counter, gazing down at the creased relationship disclosure form. I fill in my information, leaving his blank, then tuck it into my purse so I can give it to him tomorrow after the reunion. I imagine the shocked smile on his face when he sees I've filled out my part already. My first romantic weekend surprise for Tate.

twenty-three
·······

I stare at my open closet, clueless about what to wear. Do I even own an outfit that is appropriate for a high school reunion, yet still says, *Hey there, Boyfriend. Fill out this paperwork, then screw me senseless?*

I call Kaitlin for advice. It's about time I fill her in anyway.

"Hey you. Long time no talk. Need me to play nurse to you some more?"

"I'm fine actually. Look, I need to tell you something. Stuff happened. I have a boyfriend." I let out a loaded exhale. "It's Tate."

A long pause indicates Kaitlin is slowly processing my info dump. "What the . . ." There's a muffled sound, then a pause. "Okay, spill."

I give Kaitlin a quick rundown of recent events complete with gushing. "I sound like a smitten schoolgirl, don't I?"

"A little." There's amusement in her tone. "So this guy does it for you, then? Like, downstairs?"

I'm full-body blushing. Kaitlin is the only person other than Addy who knows about my past sexual relationships. "Hell to the yes."

"Now *that's* a guy worth being smitten over."

"He's worth his weight in gold when it comes to that stuff."

"Seriously?" She interrogates me about his bedroom skills, but I clarify that we've only messed around and that so far it's been focused on my pleasure.

"Well, holy hot damn." There's a long pause, then a breathy laugh. "So he kisses like a demon, you've had phone sex with him, he's gone down on you, and he puts your pleasure before his?"

"Uh-huh. But even when we're just together and not doing anything sexual, he gives me feelings I've never, ever felt with anyone before. Every single time. I'm comfortable around him, but the excitement is always there too. It's an intimacy I've never had with anyone before."

She whistles. "You lucky wench."

"No guy I've been with has even come close to making me feel the way he does, Kaitlin. Not the overly confident ones, not the sensible guys, not the ultranice guys too shy to take control. But Tate . . . Something about him . . . I really, really like him."

"I can tell." She giggles. "You two have history and tension, and that can build some serious chemistry."

I explain his introversion and the breakup that set off his tendency to hold back in relationships.

"Ah yes," Kaitlin says. "The brooding, private type who doesn't open up to just anyone, and you're the lucky woman he wants to let inside."

"I've never had chemistry with someone so closed off before. The way he opens up to me is unlike anything I've ever felt."

"Emmie, honey, I love you, but you're just like him."

I fall against the doorframe of my closet. "Excuse me?"

"Look, I know you joke about how you are this completely dif-

ferent person at work, and in a lot of ways you are. But honestly?
That hard exterior you put up during the workweek? That's a form
of being closed off."

"What do you mean?"

"I say this with love. I've been your best friend since high
school. You've always put up a hardened front to keep from getting
hurt, to keep from showing weakness. You did it during school, in
college. You're real and loyal to the people close to you, but
everyone else has to earn their way in. When someone's shown
themselves to be worthy, that's when you let your guard down.
Then you're sweet and kind."

I almost choke on my next breath. She's right.

"And for the record, you say it's all pretend, but it's not. I know
you. The real you is a sweetheart, but you're a fighter too. You have
been since you were a little kid. For some reason you think you
can't be hard and soft at the same time. You absolutely can. You've
done it your whole life; you do it every day. That's you in a nut-
shell."

In the seconds that I take to process everything, I realize Kaitlin
is spot on. I don't know why I never thought of myself as capable
or strong before. Tate even pointed it out during our make-out
session in his car, but it didn't hit me the way Kaitlin's words do
right now.

"You act like you're this tough faker when you're just being
you."

I swallow, stunned. "Thank you for the impromptu analysis,
Dr. Kaitlin."

"Addy says the same thing. Don't be so shocked that you con-
nect with a guy who harbors the same personality quirks as you.
Also, he's fucking hot. That helps."

In the background, I hear Ethan scolding her gently.

"Oh, honey, she didn't hear me. She's playing with her blocks, look!"

Slowly, I ease out of the shock. "Leave it to my best friend and little sister to know me better than I do."

"And now leave it to me to help you get dressed."

I shove a row of clothes to one side of the closet. The hangers drag loudly across the wooden rod. "Black is good, right? It's classic. Simple. Nondescript."

"Black is sexy as hell, especially on you. Wear that black shift dress, the slinky one with the long sleeves."

"It's a sauna outside," I moan.

"But you'll be indoors, and the AC will probably be cranked. You can push the sleeves up if you get hot. Wear those nude heels with it. Your legs will look a million miles long. You'll blow him away."

I glance at the clock on my nightstand. It's nearly six o'clock. I thank Kaitlin, hang up, and hurry to get ready for the evening. One look in the mirror to make sure I look presentable, and I'm off.

All along the drive to Tate's place, I think about Kaitlin's insightful words.

You're just like him.

The words that left me in disbelief an hour ago are now a source of comfort. If that had been spoken to me two months ago, I would have raged. But now? Now it makes me beam from the inside out.

When Tate answers his front door, he's a gorgeous, frazzled mess. He's frowning of course, but still manages to look exquisite. His torso is clad in a charcoal-gray dress shirt, no tie. Somehow the starkness of the dark hue against his pale skin isn't harsh. It

makes his skin glow even more than it normally does. My eyes fall
to his sleeves, which are rolled to his forearms. I jolt as the warmth
between my legs sneaks up on me. Rolled-up sleeves on a man's
thick and veiny forearms is my greatest weakness. He must have
peered into my fantasies.

Within a second, his eyes fall from my face to my chest, then
to my legs. "Holy shit." He finds my eyes again, this time with a
half-open mouth. "You look incredible."

I rest a hand on my hip. "Really?"

"Fuck yeah, really."

The light, lips-only kiss he gives me leaves me wanting way the
hell more.

There's a glint in his eyes. "Believe me, I'd love to do more than
just kiss you on the lips right now, especially when you look this
delicious."

His hand drops to my waist, and he gives it a squeeze. I shiver
despite the humidity that hangs in the air like a heavy cloud.

"But if I do anything other than closed-mouth kiss you, you're
toast. And we don't have time." Again his gaze travels down and
up the line of my body. "Tonight, however . . ."

I glide the palm of my hand to the center of his chest. "You're
looking pretty damn good yourself." I flash him my most enticing
half smile, the one I use when I'm hoping for a kiss at the end of
a date.

"Come in, then, before I ravage you in full view of the neighborhood."

He moves aside to let me in, then shuts the door. When he
ruffles his hair with both hands, I can tell just how anxious he is.

"Sorry, I guess I should have offered to pick you up. Not a very
gentlemanly move, huh? I figured since I live closer to the school,
it would make more sense . . ."

When I clutch his hand, the wrinkles of his frown disappear. The softest smile pulls at his lips.

"Don't even worry about it, okay?"

His smile widens as he taps my chin with his thumb. A giant roll of beige contact paper on the counter catches my eye. I'm about to ask about it, but then I spot a short glass filled with amber liquid near the sink.

"Self-medicating?" I ask.

"Scotch with water is the only way to pregame for a high school reunion." He walks to the kitchen, and I follow.

"That's my go-to de-stress drink," I say.

He lets out an amused hum while taking a long sip. He sets down the empty glass, and a gentle smile crawls across his face. "My girlfriend's a Scotch-drinking badass. As if I didn't adore you enough already. You ready to go?"

He drives us to a massive brick complex in the middle of the city that is apparently his old high school. A gigantic college-caliber football field takes up a major chunk of the outdoor space. There's also a cluster of tennis courts, a running track, and a meticulously maintained baseball field. It looks like some high-end sports complex.

My mouth hangs open as I step out of the car. "This is your high school?"

"You sound surprised."

I point at the football field. "Most public high schools don't have state-of-the-art athletic facilities that rival division-one colleges. This school district must have fuck-you money to afford all of this."

He lets out a chuckle. The sound brings goose bumps to my arms. "Yeah, I guess this school is pretty nice."

"Nicer than my small-town public high school. We didn't have anything close to this."

I follow a slow trickle of people making their way into the building through the front entrance. When I realize Tate isn't next to me, I spin around and reach out my hand. Relief replaces his nervous expression.

"It's okay," I say. "I'm here."

He answers with steady eyes. "Having you with me is like holding on to an anchor in rough seas."

There's a burst at the center of my chest. "Really?"

One half of his mouth curves up. I could live off the high that his brilliant crooked smiles give me.

"Really."

With another squeeze of my hand, Tate keeps pace with me while we cross the parking lot. We head through the front door, the beat of a familiar mid-2000s pop song echoing through the halls. A table covered in name tags rests against the far wall. I peer ahead and see signs directing alumni to the reunion, which seems to be taking place in the gym. Round tables dot the floor. A long table against the wall holds snacks and a giant sheet cake. The roar of conversation hovers slightly above the volume of the music. It's not a full house, but it's close. The dim lighting is reminiscent of a high school dance. The only things missing are streamers and balloons.

I start to walk inside, but Tate holds me back, fixed on his phone.

"Hang on. Brendan and his girlfriend are about to walk in the front. Let's go back and wait for them there."

There's a sizable crowd gathered at the front entrance of the school now. Brendan is the first familiar face we spot. He immediately pulls Tate into a bear hug.

"You made it!" he booms.

He releases Tate, and when I catch a side glimpse of his face, I notice he's blushing.

"And you." Brendan points to me. "You made it happen. You got this grump to show up. I owe you big-time."

He stretches his arms open for a hug. I hesitate for a moment, before walking up to him. I've never hugged one of my doctors before. I press into him and laugh.

"Consider it a thank-you for performing my surgery."

He lets out a jolly cackle and gestures to a woman standing behind him. Her light brown hair flows all the way to her elbows. "Emmie, this is my girlfriend, Jillian."

I shake her hand. She beams a warm smile back at me and immediately compliments my outfit. She's equally as friendly and welcoming as Brendan. They're a perfect match.

After a minute of milling around the front while politely conversing, I spot a tall, slim woman walk in with the exact shade of white-blond hair as Tate's. Her light skin glows, and her wavy hair falls just past her shoulders. As she walks up to us, I notice her eyes are soft gray.

She gently shoves her shoulder into Tate, who's too lost in conversation with Brendan to notice her walk up to him. He turns around to hug her, and she giggles. The nervousness in his face disappears as he smiles. Just by their greeting, it's easy to see how close they are.

"Of course you would shove me instead of saying hello. Punk," Tate says, then turns to me.

"And this must be?" She gestures at me while staring knowingly at him.

"Emmie, this is my sister, Natalie. Natalie, this is my girlfriend, Emmie."

Her face widens with a smile. Instead of shaking my out-stretched hand, she pulls me in for a tight hug. Seems like everyone in Tate's inner circle is a hugger. I like it.

"It's wonderful to finally meet you," she says, swaying back and forth with me in her embrace. "Tate's told me so much about you." She pulls back to glance at me.

My smile twitches. I can only imagine the unflattering and frustrating anecdotes Tate has shared with her.

I beam back what I hope is a sincere grin. "Oh God, I hope not."

"Don't worry. Everything he's said about you has been glow-ing." She turns back to him. "You did not do her justice, though. She's stunning, Tate."

I let out an embarrassed laugh and babble a thanks. Tate shoves his hands in his pockets, a flustered grin on his face.

"Jesus, you make it sound like I've been downplaying her. Of course she's stunning."

Inside I'm bursting. He was right. Natalie is most definitely Miss Congeniality.

"Shall we head in?" Brendan asks.

Tate leads me down the hallway, his fingers pressed gently at the small of my back.

"You ready?" I ask.

He peers down at me with cool clouds for eyes, nerves nowhere to be found. "Absolutely."

twenty-four

· · · · · · ·

W e maneuver through the crowd of bodies into the gym.
"Told you my sister would like you."

"She's incredible. A total sweetheart. I love her, and I've only known her for two minutes."

The gym is nearly full by now. Most of the tables have a handful of people sitting at them. Everyone else stands around in groups, chatting with one another. There's hugging, squealing, and laughing. Brendan and Jillian break off to join some people across the room. I notice several heads turn and stare in the direction of Tate and me. It's odd, but not surprising given what I now know about him. No one must have expected a grumpy shut-in like him to show up.

Tate, Natalie, and I find an open space near a wall on the far end of the gym. Tate offers to grab us drinks, then walks to the beverage table.

"I guess it's just me and you holding up this wall, then," Natalie says, elbowing the wall behind her. I laugh. "How are you feeling? After your surgery, I mean?"

"A lot better. Tate was so sweet to take care of me. I feel bad though that he spent so much of the holiday weekend in a hospital."

She beams. "You shouldn't. He was happy to do it."

"Oh, and I'm sorry to hear about your flat tire last night."

"It figures. The week after I get rid of Triple A to save money, I blow a tire." She flicks her hand in the air. "Tate saved the day though and changed my tire in record time. My boyfriend, Eli, is putting on a new one tomorrow. I'm all set."

"Is he coming tonight?"

She nods. "He had a work call when we pulled up, but he should be in soon."

Once our topics for small talk are exhausted, we share a few seconds of silence.

"I'm so glad you're here. I've been dying to meet you." Natalie studies me like she knows something I don't. "I've never seen him this happy with anyone. He actually laughs now. Like, daily. No one's ever gotten him to do that before. He's a totally different person with you."

I do my best not to smile so wide. "I don't know about—"

Natalie rests her hand on my arm. Her studied stare turns sincere. "I mean it. You're beyond special to him, you know."

I want to ask just what exactly Tate Rasmussen thinks is so special about me, but he's back before I can utter a word.

"Here we go." He hands me a cup full of ice and what I assume is either Sprite or 7 Up. "No alcohol, unfortunately."

Natalie takes a sip. "Lucas Waller is hosting an after-party for our class at the bar he owns. Remember him? Aced all the AP tests. Now he owns a bar. Go figure. There will be copious amounts of alcohol there, I'm sure."

I chuckle.

"What?" she says.

"It's nothing. Just, listening to you talk is like listening to your brother. I love it." I playfully knock my hip into Tate. He bites his lip, marring his widening smile.

"Really? I never noticed. How funny. I guess we're twins after all," Natalie says. "She's observant. Definite keeper."

She winks at Tate and he turns red yet again. Seeing how easily he blushes in front of family and friends makes my stomach flip.

Natalie turns to look around the room and waves down an in-shape man with dark hair and a golden tan. She introduces me to her boyfriend, Eli, and Tate shakes his hand. Before I can ask him polite introductory questions, a petite girl runs up to Natalie and pulls her into a jump hug. They both squeal, then excitedly chatter. An old classmate, I'm guessing. A handful of other people greet Natalie the exact same way over the next minute. Soon she's pulled away along with Eli into a nearby group.

"See what I mean?" Tate gestures with his cup. "Everyone loves her."

"She's like a politician. Charisma emanates from her like perfume. Only with her, it's genuine."

The two of us lean against the wall and silently observe.

"Feel free to join her. Or Brendan. I'll be fine here on my own," I say.

"Nah. I'm good right here."

"Isn't there anyone you want to see?" I point to Brendan gesturing animatedly to a group of mostly guys, then to Natalie, who is surrounded by a gaggle of peppy ladies.

"The only person I want to see is standing next to me."

He shoots me a side glance and faces ahead again. I can't help but smile. After a minute of silently standing next to each other, I realize how calm and content I am. Witnessing Tate's natural ease when he's surrounded by the people closest to him is an utter pleasure.

"This is nice." I look up at him.

"It is." He gazes at me, affection in his stare.

Our moment is interrupted when I feel a hand on my shoulder.

"You made it!" a high-pitched voice says.

When I turn around, a slender Asian woman narrows her gaze at me.

"Oh, sorry! I thought you were someone else." She lets out a string of giggles.

"No worries."

She does a double take when she spots Tate standing behind me. "Oh, hey, Tate. Long time no see." She doesn't bother to disguise her stunned tone.

"Yup." He offers a head bob and deadpan stare.

"What have you been up to? It's been years."

"Not a whole lot." He shrugs. "Rock climbing, playing rugby, revolutionizing the power tool industry. The usual."

"Um, okay, then." She furrows her brow, then turns back to me. "Sorry again for running into you."

She shuffles away. Tate grabs my hand and leads me to the snack table.

"Who was that?" I crane my neck to get a glimpse of the mystery woman, but she's lost in the crowd. A handful of people peek at us, then look away.

"Jaclyn. We weren't close," he mumbles.

"I can tell."

"We had a few friends in common. She's all about the small talk. I never was."

My stomach growls, reminding me that it's dinnertime and I've eaten nothing. "I think it's time for some cake."

The smell of sickly sweet sugar hits my nostrils. I grab the biggest piece I can find and shovel it into my mouth.

Tate watches me, amused. "Hungry?"

"I'm always hungry for cake," I say, mouth stuffed, lips shellacked in white frosting.

He laughs. "You are adorable." I start to wipe at the frosty mess with the back of my wrist, but he holds a hand up. He passes me a napkin, then steals a bite of my cake. When he crinkles his nose at me, I have to steady myself on both feet to make sure I don't fall. He's being playful, and it's more delicious than this cake.

My eyes fall to the frosting-smeared paper plate. "Your sister said something interesting to me while you were grabbing drinks."

"What was that?"

He swipes a finger full of frosting from the plate and sticks it in his mouth. Biting my bottom lip is the only way I can keep from groaning. Who knew eating cake could be so sensual?

I clear my throat. "She said I'm beyond special to you." I want to hear Tate say how he feels about me so bad, I could yowl right here in this school gym.

He raises an eyebrow. "Really?"

I nod. With his thumb, he swipes a speck of frosting from the plate and dots it on my nose.

I jerk away and laugh. "What the hell?"

With a firm hand on my waist, he pulls me against him. In a split second, his tongue slides over the tip of my nose. The frosting's gone.

He hums, then licks his lips. His face darkens. "Do I seem like the kind of guy who would lick frosting off a woman's face in full view of his high school classmates?"

"No."

He leans to my ear. "That's what you do to me, Emmie. You

make me want to do things I would have never thought to do before. You make me happier than ever. That's why you're special."

Suddenly, this gym is the last place I want to be.

My mouth inches to his ear. "Can we find someplace a bit more private?"

I understand his darkened expression perfectly now. Pulling me by the hand, he leads me out of the gym. We meander down a long, dark hallway until we reach a row of burgundy lockers at the end of the hall. The music is a distant echo.

I tug the collar of his shirt. "It's crazy isn't it? How far we've come."

He presses me against the cold metal. "A couple months ago, you couldn't stand the sight of me."

"And you were starting arguments with me constantly." I trace my finger down the hardness of his collarbone.

"Now you're my girlfriend." He presses me against the lockers, lowering his face to mine. "And the reason I finally dug out that roll of contact paper from my hall closet."

His hands are brackets pressed on either side of my waist, caging me against the lockers. I'm confused at his out-of-the-blue comment, so I kiss him. A second later, my jaw drops.

"I saw you eyeing it when you walked in the kitchen." He bumps the tip of his nose to mine. "Don't pretend you don't know."

I yank him toward me by his shirt collar. "You cleared out a drawer for me? Already?" Squeals intersperse the kisses I plant on his lips.

He nods. "For those times when a late evening turns into a lazy morning."

We pick up exactly where we left off the night before. We are our crazed selves once again, aching for each other's mouths and tongues. My fingers find their rightful spot in his thick curls. When my knuckles curl against the impossibly soft strands, I moan into his mouth. *My oh my*, his curls say to my hands. *Lovely seeing you again. How we've missed you.*

His hands remain flat on the wall behind me, not touching me at all. They don't need to. The rest of his body is doing more than enough. His entire lower half is pressed against my lower half. To call it grinding would be dirty and inaccurate. This isn't a club, and he isn't shoving his body into mine like a clumsy oaf. He's pressing ever so slightly with purpose. It's a strange way to describe it, but it's true. There's care in the way his body is making contact with mine. The rhythm is steady and slow, but deliberate. I wonder if this is how his body moves when he has a naked woman underneath him. I'll find out soon enough.

His hands don't stay away for long. They spring off the locker wall and spread against my rib cage, then up to my breasts. He gives both a gentle squeeze. His tongue curls away from mine as I feel him smile.

He grabs my hands, which are wrapped around his neck, and presses them against the wall behind me. They're shoulder level now. Our fingers interlace quickly, like they've pulled this move together countless times. I break our kiss for a second.

"Is this what you did in high school?" I manage to say after a few breaths.

He shakes his head no, then kisses me. "I'm not into PDA," he finally says with labored breath. "But I'd be into doing this in the stairwell at work."

"Yes," I gasp. "First thing Monday morning, we're sneaking away and doing exactly this."

I lean the front of my pelvis against him. There's a rock-hard bulge protruding from his pants that I don't need to see to appreciate. I wonder if we'll be one of those work couples whose productivity suffers because we're too busy fooling around in the supply closet. I hope so.

I roll my head, my hair bunching up against the metal. I'm still restrained by his thick arms and his powerful lower half. When I close my eyes, his hands drop to the backs of my thighs. In one swift motion, he lifts me up and my legs instinctively wrap around his waist. I'm still bracing my back against the locker. One of his hands runs roughly through my hair while the other strokes the side of my neck. We're locked in a stare once again. All I see is gray against a cloud of creamy white.

The way he easily keeps me pinned against this random locker is an unexpected turn-on for me. His muscled body exists as a result of impressive amounts of physical activity, and this is the reward. I squeeze my legs around him tighter. It's more than just physical attraction though. It's contentment, the feeling of safety. It's the knowledge that I've never felt more at home with anyone than when I'm in Tate's arms. It's enough to make me explode right here in this dimly lit hallway of lockers.

"Let's get out of here," I say between long, sloppy kisses. I'm clutching his face between my hands. My tan fingers pop against the whiteness of his complexion. I adore how beautifully our skin contrasts.

He nods before lowering me down slowly, my back sliding along the locker. I kick my feet to the ground and steady myself. There's an echo of laughter at the far end of the hall, and we turn in unison. A handful of people glance at us but continue walking.

"Good thing we stopped when we did." He pulls at his belt. "That would have been awkward."

I nod toward his crotch. "Are you going to be okay walking out of here or do you need a minute?"

He looks down and laughs softly. "Nothing a simple waistband tuck can't fix."

I laugh, the sharp sound ricocheting between the metal walls. "Let's say bye to Natalie and Brendan. Then we can get the hell out of here and head to my place," he says.

I follow him back into the gym, smoothing my hair down to make myself presentable. We spot them standing and chatting on the far side.

The cake table comes into my line of view, and I pull on Tate's sleeve. "One more slice. I'll catch up with you in a sec."

"Hurry back, or I'll have to come looking for you." He leaves me with a playful wink.

A dozen untouched squares sit on paper plates. I can't believe more people haven't eaten this delicious lemon crème concoction. I polish off once piece, then eye another. Tate can wait an extra minute; this cake is just too damn good.

I'm two bites in when a woman just a few feet away catches my attention. I freeze. Long, dark hair. Catlike brown eyes. Small button nose. Full lips. A similar tan shade covers her skin. This complete stranger looks almost exactly like me.

Despite there being a half dozen people between us, I zero in on only her. It's like a magnet has captured my stare. We're similar in stature and facial features—we're even both wearing black dresses—but it's not a long-lost identical twin situation. This stranger and I could pass for sisters, though. She's objectively prettier than me. And her makeup is tidier than mine too. The cat-eye she managed to pull off is more polished than my rushed smoky eye. She's a bit less curvy, and I think she might be an inch or two shorter, but it's hard to say given she's wearing wedges.

She turns, and all I can see is her back. Jaclyn races to her side, and the two hug. When a break in the music hits, I can hear Jaclyn speaking.

"You should see the girl Tate's with," she says, her unblinking eyes fixed on my doppelgänger. "She looks just like you, Camille. I mean, you two split up years ago. It's so creepy."

The last word is barely out of her mouth before everything clicks. It's like a puzzle is being solved in my brain at lightning speed.

My look-alike, Camille, is Tate's ex. Why didn't he tell me she would be here?

Now I know why he rejected me when we met face-to-face all those months ago, why he spoke those biting words his first week of work, words I was never meant to hear. Because I bear a striking resemblance to the woman who broke his heart.

Jaclyn turns away to speak to someone else, and a familiar figure cuts in. Tate's broad, pale form saunters up behind her, a smile on his face. And then it happens.

Tate's hand on her arm, his fingers caressing her skin. He leans closer, pressing his lips to her cheek.

Then his mouth is on her mouth.

An invisible vise clamps around my chest, making it impossible to breathe. My hand rises from my side to the neckline of my dress, the thud of my heartbeat shaking my palm.

I fall back, hitting the cake table with my ass. I catch myself before falling, but the whine of the metal legs dragging against the gym floor causes everyone in the immediate vicinity to spin around and stare. Normally, I'd be mortified at nearly collapsing in front of several dozen people, but right now I don't care. Nothing matters now that I've seen my boyfriend kiss his ex right in front of me.

I heave a breath and choke. If I stay in this gym a second longer, I will either vomit or scream.

The smattering of voices around me turns to muffled ringing. Every particle in my body seizes, and my throat begins to constrict. My sole focus is the bright red exit sign, my only escape.

twenty-five
....

One dim hall takes me to a short corridor, and when I shove open a set of heavy doors, I'm in what I assume is an auditorium.

I fall into one of the cushy velvet seats and stare at the floor beneath my heels. I'd crawl out of my skin if it were physically possible. Tate kissed his ex-girlfriend. In front of me. How the hell . . . why the hell . . .

A loud squeak causes me to twist around. Tate starts to head for me, but I hold up a hand to halt him.

"I can explain." His tone is placating. I hate it.

I stand. "Don't." The whisper I manage is like a cannon of anger and hurt from my mouth.

I back away, hoping with each step that the ground will open up and swallow me. It would hurt less than to watch the man I care for betray me right in front of my eyes.

I call on every boss-bitch tip I've ever read, every technique I've ever employed to try and keep it together. I stop moving and stand tall, my arms crossed, my eye contact unwavering.

"How could you do that, Tate?"

His chest heaves with a breath, like he's about to launch into a long-winded explanation. "Look, that's not . . . it's not what you think."

"Really? You're going to lie to my face on top of cheating on me?"

I employ the steady, hard rhythm I've used countless times before, yet now it feels like a needle through my throat. This man standing before me is not who I thought he was. He's a faker, too, but in the worst possible way.

Wetness hits my collarbone. When I touch my face, I realize I'm crying. Only a few tears though. I wipe them away, biting the inside of my cheek to keep the rest behind my eyelids where they belong.

"Just stay the hell away from me."

I dart out of the auditorium and into the hallway. Tate's heavy footsteps echo behind me. When he touches my shoulder, my entire body cringes.

"Emmie, wait."

I spin around. "You kiss your ex in front of me and expect me to just shrug it off?"

He opens his mouth, but nothing comes out. He stands, lips bitten into a thin line.

Another tear falls, and I scrub it away. His words, his feelings for me, it's all been a lie. If he's someone else's—his ex's—then everything between us is tainted. He clearly doesn't care about me the same way I care about him. If he ever cared about me at all.

"I guess you have a type for sure."

When I realize I've said the words out loud, I feel a stabbing pain in my chest. I can barely stomach how insecure I sound. Tate definitely has a type. He likes tall, tan Asian girls. I'm just a fetish, a kink for him to satisfy. Nothing more.

Through the shock, I somehow find my voice. "That's why you were a jerk to me when we first met. Because I look like her. I reminded you of her, didn't I?"

He stands, his face a sheet of solemn white. "That's not—"

"Just answer the question."

I think back to all those months ago when I fantasized about giving him a verbal dressing-down in high heels, staring at him face-to-face. My dream is coming true tonight, but it's mutated into a nightmare. This moment is nowhere near as satisfying as I'd thought it would be. I don't feel vindicated or triumphant. Instead, I'm a heartbroken mess wishing I could be anywhere else, wishing I could feel anything else other than this jumble of pain and anger.

This man, this man who I thought was so special, so different from every other guy I've ever been with, has hurt me in the most unimaginable way.

His chest heaves with a sigh. "Yes."

I swallow back the boulder in my throat. "So not only was I paraded around like some consolation prize in front of your classmates this evening, but I also had a front-row seat to you starting things back up with your ex."

Red seeps up his face. A huff of air follows, his shoulders rising with it. "That's not even close to the truth. If you would just stop for a second and let me explain—"

"No, Tate. No more explaining, no more excuses. You've hurt me since the day you met me. You could have just explained yourself then."

"And tell you what? Sorry I was such an immature prick to you because I was freaked out that you look exactly like my high school ex-girlfriend?"

"Yes. It's what a fucking decent person would have done." I dig my nails into the palms of my hands. "But you're not a decent person. You're with me one minute, and the next I find out you're still screwing your ex."

Every nerve in my body is firing on all cylinders. Whatever happiness I felt minutes, hours, days ago, whatever excitement I had for the future between us has vaporized like a puff of smoke in a windstorm. The only thing left is the pain pulsing from the base of my throat to my chest.

What little composure I have left I channel into my words. "You're not the person I thought you were. We're done. I never want to speak to you again."

I dig through my purse and hand Tate the Nuts & Bolts relationship disclosure form, scrawled with my handwriting. My weekend surprise is now moot.

When Tate's eyes fall to the form, I make a beeline for the women's bathroom nearby, ignoring his pleas to wait. I lean over the nearest sink and splash water on my face. When I look up at the mirror, I nearly jump. Red blotches dot my cheeks, and the skin around my clavicle is flushed. Managing not to sob has helped me avoid swollen eyes and tear streaks. Even so, I still look like the stock photo for "train wreck."

I need to figure out a way to get out of here, but I refuse to leave with Tate. Natalie or Brendan seem nice enough to give me a ride back to my car if I asked, but the awkwardness would be excruciating. It's too late in the evening to call Kaitlin. I reach for my phone and call the only other person I can think of.

TATE IS CROUCHED on the floor just outside the door when I walk out of the restroom, head in his hands, pants and shirt rumpled. He looks almost as wrecked as I do.

I don't acknowledge him as I jog through the door and to

Jamie's car parked in the front. I race to the passenger side, hoping he doesn't follow.

"Hey, you." Jamie's cheery face greets me, but it switches to concern when he gets a closer look at me. "Are you okay?"

"Peachy," I mutter. He idles for a second. "Can we go now, please? I need to get out of here."

He pulls ahead just as I catch Tate's reflection in my side view mirror. He looks around frantically, then zeros in on the car.

I give Jamie directions to Tate's house. "Thank you again for picking me up. I'm sorry it's so late."

"Don't worry about it," he says, dialing back the initial pep of his greeting. "That was Tate, wasn't it? Who ran after you just before we pulled away?"

I let out a frustrated sigh. I really don't want to get into it with Jamie, but I suppose I owe him an abbreviated explanation since he was nice enough to give me a ride on a moment's notice. I left Tate out of our conversation when I called him, but the cat's out of the bag now.

"It was. Things are complicated between us at the moment."

"I can tell."

"We've been trying to be friendlier to each other recently, I guess you'd say. It didn't work out."

"Sorry to hear that."

"Me too." I bite the inside of my cheek to keep from crying.

"His loss. You look really pretty tonight."

"You're such a liar."

"Am not. You look amazing."

"I look like hell." I yank down the overhead mirror and see that my blotchy skin isn't obvious in the darkness.

"If that's what hell looks like, I'll take seconds." He taps his thumb against the top of the steering wheel while we're stopped at a red light, then smirks at me. I can't help but laugh at his ridiculous line.

Jamie parks on the street in front of Tate's duplex, behind my car. I thank him again before stepping out. He climbs out of the driver's seat and walks around to my side.

"It was nice seeing you, even if it wasn't under the greatest circumstances. Sorry you had a bad night." He shoves his hands in his pockets.

"I'm the one who should be sorry. I interrupted your Saturday night." I dig in my purse for my keys. "Here, let me give you gas money."

"Not a chance." He takes a step toward me. When he places his hand over mine, I immediately stop rummaging through my purse. "But maybe you can interrupt my night tomorrow and let me take you out for dinner? As friends, of course."

The tilt of his head and the lift of his eyebrow imply he doesn't mean it at all when he says *friends*.

I freeze, then manage to roll my eyes in a playful way. Even though I made it clear before that I wasn't interested in pursuing anything other than friendship with Jamie, I don't want to hurt his feelings after he went out of his way for me.

Before I can think of anything to say, a sharp tire squeal pulls our focus to the end of the block. Tate's gray sedan speeds up to us, then screeches to a halt.

He darts from the car and marches up to Jamie without even bothering to turn the car off. "What the hell are you doing here?"

"Excuse me?" Jamie's initial confusion switches to hostility.

Tate's eyes dart to the space between Jamie and me, and I realize Jamie is still gripping my hand. I glance up in horror. Even though I'm pissed at Tate, I don't want him thinking I'm rebounding with Jamie minutes after walking out on him.

"Get your hands off of her," Tate says.

Jamie lets go, then turns to face him. The two of them are inches apart, exchanging intimidating scowls.

"What the hell is your problem?" Jamie says. "I was just giving her a ride to her car."

"You gave her a ride. Well done. Now leave."

"Jesus, man. You need to get a hold of yourself."

"I'm just fine. Leave. Now."

Tate's stern yet calm demeanor seems to aggravate Jamie. He clenches his fists; Tate stares him down. Their stances mimic gorillas egging each other on. I step between them before their standoff turns into a shouting match or worse.

"Stop it." I face Tate head-on, my back to Jamie. "He was just taking me to my car. That's all."

"Really? Is that why he was holding your hand? Do people hold hands now after they ride with each other in the car?"

His eyes burn with a familiar intense look. I've seen it once before when creepy Brett was trying to chat me up in the warehouse while he stood next to me.

Jamie starts to speak, but I interrupt him. "What I do is not your concern. Not anymore."

As terrible as it felt for Tate to see me holding hands with Jamie, I will not let him make me feel guilty about it. He takes a step back and thrusts a hand into his hair. The agitation in his voice translates into a rough exhale when he breathes.

"It is my concern if the guy you're with is standing in front of my house." Tate's low voice packs a punch in the stagnant summer air. We stand, misted over with sweat. Even though the temperature has dropped about ten degrees, the humidity looms like an invisible cloud.

"Quit talking like that," I groan. "I'm not with him. How many times do I have to say he just gave me a ride? I needed to get to my car."

"I would have given you a ride if you had let me."

"No way in hell I would have gotten in your car after tonight."

We're sparring back and forth, using the strain in our voices as weapons. It's the only way we can keep from yelling at each other. It's a strange game, keeping your voice at speaking volume when you actually want to scream. Whoever goes hoarse first wins.

By now we've backed up into the street, still facing each other. I turn around, remembering that Jamie is here. He's standing next to his car with his arms crossed, taking in the shitshow.

A light flicks on in the window of a nearby house. A neighbor watching our impromptu party in the street. My dignity makes an overdue appearance, and I flush with embarrassment.

A scrawny middle-aged man in a robe saunters out of the house next to Tate's duplex.

"Everything okay? Having car trouble?" he calls from his porch about ten feet away.

"Everything's fine. Thanks, Lyle," Tate replies.

"Oh. Hi, Tate. I didn't realize that was you. These peepers of mine. Not what they used to be." Lyle lets out an amused chuckle.

"We were just having a discussion. The car's fine. I was about to pull it into my driveway." Tate dials back his tone to politely sincere in record time.

Lyle waves good night before walking back inside.

I turn to Jamie. "You should go."

He shakes his head. "No way I'm leaving you alone with this guy. He's clearly unstable."

Out of the corner of my eye, I see Tate stiffen.

I roll my eyes, unable to hide my frustration. "Jamie. Listen. I appreciate your concern, but I can handle myself. Tate isn't anything to worry about."

An exasperated sigh leaves his mouth. "If you say so."

He pats my shoulder, then pauses to look at me for a few seconds. I'm paralyzed, wondering if he's going to try for a friendly cheek kiss just to spite Tate. If Tate nearly lost it at the sight of us holding hands, he will coldcock Jamie if he kisses me. Instead he climbs into his car and drives away. A loud hiss of breath signals my relief. I clench my jaw as I watch his car round the block.

I start to open the door to my car. "Good night."

"Wait." Tate's tone is gentle now, and so is his touch when he reaches for my arm.

"Tate, I can't."

"Will you please come inside and talk to me? I'll explain everything. I'll do whatever it takes to make it clear how I feel about you."

I silently weigh my options. All I want to do right now is speed home and rage-cry into my pillow until I pass out. But I also want closure. If whatever is between us ends tonight, I want to know I did it the right way. I want to know that we ended things calmly and maturely, not with an argument in the street.

"Okay."

His lips remain a neutral line, but his eyes seem hopeful. We both turn to his still-running car. He pulls into his driveway, and I follow him inside.

twenty-six

·······

Tate turns to me after shutting the front door.

"Before you say anything, let me say this. There is absolutely nothing going on between me and Camille. I haven't seen or spoken to her in years. When I walked up behind her, I honestly thought it was you. I thought I was kissing you."

I let out a laugh that sounds more like a scoff. "I saw the way you looked at her, Tate. You touched her arm; you leaned into her."

His face twists at my words, like he's swallowing bitter medicine. "I swear to you, from where I was standing, I couldn't see her face clearly. I thought it was *you*. As soon as I realized it was her, I backed away and ran after you."

He takes a breath. Seeing his chest heave up and down reminds me to inhale.

"Look, I'm a piece of shit for kissing Camille. There's no excuse for what I did, no matter how clueless I was. If the tables were turned, if I had seen you kiss some guy . . ." he trails off. His jaw tightens and his cheeks flush as if they're on fire. "I would have raged. You can hate me forever for that. I deserve it. But I need you to know that I'm not with anyone else but you. Ever since you and I started up, no other woman has even crossed my mind. I know there's no way to prove that to you, especially after what you saw tonight, but it's the truth. I promise you that, Emmie."

Despite the pain coursing through me, I believe him. Maybe it's his own pain displayed on his face or the way his gray-blue eyes glisten, as if they're pleading. He blinks before any tears can fall. And in that moment, I know he's not lying.

"Okay. If you say it's the truth, then I believe you."

He clears his throat. "I was wrong for not coming clean about Camille from the get-go. And I was wrong to let an ex—a past relationship—affect how I treated you when we first met."

Hearing him say the words is a relief, but doubt still nags at me. "Do you have some sort of fetish for Asian women?"

It sounds ridiculous spoken out loud, but I need to know. I don't want to be anyone's weird fixation, not even Tate's.

His eyebrows knit. "What? Of course not."

"You can see how it would be hard for me to believe you."

He shuts his eyes for a long second before focusing on me once again. "I understand. But I swear to you, it's just a coincidence. I've dated women from different backgrounds. I'll dig up old photos to prove it to you."

I shake my head, awareness kicking in. I let the insecurities that plagued me as a kid creep back in when I shouldn't have.

I refocus on the one thing I need to know before we go any further. "How often do you look at me and think of Camille?"

"Never." He doesn't flinch or blink when he answers.

My eyes widen.

"It's the truth, but I'll clarify. When I first met you, it took a while. I'm ashamed to admit it, but I couldn't get over the similarities. She was my first long-term relationship, and it ended because she cheated on me. The only way I could think to deal was to shut you out."

I must visibly flinch, because he holds up his hand.

"That lasted for about a month. Then I got to know you better, and from that point on, I was never, ever reminded of her when I saw you. I swear. Eventually, I just forgot about telling you because I forgot about the similarity."

"I don't believe you could forget something like that."

"I understand why you would think that." He yanks at the collar of his shirt, the skin of his neck rosy with a sheen of sweat. "When I took you home from the hospital, I thought about telling you about her. About everything."

His eyes fall to the ground. A second later they find me again.

"Remember when I sat with you while you took a bath? I almost told you then, but I didn't want to ruin the moment. I had you next to me. Finally. I didn't want to screw it all up by mentioning my ex, who I don't care about."

I recall how long he sat in silence before telling me about his failed eighth birthday party. He's right. I would have been angry had he told me in that moment.

"I forgot about her, about everything else. Except you."

His words are low and loaded with feeling. They make me ache with want.

I yank myself back to the present conversation. "What do you mean that you forgot about telling me once you got to know me better? In those first months, you never said a word to me unless it had to do with work, and even then our interaction was minimal. You spoke to me directly maybe a handful of times when we first started working together."

His chest heaves with a raspy breath before answering. "I noticed the way you talked to people. The way you interacted with them. You were tough with most. You were sweet and kind with a few. I eavesdropped a lot."

"How? Your earbuds were glued to your ears for the first six months you were at Nuts & Bolts. Or you would always shut your door."

"The walls in that place are cracker thin, and our offices are less than three feet from each other. And I never shut my door all the way. I could hear almost everything." He half smiles, then covers his mouth with his hand, wiping it away. "Whenever you would talk to someone or answer your phone, I turned off my music. I liked listening to you. You were so funny. Very sarcastic. You gave people a hard time whenever they deserved it. I loved what a ball-buster you were."

He tugs on each rolled-up sleeve of his shirt. My eyes skim over the thick, veiny lines and blond hair dotting his forearm.

"That's when things started to change. I was dying to get to know you, but I didn't know how to recover. I figured you wouldn't give me another chance, even if I explained my reason for blowing you off initially. I was embarrassed, and I didn't know how to approach you. It seemed like saying 'I'm sorry' wouldn't have been enough."

As soon as he finishes speaking, his eyes fall to the floor. He's clearly mortified to admit this to me. His explanation makes sense, and ultimately, I understand his reasons. Hearing his words though would mean everything.

"It would be enough now."

"I'm so sorry." He steps toward me. "For what I did tonight, for being a jerk to you when we first met."

I remain still.

"I'm sorry for being a jealous psycho when I saw you with Jamie."

He comes another step closer. My lips tremble, and my eyes water.

"I'm sorry for the hurt I caused you."

He fixes his gaze on me. I swallow, keeping the tears behind my eyes. Another step and we're inches apart. I can feel it in my bones that he means it. The pained way he speaks, the affection, sorrow, and hope in his eyes. Every blink is a beg for forgiveness.

"Emmie. I am so, so sorry."

"Okay," I finally say.

We're so close his chest almost touches mine. I want nothing more than to give in and rest my head on his shoulder.

The tears finally fall, and his hand finds my cheek. "Let me hold you. Please?"

His words combined with his gentle touch seal the open wound between us. When I nuzzle into his chest, it's an acceptance of his apology. I need this just as much as he does.

Despite the heaven of this hug, remaining doubts nag at me. I breathe deeply and take a step back from him.

"If we had to go through all this just to get you to be open with me—your girlfriend—this can't work." I motion between us with my arm.

He hesitates, his face twisting. I pause to steady myself. The thought of this being the end kills me, but it's the only option if we can't communicate honestly. Tears pool at the waterlines of my eyes, and I wonder how long it will be before I start crying again.

"If this can't work, I can't go back to normal," I say. "I can't see you every day at work if I have to pretend we're enemies again."

It's our worst-case scenario. The high stakes Tate was so confident about.

"Emmie, you were never my enemy," he says softly.

"I know that now, but we've treated each other like it for so long. We have to figure out a way to move forward or move on."

I'm not sure how I'd cope, but I'd have to throw on some military-grade bulletproof invisible armor at work if that became our new normal. I'd need to fake a whole new persona around Tate just to survive. Too much has happened between us, and everything has changed. Moving on most likely means one of us would quit Nuts & Bolts when we couldn't take being around the other any longer, and I have a feeling I'd throw in the towel before he did. I can already feel the crack in my heart forming, preparing for that inevitable day.

He pulls his phone out of his pocket. "Here. I want you to read all the texts I've exchanged with Natalie this past year."

"What?"

"Read them. All the way back to when I started at Nuts & Bolts."

"Why?"

"Because I want you to know everything."

"You're serious?"

He shakes his head. "I could stand here and tell you that I've never taken care of someone the way I took care of you, that you're the first woman I've had over to this apartment. I could tell you that I've never told anyone about my eighth birthday because I'm private to a fault. I could tell you that I've never let anyone in, except you."

He types the passcode on his phone and hands it to me. "But that's not good enough. I want to be open with you. I want to show you what you mean to me, Emmie."

He's weirdly calm now. I can't figure out what's going on.

I shake my head. "That's got to be hundreds of texts. No way I'm doing that."

"There's fifty texts, max. I hate texting. I hardly ever do it. If it takes you longer than fifteen minutes to read all my messages with Natalie over the past year, I'll be shocked."

"But we spent the week after my surgery texting every day."

He shrugs. "I hate texting. Except with you."

My heartbeat takes on a fluttery rhythm. "You're serious?" I repeat.

"Dead serious. Have a look. Sit on the couch if you want. I'll be in the kitchen."

He slides past me, our arms touching briefly. I move to the couch and scroll to his text messages screen. I can't find Camille's name there or in his contacts list. He was telling the truth. She hasn't been on his mind or his phone in a long while.

I scroll through his texts with Natalie. The first exchange that catches my eye is from two months after Tate and I started working together.

Natalie: Just tell her the truth. She'll understand.

Tate: Doubtful. I've been a jerk to her for too long. Nothing I say will fix that.

Natalie: Negatory. If she's a sweetie like you say she is, she'll understand.

Tate called me a sweetie to his sister all those months ago? Something next to my heart thumps. I skim the rest of her reply and scan the messages from a couple months after that exchange.

Tate: Fuck. She's pretty. Goddamn it, she's pretty. I can't focus.

Natalie: Good god. Go on about it why don't you.

The next few texts are comments about how difficult it is not to stare when he sees me. I blush. I had no clue he felt that way about me. He was always brooding and eerily quiet. I honestly thought he was funneling all his energy into keeping himself from snapping at me every day. My heartbeat quickens. I'm flattered, but I feel silly. How did I not pick up on any of this?

My finger slides down the screen to reveal another chunk of texts.

Natalie: So?? Did you get that creeper fired or not?

Tate: I did.

Natalie: Well??? Details! Come on!

Natalie: You're the worst. You arranged the firing of the sexist creeper who's been pestering the woman you're crazy about, and you go radio silent on me the whole day?

Natalie: Have you told her you like her yet?

Natalie: Quit ignoring me.

Natalie: Okay, I can handle your annoying professionalism and refusal to give me details on this prick getting fired, but I'm not going to just sit here while you blow this opportunity. Come on! Tell her you like her!

Tate: Please leave me alone. I'm trying to work.

Natalie: You've never spoken about anyone the way you talk about her. Your face lights up like a Christmas tree whenever I bring her up. I know when my twin brother is head over heels for someone.

Natalie: Your deafening silence proves I'm right. You won't say otherwise because you know it would be a lie. Just talk to her. Get to know her. Make small talk. Ease your way into it.

I inhale sharply. The relentless teasing from his sister must have gotten on his nerves. I wonder how worked up he must have felt most of this past year.

Tate: I blew it.

Natalie: Blew what exactly?

Tate: She came to the rock climbing gym. I talked her down the wall when she panicked because I guess she's afraid of heights so I calmed her down. She thanked me for helping her . . . she finally looked at me like she didn't despise me . . . and I blew it. It completely threw me off seeing her like that. She looked so scared. It wrecked me. I should have said more, but I froze.

Natalie: Crap . . . it's okay. You did a nice thing by helping her. I'm sure she appreciated that. Say something tomorrow at work to her.

Natalie: So?! Did you say anything to her today?!

Natalie: Do not ignore your sister.

Natalie: Taaaaaaate

Tate: Jesus. I don't check my phone for one afternoon and this is what I come back to?

Tate: To answer your question, no. I didn't have the nerve. She seems pretty into that contractor who asked her to the rock climbing gym. I should just leave it alone.

I can't scan the texts fast enough. It's like reading a page-turner, and I want to know how it all ends as soon as my eyes hit the first letters of each word. Only this book is about me, and I have a one-sided view of all the major plot points.

I get to the night of our first kiss.

Natalie: Work happy hour tonight, right? Perfect time to reveal your feelings for a certain coworker. Sack up, Rasmussen. Do it!

Tate: Shut up.

Natalie: Don't choke, bro. Take a risk. Tell this girl you're into her.

Tate: I'm turning my phone off now.

Natalie: Don't you dare.

Natalie: So? How goes things with Emmie?

Tate: I can't handle this. It's worse than I thought. She is . . . fucking hell, I don't even know.

Natalie: What do you mean?

Tate: I took your advice. I bought her a drink. We're playing a bar game. She's fucking hilarious. Witty. Smart. Gorgeous. Fuck, I'm screwed.

Natalie: I told you. You're a lovesick puppy. Put yourself out of your misery. Tell her how you feel.

Tate: Seriously? She'll think I'm a psycho if I admit I've been nuts about her.

Tate: I mean . . . I made up that work project just so I could spend time with her. She can't stand me. She thinks I can't stand her.

Natalie: And whose fault is that?

The next messages are from the weekend he took care of me in the hospital.

Natalie: Cookout at Eli's tonight at 6!

Natalie: Hey, are you coming or not? Everyone's asking where you are.

Tate: Sorry, no. Emmie's in the hospital. I'm going to stay with her so she's not alone.

Natalie: What?? Is she okay??? Are you okay?

Tate: I'm fine. She fell at the worksite and got a minor concussion, but it looks like she's got appendicitis too. Doctors have everything under control, though. She's pretty scared so I want to stay with her.

Natalie: Sure, of course. Wow. Poor girl. Let me know if you need anything.

Tate: I'm fine now, but I'm sure I'll need a chat later. Spending all this time with her . . . you were right. I'm a lost cause. I'm head over heels for her . . . I've been for a while. How the hell am I going to tell her?

My chest aches with a new sensation. It's numbness mixed with adrenaline and a bit of awe. There's no way. He couldn't possibly.

I hear the clink of a metal spoon and shoot up. I spin around and see Tate stirring a cup of tea while leaning against the kitchen counter. He's gazing at me expectantly.

"I made you some tea." He says it so calmly, like I haven't just been reading all of his private texts about me over the past year.

"You were head over heels for me? This whole time?" I catch my breath. I must have stopped breathing.

He's giving me the same wide-eyed stare I'm giving him. He nods. Neither of us blinks.

"No. I need to hear you say it."

"I'm crazy about you, Emmie. I have been for quite some time." He says it solemnly, like he's confessing to a crime.

Dizziness hits me, and I cradle the sides of my head with my hands. "Oh my God" is all I can say while swaying back and forth.

Tate sets the mug on the counter and rushes over to me, steadying me in his arms like he did after I fell when I wobbled in pain. He lowers me carefully onto the couch and sits at one end. I rest my head on his lap, my legs stretched out.

"Why didn't you tell me?" I sound like a wonder-stricken child who just learned that the universe is infinite. It's too much to process, and my head feels heavy, weighed down with inconceivable facts that can't possibly be true.

He strokes my hair with such gentle care I could cry. "I was afraid you'd think I was a loser. I'm a grown man and I couldn't muster the courage to tell you how I felt for so long. I made up a work project just so I could spend time with you. How uncool is that?"

Giddiness seeps into my wonderment, and I laugh. "I've thought you were many things these past several months, a lot of them not so nice, but I never once thought you were a loser. I figured you were too cool for me."

"I am the least cool person you will ever meet."

I think of his effortless confidence that has intimidated me since the day we met. I think of his killer scowl that leaves all of Nuts & Bolts nervous, the way he disarms everyone around him. He doesn't even know how far and above he is from everyone else. He has no idea how often he leaves me in awe.

"You couldn't be more wrong," I say. "You thought of that entire social media and marketing project just to be close to me?"

He nods, then tangles his fingers softly through my hair. "I know you don't feel the same way. But now you know how I feel."

"Don't say that." I stretch up and kiss him. He hesitates before engaging.

I press my head back against his lap, thinking carefully about how I want to phrase my next words now that everything has flipped. Earlier tonight I thought I cared more about him than he cared about me. I was so, so wrong. What an earth-shattering role reversal this is.

What I feel is intense, all consuming, and unlike anything I've ever experienced for anyone before. Because I'm nuts about him too.

I lose myself in his eyes for the umpteenth time. "I thought my freak-out at the reunion made it clear how I felt about you."

When he says nothing in return, I sit up and straddle his lap, my thighs flanking his hips. The steely muscle of his legs braces my body as I rest my weight on top of him. We're face-to-face, locked in an unbreakable gaze.

This time when we kiss, it's different. Our tongues resume the dirty, wet rhythm of almost all of our prior kisses, but there's a vulnerability to it now. Now I know for certain how he feels about me. I want to show him with my kiss how I feel about him.

Our mouths press together long and hard. I don't dare let go.

He doesn't either. Minutes fly by, but the intensity never fades. Our heated kisses soon seep into vulgar territory. There's nibbling and licking, followed by light biting. I love it all, and I can't get enough.

I can't get enough of him.

Our hands somehow remain measured in their conduct. My fingers settle against the back of his neck. His split their time between running through my hair and gripping my hips.

He drags his tongue gently against the side of my neck. I moan and exhale at the same time. I'm producing sounds that rival the volume and intensity of the ones I made in the hospital. It's funny how close pain and pleasure sound. But that's our existence. Tate and I have caused each other such pain in the past. When I let my mind dwell too long on it, the hurt in my chest returns. I stomp it away. Right now we're trying our best to replace it with unending bliss. I'll try as hard as I have to.

His index finger pulls down the already-low neckline of my dress. He dips his tongue into my cleavage for a long, excruciating moment, then pecks my chin softly.

"I've wanted you for so long. So much. So bad," he says quietly. He grabs me by the chin and pulls my mouth to his. It's a kiss so deep and rabid, I can hardly breathe.

I grip his shoulder, my fingers digging into the unyielding flesh. I shift against his lap. The hardness underneath me is unmistakable.

I run both my hands over his torso and bend down to kiss every bulging muscle I encounter. He leans his head back against the top of the sofa, his eyelids nearly closed. The parts of his eyes that manage to peek through are clouded over. He is drunk with pleasure. I release his shirt from his body button by button, kissing each patch of blond hair and fair flesh that comes into view as I make my way down. A soft hum emanates from the base of his throat.

"You're going to kill me," he says, eyes pressed shut this time. My lips smile against the slit of skin peeking through one of his bottom buttons. Before I can undo the last couple, he lifts his head up and pulls me back to a sitting-up position.

"Death by foreplay," I rasp. "What a way to go."

Smiling, he fingers the neckline of my dress again, this time pulling it to the side. His teeth scrape against my collarbone, and it sends a throbbing ache between my legs. It pulses harder than all the other ones he's given me. I break our kiss, surprised at the intensity.

"You turned off your phone, right?" I gasp. I don't think I can survive another night of interruptions when I'm this close to going all the way with Tate Rasmussen.

He leads me back to his mouth with a hand at the nape of my neck, pausing long enough to whisper a few raspy statements. "It's off. From this moment on, it's just me taking care of you."

He trails a line of wet kisses and feathery teeth scrapes against the side of my neck. His hot mouth lands at the top of my breast, and I hold my breath in anticipation of what he'll do next. When his fingertips pull down my bra, I let out a breathy yelp. He pauses and looks up at me, his eyes mischievous. They are the eyes of a man eager to blow my mind.

The instant his tongue slides under the cup of my bra, I'm writhing. It's just as divine as the first time he performed this move on me. Slow licks turn into soft nibbles, leaving me trembling and gasping.

I can't take it. My head falls back along with my shoulders, leaving my body limp. There's a loud noise escaping my lips. It sounds like a moan, but I can't be sure. The pleasure building inside of me is taking over all my senses, and I'm having trouble keeping my wits about me. The only thing propping me upright is his arms, which are braced securely around my body. If I can barely stand it with my clothes on, then I'm a goner the instant we're naked.

I don't know when we decide to move upstairs to his bedroom, but when we do, it's a decision we make wordlessly. We stand in the middle of his living room, refusing to break our kiss for what feels like minutes. He leads the way upstairs, tugging my hand behind him.

twenty-seven
·······

We reach Tate's bedroom and I grin. It's so him. Plain with no decorations save a lamp and a giant map of the world tacked on the wall above his bed. The bed rests on a simple steel frame with no headboard. The cotton sheets are a light slate color. The walls are the same sandy brown shade as the walls downstairs. No accent furniture; just a dresser and nightstand, both made of hardwood.

"Do you live your entire life in neutral shades?" I ask, running my hand over the top bedsheet. It's softer than it looks.

"Not anymore."

He pushes me gently by the shoulders onto the bed until I'm sitting. Another nudge and I'm laid flat. He lowers himself onto me, then uses one arm to slide me up until my head reaches his pillow. His subtle show of strength gives me a full-body tremor.

"You're so strong. I love it," I say, pulling his lips to mine.

He leans up and tugs off his shirt. Lying underneath his chest is the absolute best way to view his immaculate torso, glistening in the lamplight. All the glimpses I've gotten of his bare body until this point have been short lived. Now that we have the time, I let my eyes wander across the solid ivory surface. He's physically flaw-less, and I can't take him in fast enough. I pause at his pectorals, then move on to the toned lines of his thickly muscled stomach. I count his abs and get to six. One by one, I touch them. Everything is firm. Back, stomach, ass, thighs. There's no give or chubbiness anywhere. His entire body is wrapped in silky skin.

"All your rock climbing has paid off. You are exquisite." I catch him blushing as he sits on his knees, straddling me. "I'm jealous of every woman who got to see you up close before I did."

"Don't be. It's been a while."

"How long?" I lean up and press a featherlight kiss to his oblique. He lets out a soft groan.

"A little over a year."

"A year? Seriously?" I'm wide eyed with disbelief. How does a guy as sexy as Tate go a year without sex? "Women must throw themselves at you. How did you fight them all off?"

"It's easy when you're carrying a torch for someone else."

My cheeks heat. Instead of lowering back down onto me, he moves between my legs, his face at my thighs.

Soft kisses trail up my right thigh, then back down my left. With his head still lowered, he slides his hand to my stomach, pressing me down flat on the bed.

I bite my lip to ward off the excited giggles bubbling at the base of my throat.

"What about you?" I say through a shaky breath.

"I told you." His lips graze the hem of my lace panties. "I'm taking care of you tonight."

With the hook of his finger, my panties move to the side. His face disappears under my dress, and I gasp. He's wasting no time at all, it seems. His tongue finds me again, and the pleasure is immediate. The way his tongue slides against my most sensitive spot, it's as if we've been at it together for years.

Again with the slow circles, again with the even pace. Just like the first time, he takes his cues from me well, then tailors his technique to my reactions. After every sharp breath and moan comes another measured, delicious lick. The pressure is perfect, heavenly. Both of my hands dig into his curls, but not to lead or adjust. To hold on for dear life because this sublime friction is going to send me over the edge soon.

"Tate," I cry.

He hums a response but doesn't stop. Another half dozen swirls, and my body winds tighter. Another hum, then lightning strikes. Waves thrash through me, but he holds me steady with his face and hands. I open my eyes and see double. When my vision focuses a few seconds later, Tate is standing over me. He pulls me to the edge of the bed.

"You are way too good at that," I pant.

I gaze up and take in the visual of his bare, sweaty chest as he heaves. Aftershocks pound through my legs, and I watch intently as he wipes his mouth with the back of his hand. Damn, those lips. Those lips that kiss me like no one else can. Those lips that now own me.

"No such thing," he says. "And I'm nowhere near finished with you."

He pulls my dress over my head, then peels off my underwear and bra. They land in a small pile on the wood floor, as do my heels once I sit up and kick them off. He drinks in the sight of my naked body with eager eyes. His gaze stops at all my naughty places first, then skims over every other part, ending at my face. Wide eyes and a tense jaw indicate an expression somewhere between lust and awe. I cross my arms when I notice he's still got his pants on and I'm the naked one.

"Shy all of a sudden?" he asks.

Even though it pains me, I let my arms fall to my sides. "Kind of. It's difficult not to be when the only hard body in the room still has his pants on."

I hope my joke conceals my dash of insecurity. My physique is a poor companion to his chiseled glory. I'm healthy for sure from consistent jogging, but I'm nowhere near as defined.

He frowns with renewed intensity. "Hey." He grabs my chin gently, tilting my head up to look up at him. "Knock it off. You're beautiful."

The soft kiss he presses to my lips squashes all lingering self-doubt. I'm vibrating with lust and confidence now. I yank his belt buckle loose and unbutton his trousers. He takes over and unzips, giving me a chance to slide back up the bed. I bite my lip, eagerly awaiting his big reveal. When he lowers his gray boxer briefs, my jaw drops. All those times I pressed against his erection while we fooled around fully clothed did not prepare me. As impressive as he felt under fabric, it was nothing compared to what's in front of my face right now.

"Wow." My mouth stays open even after I finish speaking.

He smiles slightly, and a tiny bit of pink makes it onto his cheeks. Quickly, I grip his hand. I don't want him to lose his nerve.

"Well, don't just stand there." I pull him to the bed.

He chuckles and lands on top of me, propping himself on his elbows. He reaches over my head and opens the drawer of his night-stand for a condom. When he's ready, he slides in.

I gasp and my eyes widen. He seems to know I want to take this slow, because he inches into me with measured control. When I feel the full length of him, I have to take a handful of deep breaths. No man has delivered this much pleasure to my body at the mere point of entry. Normally, there are kinks to work out the first few times I'm with someone, but Tate is a master. Or an anomaly.

He begins a series of slow thrusts, and my breathing becomes desperate. I bite my lower lip to keep from yelling.

"Enjoying yourself?" He manages to sound professional and in control. If we weren't naked in his bed, I'd assume he was making small talk in the Nuts & Bolts break room.

I nod frantically. He picks up the speed, then slows down. He switches rhythm again and again until I'm yelping.

"Tell me what you want," he says with a grunt. Not so in control anymore. I moan with satisfaction.

"This. Keep doing this. Please." I claw my nails into his shoulders to demonstrate just how much I'm enjoying the present activities. His fingers slide against my scalp and fist my hair in response.

Sweat beads dot the top of his forehead. Just the sight of him causes me to tighten around him. He's hitting something inside of me no one has before. I don't know if it's his size, girth, or technique, and I don't particularly care. I'm just ecstatic it's happening. It's raw and severe and makes me cry out.

He pauses the heavenly thrusting to sit up, and I whine. But then he hooks both of my legs over his shoulders and resumes the pace.

"Holy God," I slur.

This is heavenly. This is otherworldly. This is all the adjectives I can't think of because my mind is a pleasure-filled balloon ready to burst. I've done this position in the past, but it's never, ever felt like this. Tate has mastered it. His heroic stamina puts to shame all the men I've been with previously. No man should ever attempt this move without consulting him first so he can tell them how to do it correctly.

The pleasure is building to an unfamiliar point. I can't remember a single time when it's ever felt this intense this quickly. The intensity of his heavy, even pace keeps my throat in a near-constant squeeze. I choke on a gasp.

"Don't stop," I groan. My head dips back when he hits a particularly deep spot.

For an untold number of minutes I'm on the cusp of exploding. I take in the close view of his bare shoulders and biceps, glistening with sweat.

"I want you every way I can have you," he says.

The gentle tone combined with the tickle of his breath against my ear works wonders. I have to pull from my deepest inner reserves to keep my composure underneath him. I steady my breathing. My mission, if I choose to accept it, is to keep myself from losing it too soon. And, boy, will I ever try. That's one for the record books. Never have I ever had to stop myself from reaching climax too quickly. I've always had to consciously remind myself to relax, let go, and on those rare occasions that I'm lucky and the stars align, it comes. Not tonight. Tonight my entire body is begging for release. I'm teetering on the edge, an inch from falling. I want to savor every morsel.

Just when I think I've gotten a hold of myself, he whispers into my ear how gorgeous I look, how my skin is the softest thing he's ever touched, and how he wants to feel my body against his forever. My knees tremble, and my eyes roll to the back of my head. Ecstasy is seconds away, max.

I feel the start of the inevitable drop. I wrap my legs around his waist, claw my nails into the meaty part of his shoulders, and tilt my head back for a long overdue scream.

"Harder," he moans. I obey, digging my fingers in his thick skin while squeezing my legs tighter. The distant, concentrated look in his eyes tells me he's not far off either.

The moment it hits, I'm caught off guard. I thought I had longer. My body convulses, like I've been struck by lightning while enduring the frenzied g-force of a roller coaster. I have no control over myself. My body heaves and twists around him violently, and there's nothing I can do but claw at his hair and back while screaming gibberish. When I finish, he groans, shudders, and then stops moving. He must have lost it right along with me.

I beam a pleasure-drunk grin at him. "That was . . . I don't even . . . Fuck."

He smiles back but says nothing. When he peels himself off of me, I stare at the ceiling. I can't make out any colors or shapes. A fuzzy blur is all I see. I keep blinking until I regain focus. I'm completely stripped of my old self. I am no longer made of metal, tough and hard and unrelenting. I am goo. I am slush. I am a pile of sweaty skin, pumping blood, and vibrating bones. Tate has extracted everything tough about me and replaced it with mind-blowing pleasure. Faking in bed isn't an option anymore. I'm physically unable to pretend. Everything from this moment on is real and true and painted in a blissful, postorgasmic glow.

As shaky as I am, I feel empowered. I can conquer the world. No matter the challenge, I will throw down. Air gliding. Applied mathematics. Three-dimensional origami. The intoxicating aftershocks pulsing throughout my body make it so. The bliss powering this afterglow is life changing. I can do all things after a night with Tate Rasmussen, bringer of elusive, incredible orgasms.

When I'm finally able to see again, I turn to him. His haphazard curls have been smoothed down, and his face is wiped dry. He must have gone to the bathroom to clean up.

"You've broken me," I babble.

"It was totally and completely my pleasure." He brushes a sweaty mass of hair from my face.

"We have to do this again." My eyelids droop. Exhaustion is settling in, and I'm ready for a night of heavy sleep.

"Just name the time and place."

With shaky hands, I tilt his face to mine. "No one has ever made me feel that good. And 'good' isn't even the right word, but I can't think of a better one right now because you've screwed the living daylights out of me." I peck him on the lips just as he chuckles.

Nuzzling into the pillow, I close my eyes. Tate's arm snakes around me, pulling my head into the crook between his shoulder and chest. Each breath I take tingles, his musky, evergreen scent filling my lungs. There is no better smell in the world, I think to myself as I doze.

twenty-eight

·······

It's a brand-new day when I wake, tangled in the paper-hued sheets of Tate's bed. I lie on my side; he spoons me from behind, his tree-trunk arm resting over my waist. I peel open my eyes. Morning sunlight peeks through the tilted blinds over the only window in his bedroom. It warms the light cotton sheet draped over us. Yet another stiflingly hot and humid Midwest day, but I welcome it. The morning's soft heat makes me feel cradled and secure. We're captured in an impenetrable bubble where nothing can reach us.

I roll over, still half-asleep, and let my eyes adjust to the brightness. Peering around the room, I soak in the light and the comfort. Tate stirs and moans, then pulls me closer to his chest. I smile and close my eyes again. I want to wake up like this every day.

Behind my eyelids, I imagine what we must look like. In my dreams, we are a simple image: a man and a woman floating in the middle of a bed, wrapped in cotton sheets so thin you can almost see through them. The entire room is bathed in neutral hues, but it's not boring. It's soothing.

He's pale as milk; she's tan as caramel. Her jet-black hair spills across the pillows like ink. The mess of ebony tangles with his snowy white curls. Golden sunlight streams in from the window, dancing across every surface. The conflicting shades of dark and light come together under the warm glow of orange and yellow. It creates a balance. A harmony.

It's similar to the glow I feel inside me. The longer I lie in bed, the clearer it becomes, the warmer I feel. I knew it was coming, but I wasn't prepared for the jolt. For the all-consuming, chest-tightening surge that would overtake every fiber in my skin and bones. Hot blood pulses through my veins, carrying this new sensation to the farthest reaches of my body.

After one blink, one breath, and one pulse, it's clear: I'm in love with Tate.

I don't believe it at first. How can I love someone I've only just started to get to know? But I do know him. For eleven months, I've worked with him. I know his moods and his sounds. I can differentiate the sighs he makes. I know how he's feeling depending on how deep and heavy his exhale is. I've committed to memory the number of lines that crowd his forehead whenever he frowns. I know his favorite lunch. I know the hurried way he drives, how hoodies and T-shirts are his favorite clothes to wear, the rhythm of his speech. He's got a gold mine on me too. And now I know how he truly feels.

It's a beautiful mess in my head, and I have to close my eyes to make sense of it all. Nearly a year's worth of bickering, heated emotions—it's all formed a unique foundation. That gut punch of negative feelings with every argument, every bout of silent treatment over the last several months was misdirected heat and affection. Like a haywire electrical current that caused damage until it was grounded. Now that it's contained between us, I'm buzzing with love and joy.

Our imperfect past is filled with challenges, missteps, and

complications, but look what it's led to. The most passionate night of my life and the most eye-opening morning.

When I fix my gaze on his sleeping face, my body trembles with the realization. This new feeling expands. It's faster than my thoughts or my heartbeat can keep up with. I hold my breath. Before I can inhale, he wakes.

"Good morning," he says with a sleepy smile.

I nod with dramatic lemur eyes, unable to speak.

"What's wrong?" His forehead resumes his trademark frown of concern. I bet I look terrified.

"Nothing. Just still processing everything."

He holds me tighter. "Hopefully not regretting anything?"

I nuzzle my face to his chest. "Not at all," I mumble into his skin.

"You're still my girlfriend, right?"

"If you're still my boyfriend."

"Good. Because I like this. Waking up, holding you. I want this. For as long as possible." He cradles my head in his palm. I push up to peer at him.

"As long as possible?" I ask like I'm clarifying a joke. If he can make a statement like that, I wonder if he could love me.

"At the very least."

"You want to snuggle me in your bed forever?"

He laughs, probably at my stunned tone. "Yes. I swear."

"I don't share, you know. If you say that to me, you don't get to do this with any other woman."

Gently, he grabs my chin and pulls me into a soft kiss. "I don't have any interest in anyone else. Not now, not ever."

"Tate—"

"I mean it, Emmie. I've wanted this for so long."

I pull him into a deep kiss and close my eyes. It's a heart-pounding comfort to know he feels this way about me. His words are a warm blanket over my body, soothing me.

"You're all I want," he says when we finish our minute-long kiss.

"Even when we argue? How we bicker—"

He bumps the tip of my nose with his. "We play and laugh too. Don't forget that."

I beam.

"There's a depth to us that I've never felt with anyone else. Don't you feel it?"

I nod. Our history, our flaws, our imperfect path to this perfect morning, it all works together to intrigue and satisfy.

"I don't like simple," he says. "And I don't think you do either."

He's right. I need the layers, the varying degrees of us. That's what gets me off. That's how I fall in love.

"I want this too. More than you know," I say in a hushed voice, wondering if he can tell how I truly feel.

When he beams at me, the shock leaves my body. I nuzzle back into his chest and he continues to hold me tightly. As I lie in his arms, I am elated and at peace. It's not long before we fade back to sleep, wrapped in a cocoon of sunlight and cotton.

WHAT'S THIS?" I point to a dark stain on the front of the T-shirt I'm wearing.

Men's T-shirts are my favorite weekend lounge wear, especially when my only other clothing option is a slinky black dress. The fact that the shirt smells like Tate, all spicy and foresty, is a plus.

Tate pops his head out from the hallway bathroom. A toothbrush sticks out from his mouth. "Hmm? Oh, that. I wore it when I changed the oil in my car a few weeks ago."

I walk into the bathroom as he hunches over to spit in the sink.

I hug him from behind, pressing my face into his shoulder. So far I've managed to keep my love revelation to myself. It's mind blowing enough that Tate Rasmussen is my boyfriend and that I'm wearing his T-shirt the morning after the best sex of my life. I don't need to spill my gushy feelings to complicate things.

"I like the stain. It makes the shirt look manlier," I say. Focusing on the moment helps. Teasing him eases the knot of emotion in my chest.

"I suppose it needs all the help it can get." He wipes his mouth with a hand towel. "It has Oscar the Grouch on the front of it, after all. My sister got it for me a couple Christmases ago. She said we have the same personalities."

I let out a chuckle. "Maybe on the outside, but deep down, you're a big softy like Elmo."

He reaches behind to tickle me at the waist. I squeal.

"Are you cool with using my toothbrush? I might have an unopened one in a drawer somewhere." He starts to reach for the nearest drawer, but I grab his hand to stop him. He spins around, encircling my waist with his arms.

"I'm more than happy to use your toothbrush."

I tiptoe up to give him a press on the lips. He's having none of it though and captures me in a filthy, tongue-heavy kiss.

"Don't." I push him back. "Your mouth is clean. Mine tastes like gross morning breath." I cup my hand over my mouth, hoping he can't smell anything.

"I love the way you taste," he says against my hand. I shiver so hard my knees buckle, but I don't fall. He's got me firmly in his hold. I could lift both legs off the ground and stay perfectly in place.

I playfully pull away so I can brush my teeth and wash my face.

"Here." He hands me my purse when I walk back into his bedroom. "Your phone was beeping."

He ruffles my hair before planting a kiss at the top of my head. I grin like a goober until I see a handful of frantic email messages from my sister.

"Shit."

"What's the matter?"

"My sister. She's been trying to get a hold of me all morning. Crap."

I scan through the emails:

6:02 a.m.: *You had a concussion AND surgery??!! What? You need to Skype me now!*

6:31 a.m.: *Wake up! I need to know that you're okay! I need proof of life!*

6:52 a.m.: *Okay, you're probably happily sleeping in . . . I know your coworker sent a message to me saying you're fine now, but I still need to Skype you! For my peace of mind!!!*

7:17 a.m.: *Emmie! How are you not waking up to the endless dinging noises your phone must be making at my incessant emailing?!*

I pull up Skype on my phone. "I need to Skype my sister. She must have finally read the emails you sent her when I was in the hospital, and she's freaking out."

"Gotcha. I'll be in the shower." He grabs a towel and trots back into the bathroom, leaving the door open. "Join me when you're off the phone," he hollers.

I smirk to myself just as my sister answers.

"There you are!" she yells. "What the hell? I've been trying to reach you all morning." She's bug eyed with worry.

"I'm sorry. I slept in and my phone was downstairs. Don't worry, I'm fine."

"Emmie, I was freaking out! I finally got the chance to check my email after weeks of jungle exploring and beach hopping, and I see two messages saying you had a concussion after falling at work, and you had your appendix removed. Are you okay? This is nuts." She's waving her arms around as she speaks. I recognize the drab hostel background behind her.

"It was, but I'm fine. Seriously. How was the hike in the jungle? What beaches did you go to?"

"Never mind the jungle and the beaches. You have a follow-up appointment with your doctor, right?" The bun at the top of her head wiggles along with the impatient movement of her hands.

"Yes, next week, but everything's fine. I feel almost as strong as I did before. I'm only a tiny bit sore."

"Thank God." She throws her head back and exhales. When she looks back at the screen, she squints. "What are you wearing?"

"A T-shirt." I bite my lip.

"It looks huge on you. Is it new?"

I shake my head and think of a lie. "Sort of. Borrowed it from a friend."

She raises a suspicious eyebrow at me. "Where are you right now?"

"A friend's house," I say quickly. I suddenly wish we were speaking on the phone so she couldn't see the embarrassing shade of red I suspect my face is turning.

"Really? The only friend you ever seem to visit these days is Kaitlin, and that's not her house. All the walls in her place are pastel colored. The wall you're in front of is taupe."

My silence is incriminating. I quickly sink onto the bed, bouncing slightly. "It's a new friend."

"Is this new friend a guy?"

"Um, maybe."

She claps and throws her head back before unleashing a fit of giggles. "Shit, I just busted your walk of shame, didn't I? Oh my God, I have amazing timing!"

"Addy, it's not like that."

"Oh, I'm sorry. Is he about to bring you breakfast in bed?"

"Knock it off, smart-ass. He's in the shower."

"Perfect! Now you can tell me all about him!" she says in a singsong voice as she claps her hands gleefully.

"I don't want to get into it now."

"At least tell me who he is. Oh, is it the sexy contractor you told me about?"

"Nope." I pause for a much-needed exhale. "It's Tate. My co-worker."

Addy rolls her eyes. "Come on. Be serious."

"I'm dead serious," I say with a straight face. "And it's not a walk of shame. We're . . . more than that. Way more."

"No way." Her jaw drops. "I thought you couldn't stand him."

The sharp ring of the doorbell saves me from having to explain further.

"Someone's at the door. Gotta go!"

"Emmie, don't you dare."

"I'll Skype you again later, okay?"

I end the call, thanking the universe for such a well-timed distraction. When the doorbell ringing persists, I groan. I guess I should make myself useful and answer it so Tate doesn't have to jump out of the shower and do it. When I open the door, I nearly bite my tongue off.

twenty-nine

....

Natalie's eyebrows shoot halfway up her forehead when she sees me.

"Emmie. Hello."

I stammer a few incriminating "um" and "uh" sounds before I finally return a proper hello.

"What a surprise." She lets out a good-natured laugh. "I wanted to drop by and check on Tate. I was worried when I saw you two leave last night." There's a glint in her eyes, and she's fighting a grin as it crawls across her mouth. "But I'm guessing he's all right."

I cross my arms, hoping it somehow makes me look less indecent. It's eleven a.m. Sunday morning, and I'm clad in Tate's shirt and boxers with messy bed hair. It couldn't be more obvious what we've been up to.

I shake my head and step aside. "Sorry. Come in." I shut the door, and she makes her way to stand near the couch.

My eyes feel a magnetic pull to the floor. There's no reason for me to be embarrassed. We're adults after all. Still, though. Nothing like being caught the morning after by the sister of the guy I just spent the night with.

My mouth is wide open, but I make no sound as I try to think of something proper to say. She grabs my arm in a gentle hold.

"It's okay. I was hoping you two would make up."

Her warm smile eases me. The shower turns off, and we flick our gazes to the top of the stairs.

"Beautiful, Emmie," Tate calls from the bathroom. "I thought I told you to meet me in the shower."

Natalie covers her mouth to fight back a laugh. Flames engulf my cheeks.

I attempt to drown him out by hollering, "Um, Tate. You should—"

"No, no, no. No excuses. I need you in the shower ASAP." He thuds down the stairs. When I see his lower half covered in a towel, I breathe a sigh of relief.

He halts dead in his tracks halfway down when he spots Natalie. "What are you doing here?" He tugs his towel tighter around his waist.

Natalie bursts out laughing. A second later I join her. Tate's flushed cheeks make him appear annoyed and embarrassed at first, but then he's grinning.

"That's right. Laugh it up, ladies. Natalie, what can I help you with?" He raises an impatient eyebrow to her, his arm resting on the railing.

"Just wanted to make sure you were okay after last night, but you seem just dandy," she says. "We're visiting Nana at the home this afternoon, remember? Your turn to bring coffee cake. It's her favorite, so don't forget. And don't be late. She hates that."

She spins around and pulls me in for a tight hug. "I'm so glad to see you here. He's crazy about you," she whispers in my ear before letting go.

As I close the door behind her, I'm beaming from the inside

out. His sister likes me. It makes everything feel more real, like I'm being welcomed into his private world.

Tate runs a hand through his hair. "Sorry, I didn't know she'd be by."

I bite back a grin. "It's my fault. I let her in."

"Yeah, about that."

He drops down the final few stairs to me. He grabs me by the waist and pulls me against his soaking-wet torso. I want to lick all the droplets off him, but instead I focus on his eyes.

"Next time, let the door go. Shower is first priority."

He leads me in a long, slow kiss. His breath is heated, and all I want to do is fog up the shower with him.

"I'd love for you to join me," he says in a guttural whisper.

"I don't want to make you late." I claw against his soaked back.

"We've got time. Besides." His tongue glides along his bottom lip. "I want to show you something upstairs."

He guides me by the hand to his bathroom and gestures to the filled tub. "I'd like to try this again, this time the fun way."

"You want to take a bath together?" I grin. "How romantic."

"Nah." He sits at the end of his tub, leaving me standing. "I want to watch you."

My face heats. "You want to watch me take a bath?"

He pulls me so I'm standing between his legs. "That photo of your legs in the tub has been haunting me. I'm still kicking myself for not coming over to your place that night. And that time I sat next to you while you bathed . . ." He skims the surface of the water with his fingers. "Do you have any idea how worked up I was sitting next to you, hearing you splash around, picturing you touching your body?"

I laugh to myself. "Is that why it took you a minute to come out of the bathroom?"

"Indeed, it was. I was wondering if you'd be so kind as to re-create it for me."

His hand glides up my thigh and under his boxers, his fingers wet with bathwater. Before he can graze any sensitive parts, he pulls away, resting his hand at the waistband.

"I'd love to," I purr.

As I pull off his T-shirt and boxers, his eyes never leave my body. I tie my hair up in a topknot before lowering myself in the tub.

"Messy hair," he mumbles. "I like."

I flash what I hope is a sexy smile. Pressing against the back wall, I let my head and back rest against the cold tile.

My hands run across my stomach. "You want me to do exactly what I did to myself the night I talked to you from the bathtub?"

"Yes, please." His eyebrows knit together, like he's concentrating. His eyes run the length of me before ending at my face.

With wet hands, I massage my breasts and moan. The ache between my leg starts.

"Christ," he mutters. "You were doing that on the phone too?"

I shake my head. "I'm freestyling a bit. Hope that's okay."

His eyebrows knit. That frown. I used to think it was always rooted in anger and frustration, but arousal seems to be a common culprit.

With closed eyes, I feel down my body. Using my fingertips, I draw a line down the side of my stomach. The tickle it causes makes me jerk. When my breath starts to quicken, I open my eyes to check on Tate. He sports that half-lidded, dazed stare complete with bulging jaw muscles.

"You have the most adorable turned-on face." I chuckle. He grunts.

Finally, I let my hand fall between my legs. Before, I needed more than just a hot body to get me going, and Tate is so much more than a hot body. He's sweet, caring, and protective. And the way he stares at me, the entire sky in his eyes, makes me dizzy with want.

The ache strengthens. My breath turns rapid. It's silly, but the squeals I let loose make me self-conscious. I shouldn't be. We spent last night naked in his bed, and I made all the noises. But we were together then. Now it's just me, the spotlight's on, and I don't want to disappoint him. I want him to watch, to savor, to draw pleasure from every moment.

"Fuck, Emmie," he growls. "I don't know how much longer I can sit here and watch."

"A little longer."

The pleasure my hand brings is nice, but it's nothing compared to Tate. Even as I work myself into a tizzy, I wish it were him instead.

Heat builds at the center of my core. My hand moves faster and faster until my chest heaves and my mouth falls open. No words leave me. Only desperate, carnal moans.

I sling my leg over the side of the tub, barely missing Tate's towel-clad thigh. Both his hands grip the side of the tub with iron strength. I can almost feel how hard he's pressing into the porcelain.

My toes curl and my leg quivers.

He places a hand on my calf, and our stares meet. "I want you. Now."

"Then take me. Now."

The word "now" is barely out of my mouth before Tate jolts up and pulls me out of the tub. Soaking wet, I must spill a bucket of bathwater onto the tile floor when I stand up. He doesn't seem to care, though. Instead he yanks the towel from his waist and half-heartedly dries me off. Scooping me up, he carries me back to his bed. I'm unceremoniously dropped in the center.

"We're definitely doing that again," he growls.

With gentle hands, he touches me. There's urgency in the contact, but it's not rough. It's full of intention. He takes his time caressing, kissing everywhere. He starts at my neck, then trails down my chest, my breasts, my stomach. When his mouth reaches between my legs, his tongue works in slow, steady circles. I'm reduced to breaths and moans, just like I was last night.

It doesn't take long before I'm screaming in pleasure, and I know why. There's something more behind the dirty deeds we commit now. It's not just arousal; it's emotion running deep within me, within him. All the feelings of my early-morning revelation surge ahead. So this is what it feels like when you have sex with someone you love.

When I come down, he lifts his head up. The half smile he greets me with makes the butterflies in my stomach dance once more. He moves quickly and smoothly, sheathing a condom over himself before sliding in. That full feeling hits. That delicious, heavy, complete sensation will never, ever get old.

I mutter something about wanting to use my mouth on him, to make him feel as good as he's made me feel.

"Next time." He leans forward, speaking through a moan. "Right now, I want this. And I want you."

My back arches the instant he hits that deep spot. I can't help but howl. Over and over he hits it, and again it's not long. My brain is a fuzzy mess, trying to process every single second of this heaven. It's the off-the-charts physical pleasure combined with what I feel for him that must be responsible for this level of intensity. Sex has never been this good, this fulfilling, this stripped down. Love is a game changer for me, it seems.

Tate's body tenses above me, and I wrap all of myself around him. My legs and arms cocoon him as I come down, hopefully giving him the same comfort and satisfaction that his body gives me.

He collapses on top of me, tucking his head at the side of my neck. He moans. "I want to stay in bed with you all day."

"Me too." I run my fingers through his damp curls. "But your nana."

Moist breath hits my neck when he laughs. Twisting to the nightstand clock, I see that he has less than an hour until he's due at his nana's. I tell him, and he groans.

"You will not be late to visit your grandma."

He settles on his back. I cuddle into his chest.

Wet lips land on my forehead, then slide to my mouth. We kiss again for minutes, barely pausing to breathe. With my hands cupping his face, I break us apart. "If we keep this up, you're going to be late."

His hand on my chin, he guides my mouth to his. "Come with me."

I pull back. "To meet your grandma? No way," I chuckle.

"Why not? My parents will be there too. They'll all love you. And they'll love me more for snagging someone like you."

My heart flutters at his eagerness to have me meet his family, but deep down I know the timing isn't right. "I'd love to meet your family, but not during my walk of shame after our first night together." I kiss the tip of his nose. "It's been a whirlwind the past eighteen hours, don't you think? Give me more than half an hour to prep."

He squints, then smiles, seeming to understand. "All the time you need."

"Maybe next weekend."

His lips purse. "I don't know. Don't you think that's a bit soon?"

I nudge his rock-hard stomach with my elbow, and he booms a throaty laugh, pinning me against his chest with both arms.

"Do you hear that?" Tate says.

It takes a few seconds, but I zero in on a faint beeping sound.

"That's your phone," he says. "It's been beeping for the past few minutes."

I was clearly caught up in the moment, because I didn't hear a thing. "It's my sister. I hung up on her earlier to answer the door. She's going to blow up my phone till I call her back."

He gathers my hair off my shoulder and brushes his lips against my bare flesh. Another phone beep. I close my eyes, wishing we could enjoy each other without any more interruptions.

"She probably wants to make sure you're okay. You should talk to her. And you're right, I need to get going." He rolls away and sits up, pulling me up to stand with him.

I turn playful and pull him to face me. "One more kiss. Please?" My voice is a breathy whisper. There's a flame in his eyes.

The heat between us reignites, and he grabs at my naked body with urgency. If I were wearing clothes, they'd be torn off in an instant. I reach for him, but he holds both of my wrists in a firm grip. Our foreheads press together while we take deep gulps of air, waiting for our breaths to steady. By the heat of this kiss, you'd never guess we'd just finished ravaging each other in his bed.

His grip moves to my waist. It's firm yet soft, just like him. Our bodies work so well together whether we're lying down or standing.

"Emmie, I . . ."

The low, gentle tone of his voice is a cloud floating between us.

He runs his fingers through my hair again. I savor the sweet contact. A minute passes without him saying anything. Heavy panting is the only sound we make.

"What is it?" I say, opening my eyes.

His stare jolts me. He's stripped a layer of himself and is letting me see through his eyes. I feel like I can peer miles inside of him. There's affection, longing, and something else. Something deep and far off. I want him to tell me exactly what it is.

"Just say it," I whisper. I'm shaking so hard on the inside, my fingertips twitch.

"You should get dressed and go home," he says quietly. "Skype with your sister. She needs to see you."

I nod, disappointed. He was about to say something important but chickened out. His take-it-slow nature wins out once more.

We dress in silence, our backs to each other. It's probably better this way. If we made eye contact, we'd end up sidetracked in his bed or shower. I slip on my black dress and heels while he grabs the Oscar the Grouch T-shirt I dropped on the bathroom floor and pulls it on.

"You should wear something else," I say while rifling in my purse for my keys. "I hadn't showered when I wore that."

"I like it though. It smells like you. This way I'll have you with me the rest of the day." His tender tone compels me to turn around.

Last night, he was the one to put himself on the line when he revealed his feelings to me. And now there's something I can do to show him just how strongly I feel. I tackle him with a bear hug.

"What's this all about?" he asks with a chuckle.

"You'll see tomorrow." I dart down the staircase and walk out the door.

thirty

. . . .

Monday morning begins with my knee shaking against a chair. I can't help it; I'm so excited I could burst. Luckily, no one is nearby to notice. I'm fifteen minutes early on the first day of my new work life. Everything is the same except how I feel about my across-the-hall office neighbor. I had all of Sunday, a two-hour Skype conversation with Addy, and an hour phone call with Kaitlin to bathe in my newfound bliss. There is zero doubt, and I want everyone to know.

The piece of paper lying in my lap is the first step. Every time I hear footsteps down the hall, my head nearly snaps off my neck to see if it's Tate. My neck is starting to cramp due to all the false starts, but this time when I turn it's him.

He stops short at the front of his desk, a question on his face. Before he can ask me why I'm sitting in his office instead of my own, I stand up and hand him a crisp new copy of the Nuts & Bolts relationship disclosure form, complete with my information written on it.

"My weekend surprise is a day late. Sorry."

He responds with wide eyes and a slow smile.

"All that's left is you."

He scans the paper with bright eyes, then reaches into his messenger bag. He pulls out a book with a folded piece of paper sticking out of it. When he smooths it flat onto his desk, I recognize the crumpled edges and my handwriting.

"You saved it." I skim my fingers across the employee relationship disclosure form I handed to Tate on Saturday night during our blowout.

"I was hopeful." He huffs out a sigh through smiling lips. "I love your weekend surprise more, though. It's the bee's knees."

"There you go again sounding like you're from another era."

He lifts a single knowing eyebrow at me. "I seem to remember a beautiful dark-haired woman saying on Saturday evening that she likes the way I talk."

My head falls back as I laugh. "We're something else, aren't we?"

"Indeed. And now everyone will know you're my something else, and I'm yours."

"So lovey-dovey. Have we lost our edge already?"

"Nah. We'll still bicker. Someone's gotta call me on my typing and tapping and slurping."

This time when I try to push him, he catches my hand and laces his fingers in mine. "I knew you did that on purpose."

"I couldn't help it. Your annoyed face is the cutest damn thing I've ever seen."

With my free hand, I palm his cheek, savoring the rough feel of his stubble. Leaning over his desk, he fills out the form. I can't help but fidget, the bottomless joy simmering underneath my skin. The impossible is happening. The man I used to loathe with such ease is now the object of my affection.

"Don't forget to write the date on it," I say. "When Scott in Accounting goes through the paperwork, he's always miffed if people forget."

I reach to point out the date line, and knock into the book on Tate's desk. It's a copy of *Hawaii: The Big Island Revealed*.

"Are you reading this?" I ask.

Tate stops writing, then looks at the book. Something extra rests under the smile he flashes me. "I finished it a few months ago." He shoves it into his bag.

A light pops on in my head. "That's why you knew so much about the Big Island when you asked me to talk about it in the hospital, isn't it? The questions you asked were so specific. You were learning about where I came from, weren't you?"

One corner of his light pink mouth quirks up. "You didn't give up much the times I asked you about it at work. I had to forage for info on my own."

I ruffle his curls with my fingers. The soft moan that slips out of his mouth makes me shiver. I press a light kiss to his lips.

"We should probably head to Will's office. We've got a meeting with him and Lynn, remember?" he says against my mouth.

"Crap—that reminds me. Jamie."

"What about him?" Tate's jaw tenses.

I run a hand over his face. He relaxes instantly. "Things are going to be so awkward when we see him at the worksite."

"I can be professional," Tate says.

I raise a doubtful eyebrow.

"I can try to be professional," he amends. "We're all adults. If he can't deal with us, he can quit."

I follow him to Will's office, where Will greets us with a star-tled snort before spinning away from his computer screen. I recognize the eBay logo before he minimizes the window. Lynn trots in seconds later and moves a chair next to Will.

She beams her signature megawatt smile. "My dream team!"

Tate shoots me a heart-melting sideways smile that Lynn can't see because she's rummaging through the notepad she brought with her. Will doesn't notice, either, because he's discreetly kicking his box of *Star Wars* action figures farther underneath his desk so Lynn can't see. My insides quiver with the knowledge that from now on, Tate can give me as many sweet looks Monday through Friday as he pleases. I grip the arms of the chair, vibrating with joy.

"So! I'd love to hear an update on how things are going on the social media and marketing fronts regarding the homebuilding project," Lynn says.

I grab the relationship disclosure form from Tate. "Before we get into that, we want to give you this."

I slide the paper onto Will's desk. He and Lynn do identical jaw drops.

"You two are dating?" Lynn says.

We both nod with tight-lipped smiles.

Will makes a "huh" sound.

"Well. I can safely say I did not see this coming." Lynn smiles warmly and makes eye contact with both of us. "How's that for romance in the workplace?"

"Thank you," I say. "Now, as far as the social media and marketing efforts for the homebuilding project are concerned, Tate and I have some excellent ideas and plans for the upcoming months. We've already put a lot of work into it."

"Every time we post a hashtag, it trends locally for the entire workweek," Tate adds. "And Nuts & Bolts has doubled its number of social media followers since the charity homebuilding project kicked off almost two months ago."

"And from those press releases I've written and sent, I've scheduled two upcoming interviews with local news stations," I say. "Nuts & Bolts' homebuilding project is being included in a community magazine feature about community service too. The local newspaper is also going to do a write-up about us next month."

"How wonderful," Lynn interjects in happy tones. Will nods along.

"It is. And I think Tate and I should be compensated fairly for the additional work we're doing. We appreciate the extra vacation, but building the home is projected to take about a year. That means at least a year of carrying out this extra work for the marketing and social media project. Both of us feel a raise is justified."

The words fall from my mouth with natural ease. It's no effort at all to speak so assertively. This is me. I can be soft, hard, assertive, sensitive, thoughtful, decisive, and more.

Tate chimes his agreement.

Lynn responds with a smile. "Spoken like a true boss. I always knew you had it in you, Emmie. It's a pleasure to see it come out with this project. I have a feeling you'll go far at Nuts & Bolts if you keep this up. So encouraging to see a young lady like you carve out a place for herself here."

Lynn's reply has me glowing. In this moment, we're more than just coworkers. We're women in a mostly male workforce at different points in our career, but with the same goal: to succeed. I see Lynn in a new light now. With her take-charge attitude and cheery spirit, she's established a meaningful and powerful position as a manager. The fact she recognizes a similar drive within me means everything.

"Why don't you two email Will and me later today with an official wage proposal? I'll see what we can do."

Tate clears his throat. "There will also be a vacation request for you to approve."

"Oh yes, I remember your vacation request, Tate. That's already been cleared. You're good to go," Lynn says.

"I meant Emmie. We're going on vacation together. I want to make sure it's okay for her to take the time off too."

I whip my head to him. I am?

"Sure, that won't be a problem. Where are you kids going?" Lynn's eyes glisten with excitement. Her enthusiasm for our new relationship is sweet, but I'd like to be clued in to whatever Tate is talking about.

The mix of mischief and joy on his face when he turns to face me makes my stomach flip.

"The Big Island of Hawaii. Emmie grew up there, and she's graciously agreed to show me her old stomping grounds."

"How exciting!" The sound of Lynn joyfully clapping her hands is interrupted by her cell phone. It's one of the few times I've seen her frown. "I'm sorry, my son is home sick from school today and is calling me for the third time this morning. Good Lord, teenagers. I have to take this."

She steps out into the hallway and shuts the door, leaving me to work out the surprise Tate's sprung on me in front of Will. But then Will pops out of his seat, phone in hand.

"I've got an online auction to commandeer. You two take your time. Oh, and congrats! Happy for you kids!"

Will flies out of his office, shutting the door behind him.

I turn to Tate. "Are you serious? How did you . . . What are you . . . What the hell?" I'm a string of incomplete questions. I scoff and laugh at once. "You're crazy."

"Maybe. But you already said you'd go away with me."

"What in the world are you talking about?" I would remember if I had agreed to go on vacation with my work-enemy-turned-boyfriend.

"At the hospital, you said the two of us could never work. Remember?"

"Yes." I'm chuckling in that uncontrollable, giddy way where the more I try to stop myself, the harder I laugh.

"Then I asked if we could go away and make things right. You said you would."

Knowing that Tate flipped it into a reality makes me beam from the inside out. He reaches over and wipes a tear from my cheek. I must be crying.

"They're happy tears," I sniffle.

He leans over and kisses my cheek just as another tear rolls down.

"You must have been planning this trip for a while," I say. He nods.

Then it dawns on me. "The travel book on your desk! So sneaky."

He turns his chair so he's facing me.

"This will cost a fortune, Tate. I'm not letting you pay for it all. I'll write you a check—"

He tucks my hair behind my ear. "No, you won't. This is my gift to you. You're letting me into your life."

I shake my head until I start to feel dizzy. This has to be a dream.

"My parents had a bunch of frequent-flier miles they weren't going to use. When I told them about the vacation, they insisted on giving them to me. The flights won't cost a cent. I found an affordable condo rental not far from Magic Sands. It's all taken care of. You just have to pack a bag and come with me."

"You say you want me to show you around, but I don't know how much I'll remember. I haven't visited since I was a teenager." I can barely sputter out the words. I'm still stunned in disbelief.

"You'll manage. Besides, this *haole* can't handle big bad Hawaii on his own."

I snort a snotty laugh.

"I want to see where you grew up. I want to go to the farmers markets with you." He kisses the side of my neck, and I shiver. "I want to climb a palm tree and fetch a pineapple for you." His tone is soft, encouraging.

"Pineapples don't grow on trees."

"Then I'll buy you one at a fruit stand."

He grabs my hand and gives me the most loving, gentle squeeze. I imagine he'll hold me the exact same way when we're walking along the sugar-sand beaches.

"And then we'll turn it into a paperweight for your desk," I say.

He beams at me, the joy reaching all the way to his eyes. "I would love that."

"When are we going?"

He grabs a tissue from Will's desk and wipes my face with it. "In two weeks. We're staying for ten days. We'll be there during the Ironman race."

"What? I've been dying to go back for Ironman since forever."

He runs a hand through my hair. "One downside though. Our flight leaves at like five in the morning, and we have a four-hour layover. It's going to be an exhausting travel day. Think you can handle it?"

"Absolutely," I say. "How on earth did you manage all this? How did you know how happy this would make me?"

"Pining after you for the past several months was a good start. The expression on your face every time you looked at that photo on your desk was a dead giveaway of how much you wanted to be back in Hawaii."

I lean over and pull his face into my hands. The kiss I plant on him is heated, wet, sloppy, and salty. This level of smooch should never be allowed in any workplace, but he doesn't seem to mind. He returns it with equal passion and affection. It reminds me that no one has ever kissed me like he does, and no one ever will.

"You're happy, then?" He smiles against my mouth.

"The happiest. This is too much."

He pulls back, cradling my face in his hands. "For the woman I love, it's worth it."

I open my mouth to speak, but there are no words. Just hot, stunned breath. "You love me?" I can barely get it out.

"I love you, Emmie."

"Hang on." I grip his forearm like it's a life preserver and I'm drowning. "But I—"

He holds up a hand. "It's okay."

I'm aching to tell him. "No, what I mean to say is—"

"Emmie. I know."

"You can't possibly."

"Listen, I don't want you to tell me you love me now just because I told you I love you, or because I booked us a trip."

"I would never."

"I just want you to have this moment for yourself. Soak it in. Don't say anything. We'll talk love stuff later."

"Why do you get to say it?"

"Because I'm ready. I've known for a while."

"How long's a while?"

He leans forward to kiss my forehead. "I've had feelings for you for the past several months, but the first time we kissed, I knew I loved you."

He's perfectly composed in this moment. It's both impressive and maddening, given my snotty state.

My natural urge is to ask, to question how and why and are you sure. But I don't. Because I know exactly how it feels. In the moment, when it hits, there's no doubt. It's love, it's real, and it is everything. I felt it yesterday when I woke in his arms.

"I told you we'd still argue," he says.

My pursed lips give way to a smile. "I can't believe you're not letting me say it."

His thumb grazes my lips.

"And I can't believe you love me," I say.

"Believe it. I thought my behavior these past couple weeks would be a clear indicator. I came so close to telling you yesterday."

I shake my head, recalling that moment when he looked at me, emotion coursing through his eyes. It's back today, only this time brighter. Now his blue-gray eyes focus, his teeth sparkle whiter, and his lips flush pink. He beams at me. We say nothing, taking comfort in the silence. Affection runs like a current between our bodies. We can thrive forever on this new electricity.

Finally, all bets are off, all shields are dropped, and we can fake no more. He's flushed and giddy; I'm teary and overcome with joy. It's the only way I ever want to exist with him.

When he runs his hand through my hair, I stop him with a hand on his arm. I press a kiss to the inside of his milky wrist.

"You'll have to slather sunscreen on me nonstop," he says. "It's going to be annoying as hell."

"I don't care. I love it all." It's the closest I can get away with saying it right now.

In my head, I scramble to figure out the right moment to drop my love bomb on him. Maybe while walking along Hapuna Beach, just before sunset. Maybe during a swim at Magic Sands,

the waves crashing over us. Or maybe when we're huddled together in the crowds, watching the Ironman competitors race by.
I'll whisper it in his ear, so only he can hear.

For the millionth time, emotion has me by the throat, and I
can barely speak. I shake with an unending amount of love I didn't
know I could feel until the person I least expected triggered it in
me. My body is overwhelmed processing it all. By the way Tate
stares at me, he can tell. And I can tell by how he holds me in his
arms that he can barely take it either.

We kiss for the millionth time.

"It's all perfect," I whisper as I hug him. And it is. When I
speak, it's the truth. There's no need to fake anything, not anymore.

Acknowledgments

I cannot believe I actually get to write acknowledgments for my first book . . . HOLY CRAP!

The very first person I need to thank is Steph Mills. Steph, thank you for recommending Gemma Burgess's *A Girl Like You* all those years ago. Reading that book changed my life. Something in my brain clicked when I read it. A voice inside my head said, "See this? This is what you should be writing!" The moment I finished it, I started writing and haven't stopped. I owe you everything for leading me to that book and helping me discover my passion.

On that note, thank you to Gemma Burgess for writing *A Girl Like You* and all of your other brilliant books. You are a goddess in every sense of the word. I was so nervous the first time I emailed you to fangirl over your book, but you responded with a kindness and graciousness that still leaves me in awe. Thank you for your guidance, for your support, and for your never-ending encouragement.

Thank you to the remarkable Lexi Banner, who read the very first version of *Faker*. Lexi, you were my first ever beta reader and critique partner. I had no idea what I was doing, and it showed in my writing. Thank you for being patient, for never holding back when you critiqued my work, for calling me out on my bad writing habits, for pushing me to do better even when I didn't think I could.

Thank you to Katie Ryan, Sophie Berti, and Pamela Castro, who read early versions of *Faker*. It was a mess back then, but your encouragement and critiques kept me going.

Thank you to Stefanie Simpson, one of the most incredible human beings on this planet. Meeting you in person, an author I admire and respect so deeply, was a life highlight. The fact that we're now friends and read for each other blows me away every time I think about it. I'm lucky to know you.

Skye McDonald, thank you for your friendship, your honesty, and your kindness. You read so many versions of *Faker*, I've lost count. It wouldn't be the book it is today without you. I owe you ten thousand drinks, and someday I will meet you in person and actually buy you one.

Evie Drae, thank you for being the kind of person who can offer thoughtful feedback while also making me laugh until my sides hurt.

JL Peridot, you are one of the most poetic and brilliant writers I know. Your feedback and friendship during my revising process helped me so much, thank you.

To the All The Kissing Facebook group, thank you for existing. I've connected with so many of you wonderful writers. And thank you for hosting the fan-freaking-tastic #KissPitch event in 2018. Without that, I would have never landed my agent. I owe this group everything for the opportunities you created.

Thank you to Helen Hoang for being kind enough to give me feedback when I posted my pitches in the All The Kissing forum in the run-up to #KissPitch. From your comments, I fixed my pitches and got an agent out of it. I will be eternally grateful to you for that.

To my agent, Sarah Elizabeth Younger, at Nancy Yost Literary

Agency, thank you for taking a chance on me and for thinking that my book deserved a shot at being published. Thank you, thank you, thank you for your heroic patience during my multiple revisions. (Especially to your otherworldly interns. I want to hug each and every one of you!) I will never be able to fully articulate what it means to have someone like you believe in me. You are beyond amazing.

Thank you to my editor, Sarah Blumenstock, and everyone at Berkley and Penguin Random House. Sarah, you are hands-down the most amazing editor on planet Earth. This book is better than I ever thought it could be thanks to your insight and input. Thank you for loving *Faker* as much as I do.

Team Awesome (aka Jen, Jessica, L-Dog, and Steven), you guys freaking rock. I hope reading this book brings back all the hilarious and ridiculous times we had while working together. A million thanks for cheering me on through every step of this journey. I love you guys.

Thank you to the writing community on Twitter. Connecting with you all has helped me so much. You are some of the most intelligent, passionate, supportive, and loyal people I know.

Thank you to my family and friends for the endless support and love you've shown me. I love you all more than words can express.

To my husband, Alex, thank you for being my biggest cheerleader and for always being proud of me. I'm working very hard to make your house-husband dreams come true. It may take a few more books, though.

And last but not even close to least, thank you to everyone who reads this book. For the longest time, the idea of me publishing a book that people would actually want to read seemed like a pipe dream. But you all have made it a reality, and for that, I am forever grateful. I love each and every one of you.

Photo by Daniel Muller

SARAH SMITH is a copywriter turned author who wants to make the world a lovelier place one kissing story at a time. Her love of romance began when she was eight and she discovered her auntie's stash of romance novels. She's been hooked ever since. When she's not writing, you can find her hiking, eating chocolate, and perfecting her *lumpia* recipe. She lives in Bend, Oregon, with her husband and adorable cat, Salem. *Faker* is her debut novel.

CONNECT ONLINE

sarahsmithbooks.com
🐦 AuthorSarahS
📷 AuthorSarahS

Ready to find
your next great read?

Let us help.

Visit prh.com/nextread